ISBN 9798459946192

BIRTHDAY TREAT

ANTHONY SELF

For Pops – for teaching me how to read

PART I

PROLOGUE

She walks quickly down the street, cradling the bundle to her chest.

It's better to do this now then later, she tells herself. It's not yet 4am. She glances nervously over her shoulder, just in case. Although it's late November her face feels like a blast furnace. She's sweating from her forehead and armpits. She feels a flutter of panic. Guilty people sweat. She'd read that somewhere, and the one thing she was desperate to avoid was looking guilty.

Guilt would come later.

She looks ahead of her, where a homeless man sits against the glass pane of a supermarket. The wide yellow banners adorning the glass exclaim: 'Last days of SALE! Everything must GO!'

All the shops were shutting, now. Laws had been changed. Less people outside. Only gangs and low-life scum. Maybe she should head back.

She puts the thought to the back of her mind.

No. It'll only get worse.

That's why she came out at this time, so there wouldn't be anyone around. Less drones in the sky.

She doesn't know if the homeless man is watching her or has simply fallen asleep. His head is craned back but she can't see his chest move. She wonders for a moment if the man is dead. Could she ever fall asleep in a sitting position? She's been so tired these last few months, she thinks she could fall asleep standing up. Fatigue gnaws at her constantly, and most days she doesn't want to get out of bed. Most days she doesn't want to wake up at all.

She picks up the pace.

The bundle shuffles in her arms and she stares down at it, coldly.

She and her husband had celebrated their first wedding anniversary last April. She had been eight months' pregnant and looked like a goddamned blimp. She had always been a slender girl, but since she had given birth she'd never managed to get back to her original weight. She tried diets, exercising, and fasting, but nothing worked. As if the child she spawned into this world had involuntarily cursed her body. She knew she was losing whatever marginal prettiness she might once have had.

The bundle starts to whine, and she hisses for it to be quiet.

"Shut up, shut up, shut up." She says, like a mantra. It's the chant she's been using during these sleepless months. Sometimes she screams it, other times she whispers it in a fugue state. Most of the time she opens her mouth to say it, but nothing comes out.

Her vision starts to blur with tears. Soon the whining will become a wail, then the wail into shrieking.

She knows this.

She crosses the road, away from the homeless man. She's been walking for an hour now, away from her home and husband. She didn't have any clear indication when she left of her destination. Earlier, when she was staring at the ceiling willing herself to sleep, she knew she had to do something. She just couldn't tell what. She's about to pass a bus stop where there is a bin and a few discarded boxes lying haphazardly.

A bottle smashes somewhere down the street.

She gambles. It's the sort of instinctive gamble you take so fast that to call it a split-second decision would understate the speed by an absurd factor.

As she passes the bus stop and the bins, she glances at the open receptacle.

She drops the wailing bundle in and carries on walking.

She covers her ears with her hands and starts running as she hears the shrieking baby. Someone will soon discover it, she tells herself.

Better to do it now, before it started crawling. Before it started stringing words together. Before it called her mother. It would be harder then.

Better to do it now.

(Page extract from The Network's Terms and Conditions 'Birthday Treat' instruction sheet – emailed and signed by the user before commencement of their Birthday Treat.)

RULE #5

SCOOP SUIT

If a S.C.O.O.P. (**Self Contained Ordinance and Optimum Paragon**) Suit wearer breaches, violates or fails to follow, or act inconsistently with the rules, restrictions, limitations, terms and/or conditions that apply to '**The Network**' within twenty-four hours (24 hours) of their **BIRTHDAY TREAT**, whether listed in this User Agreement and Privacy Policy, posted at various points in the Service, or otherwise communicated to users of the Service (collectively, the "Agreement"), **The Network** will terminate, discontinue, suspend, and/or restrict your account/profile, your ability to access, visit, and/or use **The Network** or any portion thereof, and/or the Agreement, including without limitation any of our purported obligations hereunder, with or without notice, in addition to our other remedies. The wearer of the SCOOP suit will be entered automatically into the **HUNTED TV** programme as per **BIRTHDAY TREAT** protocols.

The wearer of the S.C.O.O.P. Suit will have five days to remain undetected by the general public and **Network Agents** in accordance with The Network's protocol. We reserve the right, in addition to our other remedies, to take any technical, legal, and/or other action(s) that we deem necessary and/or appropriate, with or without notice, to prevent violations to The Network and enforce the Agreement and remediate any purported violations. Weapons of class 4 and below will be authorised by the general public during this time.

A. CAUTION: ANY ATTEMPT TO OTHERWISE UNDERMINE THE OPERATION OF THE NETWORK, MAY BE A VIOLATION OF CRIMINAL AND CIVIL LAW. SHOULD SUCH AN ATTEMPT BE MADE, WE RESERVE THE RIGHT, IN ADDITION TO OUR OTHER REMEDIES, TO SEEK ANY REPARATIONS DEEMD NECESSARY (INCLUDING USE OF M.O.W. SQUAD SERVICES) FROM ANY SUCH INDIVIDUAL OR ENTITY TO THE FULLEST EXTENT PERMITTED BY LAW, INCLUDING MILITARY GROUPS.

If, after five days of continued concealment, the wearer of the S.C.O.O.P. suit will receive 500 Social Credits into their account and a monetary investment into their personal account of £500,000.

In addition, we may curtail, restrict, or refuse to provide you with any future access, visitation, and/or use of The Network.

1

KAVANAGH

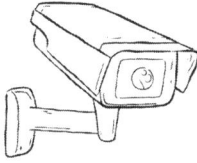

SUNDAY

Mrs. Bowerman sat in the corner of her small flat, swiping through the latest copy of 'Women's Weekly' on her tablet. She was filling out a 'Does He Find You Sexually Desirable,' questionnaire. Occasionally, she would flick to the back to check the answers before making up her mind as to how she would respond.

The doorbell rang.

Mrs. Bowerman glanced at the clock on the mantelpiece. They were sticklers for timekeeping, she thought absently. She called to her nephew, Brian.

"Could you answer the door, please?"

A deaf observer may have thought at first that the floorboards were merely vibrating with the passing of a train outside, but even a deaf man would have seen the slow gait of her nephew as he lumbered sluggishly from the bathroom to his bedroom, dragging his feet and grunting inaudibly. He stuck out his tongue and flipped her the bird. He may have only recently turned seventeen but had the physique of a mountain bear that had eaten far too many goats. His bedroom door slammed shut and then she heard the muffled sound of pots banging, or whatever they considered music nowadays. Mrs. Bowerman sighed heavily and got up slowly, like the palsied old lady she was. The tendons in her ankles thrummed like high voltage wires. She left the tablet on the coffee table next to her birth certificate and made her way to the hallway, momentarily pausing to adjust the plate of Jaffa Cakes she laid out when expecting guests. She glanced back at the floor panelling underneath her favourite chair. It looked secure.

It was a young man at the door, dressed in a fashionable suit, carrying a briefcase. His face was awfully long, and pale. His black hair was combed tight against his skull and parted with rigorous care on the right side of his narrow head. Mrs. Bowman felt a little inward shudder when she looked into his eyes...and she didn't shudder easily.

"Hello." He said.

"Hello," Mrs. Bowerman replied.

"May I come in?"

Mrs. Bowerman hesitated. "Do you have any identification?"

She'd spent the last thirty years on the council estate and knew it was unwise to let anybody in without credentials. Maureen, her friend from 78B had once let in a young man that claimed to be an electrician. When she next looked in her purse thirty pounds had mysteriously vanished. But she also had Alzheimer's, poor love, so it was quite possible she'd given the money away. It reminded her of an old joke: *How many Alzheimer's patients does it take to change a lightbulb?*

To get to the other side.

Under normal circumstances she would have cackled outright – the laugh of an aging, cynical bawd.

But these were not normal circumstances.

She saw a smile surface on the man's lips – a smile as thin and white and cold as the freezer in the kitchen. It troubled her for a moment, as if he had read her mind. She had to remember herself. He fished in his jacket pocket and produced a photo ID. She scrutinised it with narrow eyes. The picture did him justice; he was the type of man that photographed well, but she was disappointed. She hoped for a badge, something like on the Free-Vee. He possessed the appearance of someone that could be on television, she thought. High eyebrows and aquiline nose. Piercing eyes. Yes, she could see him playing a villain on her favourite soap.

She had seen the type before, working in The Network – always with a spare minute or two to lean on a railing without a care in the world, able to laugh appropriately at one of your jokes but then sleep with your daughter any time they wanted to.

Instinctively, she did not like him.

"Come in," she said.

The young man turned and nodded. Another person appeared at the entrance, his partner – she assumed. From the cobweb of lines around his eyes she guessed he was middle aged and looked far from healthy. He seemed flushed, as if he had just completed a circuit of laps around the courtyard.

"My associate, Agent Williams." The young man said, as way of explanation.

Mrs. Bowerman shrugged. It didn't really matter, she supposed.

She walked them through into the living room.

"Would you like some Jaffa Cakes?" She asked.

The Agent considered the offer, as he looked around the austere little flat. "That would be lovely," he finally said in a mellow, pleasing voice.

They sat in the living room, plates resting on laps. She'd used her best serving dishes. Once he'd finished eating, the young man deferentially positioned the plate on the arm of the sofa and leaned forward. "Mrs. Bowerman, my name is Agent Kavanagh. I'm from the Ministry of Waste, part of The Network. You understand why we're here?"

Mrs. Bowerman nodded. Kavanagh had hawkish eyes, she concluded. He had the cool intelligence of someone who would be five moves ahead in a game of chess. She would have to be careful. Unfortunately, she couldn't say the same for his associate, Williams. He sat on the other end of the sofa; legs splayed out in front of him. Whenever she made eye contact, he exuded a stolid, unfriendly, and obstinate expression.

Agent Kavanagh produced a notebook from his coat. "I have to ask a few questions before we start the procedure. Is that okay with you?"

"Oh, yes of course." She said.

"Jolly good," he said, beaming a wide smile. "I must say, Mrs. Bowerman-"

"Call me Eleanor, dear."

"Mrs. Bowerman," he said, narrowing his eyes, "you're our fifth visit this morning, and you seem very...composed about the matter."

"Well," she began, "my late husband, Henry...he would always get into a tizzy about such things. When they privatised the NHS, he would shout at the Free-Vee. It only raised his blood pressure, which I guess is ironic in a way. He was a man of...principles. He wanted to march with the protestors...to sign the petition, you know?"

Kavanagh nodded.

"But *I'm* a realist. 'You can't fight progress,' I told him. Even after the pandemic and the riots...I mean really, what did that solve? I have no orthodox beliefs, I guess. I have no pictures in my mind of an after world for myself. Or for him, for that matter. Towards the end...I could see it in his eyes. He was scared."

"Scared of what?" Kavanagh asked.

Eleanor waved a dismissive hand, "Of death, of course. You see, we convince ourselves that something else exists afterwards. It's ingrained into us from an early age...but everyone's afraid of the reality. That this is all there is. There's nothing beyond. Nothing, but oblivion. You either make the best of the life you have now, or you rattle along, like a cog in the wheel." She purposefully looked at the birth certificate on the coffee table. Her foot slid over the wooden floorboard beneath her. It gave her comfort to know her precious things were close to her.

Kavanagh considered this for a moment and cleared his throat. His eyes darted down to his notepad.

"You are Mrs. Eleanor Bowerman of flat 55C, Hammersmith Estate?"

"I am."

"And you're the proprietor of this flat?"

"I am."

"A widower."

"Yes."

"Tell me, Mrs. Bowerman – have you ever learnt programming?"

"Programming? Why no dear...I was a secretary once for a VP, but that was years ago."

Kavanagh nodded his head, scribbling notes down in his pad.

"You've never been taught advanced C++?"

Eleanor laughed. "I don't even know what those words mean."

"You are sixty-four years old?" Kavanagh said quietly, almost a whisper.

"I am not. I am fifty-eight."

Kavanagh peered at Eleanor from his notepad. There was a flashing glow that was gone an instant later, as if his face had momentarily twisted into a vulpine mask of rage and hate. It was like she had caught something uncanny out of the corner of her eye. When she looked at him again, his thin smile was back in place. He slowly closed his notepad and rested back on the sofa, steepling his fingers and purposefully crossing his legs. He sighed heavily.

"Mrs. Bowerman...are you familiar with the work we do?"

"Yes."

"Please tell me what you've heard?"

Eleanor shifted uncomfortably in her seat. The last interview wasn't like this. The last interview had been straightforward, and the Agents had left within ten minutes after looking at the birth certificate. Her ears started to feel hot and the cardigan she wore now felt restrictive and scratchy. She licked her thumb and started scrubbing at a little fleck of dirt on the coffee table.

"There are lots of things The Network does." She said defiantly, as if this taciturn answer sufficed. "Lots of different departments."

"But there's something that *I* do specifically. You saw my ID card, yes?"

"I did see that."

"So, I'd be obliged if you could indulge me on the matter, just so that we don't have any crossed wires on the subject."

She scrubbed harder at the bit of dirt. It wasn't coming off. "You're a Retirement Agent."

Kavanagh clapped his hands together. "Brilliant, Mrs. Bowerman. The CEO of The Network couldn't have said it better himself."

Mrs. Bowerman frowned. She didn't know how to read this Agent. One moment he seemed to be looking through her eyes to the back of her head in scrutiny, and the next moment act jovial with child-like glee. She didn't know whether to believe him or not; she didn't know if he was serious or leading her on for reasons of his own.

"But the meaning of your visit, Agent Kavanagh, although pleasant...eludes me. I had a Retirement Agent interview me two years ago." She enunciated the next words slowly. "When I was *fifty-six*." She left the piece of dirt but was perturbed by its tenacity of not being obliterated under her thumb.

Kavanagh's lips curled into a mirthless grin, showing a big set of perfectly white teeth – *shark's teeth*, she thought.

"I'm aware of that," Kavanagh said, still smiling. "I read the testimonials on the area, but *I* was not a Retirement Agent two years ago. I'm a stickler for the particulars, you see."

Eleanor considered this, nodding her head in agreement.

"Now, my orders are that I must have Agent Williams here conduct a thorough search of your house before I can officially cross your name off my list." At this, he waved a hand at Agent Williams. The overweight man just stared at the wall vacantly, as if waiting for the string in his back to be pulled. "If there are any irregularities to be found," Kavanagh continued, "rest assured Mrs. Bowerman, they will be. I have a strict schedule to keep, and I would like nothing else to be merrily on my way – so if there's something you want to tell me now,

I'm all ears. I would like to use this moment to add that any information that makes performing my duty easier will not be met with penalties."

Mrs. Bowerman wondered what Brian would eat for supper tonight.

"In fact, your family would be rewarded, Eleanor. You might want to think of your nephew in this situation."

There was a silence that permeated the small living room like an awkward estranged family gathering. She planted both feet on the floor panelling below her chair and used the tips of her fingers to slide the birth certificate forward. Somehow, she felt at ease with her feet on that floorboard.

"I'm fifty-eight." She prickled at the thought of being accused of lying. "I did my duty. It's not *my* fault that your records haven't been updated."

Kavanagh smiled – the sad, patient smile of a man who had often heard this line before. "What's your Social Credit Score?"

"One hundred and Forty-Three."

Agent Kavanagh re-opened his notepad, eyebrows arched. "That's quite impressive."

Eleanor smiled at the compliment.

Kavanagh leaned forward, towards Eleanor with his nose stuck out, like someone who was meaning to smell a flower. "But you realise that the reason for my visit includes a spattering of falsified birth certificates in the area. Quite high-grade stuff. We caught the deviant selling them. An impressive list of names, we found. But it would take someone with advanced programming skills to create these. Someone who could easily make their previous employment history look mundane and rudimentary. Say that of a secretary." His glaring eyes were half-closed, as if he had inhaled some sublime aroma and wanted to concentrate on nothing but that. He let the veiled threat hang.

Under normal circumstances, Eleanor would have argued the point. Instead, she stoically lifted her chin and cleared her throat, which suddenly seemed clogged. Her feet shifted uncomfortably beneath her. Kavanagh shrugged in a 'what are you going to do?' kind of way and continued with the questions.

"You have no means of income from The Network or outside sources?"

"No."

"Family?"

Eleanor sucked in some air. "My daughter, Sophie and her husband...they're currently..."

"Incarcerated." Agent Kavanagh said, without missing a beat.

Eleanor felt her face reddening. She bit her bottom lip and nodded. "They found it hard to adjust," she said in her most conciliatory voice. "You can't expect people who enjoy the odd social tipple to suddenly stop because their credit score -"

Agent Kavanagh raised a hand. He closed his flip book for a moment and looked up. She marvelled again at those belligerent, penetrating eyes. When he began to talk it was as if he was shining, like someone inspired.

"You know, my father used to be an explorer."

Silence descended again over the room. Williams turned his chubby head and looked at Kavanagh. Mrs. Bowerman remained silent. This wasn't part of the script.

"He once travelled to Antarctica. I was noticeably young at the time, so when he returned, I was always eager to hear of his adventures. His stories. But they weren't about the penguins, or the polar bears...no, no. He taught me about hypothermia. About the way it would invade a person's body if they were foolish enough to stay out in the cold for too long. The way it set in someone's body. A shiver, at first. Then a little more, until the body started shaking, desperate to let any warmth in. Your heart rate and blood pressure rise imperceptibly, you see? It's amazing, what the human body can do, under such adverse conditions. Your blood vessels constrict, with less and less blood reaching the skin, trying to preserve what little heat they have. The body defends itself, cutting off any unnecessary function to try and stay alive for as long as possible.

But...like life, it's a losing battle. As the temperature drops, the shivering becomes more violent and the muscles stop behaving as they should. The person slows, unable to process muscular movements. The person becomes confused, their brain starting to shut down. But the cold doesn't retreat, Mrs. Bowerman. Oh no... heart rate, respiratory rate and blood pressure all start slowing down. Just so the body can maintain something...anything to try and stay alive. Age is like that. It's the inevitability of things. We are here to simply remove that last human indignity."

All three sat in a moment of reverie.

"I need a piss. All this talk of cold." Williams said.

A sudden wave of anger shuddered through Mrs. Bowerman like a boot to the throat. She felt like she had been quite co-operative during this ordeal but couldn't contain her frustration any longer. "I would like you to leave now," she said, with a wedge of emotion stuck in her throat. "I have to start getting supper ready for Brian," her voice trembled to a whisper. Agent Kavanagh flinched as if slapped by her rebuke. He turned and hissed something to the man splayed on the sofa.

Williams mumbled and stood. "I didn't mean..." he started, eyes darting from Kavanagh to Eleanor, but stopped – not all at once, but wound down the way a record player does when someone turns off the power without taking the needle from the disc.

"Wait for me downstairs," Kavanagh said curtly.

"But the lift's out of order."

Kavanagh glared at Williams. Without another word he left.

"I'm sorry," Eleanor said. She had never been the type of person to behave cruelly to someone, even if they deserved it. "I guess this situation troubles me more than I anticipated."

"No need to apologise," Kavanagh said, noting the time on his watch and flicking the notepad again. "Do you mind if we continue?"

After collecting herself, Eleanor signified that she did not.

"So, it's just you and..."

"Brian. My nephew."

"Ah yes. He's a Grade Two, is that correct?"

Mrs. Bowerman winced. "When he was young...that is, when

terms like ADHD were still being used, the doctors prescribed him medicine. As he grew older, they gave him testosterone and other such things."

Agent Kavanagh clicked his tongue, shaking his head.

"We just refer to them as 'Degenerates' these days. Doctor's didn't know what they were doing back then. Brian's been arrested a couple of times on account of anti-social behaviour and delivering contraband..."

"That's not his fault!" Eleanor cried, in a voice that didn't seem her own. "It's that Charlie Ricoh from the other side of the estate. He's always getting my Brian into trouble with his scheming. Nasty piece of work that boy, let me tell you." Her lip trembled, wondering if her outburst had cost her something pivotal at this crucial stage.

"Hey," Kavanagh said, with the soothing ease of someone placating a child that had just thrown a tantrum, "I'm not here to judge, *Eleanor*." In one swift movement he was kneeling in front of her, a deferential hand on her knee.

"In fact, I must commend you...it seems with your guidance and his willingness for the ERD programme he's just about managed to limp across the acceptable Social Credit Scoring limit. Now..."

His eyes went down to the panelling that the old woman's feet were trying desperately to conceal from him. "I wouldn't be particularly good at my job unless I knew certain things about people. Sometimes it's like playing a game of poker. And do you know what I've learnt about you, Eleanor?"

The tears came then. They came in fat streams down a wrinkly face. Kavanagh allowed this for a moment, rolling his eyes when she bent down to wail silently into her knees.

"Wha...what have you learnt about me, Agent Kavanagh?"

"Your tell. I saw it as soon as I sat down here. Some people blink a lot. Some people remain perfectly still. Your feet gave you away. You've got a little secret compartment underneath your chair, haven't you?"

Eleanor's shoulders shuddered with her sobbing.

"It's okay...it's okay," he whispered. He carefully pushed the chair away from the table, with Mrs. Bowerman still weeping on it. It didn't take him long to find the catch and remove the loose board.

"A few laptops...near state of the art. I must hand it to you, Mrs. Bowerman...you're good. Now, I'm sure the lab boys will have fun with these, but am I right to presume you have been doctoring birth certificates for some of the residents of the estate?"

Eleanor started to collect herself. Wiping the tears away from her eyes with the balls of her hands she merely nodded. That was that, then. The jig was up. Like she had told the Agent when he had first sat down, she was a realist. She knew what was to come.

"And you are sixty-four years of age, correct?"

Mrs. Bowerman studied the floor, shuttering the last few moments of uneasiness out of her mind. She lifted the birth certificate from the coffee table and ripped it in half. Then she forced her tongue and larynx into action.

"Yes."

Kavanagh jotted down some notes, standing back up.

"I see. My predecessor was a little light on his inspection. Not a problem, Mrs. Bowerman. You're doing the right thing. The right thing for Brian."

He scanned his flipbook and then observed Eleanor intensely.

"Well, that pretty much sums everything up. Apologies for the questions, but you understand we must be thorough. The computers sometimes miss the finer details."

Her resentment and disgust for Agent Kavanagh had grown exponentially in proportion to one another during their interview, but she had to admire his fastidious attention to detail. He was a shark alright, that was certain. He was a survivor, like her. She asked him if he wanted a cup of tea.

"That would be lovely," Kavanagh replied.

As she made her way to put the kettle on, the bedroom door flung open and Brian stood motionless in front of her with red puffy eyes. She studied her nephew with a mixture of pity, reverence, and anxiety. Brian had a round face, not ugly by any standards, just alarmingly ordinary. Three years ago, he'd been one of the first groups of Grade Two's to have an Emotional Response Disc, or ERD for short, surgically grafted onto his forehead. The concave metallic disc, with a texture like stainless steel and no bigger than a 10p coin - indicated the wearer's mood by changing colour. If they were feeling depressed its surface would pulsate a dull cobalt. If the wearer were feeling sick, a green pallor would emanate from the disc's surface. It was a way for the user to communicate their feelings to other people. The general populace heralded the ERD's a scientific marvel. A badge of liberty. A device to bring Grade Two patrons closer to their fellow man. For Eleanor, however, it was simply a way to understand what her sullen nephew was thinking. But right now, she didn't need the ERD to indicate his current state of mind.

"It's not *right*," he spat, childishly.

"Oh, now hush. You sound like your Grandfather."

Brian stood at the door; fists curled into balls.

"Everything's arranged," she said in a mollifying voice. "Now you go and keep Agent Kavanagh company while I make us a nice cuppa."

Brian's ERD flashed yellow, indicating apprehension.

"He needs to talk to you," she whispered.

Brian's head sagged as he trudged into the living room.

"The man of the hour," Kavanagh declared, clapping his hands once as Brian sat on the sofa, glowering at the floor. Kavanagh opened his briefcase and removed a stack of papers which he arranged in neat rows on the coffee table.

"Brian, can you tell me...currently, what is your Social Credit Score?"

Brian's ERD flashed a brilliant golden.

"Thirty-two," he muttered.

"Thirty-two, eh? Not exactly the strengthening of social sincerity that our glorious leader envisioned, is it Brian?"

Brian did not return Kavanagh's grin. "No," he mumbled, eyes fixed on the floor.

"You know Brian, you have a certain look about you," Kavanagh continued, "you look like you're hungry but unsure if you'll be fed or not. Do you understand what I mean?"

Brian remained quiet.

Eleanor arrived with a tray of tea. After several sips, Kavanagh motioned to the papers.

Eleanor perused the paperwork, muttering under her breath as she studied the terms and conditions.

"Oh my," she said, "I didn't realise it was going to be so expensive." She turned to Brian, but he wouldn't meet her gaze.

"Agent Kavanagh...I don't think I can afford this."

Kavanagh brought a steady finger to his lower lip, deep in thought. "It may seem like a lot, but what with transportation, servicing fees and so on, it all balances out. If you'd used the appropriate booth when you turned sixty," he shot her a meaningful look, "Then we wouldn't be in this predicament now, would we Mrs. Bowerman?"

"I don't have fifteen thousand pounds!"

Kavanagh nodded slowly. "We do offer an in-house package, at a tenth of the price if that suits?"

Mrs. Bowerman sighed. Shrugged her shoulders.

"Wonderful," he said, tapping his ear. "Agent Williams, would you bring up Bertha, please." He sat back in his seat, quietness descending upon the room. Mrs. Bowerman signed the papers. A few minutes passed until the doorbell rang. Mrs. Bowerman began to rise, but Kavanagh gestured for her to remain seated.

"Brian, would you answer the door?" He said.

Brian's ERD flickered a dim scarlet, and Eleanor thought that he would disobey the Agent's command. A small silence played out, but in the end he conceded. Williams entered the living room, carrying a compressed gas cylinder and some dust sheets.

"Those stairs will be the death of me," he panted, placing the tank on the floor.

Kavanagh checked the time again. "Mrs. Bowerman...Eleanor, would you stand with me, please?"

Mrs. Bowerman stood up.

"Is there anything you would like to say to Brian?"

Mrs. Bowerman wasn't sentimental - when her Henry passed away, she didn't cry over him, because they had shared a good life together. Such memories elicited little emotion because they belonged in a different age. She cauterised herself to such feelings. She looked at her nephew, his large eyes staring at her. He looked so lost. The only thing she could think was to give her nephew sage advice. Williams twisted a valve on the tank and a thin hiss of air escaped.

"Brian," she began, "Whenever you meet anybody, look for something nice to say about them, because even if they've got a hideous face they might have fantastic ankles or lovely hair, and compliments do cheer people up. Be confident and not arrogant, and don't be arrogant and unconfident...Now, you'll be getting half of my Social Credits, but you can't waste them. You can't get yourself involved in trouble again, do you hear me? Otherwise...well...look at me prattling on. You know already what will happen, don't you? Lastly, always remember to eat your vegetables. Promise me you'll eat your vegetables."

"I promise." Brian said slowly.

Eleanor smiled. It was the worried kind of smile she always seemed to make. During her speech, Williams had moved the coffee table out of the way, flapped the dust sheet and laid it on the floor. He was wheezing by the time he went back to the gas cylinder.

Eleanor signalled to Kavanagh. Williams stepped forward, aimed the bolt gun and pressed the nuzzle against her forehead.

This was the moment.

Kavanagh leaned forward and studied Eleanor's eyes with eagerness. But it was always the same. The eyes seemed to lose their fear and instead fill with a great puzzlement. Every time.

There was a snapping sound, very thin, like a twig. Something coral-coloured and soggy flew out the back of Eleanor's head and she fell to the floor.

Kavanagh sighed and retrieved the papers. He required something slower perhaps. Something that would capture the moment longer.

"Well now, Brian," he said, snapping the latches shut of his briefcase, "You're the proprietor of this flat now. As an employee of The Network, it's my duty to inform you that if your Social Credit Score falls below thirty, we'll have no choice but to repossess this property and re-house you in an area that befits your...standing. Do you understand what I'm telling you?"

Brian gawped at his Grandmother. She looked peaceful. His ERD throbbed a dark teal.

"Cheer up, Brian. Your Gran just provided a worthwhile service to the country. Think of all the detergents, plastics and nuclear fuels she's saved us. Granted, she managed to evade us for years...and that will affect the number of Credits that will deposited in your name from her account...but overall, it's our responsibility to this planet to ensure we minimise the waste we create. Our goal is to reduce the carbon footprint of the UK by five hundred and fifteen tonnes per family household, and we're making good on that promise."

Brian finally lifted his head. "Is it true that they're bringing the retirement of life age down to fifty-five?"

Kavanagh threw his head back and laughed wildly. It was the sound of a lunatic. Brian stared at Kavanagh with dazed incomprehension and vacancy. The Agent put a hand to his chest, as if the Grade Two just made the funniest joke he'd ever heard. Kavanagh surveyed the flat again, as if planning where new furniture might fit. "Well, we can only hope, Brian. We can only hope. Listen, we'll be back in a few weeks to check on you, see how you're getting along." He picked up his briefcase and walked to the front door. Brian watched as the other Agent started removing the body of his Nan.

"But I think we both know," Kavanagh said, both petulant and teasing, "that it won't take *that* long for your Score to drop below the threshold." And with that, he flashed a grin at the young boy and left.

Brian watched on dismally as Williams folded the dust sheets over his Nan's corpse. A rivulet of blood escaped and the portly Agent smeared it into the carpet with his boot.

After Williams left the flat, Brian plodded into the kitchen. His belly was rumbling, and he wondered what he would have for dinner. His Nan usually made him fish fingers and beans, that was his favourite. Despondently, he realised she hadn't left anything out for him, and he would have to make his own dinner. He'd never made his own dinner before. Brian felt both anxious and excited at the same time.

He laid his hands palm-down on the counter. Thought for a moment what he would like to eat and how he would go about making it. His hands left two palm-shaped patches of dampness on the laminate as he reached for the drawer to find the shiny thing that peeled the tin open. He'd been shown countless times how to use it but could never remember. He was always forgetting things. He rummaged through the cutlery drawer with heavy, clammy hands and became frustrated when he couldn't find it and took a sharp knife out instead. He jabbed the lid with little effect.

He prodded it a few more times. Scared that he would cut himself if he used more force than necessary, he tried slicing the side of tin. That didn't work, either. He scratched his head, contemplating the difficult procedure, before an idea struck him.

Charlie would be able to open the can. His friend from the other side of the estate had always been able to help him out with these problems. He'd likely have to deliver a few packages for him, but that was okay – Brian knew he was a great delivery man. He always delivered the packages that Charlie gave him.

"Always at night, never to be seen, always take flight and remain keen!" Brian cried, repeating the deliveryman mantra. Smiling now, he picked up the tin of beans and headed for the door. He was sure everything was going to be alright.

CALLER: All I'm sayin' man…is that Birthday Treats are the way forward, innit? I *agree* with The Network bruv – it's been proven that crime in the UK 'ave been slashed because of Birthday Treats.

HAPPY HORGAN: What statistics are you referring to, exactly?

CALLER: The stats, bruv! The stats! On the Free-Vees. 75% crime wiped out in the first year when it came online, yeh get me? You can't argue with the numbers, bruv.

HAPPY HORGAN: But the statistics come from The Ministries, right? Who are owned by The Network. You believe everything you watch on the Free-Vees? And what's with that, anyway? Free 8K televisions for everyone, on the condition they're always on, 24/7. Mining data from what's said inside your house to project algorithmic flows and feed you, the viewer, preferential adverts. Who knows what other information they pick up from you?

CALLER: Listen, I don't know nothin' about all that…what I know is I've got my birthday later this week and I can't wait to see if I get mine, innit?

HAPPY HORGAN: You realise that the chances of being selected are like winning the lottery?

CALLER: More and more people gettin' selected each week, bruv. It's all in the -

HAPPY HORGAN: Stats. Right, yeah I heard you the first time.

CALLER: If I got my Treat, y'know what I'd do with it?

HAPPY HORGAN: I didn't ask but I'm sure you're going to tell me.

CALLER: You're jokes, Happy. Nah, nah, 'fin is -I wouldn't even take my Treat. Wait it out, innit? Enter the TV show as a runner.

HAPPY HORGAN: You'd forego your twenty-four-hour period of 'anything goes' ultraviolence to be hunted by everyone in the country?

CALLER: Bruv, you know how much skit you get if you survive the five days?

HAPPY HORGAN: *Broski*, do you know how killed you get if you don't? Only one person has survived the show. Freddy Henshaw. I'll be honest, I don't think you have it in you.

CALLER: What sayin', Happy?

HAPPY HORGAN: I'm saying that you sound like a dragger. All talk. I bet you've been telling everyone you know that it's your birthday this week, haven't you?

CALLER: I ain't no dragger, ya dickhead!

HAPPY HORGAN: Sure you are! I bet you've been telling your mama that you'll enter the show, buy her some nice clothes, and set her up for life, but when it comes down to it, when the chips are on the table you'll fold, my man. You'll fold like a cheap hooker being sucker punched by her pimp and you'll be sucking my veiny cock just so you don't get drafted into the show. I've seen your type before. You. Are. A. Dragger.

CALLER: You…You know what, Happy? You know [CENSORED] WHAT? When I get my Treat, I'm coming to your studio, fella. Yeah…I'll be coming armed to the teeth and you know what I'll do? I'll –

HAPPY HORGAN: Uh-oh, we seem to have lost you there, caller. And what a shame too, you sounded like such a polite, upstanding member of our grand society. Ha-ha, I tell you folks, if I had a penny for every Degenerate threatening me and the show. But that's what you want, isn't it? That's what you crave? And I am your humble servant, Happy Hogan. Let's get the day started with a little music, shall we?

- From The Happy Horgan Live Show
@Happyhorgan

Case #254

NetworkID: 8716367 Bryant, G.

Time: 14:12

8716367: Hi [REDACTED] – how are you today?

#254: Yeah, better today, thanks.

8716367: Have you been taking the medication prescribed by your GP?

#254: Yeah, have one more week left and then I should be off them.

8716367: And how does that make you feel?

#254: Uhh…good.

8716367: Are you sure? When we last spoke, you seemed a little unsure about the consequences of your Birthday Treat. Do you still feel the same way? It's important not to withhold.

#254: Quite the opposite.

8716367: Oh?

#254: Yeah…I mean, I guess the medication's helping, but -

8716367: The medication prescribed by The Network is only to counter the initial shock and possible instability one may feel after having conducted their Treat.

#254: Do they get you to say that Mr. Bryant? That sounded a little…artificial.

8716367: Haha, you caught me.

#254: Are there scripts for everything involving this, or do you –

27

8716367: No, no, not at all. I used to be a psychologist - you see. But when someone asks a specific question about The Network's -

#254: Gotcha. You've got to recite some bullshit T and C details.

8716367: Exactly. So tell me [REDACTED], how do you feel now? About the actions you took.

#254: Well…for the first week I felt like I'd killed someone, you know? Like, in cold blood. But then…then it made sense.

8716367: In what way?

#254: The guy raped me back in college, Mr. Bryant. I spent so many years…blaming myself. Do you know what that's like? To constantly think you're wrong…to constantly feel like it's your fault. What I could have done differently?

8716367: I do. Yes. So when you got your Birthday Treat…

#254: I felt like I had control. I was taking back control.

8716367: You know, part of my job here is to rehabilitate people who can't quite seem to grapple with the ramifications of what these laws mean. The younger generation are seeming to adapt well to it…but older people…We've spent so long of our lives learning one thing, to adhere to laws and religions of old, that it can seem quite jarring when we're finally given an opportunity to do the exact opposite. You can set the balance. Is that how you feel?

#254: …yes. Strangely, yes. That's exactly how I feel.

8716367: Good. That's good then.

#254: But like…what about his family? He had a few kids, you know?

8716367: Legally, they can't touch you. We've spoken about this before. Of the millions of people in this country, getting a Birthday Treat in your lifetime is like winning the lottery.

And if any action were taken against you by a member of his family, they would be purging themselves.

#254: But it has happened before, right?

8716367: Fortunately, no. The consequences are too grim. Affect too many people.

#254: But I still killed the guy.

8716367: Let's review this once you're off the meds, okay?

2

GEORGE

MONDAY

111 HOURS REMAIN...

George Bryant stared at his reflection in the bathroom mirror, dubiously contemplating the waxy pallor of his face. Since the crows-feet and the lines that ran from his nose to his thinning lips became more pronounced, he'd felt like his skin had been coated beige, like his mother's sitting room. It brought back an old memory from the corner of his mind, when he was young and enjoyed camping out in the garden. He would become transfixed with holding a torchlight to the palm of his hand and marvelling at his translucent skin.

He perceived the colour of his eyes, as if someone had dropped half a fingernail's worth of blue wax into a white platter. He pulled down an eyelid.

Conjunctival lymphoma.

Conjunctival hemorrhage.
Conjunctival hemangioma.
Conjunctival nevus.
Conjunctival melanoma.

George blinked several times. *No.*

He wouldn't put himself through this again. He was thirty-eight, not sixty. He still had a good portion of life to live until retirement. He stared at his haggard reflection, noting the loose pouches under the eyes. Jutting out his chin, he wasn't startled in the slightest to find his cheeks runneled like potholes, as if his middle-aged face was the rusted-out bonnet of a car. *That car,* he thought, is called *mid-life crisis. No one in their right mind ever thinks they'll buy that model and ride around in it, but the dealership's closed down, yes sir-ee. Company's liquidated. No takebacks. You get what you sign for.* Sighing, he looked down at the paunch of his belly, his little reminder of the last few years of unhealthy eating. And forget about exercise. He exhaled slowly, letting his stomach expand like a full colostomy bag. He slapped his belly, taking an odious pleasure in the wet smacking sound of flesh upon flesh.

Time to wake up, he considered dourly.

He attempted smiling at his reflection. At first, it took him a moment to summon the strength to curl his lips into a grimace. He mouthed a few words in greeting, as if speaking to someone on the street, or someone in a coffee shop -

(*Carina*)

- and then the scowl turned into a mild wince. He usually took a moment each morning in the bathroom to put on his mask – his layer of feigned nonchalance. It had taken years to practice the look, but the routine was always the same. It was the disguise of someone who had been shamed so many times that he had simply adapted to never showing his genuine appearance.

A sudden cackle of laughter from the living room disturbed his routine momentarily, and his mild wince twitched spasmodically so it appeared as if he was having an embolism.

The fact she's laughing is a good sign.

It means she would be settling in to watch her morning stories, as she lovingly called them. Nevertheless, the sound made his skin crawl. There was once a time when he found her laughter endearing. There was also once a time when he found the braying wail of a donkey hilarious. It was as if a hyena and donkey had fucked and created a bastard hybrid creature.

A Hyonkey.

Or a Donkeena.

It's odd, he thought to himself, *how diluted a sound can be by the continuance of the necessary routines of day-to-day living.*

George opened the medicine cabinet and popped several vitamin pills. Brushed his teeth, checked his receding hairline. That was the routine.

George Bryant was a man of routine.

Elspeth usually clipped her toenails as she watched her shows. George shuddered at the thought of the sickle-cell shaped bullets sniping the picture of his dead mother on the mantelpiece. He took one final glance in the mirror of the bathroom for composure before he padded his way back to the bedroom and dressed. Before he got there however, he noticed the pile of unwashed dishes in the kitchen sink. The first fracture of his carefully painted mask flared brilliantly like a wasp's sting. Rolling his eyes, he began mentally counting down from fifty as he dressed.

There was a hole in his sock.

George sighed and hoped that this wasn't going to be one of those days, full of unexpected small things that went wrong.

When George entered the living room his wife was staring at the Free-Vee with steady, vacant concentration. All the development flats had a Free-Vee box now; it was the law – the sixty-inch monstrosity bolted to the peeling wallpaper, broadcasting thousands of channels of game shows, blogger channels and big money giveaways. He felt bile rise in his throat.

Sure enough, she was already nestled in for the day ahead – catching up on episodes of *Hunted TV* from the night before. His eyes swiveled hypnotically from the dressing gown she was enveloped in, the flab around her middle spilling out, to the screen – some handsome announcer speaking with machine gun rapidity to emphasise the dramatic action occurring onscreen. George stood there for a moment, wondering if she would acknowledge his presence in the room.

She did not.

He held a firm belief that never saying anything that did not improve on silence was a good thing.

In the end though, he knew he would have to say something.

"What's the latest?" he asked.

"Emo girl hasn't taken her birthday treat. First day on the run."

At that, the announcer was swiftly replaced with a transitional banner of the *Hunted TV* show, before a young girl's face appeared on the screen, staring antagonistically into the camera, as if posing for a police mug shot rather than a photograph for the world to see. She had coal-coloured hair, falling freely over her shoulders. Her skin was porcelain white, with just the faintest bloodied touch underneath the surface of the skin. *Like holding a torchlight to the palm of my hand...*

The girl's stats were printed out on the right side of the photo in vermillion text, accompanied by an old typewriter sound effect to enhance the drama unfolding onscreen. The announcer's voice piped through the surround sound stereo speakers.

"Alice Paige. Nineteen years of age. Social Credit score of 107. What would make this exemplary young woman fail to comply with her moral duties to the people of the United Kingdom and neglect the operation of The Network?"

George couldn't help but notice the host had surreptitiously enunciated 'fail' and 'neglect' on a higher octave in the sentence. Alice Paige's photo dissolved into other pictures now, old snapshots of the girl as a toddler. Smiling. Innocent. George felt a pang of revulsion and dread pass through him, before feeling his mortality whispering through his bones like a cold draft on a late January evening. He did not want to see anymore. He dawdled for a while, before recollecting himself. Then he could not remember what his thoughts had been.

The dishes.

He glanced at his watch. If he took the time to clean them now, he would be late for work. A rebellious thought crossed his mind.

Let her fucking do it.

"Do you think you'll be able to wash the dishes today?"

Elspeth had lapsed into a complete Free-Vee stupor. She stared blankly at the TV set with shiny, doorknob eyes. George remained still, peering down at his wife of eighteen years with disdain and contempt. When she finally noticed that his eyes were blazing into the side of her skull, she grunted a monosyllabic, "Fine."

Fine.

Well, lah-dee-fucking-lah! That will take care of everything, won't it? George thought as he picked up his briefcase from the side of the sofa. *'Fine' sorts out all of life's problems, doesn't it? Ask her to change the duvet covers and she says fine. Then you come home from work and pop your head in the bedroom and the sheets are all twisted and crumpled, just as they were left in the morning. Ask her to put a wash on so I have a clean shirt for the next day and she says 'fine,' but when you look at the basket in the evening the same shirt is there, almost staring at you in a mocking way chiding, 'See Georgie boy, I'm still here. Still covered in your sweat and tears and you and I both know you are going to put me in the washer, don't we?'*

Fine. He picked up his briefcase that he always left beside the sofa. He thought that she had another three episodes to get through until she was into her afternoon regime.

George turned and was about to leave when a wailing stopped him cold.

"Geooooorge, you haven't given me a goodbye kiss!"

The second fissure of George's mask splintered down the side of his face, like a lightning bolt.

Two in the same morning. What a treat.

He glanced over his shoulder and trembled inwardly as she splayed her legs out from underneath her robe, revealing black underwear. Through the silk fabric, he could see the dark tuft of hair and smelled the mingled aroma of sweat and baby powder, and he involuntarily stiffened in his work trousers.

Suddenly George wanted to grab her off the sofa, throw her down on the carpet, slamming the breath out of her in a terrified gasp. He wanted to tear off those black panties, one hand clamped down on her neck while the other forced her legs wide apart. Then he would thrust his face deep into her cunt. The idea repulsed him, or perhaps it was the abrupt violence that had so easily seeped through that had disgusted him, but when he searched his heart for a reason not to replay the vivid image in his mind he found it empty. He would need to shutter those thoughts away before work. It wouldn't help him with the people he had to evaluate today.

He swiftly planted a kiss on her forehead, turning to leave. He was almost free and shrugging into his coat when she started imploring him in a mechanical, pedagogical voice to eat some fruit at the office. He left her with her stories.

Some districts of the town showed evidence of wear and tear, though an attempt had been made to cover the desolation with large advertisement hoardings. Like all the great cities of the world, this one, behind its smile, revealed the rotting cavities that nobody was able to fill.

He coughed and sent a gob of green phlegm flapping toward the pavement. Soon he was ordering an Americano from the coffee shop with the pretty girl that always smiled at him as she handed over his coffee.

Ah, Carina.

She had a nose ring - George once complimented her on it. He said it looked nice. She gave him a wan smile, as though she had heard that flattering remark thousands of times. *And heard it from younger, attractive men,* he thought sourly. The sleeves of her uniform just about covered a tattoo that he had stared at longer than was appropriate during an exchange for coffee. George tried to figure out what it may be, but he could never manage it. Tribal, maybe...but it could also be the tail of a dragon. He never asked her. The girl handed him his coffee, and as she clicked the plastic lid onto his cup, he noticed she'd created a little frothy heart on the top, and when he looked up in surprise their eyes met. Instinctively he averted his gaze and felt his cheeks flush.

'There you go, Gary. Have a good day.'

It had gone well beyond the point of correcting her, several weeks now, so he just smiled and nodded appreciatively. It was easier to be polite.

He wondered if she had a boyfriend...perhaps a musician in a rock band. George could imagine her moshing in a crowd of Degenerate youths, flinging her hair back and forth and flailing rhythmically to the beats of whatever music she listened to. He liked to think it was Rock. George had always liked Rock. The 80's stuff, way, way back in the day. Now it was all Bing! Bop! Swoosh! noises that sounded like they came from a bad alien invasion movie.

He felt old again. All events, no matter how earth shattering or bizarre, are diluted within moments of their occurrence by the continuance of the necessary routines of day-to-day living. Had he read that somewhere? When had life become so repetitive and dull?

Routine, he told himself. Stick to the routine and everything will be fine in the end.

⊕

George was hunkered behind a pillar when he witnessed the man in the orange SCOOP suit throw the girl from the platform.

He usually stood at the end of the platform, away from the crowds and the people - he didn't like to sit on the benches as he'd read somewhere that older gentlemen...older and *overweight* gentlemen, shouldn't sit down for too long in one place. He mentally counted the hours in the day that he sat behind a desk. Imagining the blood clots forming behind the kneecap. He multiplied the hours in a week. He thought about those dramatic medical TV shows where the doctors were sleeping with the attractive nurses and when the camera zoomed inside the victim's body to see a perforated lung or a heart as it stopped beating. Now he viewed himself standing up, releasing the clot, letting it zip straight to the heart.

A one-way trip to the old freezerino.

He had a whole day of sitting, so he liked to take the opportunity to stand.

Other commuters were staring up fixedly at the arrivals board in the hope that somehow the digital read-out might speed up the appearance of the next train. He used this time to enjoy his morning coffee without being sardined against the railing, so the end of the platform was usually the best position.

"Passengers are reminded that smoking tobacco, marijuana and opiate cigarettes is prohibited at all stations and on all train services," a clipped voice announced over the PA system.

He noticed something odd as the people nearest to him started flittering away in zig-zag patterns, like a school of fish darting away from a predatory shark. George instinctively followed the anxious glances being thrown at the stairwell and looked below the railing to view the man in the brightly coloured SCOOP suit, trudging up the stairs with a mirthless, rictus grin.

The man was going to take his birthday treat early in the day, it would seem. He had dark hair slicked back into a ponytail, making him look like a member of a grunge band, or worse...an IT technician. He could see his scalp through the groves his comb had laid down. George noted his long face, accentuating gaunt cheeks. His lips were a crimson red, as if lipstick had been applied to them.

But it was the eyes that chilled George to the core.

The eyes always gave it away.

Those wide, grey orbs beginning to glaze over. The eyes of someone with a Birthday Treat surprise in mind. Being the cautious type, George slunk behind the pillar he was resting against, careful not to spill his coffee. Last thing he needed right now was a stain on his white shirt. Elspeth would be livid if he came home with a blemished shirt. But then for the second time that day another defiant thought crossed his mind.

Let her fucking take care of it.

He'd just woken up on the wrong side of bed today, that was all. That's what he told himself.

He noticed the commuters eying the ponytailed man with scrutiny and they moved quickly away from his general proximity. George glanced down the track to see the approaching train; he estimated it would be ten seconds before it stopped at the platform. The man in the SCOOP suit was at the top of the stairs, scanning the crowd of people like an automated turret. George kept his body against the pillar and managed to swig some coffee without making a sound.

Damn, that's good.

An image of Carina flashing a smile at him from the coffee shop popped into his mind. George didn't care that she got his name wrong. Screw it, he would change his name to Gary for her. A blazing vision scorched into his mind then; spreading her thick, muscular legs, his fingers wedging into her, out and in, in and out, pulling out entirely and sucking the digits before the velvet head of his cock spread her wider. His hip bones smacking up against her ass as he fucked her – twisting her round so that her long, strong calves wrapped around his body, sweat glistening. She would scream his name…or in this case, she would wail the name Gary – over and over again. He would bite her nose, make her gasp. He would hook the nose ring between his teeth and snap his head back. Blood would spray, but she liked it. She was a punk. She was cool.

She understood.

He took another sip of his coffee. Did she like doggy style?

What was up with him today? Sex fantasies and rebellious inclinations all before 9am. Perhaps he had slept in a funny position last night…

Furtively peeping his head round the pillar, George could see the man with the red lips pick someone from the crowded platform: a girl precariously close to the platform edge, her eyes closed, tapping her foot by the thick yellow safety line, massive headphones wrapped around her teenage head, presumably to block out the bustle of the morning travel.

"*May I have you attention please,*" the PA announcement

squawked. *"The train now approaching platform 2 will not be stopping, due to legislation policies. Please stand well clear of the edge."*

George glanced at the cameras mounted on the station ceiling, following the gaunt man with the long ponytail swishing past the nape of his neck. *Yeah*, thinks George, *they know what's about to happen. Probably happens once a week. Going to be late now. First appointment will be delayed, causing a domino effect for the rest of the day. Going to be working late tonight, George old boy.*

The man in the orange SCOOP suit seemed galvanised, as he zoned in on the girl with the big headphones. He walked with purpose and George noticed his hefty gait as he zeroed in on his prey. Many of the other people on the platform were practically tripping over themselves to get out of the way, because you never really know what was going through a Boiler's mind. No one looked at their neighbour, for fear or seeing their own worries reflected there. George had been accustomed over the years to the search for indicators; the glazed over expression of someone who is about to commit an atrocious act, as if they are about to plunge their finger down on a detonator and blow themselves and everyone around them to little chunks of globular viscera.

He'd once gone on a course at work to learn that particular skill set. Watching films, checking to see the whites of terrorists' eyes before they committed to an act of unspeakable horror.

That was in Scotland, he thinks. *I wonder if Elspeth would like Scotland? Probably not. Probably too wet for her, even though she would never dare leave the hotel. Too infatuated with her stories.*

George watched with rapturous awe as the pony-tailed man clamped a hand down on the girl's shoulder. He did not take a sinister pleasure in watching these events unfold; it was more a Darwinian lesson – the lesser, unintelligent masses being culled for the Greater Good. He read somewhere that the diminished, less responsive brain cells in a person's head just disintegrate, making way for the stronger cells. They are the weakest link in the cerebral cortex. Birthday Treats were like this; they simply rid the population of the weakest individuals.

He thought about embolisms. One minute, you're standing on a train platform, sipping coffee and then the next a weak vein snaps and you're keeled over, dead before your body hits the ground.

George had been thinking a lot about death recently.

The girl's eyes snapped open and half a second passed before she registered what was happening. *Stupid really*, George thought, *you should never let your guard down in public.*

Because you never know when you might bump into a Boiler. They're everywhere. And they're here, every day. The girl turned sharply to run, opening her mouth to scream, but the man in the SCOOP suit was faster, securing his other hand down firmly with a vice-like grip on her satchel and pulling her into him. The sound of the approaching train was building to a crescendo. His arms wrapped around her and he brought his face down close to hers. He lifted one of the massive ear cushions and reverently whispered something into her ear.

At that moment George wondered what he was saying. It looked almost confessional, as if he were unburdening himself to her, using her as a vessel for all sins committed, past and present. Maybe it *was* his confessional. His mouth was trembling rapidly, so it could have just been gibberish.

George took another sip from his coffee. The train was almost on top of them; he could hear the taut coiled wires from the tracks whipping with that unmistakable sound. In a moment he would feel the rush of air as the train whizzed by.

"Clean up on aisle number five!" the Boiler suddenly screamed, pushing towards the edge. George's eyes dropped to the stenciled 'Mind the Gap,' moniker etched along the beige line. He speculated why a warning so perfunctory should still exist.

Struggling to be free of the man's grasp, the girl kicked out with her legs and screamed for help at the morning commuters, huddled like sheep at the other end of the platform. She knew it was useless though; most of them had already turned their heads and were looking away, pretending not to hear the wails and ear-piercing shrieks. Like George, they were contemplating whether the holdup would make them late for work.

But another part of George awakened. Perhaps it was the restless contemplations of anarchic agitation he was experiencing that morning, or the final realisation that he had been daydreaming for the last decade, but in that moment, when the girl with the headphones screamed one last time...there was a schism. George leapt forward from his hiding position, wrestled the Boiler to the ground, and started pummeling his fists into his face. Not just until the man was unconscious, but until the pony-tailed, rat-shit, red-lipped sonofabitch's face was pulp on the platform ground. As George arced his arm to give another blow, he saw Elspeth's face underneath him. He saw the chiseled jawline and fantastic, meticulous teeth of the commentator Ryan Lando from *Hunted TV* below him. He saw his boss at work below him. He saw everything that he wanted to break in that instant and he smashed his fist down with all his power and might.

After he neutralised the Boiler, the teenage girl tearfully thanked him, saying that she was so stupid to have her headphones on, but she just wanted to cancel out the noise of everything around her. George understood – he knew only too well how things could become overwhelming. The girl suddenly threw herself on him and started sobbing into his chest. George was acutely aware of the blood on his knuckles but embraced the girl in an endearing hug. The daily commuters on the platform started to clap. It was just one person to begin with, like the way in the films, a slow patter of two hands – everyone was still in bemused shock and he could understand that... no-one had ever interrupted a Boiler from taking their Birthday Treat before...the consequences were too severe to think about, but the solitary clap soon started to reverberate throughout the crowd like a pebble eddying through a pond and as tears started to stream from George's eyes the whole station applauded him.

Lowly George Bryant. Debriefer of Birthday Treats for The Network. Level Two clearance.

He hugged the girl tighter and he could feel her body quivering within his protective hug.

"Don't you worry pumpkin," he said, his voice shaking as they both cried together. "I'll never let anyone hurt you."

The applause of the platform was deafening. George took a moment to savour the feeling of adulation...of admiration. Of respect. It was a feeling he had not felt for a long time.

It felt good.

The girl pulled away from him then and looked him in the eye. Something wasn't right. Her eyes were bloodshot, her mouth contorted into a void of terror. The girl made a noise, like a moan or bellow made underwater. George's muscle's contracted and he sprang backward, some reptilian side of his brain taking control and striving for safety.

"Why did you let me go?" The girl whispered, before blood sprayed from her open mouth.

George was shot back into reality.

The Boiler shouted something about cleaning up on an aisle. Then he had thrown her onto the track.

From his spot behind the pillar, George didn't see the intensity of what twenty-seven tonnes worth of metal travelling at speed could do to human flesh. He didn't think about the way her skull smashed against the front of the carriage as it whizzed past him. Her legs flailed wildly in the air. Almost like a gymnast performing an acrobatic pivot for the Olympics. He didn't factor in the jaunty, forty-five-degree angle she'd been propelled, or had been lobbed, much in the same manner a labourer would toss a bag of cement onto a wagon – he didn't think about the sound of her thrashing legs snapping like twigs as they went under, the way her pulverised body dragged like a rag doll under the plethora of wired pipe work and tubes, under the grease-stained cables and jagged edges. The way her scalp sheered away from her skull just as easy as an orange being peeled. Appendages from her body tearing like a petulant child cleaving a doll's plastic torso in glee – the remaining limbs caught like a silk scarf in a fan and shredded beyond recognition. George shivered as her screams were abruptly cut. He blocked out the noise of grinding bone as the girl was finally crushed under the mighty weight of industrial metal.

He didn't think about these things in the several seconds they happened.

No.

Of course not.

George looked back at the platform, where all the morning commuters stared at the sky, or the other side of the track. His eyes glanced over to where the girl had been a few seconds earlier and observed her headphones, now left eerily on the platform floor. *They must have fallen from her as she flew,* he thought. He heard several other people mumble under their breath, a few even shake their heads, but they knew better than to linger on it. For them, and George – the moment was over. Like the few seconds of guilt that pass after walking past a homeless person on the street without giving any change, they would go about their daily lives. Such was the way under Network living.

George kept the Boiler in his periphery. He watched the gaunt man exhale sharply, as if he had kept the last few seconds of air trapped in his lungs. George noted the small camera attached to the chest piece and wondered if Elspeth would watch this later in the evening. She might have even seen George on the platform.

The Boiler ripped off a strip at his breast pocket. A bright light started flashing in recurrent intervals. As the pale man with striking red lips took a seat on one of the benches, holding his head in his hands, George likened the flashing light to the life jackets worn by plane crash survivors, lost at sea. Soon the proper authorities would arrive, and the Boiler would be taken home. He would resume his job tomorrow like a normal person and colleagues would nod and talk to him like nothing had ever happened. Safe in the knowledge that this man had not targeted them. Because today was his birthday, and now he'd completed his treat. George would later learn that the man was a caretaker of a local comprehensive All Girl's school.

George wondered if he would be debriefing the man tomorrow.

No one looked at the track once the train whistled by.

That Alice Paige looks like some Joan Jett reject, son. She ain't gonna last 5 mins on #HuntedTV

¬

Gonna get the boys out tonight and go A-HUNTING!

Get your rifle's and guns. Gonna BLAP BLAP that hoe like Modern Warfare

¬

Skinny ass byatch don't stand a chance. #wasted

@CRicoh

175 replies 450 RTs 208 Likes

I can't believe she didn't take her Birthday Treat! WHAT THE HELL WAS SHE THINKING? #craycraylife

@prrrrtygrl149

678 replies 2478 RTs 1067 Likes

Good for her. Can sumone help me get these beanz open?*@Brian_Bowerman*

2 replies 0 RTs 11 Likes

Have you heard she's in a band? I mean, like proper back in the day punk stuff. Don't know whether I'm in love or not. #jurystillout

@ShortCircuit99

255 replies 2835 RTs 766 Likes

I WANT that leather jacket. It's sooooo retro it's not even true.

She is totes vibing 80's chic. Girl is lit. Subscribe to my YouTube channel and let me know where I can get it. #hannahvintage #vintage #leatherjacket

@hannah_vintage

879 replies 5467 RTs 4776 Likes

Dude, she's not going to last 17 hours, let alone 17 days #aliensquotes

¬

We're mostly coming out to hunt her tonight. Mostly. #aliensquotes

¬

She's on an expressway elevator to hell – GOING DOWN! #aliensquotes

@Aliensfan616

654 replies 8765 RTs 3398 Likes

So, if I catch her: can I keep her in my basement and do what I want with her? I mean, there's nothing in the rules against that, right?

@Capt_paedo

457 replies 1650 RTs 2879 Likes

FIGHT THE SYSTEM. EVERYTHING ABOUT THE NETWORK IS A LIE

#thenetworklies

@For_The_Movement

378 replies 978 RTs 1421 Likes

3

ALICE

MONDAY

109 HOURS REMAIN...

Alice Paige was running.

She didn't want to admit to herself that she was currently running for her life, not because it conformed to some nonsensical platitude she'd seen a thousand times on the *Hunted* TV programme, but because it would confirm the steadily growing affirmation that she was vulnerable.

Alice Paige never felt vulnerable.

She was out of her SCOOP suit however, which was something at least.

His screams still lingered in her mind, but she couldn't think about that right now. Those nightmares would come later. *Future Alice will have to deal with that*, Boss Bitch commanded. *Present Alice needs to find a fucking way out of here alive.*

Coming into central London had been a huge risk, but one she knew had to be taken. She'd left the 'clinic' via the back door, which led onto Hopkins Street, a narrow alley. She'd need to keep to the back streets, where less people were likely to spot her. She'd left her backpack with supplies and sunglasses back in the clinic, but she didn't dare go back in case she'd tripped a silent alarm. *The creepy fucker probably had a camera wired up, too,* she thought with a mild gut pull of disgust. Alice swore vehemently under her breath – she'd been so stupid to go against her instinct. She rounded the corner onto Peter Street and looked to her right – it was a dead end with shuttered garages, but there appeared to be a small building with boarded-up windows. She mentally noted that as she quickly turned left, continuing down the constricted thoroughfare. She kept her head down, darting through the shoppers and market stall owners that appeared before her. Hiding in plain sight would only last her so long. She knew the drones flying overhead would have cameras. Agents would be looking out for her. She passed a comic book shop and a myoclonic jerk shuddered through her body as she saw an image of herself on a Free-Vee screen inside the store.

She stopped in her tracks as she gazed at the former shell of herself on the television. She couldn't quite believe that the scrawny, dark haired girl on the screen was her, just a few days ago. The incredulity of the whole situation hit her in the pit of the stomach like a deranged mountain goat ramming her with its long black horns.

How did they get that picture of me? Was the first cold thought that sprang to mind. *It's the Network,* Boss Bitch summarised, trying to fight against the onslaught of panic and despair. *They know everything about you. But that's the point, isn't it? That's why you're here, right? They know everything about everyone. Remember why you're doing this.*

Was the comic book guy staring at her? She lifted her hand to her face, pretending to play with her recently dyed blonde hair. She needed to do something, she needed to move - but terror had frozen her to the spot and now there was something else bubbling inside her. Anxiety tasted like acid and she swallowed hard to hold it down rather than risk having it consume her. Blood pounded in her ears, and her fingers tingled. She attempted to ignore the commotion surrounding her and tried to keep herself steady despite the disorientation she was feeling. Her chest was sweating. She had to get away; she couldn't stand near the damned comic book shop any longer. The noise and traffic around her gradually increased, swelling into a tornado roar of sound and bustle. An overwhelming sense of dread engulfed her, constricting her throat tightly.

Don't worry, Boss Bitch soothingly whispered. *It's just a panic attack. You've had them before. You know how to deal with them. Ride it out. It's not going to kill you. You're not having a heart attack.*

But what if this wasn't a panic attack? Alice had been advised that having someone with her during an episode might help to reassure her. But there was no-one she trusted. She couldn't even trust Dave now, not after what she'd just been through. She would have to assume that The Network would pick him up sooner rather than later. That's what they did. They would investigate every person she ever knew, squeezing the ones she knew intimately.

Don't think about that now! Screamed Boss Bitch. *Facts: Your time to take your Birthday Treat has elapsed. You have five days to stay hidden from everyone. Network Agents will be after you. Glorified online bloggers wanting a spike in their avenue stream will be after you. Friends and family will be after you. Trust no-one.*

She took a deep breath. She wore skinny grey jeans, but in the back pocket she always carried a mask. Since COVID-19 everyone wore masks. She remembered her last foster mother telling her about a time when everyone stayed inside of their houses for almost two years. That terrified Alice more than anything else, being locked up with family.

Yeah, family.

She slipped her mask on. It would conceal her face for a while, but it wouldn't be a sure-fire way of eluding people. She had to admit it, people loved *Hunted TV* – there were clans out there, militia groups that thrived on hunting runners down. That's what they did. As a hobby.

Apart from Dave, no one else knew that she had come to this place to get her SCOOP suit removed. Alice was unnerved even by that amount of information he had, but it was Dave that put her in touch with the sleazeball in the first place. The only guy that could do it, apparently. They had discussed it before she let the 24 hours elapse without having committed her Birthday Treat. She knew that Network Agents would be knocking on his door, so she didn't tell him what she had been planning.

She felt nauseous and found herself staggering to steady herself by the comic bookstore window frame. What if this was a full blown, all-out, artery clogging heart attack?

I mean, I just killed a guy. Not something you do every day.

That one solitary thought made the wave of anxiety come crashing through her mental defences like a pack of hyenas scrabbling for the meat – she had killed someone.

Fuck. Oh Fuck. Oh dear Lord Fuck. What have I done? What have I done?

The irony wasn't lost on her either. If she had committed the act a few hours earlier, she could just go home now, and everything would go back to normal. Same as it ever was. Just like the Talking Heads song.

It was an accident.

She closed her eyes as she tried to breathe through the mask.

It's irrelevant now, stated Boss Bitch. *The SCOOP suit had already been taken off. The camera wouldn't have filmed it. The guy was a fucking cunt and the world is better off without him. You did the world a favour. You know it wasn't the first time he'd done that, right? How many bodies do you think they'll find in his basement?*

Alice inhaled quietly through her nose for four seconds. She held it for seven seconds. Exhaled completely through the mouth for eight seconds. It felt tranquil to hear it against the mask, even if it did make breathing slightly harder. It would be simpler, wouldn't it? Just to lie down on the floor now and call it quits...yes that would possibly be the best thing to do now…just to let the painful throbbing of her chest subside as she lay down on the cool pavement.

No. Don't shut down. Not here. Anywhere but here. That was the warrior voice again. She needed that boss bitch.

Those dots you're seeing behind your closed eyes, it's just tension. It'll pass. You will not pass out. Freddy Henshaw survived the five days, remember that. He was a lowly Degenerate with an IQ in double figures. You're better than he was. Remember when you first performed at The Pit? Quiet, deep inhales, now girly. Remember that lovely moment of silence – of anticipation – before the drumsticks clacked together cueing you in. Then the onrush of adrenaline as the first deep bass tones thundered from the amps. Same thing. Same thing.

Alice opened her eyes.

The movement of people seemed to organically align again. The market stalls were still there, the bustle of the London streets thronged as they always did. No one was staring at her, no one was paying her any attention.

Breathe. Remember the technique. Inhale quietly through the nose for four seconds. Hold for seven seconds. Exhale completely through the mouth for eight seconds.

Alice did this several times.

She sharply turned and ran back towards the clinic. The crowd started to disperse, and she found herself at the dead end with the shuttered garages. She chided herself for thinking that she should do this during the day. It was too populated, with far too many people roaming the streets. Making sure that no one was watching her, she slipped through a narrow opening of the chain-link fence protecting the dilapidated building.

The abandoned house stood in a serene way amongst the rest of the hustle of the street, as if it had chosen solitude for itself, as if residents were a luxury it could forgo. The windows were covered with a thick layer of dust that looked like it has been untouched for years. The entrance door was framed with what looked like a plank of wood around the outside edges and one across the middle for strength. A flimsy piece of plywood had been nailed in place, covering the door itself. Luckily, it seemed like someone had the idea a while ago to use this decrepit structure for sanctuary, and Alice noted the bottom corner had been wrenched away. She furtively scanned the area one more time to check there weren't any CCTV cameras pointing in her direction, or any drones in the air. When she felt relatively out of sight, she fell to her knees and yanked the corner of plywood away from its anchorage. It was a tight squeeze, but she managed to sprawl through the small hole.

Alice crouched in the darkness of the entrance, listening. She didn't hear any voices. Even the distant noise of cars and vans from the roads outside was absent. As her eyes adjusted to the dark, she could make out fragments of plaster lying damp over a long un-trodden floor, their only purpose to soak in the seasonal rain. The walls appeared rotten and blistered, nursing the mildew that ran up the peeling wallpaper. Alice was alert and tense, every muscle bunched and ready to spring at the slightest unfamiliar noise. She listened intently. There was a damp smell, mixed with something sweet and cloying, like decomposed meat. She noted a few cans attached to string in the middle of the hallway and she slowly avoided them.

Someone's been here. Someone's been here for a while and has set up noise alarms. That someone could still be here. Boss Bitch again for the win.

She looked back. Alice became acutely aware of the dust motes moving sluggishly in the shaft of light from the opening she had created and wondered if she could go back and hide amongst the crowds of the London streets.

No. Too risky. Her face would already be plastered over every digital billboard in the area. Even with the mask, people would be looking for her, and that's what scared her most. It wasn't the faceless Network Agents or the people that used to know her when she played in a band. No, it was the Degenerate fanatics. The ones who would sell their own mother for a few Social Credits that month. The ones she'd seen so many times in The Pit, headbanging and thrashing away to their music, giving her high-fives and devil horns one minute and then throwing bottles at her onstage the next because they were crashing and wanted to score more drugs. They were the ones that had nothing to lose and would be out searching for her, looking for that sweet prize skit.

She'd have to wait until night fall. At least then she'd stand more of a chance of not being recognised. Nodding to herself, she tentatively passed through into a circular vestibule, careful not to step on anything that could give away her location. Nothing but cracked windows and mouldy, browned wooden walls with water stains painting as scars upon skin. Stairs led up, and she forced herself to ignore the discarded syringes and beer cans that littered the floor. She could stay here for a few hours and then slip away under the cover of darkness. Her plan had only been momentarily disrupted, nothing more. Alice even started to think that maybe this could be her hideout for the next couple of days.

The sound alarm made of tin-cans made her cautious though. Who would set up an alarm system in this place?

The stairs were slapped against the eviscerated wall as if they were an afterthought. They were uncommonly narrow, which gave Alice the terrible impression that they had been haphazardly installed after the building had been boarded up. If there had once been a banister it had long ago been salvaged or burnt for firewood. She disbelieved that it would hold the weight of a child let alone an adult, but she took a deep breath before placing even some of her weight on the lowest step. The squeak did not surprise her, but it was immediate and loud, so if there was anyone upstairs, they'd know she was there. Frozen, she waited for any signs of stirring or commotion from the level upstairs. *Give it two minutes, then one minute more.*

She began to ascend against the advice of her anxiety. Slivers of light penetrated from outside, as if invited in to ignite the dust motes swirling in the blackness.

At the top, the bad odour of the house was strongest. Even through her mask, Alice covered her face with the sleeve of her leather jacket, but even then, the stench was overwhelming.

It's okay. Dead rats. Fungus growing from the walls. Not a dead body at all. This will be fine for a few hours. This. Will. Be. Fine.

Alice traversed the crumpled newspapers, broken beer bottles and mottled patches of carpet to arrive at the first room on the upper floor. Four concrete walls with a dirty, blood-stained linoleum floor. She hadn't expected anything less. There was a toilet here with no lid and a soiled bare mattress. There were some crumpled crisp packets and an open can of beans. Alice's mind reeled with the possibility of intruding on a homeless person's refuge and felt a pang of guilt that she was intruding in someone else's house.

And what do you think hobo Joe would do if he recognised you? Boss Bitch chided. *They'd cut your little toes off with a rusty razor, girly. Rape you and keep you here to spawn their hell child. You've dealt with Degenerates before. Most are harmless and can't express themselves properly. But the ones that are aggressive and mean? Well darling, you've also dealt with them before too. A straight punt from the Doc Martens to the proverbial goolies always straightens out the status quo.*

Alice surreptitiously nodded to herself in the darkness, agreeing with the cold sided nature of herself, carrying on and stopping only when she came to a collapsed doorway. Wooden planks barred her from entering, where it looked like the house had fallen in on itself. Or perhaps someone had constructed a rudimentary obstruction to deter potential thieves.

Alice felt cold. Cold all over. The boards were cracked and splintered fresh, enough that she could tell it was a recent blockade.

Still, she had to check. She approached, peering through the slats. It looked just like the rest: quaint in size, aging, and creepy. Cobwebs draped off the walls, their owners nowhere to be seen. Damp seeped across the ceiling, like reaching fingers, the smell of mildew and mould permeating through her mask and making Alice retch. It was unbearable. Thick brown and green moss covered every surface. A small bed, fitted for a kid, sat at one end, with a broken night table plopped next to it. The floorboards were caved and broken, leaving the two simple pieces of furniture sloped towards the dirt waiting for them.

"Slippery Jim's hit the jackpot."

Alice swirled on her feet and was surprised to see a leering face staring back at her. The man's rotted teeth gleamed wetly in the dark. She was about to say something but was robbed of the chance as a bee stung the side of her neck. Her throat constricted instantly.

"Old Slippery Jim is gonna have some fun alright," hissed the raggedy man in front of her. Alice tried to move but she only managed a lazy half-turn before sloping down to the floor and folding in on herself. Her field of vision was starting to blacken, and the last thing she remembered before the room rushed away from her was two rheumy eyes looking down at her.

What do you think hobo Joe would do if he recognised you?

Then everything went black.

6.00pm: Hunted TV

All the Action! Live! Get your daily dose of up-to-the-minute reports from your host, Ryan Lando and join in the search for Hunted's most recent contestant! Witness the mayhem and fun as Ryan interviews guest celebrities as they share their thoughts on the Alice Paige events as they unfold!

7.00pm: Flog It! Live!

The Romans used to flog their victims, and now SO CAN YOU! 10 criminals are put to the public vote – these dastardly deviants have been a scourge on the system for too long! Now YOU get to cast your vote and help decide who gets flagellated and who gets spared the cat-o-nine lash! Catherine Bee puts the sting in this tale!

7.30pm: Top of The Poppers

New! An old concept gets redefined for a new generation! 50 Contestants are given a cocktail of amphetamines and must dance, dance, dance the night away to the UK's latest pop songs! Pick up those feet though, because if you stop moving for more than 3 seconds you get a warning shot. Literally! Those Agents have their rifles trained on you! Three and you're out! Permanently! Who will be the last person standing? Tune in to channel 567 for live coverage 24/7!

8.00pm: Hunted TV

All the Action! Live! Ryan Lando gives you up-to-the-minute coverage of events as they unfold!

8.30pm: Hate Island

TV reality show where single participants are taken to a gorgeous villa in Majorca but must team up with their ex's in order to survive! It's a battle royale with constant video surveillance. Viewers get to vote on their best couple! Only the most barbed, miserable pair of haters win!

9.30pm: Silent Babies

Join psychologist and world-famous body sculptor (yes, that's real human flesh!) Dr. Horatio Dahmer as he takes you on an epic journey of the mind. A journey of silence and intrigue. Five mothers have agreed to give their recently born babies to Dr. Dahmer to keep locked in a sound proofed isolation booth with no light or movement for 6 months! Tune in to find out the results…

10.30pm: How to Break Into the Higher Social Credit Score

Sachin Rajan investigates how much class still matters in Britain's leading professions, finding out what it takes for young working-class people with ERD's to break into the elite as he spends time with Degenerates looking for prestigious positions.

11.30pm: I Love Lucy

Lucy Gallop wants to beat the world record for having sex with the most people in a day. But time is against her! She'll have 24-hours to beat the current record of 919 males. That means she'll need to spend less than 60 seconds with each guy! Can you feel the heat in this room? Tune in to channel 738 for live coverage 24/7!

12.30am: Hunted TV

All the Action! Live! Ryan Lando gives you up-to-the-minute coverage of events as they unfold!

- Radio Times UK

4

THE OLD MAN

MONDAY

108 HOURS REMAIN...

I like to go for long walks.

Not many people know that about me. They see the monolithic Network Building based in central London and they think I'm perched at the very top, like some divine emperor that never leaves. Don't worry, I've seen the sketches comparing me to Howard Hughes on the Free-Vee. To be honest, I think it's a riot! For the younger kids reading this, Howard Hughes was an American business magnate, investor, record-setting pilot, engineer film director, and philanthropist, known during his lifetime as one of the most financially successful individuals in the world.

I guess I can see why they make the comparisons.

Well folks, the reason for this blog is to let you all know some news. Some good. Some bad.

Let's start with the bad, shall we?

I'm dying.

Now, theoretically speaking – we're all dying. A pessimistic person would opinion that as soon as we're born, the pistol has been shot and we're on the conveyer belt towards death. But I think that's quite a morbid way of looking at life. I've always been an optimist at heart, and that's why I started to write this blog. You see, I'm not going to have enough time to write my memoirs. The quacks tell me I probably have a year left, and I don't want to spend all that time hunched over a computer, writing things down. A king rules, and then he dies. It's that simple. I just thought it would be good to record some of my rambling thoughts in a coherent way and educate the good people of the world with some of my life experiences, to give you all an insight into how I became the man I am today.

Also it's a way to tell you how The Network was created and where it's heading in the future. It's strange to think that not so long from now I'll be gone and the company I built will continue without me. But just in the way that a parent raises a child to an age where they're ready to strike it lucky on their own, I must do the same. I must wave that child away as it stares bright eyed and awe inspired at the world.

I thought a long time about writing this. We live in strange times, and with the media being what it is, things I could write could be misinterpreted, or represented in a way that would be damaging to The Network. My lovely PA Cassandra was a little worried that certain factions would try to manipulate what I jotted down to besmirch my name, or at the very least slander what it is we've achieved over the last twenty odd years.

But then I thought about it and decided that was *exactly* the reason why I had to write this. It's with great humility to say that The Network has been the kind of grand accomplishment I can be proud of. It's the kind of dream that most people don't get to make in their lifetime. I sometimes sit here and think to myself that it's all a dream, really – that if I try to reach out and grab it it'll drift away in a puff of smoke. The things we've accomplished, the barriers we've smashed down...it's all very awe-inspiring.

It's my legacy, you see. My wife Beatrice and I never had children of our own...so in a strange way I've always looked at the business as a facsimile of the child-like entity. You might laugh at that, but it's true. I've moulded this company from its early years, just in the same way a parent teaches their offspring right from wrong. We've both made mistakes along the way, but we've both learnt from them. Sometimes we stumble, sometimes we fall, but we've always managed to pick ourselves up and strive for greatness. So, laugh all you like, dear reader – but know this to be true: I've given all my heart to this venture.

But I'm getting ahead of myself.

You may have read some articles about my modest origins, how I went from owning a simple pharmaceutical store in Ealing to founding the most entertaining, prosperous and advanced conglomerate in the world, but I wanted to set the record straight, so to speak. In future blogs, I'll be telling you my superhero origin story (harhar) – but for now I just wanted to talk to you about how The Network became the best solution for a nation in turmoil.

It may be hard to remember, but over twenty years ago, we were at breaking point. The world was literally imploding. Do you remember that? Do you remember the pandemic? The fear? The rioting? Perhaps some of you reading this will be too young to recollect but let me assure you when I say that we were on the precipice of economic, political, social and ecological disaster. Most people had given up, thinking that we were going to star in our very own dystopian, post-apocalyptic film. And they would have been right. Crime was rampant, the police forces were striking, and lawlessness had descended over this once beautiful country. Overpopulation had dwindled the earth's resources to dangerously low proportions.

But I had a dream.

I realised that The Network could be more than a band aid for a gaping wound. It could be a *solution*. It could provide worldwide relief. It could give people the hope they so drastically required. Little by little I tried to achieve that dream. I became fanatical.

Soon, I was able to share my dream with other people. It gave them hope. It gave them an escape. It gave them freedom. We started off small, but I had a fierce and loyal team behind me. There's a great saying that behind every great man is a woman, and that's no joke. I wouldn't be here today without the love and grace from my wife, Beatrice. As I'm writing this, I can hear her softly snoring in the next room. She'll throttle me when she reads that, but I find it reassuring to know that she's been by my side from the very beginning, and I'll die a happy man knowing that she'll be there with me at the very end.

The dream continued to soar.

We gave people jobs. In a time when pandemics were forcing people into a life of squalid solitude, we were able to reconnect people. I sold the pharmaceutical store and we evolved into a tech company, which then branched out across multiple umbrellas of research and development. We gave people affordable healthcare and a system that worked for *them*. No more politicians lying to line their own pockets. I said from the very beginning that there were going to be some tough choices to make, but it would be the only way we could save this planet. The decisions of our past are the architects of our present. We started to generate billions in tax revenue. Soon after that we were able to create technology that would help save our dying planet. We were so big by then that we were able to jam our feet in the doorstop of the political world and start addressing the real problems. And then the biggest issues to tackle. The overpopulation and the crime.

A lot of people have differing opinions on some of the choices that we made over the years, but to them I would say this: It works.

Did you know that it took thousands of years all the way up to the 1800's to reach one billion people? Then it only took about a hundred years to double the population to two billion in the 1920's. After that it was only fifty years for the population to double again in the 70's. We were well on our way to eight billion. If the numbers are a little overwhelming, just think of it as a picture: every year we were adding the equivalent of the entire country of Germany into the world. Just take a moment and think about that. Let it sink in.

The world's resources were being pulled out of its roots. World leaders weren't doing anything about it, so we had to act. It would be revolutionary and radical, but as I said before, tough choices had to be made.

And the dream continued.

I'm not saying we live in a perfect world, but I like to think that we've managed to make a world that works best for the people living in it. My recent prognosis has given me time to reflect on a few things, and I've taken more time to go on walks and think about the future.

Because really, that's what it's all about, isn't it? The future. I've built my legacy and I'm proud of it. Damned proud. But I won't be around for much longer. Therefore, my thoughts are moving forwards. You should always be moving forwards. How can I be sure that we won't fall into the same traps again? How can we ensure the safety of humanity and that we never make the mistakes of the past?

I think I know.

But, just like any good entertainer, it's only customary to leave the audience wanting more. Maybe I'll explain in my next blog post. Maybe I won't. Let's see how I feel. Until then, I'm going back to bed to join my lovely wife and hopefully sleep as peacefully. I wish you all the very best.

Until next time, stay safe.

PATRICIA O'NEIL: We're with Ryan Lando, host of the popular show *Hunted TV* – how are you doing today Ryan?

RYAN LANDO: I'm pumped, Patricia. Absolutely pumped. There's electricity in the air. We're on the first day of Alice Paige's hunt, and the scent is strong. By the way, I watch all your news broadcasts – you always look fantastic.

PATRICIA O'NEIL: (Laughs sheepishly) Ha-ha, why thank you Ryan – you charmer. What can you tell us about the events unfolding so far?

RYAN LANDO: Well, it seems that Ms. Paige has been able to nullify her SCOOP Suit.

PATRICIA O'NEIL: Nullify?

RYAN LANDO: Simply put, she's managed to get the SCOOP Suit off.

PATRICIA O'NEIL: Is that possible?

RYAN LANDO: Well, it's extremely difficult, let's put it that way. Her camera feed went dead earlier this morning and we haven't been able to re-establish a connection. There's no way she would have been able to do this by herself, so we know she's had help. That gives The Network Agents some strong leads, as they're aware of certain illegal chop shops that cater for this specifically.

PATRICIA O'NEIL: But if she's removed her SCOOP suit, won't it be harder for people to recognise her?

RYAN LANDO: That's the double-edged sword in this case.

PATRICIA O'NEIL: Talk to us about the cameras, Ryan.

RYAN LANDO: Well, to give the contestant a sporting chance, the HD camera on the SCOOP Suit emits live bursts once every couple of hours. It keeps the contestant on their toes but also shows where they are.

PATRICIA O'NEIL: Couldn't the contestant just block the camera with some gum or something similar?

RYAN LANDO: Yeah, that was a problem we faced in the first year of *Hunted TV*. The suits were fitted with safeguards after that.

PATRICIA O'NEIL: Safeguards?

RYAN LANDO: If the contestant decided to block the camera feed in any way, the suit would shock them. If they continue, the shock voltage increases.

PATRICIA O'NEIL: Interesting. There's always been talk that the suits have been fitted with tracking devices. What do you have to say about that?

RYAN LANDO: That's baloney, Patricia. The Network gives the contestant a fair and sporting chance that they'll be able to last the whole five days. It doesn't state anywhere in the contract that the contestant can't remove the suit…so there's a loophole I guess, but maybe next year we'll bring in a new clause. That's what I love about you, Patricia. Your investigative skills. And your eyes.

PATRICIA O'NEIL: Umm, thank you, Ryan. We're coming up to the fifth anniversary of Frederick Henshaw's infamous run, the only known survivor of the *Hunted TV* programme. He managed to stay ahead of the general public and Network Agents for five days, so we know it can be done. Do you still think about Freddy's success?

RYAN LANDO: I'd be lying if I didn't say that Freddy's escape still leaves a bittersweet taste in the mouth. We've had a 99% success rate on *Hunted TV*, and Freddy is that stain that will forever be held on the record. But it just goes to show that people can win this game.

PATRICIA O'NEIL: Some people speculate that Freddy didn't win, that it was all a publicity stunt to give people a little hope as the retirement rates have increased exponentially over the last decade.

RYAN LANDO: (Laughs) Ha-ha – wow…that's…that's just insane. Conspiracy theory time, eh?

PATRICIA O'NEIL: But you're not denying it?

RYAN LANDO: I'm just so mesmerised by your eyes, Patricia. I could get lost in them.

5

KAVANAGH

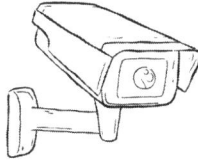

MONDAY

107 HOURS REMAIN...

Agent Kavanagh logged into his terminal at The Network command centre.

Fifteen retirements this morning. Not a bad result. By no means a personal best, but there was still the afternoon to make up the difference. Before he started typing on his keyboard, he positioned his phone and pens, so they sat perpendicular to the base of his laptop. His desk was all straight lines and everything on it was orderly arranged and aligned. Kavanagh believed that a man was a method, a progressive arrangement, a selecting principle. He also believed that to be respected, authority had to be respectable. Everything had its place.

The Network headquarters was a cloud-capped colossal tower

located in central London, a monument to the modern age with acres of glass welded together with shiny steel. Kavanagh felt that the city below was so far away it felt almost like another world, with all those ant-like people shuffling about alongside all their problems being of no more consequence in Kavanagh's opinion than temporary static on the intercom. The Department of Waste was located on the thirty-seventh floor.

He started tapping names into the database inside his soundproof glass cubicle, categorising addresses, next of kin and respective times and dates. He didn't see people and faces as he went about his work, in the same manner that a butcher wouldn't stop to think about how many fowls he would hang inside his shop that day. Humans, as far as Kavanagh was concerned, were overridden by primitive emotions and had yet much to discover without their small headed minds celebrating the vacuous vices in their insignificant universes. They could be so much more if they simply put their pasts behind them and investigated the future because without distractions, they could be anything and do anything.

Kavanagh peered over the lip of his laptop and saw Agent Williams slouched over his terminal, a few cubicles down scratching at his stubbled jowls, checking his phone the fifth time in two minutes. Kavanagh continued with his work, no faster, no slower. As far as he was concerned, the inept agent could check his phone a hundred times in his indiscreet way, huffing and puffing like the nuisance he was. He glanced at his own phone, annoyed with its silence.

There was going to be an announcement by The Old Man soon.

An email alert had gone out to every Agent that morning, regarding the Alice Paige case. It was her first day having decided not to engage with her Birthday Treat and, in the process, entering the *Hunted* TV programme, and there had been no sightings of the girl in London as of yet. The keyboard on his laptop was entirely flat and in the darkness of the office it was only the under-lit keys that glowed. Kavanagh felt like he was typing on a table than the machines of old. He preferred the bulkier versions to the slim-line portable devices they could carry in their cases, as he found a certain satisfaction to the give of the keys, like you were pressing a button. It let you know you had made contact. Now it was just the feeling of something solid and cold under the fingertip. As Kavanagh typed in Mrs. Bowerman's details into the central database, he made a note about her grandson and diarised a follow up appointment in his calendar. The unfortunate Degenerate would likely foul up sometime between then and now and Kavanagh wanted his name on the claim when it came time to repossess the house.

His phone chimed.

A short message, but nonetheless an important one. Probably the most important of his career.

Agent 8718669.

Meeting Scheduled.

20 mins.

Floor 350.

Replying too soon would show anxiety, not a trait he wished to advertise. Kavanagh's fingers froze mid-way through his report. If he were being promoted to find Alice Paige, he would get the opportunity to retire her. He thought about that for a moment. The last two years he'd been retiring old people, people of no consequence. He found himself wondering what it would be like to retire a young person. A child, really. Perhaps with Alice Paige the result would be different. There might be a different expression in her eyes at the end, something besides the bemused countenance that vexed him every time he saw it. He would quite like to see her lights go out.

He re-read the text, to ensure he understood perfectly well the meaning behind it. He leaned back on his chair and exhaled, realising he had been holding his breath. This was it, then. Clearing his throat, he pocketed his phone and set his laptop to standby. Exiting his glass cubicle, he walked past a half-dozen other chambers – some transparent, some opaque – in which other agents were handling other aspects of Waste assignments. He glanced over at Williams as he walked down the narrow-carpeted aisle. His incompetent colleague was tapping his fingers on his desk, waiting for a text that would never come.

You're trash. I'm better than you. Kavanagh started walking with a ranging stride, even and quick paced. *How do I know I'm superior to you, Williams? The way you conduct yourself. I know from comparing your clothes to mine, your shoes, your hair, your car. You are trash. Everybody has a right to be stupid, but some people just abuse that privilege. Stop snivelling and crawl back to whatever bin you sleep in.*

Kavanagh waved his hand to his underling. Williams took it as a passing gesture, but Kavanagh sneered at the real meaning. That one gesture meant unsalvageable. Thanks for all the fish. Williams flipped a switch on his cubicle wall and it instantly turned opaque. *Suit yourself,* Kavanagh sneered.

As he left the office and made his way across the atrium, he felt the soft clicks of his heels hitting the marble floor. The walls were covered with grey wallpaper, interspersed with framed motivational posters about carbon waste and elderly people walking into a doorway with light emanating from it, with the simple words: KNOW YOUR ROLE. Entering the toilets, he checked to make sure that none of the cubicles were in use. The light in the bathroom was bright and sterile, lacking even a trace of warmth. He stood in front of one of the mirrors and unbuttoned his jacket, folding it carefully and laying it next to the sink. He stared at his reflection as he started rolling up his sleeve.

"With self-discipline almost anything is possible."

His pale arm revealed a criss-cross patchwork of scars, old and new. There were even some cuts still fresh, red and puffy and deep. He presented his underarm forward towards the mirror, as if offering it a gift. With his free hand, he reached inside his folded jacket and produced a small razor. So small, but sharp.

"Force has no place where there is need of skill." Kavanagh pressed the razor's edge just below the nook where the forearm and elbow meet.

"You must submit to complete suffering in order to discover the completion of joy."

He dragged the razor into his flesh until blood welled. The colour was a dark red against the blue-white skin there. It wasn't a noticeably big cut, he'd made bigger in his time, but the sting of it focused everything to an acute point. There was something about the act that warmed his core, bringing a surge of energy that was purer than anything he'd felt. It gave him that extra spark, the catalyst that would fire synapses in his mind and keep him on edge. Keeping him focused. The blood seeped dark and crimson. He didn't need to go too deep today; he just needed a boost – something to prepare him for the meeting. Cautious that anyone could enter the lavatory, he pressed his lips snugly against the opened wound and sucked to stop the free-flowing surge of sticky blood. There was a discreet, metallic tang. He unrolled tissue from the nearby dispenser and wrapping it around his arm. He rolled down the shirtsleeve, checked himself, carefully preening any unwarranted grey hairs from his scalp, which was tightly combed to his skull. He shrugged on his jacket.

His phone beeped again.

Agent 8718669.

Meeting Scheduled.

10 mins.

He replied he was on his way.

The lift opened directly into an alcove with an ornate door in front of him. The gold-plated name above the frame made Kavanagh collect himself for a moment before knocking.

"Come!" Came the brisk, impatient cadence of a person accustomed to getting her way.

The private office was an immense room occupying the upper-most corner of the building with floor-to-ceiling windows, giving a stunning panoramic view of the city below it. The two remaining walls were covered with intricate filigree wallpaper and monitors showcasing the latest news with regards to Alice Paige. On the grand mahogany desk sat a desktop computer and a stack of papers sitting under a *Hunted TV* paperweight. A bookshelf, overflowing with books was in a corner, with a single oil painting – The Medusa by Caravaggio. Cassandra Rey sat behind the desk, her business suit as crisp as a new banknote and dyed to a uniform shade of bleak grey. Her face was made up, but not overdone and her long black hair was pulled back into a ponytail. She was scribbling something on a piece of paper as Kavanagh approached, not looking at him or acknowledging his presence. Kavanagh stood before her, hands behind his back like a soldier awaiting a command. Finally, she finished whatever paperwork and cocked her head slightly towards him, as if appreciating a round of applause which only she could hear.

Kavanagh met her at the desk and stretched out his hand. He was momentarily surprised that Cassandra's grip was vice-like. *But then again,* he thought, *she didn't get to this position via the soft approach.* She waved a hand to the seat in front of his desk. "Agent Kavanagh," she said, "please, take a seat."

Kavanagh did so.

"I've heard about your work, Agent Kavanagh."

Kavanagh stared at her.

"Your records and your recent field work results indicate that you're a very bright boy indeed. So...indulge me...do you know why you're here?"

The fresh cut on his arm stung as he folded his arms. *No small talk, no chit-chat. This PA gets straight down to the meat and potatoes.* His eyes flicked to the monitor on the wall where Alice Paige's mug shot was displayed. The compulsive shrieking of the announcer couldn't be heard, so Kavanagh assumed that Cassandra had special privileges to have it muted or turned down. *Quite a sweet set-up.* Kavanagh couldn't help but feel that perhaps in a few years from now he may also have an office just like this one. If he played his cards right.

"I assume you're going to give me the Alice Paige job."

Cassandra's face held a distasteful squint that Kavanagh found revulsive. In truth though, he found most people revulsive. The PA of The Old Man let the moment linger for a moment, teetering into uncomfortable silence. Perhaps she was playing with Kavanagh's perceptions of her. Or perhaps she was merely trying to unnerve him. Her mouth curled into a thin smile as if she were in possession of a wonderful secret.

"Right," she said, following his gaze to the monitors, "she's becoming quite the burden. But never assume things, Agent. It makes an ass out of you and me." She chuckled at this.

Kavanagh bristled at the remark, but he let it slide, opting to smile benignly at the joke aimed at his expense. He watched intently as Cassandra's hand produced a dossier file from the desk and languidly slid it towards him. As Kavanagh flipped it open, Cassandra leaned back in her seat, turning slightly to take in the sweeping view of the city. "Alice Paige. Age twenty-one. Social Credit score of 107. Attended Manchester University for several years before becoming suspended for failing to respect authority. She slapped a teacher citing unwarranted advances. She moved to London and her work record has been spotty at best. Joined a punk band and has been playing in dive bars for the last couple of years. Failed to participate with her Birthday treat and was officially transferred to the *Hunter* TV programme eleven hours ago."

Kavanagh leafed through the documents. "Her Social Credit score has never dipped below 100," he remarked.

Cassandra smiled briefly, white teeth glittering. "Indeed. Smart cookie. Credit rating not high enough to enforce tax brackets, but not too low to warrant Degenerate status, even though all of her song lyrics promote anarchy and chaos."

"You say she's been on the run for eleven hours?"

"Hence your promotion, approved from now."

Kavanagh peered over the file to meet Cassandra's eyes.

"You're not surprised. It's a character trait I admire. I loathe false sentimentality. But frankly, Agent Kavanagh, I didn't want a Waste agent assigned to this. There's a finite stage where a Waste Agent becomes...desensitised to the work they do. You've been conducting your role admirably for the last two years. But I believe you have become nonchalant to it. You have become numb to it."

Kavanagh let his arms fall to his side, so she couldn't see him balling up his fists so tightly he felt new blood trickle from his arm. *You must submit to complete suffering to discover the completion of joy. You must submit to complete suffering to discover the completion of joy. You must...*

"Let me be franker...I didn't want *you* assigned to this. Unfortunately, I must contend with the big man, and he's made his wishes perfectly clear on this matter."

Her eyes flicked to the far end of the room, where double lift doors remained shut. Kavanagh assumed the Old Man was in the penthouse on the floor above. He didn't know until this moment that there was another floor above. He mildly wondered if The Old Man was up there now, staring at several screens. He'd heard rumours that he peed in mason jars and only showed his face on rare appearances.

"Is it true?" Kavanagh asked.

"Stomach cancer," Cassandra replied. "The doctors say he may have a year left, but that's hopeful at best. I would say six months, tops."

Kavanagh nodded his head. He tried to muster a little sympathy for The Old Man but found it hard to feel bad about a person he'd never met. Kavanagh often wondered if he was heartless. He knew he had a heart, because if he pressed his hand to his chest he could feel it pumping.

"He likes your attention to detail. You're efficient." Cassandra continued, "If I'd have full reign on this matter it would have gone to someone a little more...ruthless. Your results come from the elderly and frail. This girl is young...pugnacious."

"I can be ruthless." Kavanagh said flatly.

"Our last Hunter became...sloppy. The Hunted Programme is one of our surest ways of eliminating troublemakers such as Alice Paige. The last person to waylay their Birthday Treat made it to the fourth day. It's unacceptable. We've been on the air for over a decade and to date we've had no survivors."

Kavanagh blinked. "What about Frederick Henshaw? He won five years ago."

Cassandra made a sound: not exactly a laugh, exactly; more of a shrill giggle. "We made it look like Frederick Henshaw succeeded to keep the populace in check, Agent Kavanagh. You give people a small amount of hope, just a slither, you see? You do this to keep their heads above the water. To make them think it's all balanced. But nearly impossible. You want them to think that it *could* happen, but only once in a millennium. You think Freddy Henshaw is sipping cocktails on a beach somewhere? The poor fool was shot down on the third day. We made tapes and deep faked the rest."

Kavanagh considered this.

"You remember the old days, Agent Kavanagh?"

Kavanagh grimaced. He did.

"I remember what it was like." He said, tactfully.

Cassandra narrowed her eyes at Kavanagh. She swept her arm across the windows behind him. "Tell me what you see out there, Agent."

Careful, he told himself. *This is a test, just like everything else.*

Kavanagh took a moment to think of the question and flashed a big PR smile. "Potential."

Cassandra clucked her tongue. "Don't tell me what you *think* I want to hear, Agent Kavanagh. I didn't get to this position surrounding myself with people telling me what I wanted to hear."

Kavanagh didn't return her grin. Something in her expression comported a mix of displeasure and anxiety. *With self-discipline almost anything is possible.*

"Perhaps I should clarify. I came to realise at a young age that the world is made up mostly of fools and liars," he said carefully. "The world before The Network seemed to be jammed in a perpetual gridlock of snarling stagnation, with leaders too absent-minded and fundamentally ill-prepared to lead this country. They stood snivelling and shuffling, pissing vinegar into the buttery jar of milk that the plebs outside those windows lapped up. Only they didn't know that the jar had been shaken and was curdled. They always promised new things, didn't they? A fresh start, a new beginning, a shiny tomorrow, but they always spoon-fed gruel until we choked on it. Domestic violence had risen, and cuts had left the city at breaking point. You were the tip of the spearhead that this country so desperately craved. In time people have been able to ascertain the importance...the fundamental significance of what we're trying to achieve here. When I said potential earlier, it wasn't the hopes and dreams of the residents of this country. It was the heavy boot on their necks. It's the people with their camera phones, rooting for Alice Paige to be caught. They want to see her wiped out and they'll enjoy stomping on her face if they can."

Kavanagh stopped. He hadn't realised during his ramble that his voice had risen and was trembling. He felt his cheeks flush. The new cut on his arm stung against the haphazard wrapping of tissue paper. He clamped down his tongue between his teeth to keep a yelp from escaping his mouth.

Cassandra looked at him with blank eyes. She pressed her lips together. "I want this girl caught, Agent Kavanagh. Eleven hours has been long enough. If she makes seventy-two hours, we start looking incompetent and bungling. Each day that she survives, we lose the power of the people. They'll start to chant for her, they'll start to love her. Then the unruliness and abhorrent behaviour rises again. If she ever reached the fifth day -"

"She won't."

"If she ever reached the fifth day," she continued, the tambour of her voice deepening from the interruption, "it wouldn't be good for us. You'll have all means at your disposal to get the job done. We usually assign a point agent and secondary to hunting down the perpetrator. You're with Williams, are you not?"

Force has no place where there is need of skill.

"With all due respect, ...Williams is an imbecile. A bouncer at the door of a nightclub, at best. From this dossier, Alice Paige will scurry underground and try to blend in with her people. Those good middle-class folks out there," he said, jutting a chin at the windows, "they hate her with every fibre of her being...she symbolises all the fears and darkness they can only dream about if they get a Birthday Treat. No...the way to catch a rat is to think like one."

Cassandra laughed softly. "Maybe I'm wrong about you, Agent Kavanagh. Who would you choose as your secondary, then?"

Kavanagh didn't hesitate. He'd already thought this through. "Agent Valentine, sir."

Cassandra considered this, staring up at the ceiling as if trying to solve an answer to a puzzle. Her face wore an irritable look. "Valentine is on indefinite suspension."

Deliberately, Kavanagh slowed his thoughts. "That's correct. He's suspended for the exact reasons I need him as my secondary for this particular assignment." He flashed another grin, this one beaming and toothy.

"You need to be careful," Cassandra said, hardly raising her voice. She looked directly at Kavanagh, "you've shown acute perspicacity for coming this far...to be in this room. I don't believe you care much for me, Agent Kavanagh."

Kavanagh could feel blood pooling at his wrist. He felt his forehead was slick with sweat. *You must submit to complete suffering to discover the completion of joy.*

"I don't care one jot about that," Cassandra continued, in a scholarly voice. "In fact, it's a welcoming relief. I suspect that most of my staff consider me somewhat of a bitch, and they'd be correct in their judgement of my character. I have to be conniving, manipulative and a bit of a bitch to run things around here."

She looked at Kavanagh for comment. The Agent remained wisely silent.

"We've got the boyfriend downstairs in interrogation. Every SCOOP suit has a tracker, unbeknown to the user. Preliminary intel suggests that she's used a backstreet vendor to forcibly remove her SCOOP suit. We need to find out who and where she's gone. You should be able to pick up the trail from there."

Kavanagh stood, trying to look composed and appraising.

"There's nothing personal in the things said in this room, Agent Kavanagh. But just remember one thing," Cassandra said, elbows on the desk and the tips of her fingers tenting together. "Don't you ever try to fuck me. Get the girl and I see bright things for you in the future." Cassandra was done with him then, returning to her work.

Kavanagh walked back to the door, imperceptibly scratching the area where he had made a cut. *Nothing personal taken,* he thought to himself. *I also see bright things ahead in my future.*

CALLER: It's the end times, Happy. I kid you not. We must prepare for Eternal Life.

HAPPY HORGAN: That's a tad…extreme.

CALLER: Oh, there are signs. There are signs all around us. Isaiah 13:9 "Behold, the day of the Lord comes, cruel, with wrath and fierce anger, to make the land a desolation and to destroy its sinners from it." It's right there in the bible. We must rejoice in His name and prepare ourselves for the life after this one. I'm talking about repentance.

HAPPY HORGAN: Hang on a second…let me see if I've got this right. You think we're heading for Armageddon?

CALLER: It's already here, Happy. Global warming? The insidious fiery beast that crept into our beds without us acting. Moral decay? It's running rampant - from the filth on the television to those poor Degenerates on the streets. Years ago, we would have helped them. Not vilified them, categorised them and stuck glowing lights on their foreheads. Then there's the False prophets.

HAPPY HORGAN: I assume you're saying that The Network are the-

CALLER: Yes! Exactly! Revelation 20:9-10 "And they marched up over the broad plain of the earth and surrounded the camp of the saints and the beloved city, but fire came down from heaven and consumed them, and the devil who had deceived them was thrown into the lake of fire and sulphur where the beast and the false prophet were, and they will be tormented day and night forever and ever."

HAPPY HORGAN: …

CALLER: Here is the FINAL destination of Satan and all his evil demons. Right here, Happy. Today. For our eternal destiny is sealed and nothing can prevent it from occurring for God has ordained the end. And we must prepare.

HAPPY HORGAN: Well, let's backtrack a little so I can wrap my head around all of this.

You're saying that our land...the UK, is currently a desolation. And the sinners, I'm going for broke here and say that WE'RE the sinners, will be destroyed by The Network. Who is the devil? Is that right?

CALLER: TV's constantly on. Antibiotics that don't work anymore. Gameshows that glorify death and destruction like some Roman Colosseum. Marijuana cigarettes, for Christ's sake! The bugs are gone, have you noticed that, Happy?

HAPPY HORGAN: The bugs?

CALLER: Took a drive to Wales last weekend. On the motorway for about three hours. Turned into country roads. When I got out of the car, didn't see a single bug splatter on the car. The world's insects are hurtling down the path to extinction, threatening a catastrophic collapse of nature's ecosystems. More than 40% of insect species are declining and a third are endangered. So, when the bugs die out, the birds die out. And that causes a chain reaction which ends with us. Cause and effect.

HAPPY HORGAN: Maybe it's all a conspiracy.

CALLER: ...

HAPPY HORGAN: You still with me?

CALLER: It's not a conspiracy, Happy. It's not China...it's not any of that.

HAPPY HORGAN: Right! It's not. But you were happy to chalk it up to the devil a minute ago, right? You're talking about eternal life and repentance? Good God, man. Show me a religion that prepares one for death. For nothingness. For oblivion. Sign me up to that Church, because that's what I believe, brother.

CALLER: You're being facetious.

HAPPY HORGAN: Because I don't believe what you believe? Every road ends in death. To think otherwise is just foolish.

Birthday Treat

- From The Happy Horgan Live Show

@Happyhorgan

Case #289

NetworkID: 8716367 Bryant, G.

Time: 13:07

#**289**: Where does our soul go when you die, do you think?

8716367: Are you religious?

#**289**: Plato believed in the transmigration of our eternal selves. But where do they go? That's the question, isn't it?

8716367: Where do you think they go?

#**289**: Hmm. Christianity, Buddhism, Islam…even Taoism…they all believed the soul…moves on.

8716367: But you don't think it does?

#**289**: I have become an expert in the soul, Network man.

8716367: You can call me George, if you like. Have you been feeling this way since your Birthday Treat?

#**289**: Where is she now, I wonder? Will I meet here again when I'm gone?

8716367: Can you confirm you have been taking your prescribed medication following your Treat?

#**289**: Drugs are for the weak, Network man. In Latin, they called the spirit the Anima. It means the soul…the mind. I feel like maybe I have lost mine.

8716367: …your mind? Or your soul?

#**289**: I feel like I'm searching for what remains of me. Do you understand?

8716367: Have you been feeling this way since you poisoned your wife?

#289: I freed her spirit. It's what she wanted.

8716367: She was quadriplegic, is that correct?

#289: What are we, underneath the tissue? Hmm. Are we made up of billions of atoms that simply cease when the body finally decays to a point of uselessness? My wife had a good spirit, I think. But have I damned myself in the process?

8716367: Descartes famously believed in the dualistic nature of the soul and mind.

#289: Hmm.

8716367: You say that you freed her. Did she communicate this with you?

#289: She was my wife. I could tell.

8716367: I can imagine…the strain. Years of having to look after someone that way.

#289: It was my job. My position as a loyal husband.

8716367: What you're feeling is guilt. Maybe that's why you're trying to find yourself. A burden that was weighing heavily on your shoulders has now been lifted and perhaps you don't know what to do with that?

#289: Perhaps, Network man. Perhaps.

6

GEORGE

MONDAY

106 HOURS REMAIN...

George was late for work. He'd spent the entire morning on diverted routes towards London. As the automatic doors swished open, he could already see Sebastian Faulkner peering down at him with contemptuous, reptilian eyes from the balcony. Muttering crude and incomprehensible words under his breath, he passed the security guard with the buzz-cut hair, swiped his ID card across the turnstile panel and reached the lifts, punching the UP button multiple times with a podgy digit. The wall-mounted Free-Vee was showing an episode of *Frogger!* where a fat man was currently deliberating when to try and run past the screaming lanes of traffic. As George waited for the lift to arrive, he found himself absent mindedly shaking his head as the portly man decided to make a mad dash across but failed to see the 18-wheeler that pulverized him into a gooey puddle.

He considered taking the staircase up to the fourth floor, to burn off some calories and make a point of tackling the paunch issue that had manifested into a gut problem, but he wasn't in the mood. Especially now, under the scrutiny of Sebastian's gaze, boring lasers into the back of his skull. There had once been a time when George had an office on the seventh floor of The Network building. He had a resplendent view of the Gherkin and the Millennium Wheel – he felt like he was in a different part of the world in that office; the glass curtainwall separating him and the normal people of the world. Often, he would look down at the ant-like specks of people going on about their normal life and he would feel content in the knowledge that he was safe in his own little bubble, his own little paradise. Away from Elspeth...away from everyone.

Words like 'open-space environment,' had been thrown around like recreational drugs at a hippy festival: CAD designs had been drawn up and that was all she wrote; offices were demolished and rows upon rows of desks were implemented into the building. George had been quite content sitting in his office, not talking to anyone. The lift finally came, and George found himself staring at the wall to avoid eye contact with his colleagues. He wondered if he would be able to grab a quick nap in the toilets later. He tried to get the handicapped stall, as it was clean and spacious. It was also at the end of the row against the wall so he wouldn't have two people flanking him whilst they grunted and shat like hogs.

When the lift opened on the fourth floor, he found himself staring at the bulky shape of Sebastian Faulkner.

'George!' he said, throwing his hands out in a mock gesture of welcome. George likened it to a vampire about to suck the life force out of his body. Faulkner was the kind of guy that laughed after everything he spewed from his mouth, a staccato *yuk-yuk-yuk* that drilled into the brain like a violent buzz saw. George nodded his head which was already starting to thrum like a bad tooth and started walking towards the doors of the large office space, wondering what this uncharacteristic morning greeting concealed.

"How's it going?" Sebastian asked. *Yuk-yuk-yuk.*

George hesitated for a moment. He had not mentioned anything about his lateness, which meant that he was after something.

"Oh, just fine," George replied, not breaking stride so that the vampire couldn't hypnotize him with his unusual supplicating temperament. George noticed his elegant suit and his shoes that were buffed to distraction and he unconsciously looked down at his own scuffed shoes. For a split second his mind hurtled back to the ponytailed man on the platform, the man with the red ruby lips – the way he calmly and proficiently lifted the girl's headphones to whisper something sweetly into her ear before throwing her in front of the train. George thought now to himself whether *he* was the girl with the headphones, about to be thrown under the train.

"Yes, let's walk and talk. I know you're a busy man," Faulkner said, coolly turning on his heels to keep pace. "George, something's come up that we need to discuss," he whispered, leaning in and staring with those black, dead eyes. "Something very important."

George pushed through the doors and into the office space. It was Monday, and he hadn't even turned on his laptop. He thought again of the handicapped stall and the bars on the wall that sometimes made him feel like a quadriplegic or a ballerina, depending on his mood. It was Monday, and he was late and didn't even have time to sit down and take off his coat. The headache he was trying to suppress clawed at his skull like a wild panther attacking its prey. He was not in the mood for Faulkner's games.

"What is it, Sebastian?"

George noted Sebastian's eyelid twitch at this – *probably had a whole speech ready for me,* he thinks, *and the officious little prick doesn't like to be hurried on.* Within a microsecond of the thrombotic twitch, his mouth twisted cruelly into a leer.

"Well, it's Parker." *Yuk-yuk-yuk.*

Like a dial-up modem, George's brain started screeching noises as his brain tried to connect to the worldwide web of forewarning.

George had once assumed that every office in the world had a Parker, the kind of guy that's never really given any worthwhile tasks to complete, as he can't thoroughly comprehend them. Slow of reaction, he wasn't particularly agile on his feet in a mental capacity. He was the kind of person that you avoided trying to have a conversation with at work because you didn't have the grace or the inclination to humor the village idiot as he whacked chicken drumsticks against his knees attempting to emulate the beat of *The Macarena*.

He had a good heart, though. Spoke his mind, which George respected.

They passed a couple of whiteboards in the middle of the room scribbled with writing and work diagrams.

"What about him?"

"Well...the higher uppers want him to take on a more... substantial role. It's quite an embarrassing situation really. I'm mortified. Ha-ha. But we've got to keep the cog turning, so to speak."

They had reached George's desk. He placed his briefcase on the table, snapping the latches open. George's mind was still whirring as he took out his laptop. Parker came under his remit, so he was wondering what Faulkner was about to propose. Faulkner continued: "They want him to start taking on cases. I thought it would be a good idea to let him listen in on your calls."

George took out a few files and slowly closed the lid.

He knew the tell-tale signs of a restructure within the group when he saw them. Cut backs. Departmentalizing. Same old tricks.

George slapped the files down at his desk. "He's only been here a few months, Sebastian. He's not ready."

It was important to use Sebastian's name whenever possible during this conversation. He knew he would not win the argument, but he wanted the little shit to feel partly bad about it. Using people's names relayed a kind of 'we're in this together,' feel. George hadn't studied psychology for nothing.

"Yeah. As I said, I'm *mortified*."

George looked at Faulkner. An uncomfortable moment passed,

and the headache that had started as a small throb was threatening to go nuclear.

There were too many things crisscrossing to make sense here; Parker was too immature and stubborn to make the right calls when it came to evaluating Birthday Treaters and debriefing them after an event. Something was up. He wondered about his own role, and what had prompted this act of blatant destabilization.

"This wouldn't have anything to do with the cutbacks mentioned in the annual report, would it? I'm not training him to do my job for you guys only to fire me in a month's time, Sebastian." George said.

Faulkner clapped a heavy, sausage fingered hand on his shoulder. "No! Not at all, George. But I do need you to get him up to speed and ready for a presentation with the managers within the week. That okay, George?"

Adding substantial salt to the wound, Parker sauntered around the corner just at that moment and provided Sebastian and George a churlish two-fingered wave.

"All right, fucktards?" he said, unburdening his Hello Kitty backpack from his shoulders onto the desk.

Faulkner grimaced at the comment and for a moment George took childish glee in watching the twitch returning to his eyelid, but the moment was short lived. Faulkner looked at George for so long that he thought he may have suffered a sudden embolism.

"Remember George," he said, eyeing him wearily, "management will be looking at *all* of us with this presentation."

"Well, it's a good thing that management doesn't hate *all* of us," Parker nonchalantly murmured as he set up his station.

George had to hand it to the kid, he may have been simple in the ways of the world, but he said what he thought. Faulkner snapped his lizard-like head to Parker and hissed quickly, "Mr. Parker, I may remind you that you're talking to your superiors."

Parker nodded, indicating something behind George and Faulkner. "And may I remind you, *Mr. Faulkner* – that it's George's birthday this week."

George and Faulkner simultaneously swiveled their heads round to see the whiteboard in the middle of the room. In crude red lettering, a few names had been scrawled against dates. George noticed the following:

HOLLY LUCAS: 26th

GEORGE BRYANT: 29th

Faulkner took a moment to absorb this information. Parker switched on his laptop, humming a listless tune, which George thought may be *Ode to Joy.*

"I...I didn't know it was...your...your birthday this week, George," Faulkner stuttered. His face turned beetroot.

"The board never lies," George said flatly.

Faulkner took an imperceptible step back from George. "And," he said, trying to maintain an air of conviction, "You've never had a Birthday Treat?"

George shook his head.

"Well...maybe this year, eh?" He laughed after this, another *yuk-yuk-yuk,* but this time there was a discernible hollowness to it.

George glanced over at Parker. Still humming away, he simply raised his eyebrows.

"Maybe," George said, turning on his laptop. Faulkner soon retreated, saying something about an important meeting that he had to attend.

"I'd put that guy out of his misery," Parker said matter-of-factly. "If it was *my* Birthday Treat, I mean."

George muttered in agreement, looking at all the files that he had to delegate to Parker. He was still processing the information. He realised that his hands were shaking.

"Are you not worried that I'd come after you?" George said.

Parker shrugged. "Shit rolls downhill, Georgy boy. What would be the point of you taking your Treat out on me? I'm sure you'd prefer to go after your bosses."

George gave a noncommittal nod. He was right. Again. *What is happening to the world?*

Parker extracted a Tupperware box and started digging into what could only be described as last night's grisly remnants. "Who's Holly Lucas, anyway?"

George shook his head. "No idea. But it's her birthday tomorrow," he said glumly.

Parker eyed him from across the desk.

"You okay, George? You're looking a bit peaky this morning, mate. More so then usual."

George sighed. "I saw a girl get thrown on the train tracks this morning by a Boiler."

Parker looked at him horror-struck. "Fuck."

"Turned out he was a janitor for a comprehensive school. He's probably been thinking about killing one of those girls for a while."

Parker thought it over. "Do you ever think we're in the wrong job?"

George felt old and tired and at a complete loss. "Have to pay the bills somehow, right?"

Parker mulled that over as he stabbed some pasta and wolfed it down. "Doesn't have to be that way," he said lightly. "Think about it. We've become so desensitized to everything happening in the world now. There used to be a time when people gave a shit. Look at us. You speak with people that have been affected by a Birthday Treat. You listen to their problems and you hand out fortune cookie platitudes to make them feel better for having caved in their mother's head. Some of them listen. And most of these people secretly desire to get a Birthday Treat once in their lives, anyway. What's the usual percentage that get picked anyway? Degenerates. Young people. People with axes to grind. People with bad health that live in poverty. When was the last time you saw a social elite get a Birthday Treat? It's all rigged, man." He stuffed more pasta into his mouth, but leant forward and whispered, "It's The Network keeping the people in check, George. You know it, and I know it."

George shook his head. "Dangerous talk, Parker."

Parker sat back and continued eating. "Dangerous times to live in, amigo."

It was then that George noticed the small envelope with his name written in fine handwriting on his desk.

"Did you see who left this?" George asked. Parker had already put his headphones in, engrossed with his laptop. He opened it and slowly read:

Dear George,

You'll be receiving your Birthday Treat on Friday.
I would like to meet you to discuss what you could do with it.
We also know where your daughter is.

A Friend

George stared numbly at the piece of paper in his hands. How long had he been looking at it? It felt like half an hour had passed. It was only when Parker asked him to stop grinding his teeth that he came out of his stupor.

He remembered putting on his sock that morning. The one with the hole in it and hoping that this wouldn't be a day of small, unexpected surprises. But the universe had a funny way of shitting all over your preconceived plans.

The toilet cubicle was calling to him. He stood from his station and drifted through the office as if in an ethereal dream. He looked at his reflection in the mirror. He took his index finger and pulled down an eyelid.

Conjunctival lymphoma.
Conjunctival hemorrhage.
Conjunctival hemangioma.
Conjunctival nevus.
Conjunctival melanoma.

George blinked several times. How could someone know he was

going to get a Birthday Treat? The Network contacted each individual twenty-four hours before their allocation of a SCOOP suit.

How had they known about his *daughter*?

There were too many questions, and George's head felt ready to explode. His chest tightened and he suddenly felt numb down one side of his body. Was this it? Was he about to have a heart attack? The colour drained from his face and he limply went to the handicapped stall at the end of the bathroom. He rested his head in his hands and rocked back and forth on the toilet seat. The pain in his chest swelled and he felt himself breathing in and out loudly.

Relax, Georgie boy. Breathe in. You're not having a heart attack. Breathe out. Someone is playing a cruel prank on you...How could they know about...no...it's just someone fucking with you. Breathe in. Think of good things. Think happy thoughts. Breathe out.

He went into a mantra like state and focused on a club sandwich. That would help. He pictured eating it slowly and thinking after every bite, 'this is a good sandwich.' He zoned in on the mayonnaise and the texture of the bread. Yes. That was good. He was in control.

He was in control.

At lunchtime, George met Holly Lucas in an underwhelming, prosaic fashion. Following his meltdown in the toilet cubicle, George had gone back to his desk and made several calls, listening to a woman who had burnt her dog to death as her Birthday Treat – "she kept on yip, yip, yipping at me. I couldn't take it anymore!" to a Degenerate teenager that had amputated his sister's hand because she 'stole a cookie from me the other day,' and finally a man who had raped his neighbour because she 'walked around like a hooker and was asking for it.'

George talked to these people in a mechanical, clipped voice. His thoughts kept on coming back to the letter. There had once been a time when he had an office and met the clients he was dealing with. Had the whole leather sofa and everything. That had been years ago.

Before The Network had forced small business into their multinational machine.

By lunchtime his belly rumbled. He realised he had missed breakfast, so he ventured to the staff canteen to find himself morosely chewing on a stale egg and cress sandwich. Then he realised that no one was sitting near him.

He looked up from his slumber, in the way a man who has just been found with his hands down his pants at a Toddler Of The Year Award and was surprised to see the bench completely deserted. He thought this strange as it should have been crammed at this time.

There was a slender, redheaded girl sitting on the bench opposite him, however. He noted that she'd been staring him with keen eyes, like a predator surveying its prey, too bloated to feast further at the moment but seriously considering a second helping. George found himself laughing nervously, not looking in her eyes except for a quick flash, trying to gauge her intentions. He wondered how old she was, her face strong, intelligent and sharp in a forbidding sort of way.

A tinny *ping* made George slyly glance at the girl as she picked up her phone and tapped a few buttons, before replacing it back on the table.

She caught his eyes.

"Do you mind picking that up for me?" she asked innocuously enough, pointing to a napkin on the floor. George's gaze flitted from her pursed full lips to the discarded serviette. He had no idea how long it had been there. It was crumpled up, as though someone already used it. George was sure he could make out a smear of ketchup on the underside. He looked back at her anticipating smile, a thousand thoughts dancing in his mind like a kaleidoscope.

"Sure," he said finally, slowly standing from the bench. His eye line was drawn to two employees with coffee cups entering the canteen area, talking amiably enough to one another until they spotted the red headed girl sitting on the bench. Without a word, they quickly turned on their heels and left.

George bent down, picked up the napkin with all the subtlety of a tap-dancing hippo, the effort leaving him breathless and dizzy. He sauntered over to her bench in a hopefully nonchalant manner and placed the serviette delicately on the table. George noticed that she wore a tortured expression as if she were sucking on an incredibly sour sweet, one she dare not spit out.

He turned to go back to his seat, but she wasn't finished with him yet.

"Do you mind doing something else for me?" she asked, blinking a few times for dramatic effect. She clasped her hands together, as if in prayer.

George smiled weakly, raising his eyebrows.

"Do you mind getting it out for me?"

George tilted his head to the side. "Excuse me?"

The red head pointed a finger at his crotch. "Your penis," she said, matter-of-factly. "I'd like to see it."

George felt his head swell alarmingly. And not the one in his trousers. Heat rushed to his cheeks and there was a slight buzzing noise in his ears. He could no longer hear her voice. This day had started on a bum note and it was getting procedurally worse. For a moment he wondered if he was still in the toilet cubicle, asleep, and this was all a dream. He mentally pinched himself and recoiled when he found that no, this was real life. He wondered if Parker was standing in the galleries somewhere, pissing himself with laughter.

He snapped out of his daydream and became conscious that the red head was expecting some kind of response from him.

"I said: I don't have all day." Those luscious lips twisted into a grimace of animal hate.

"Who are you?" he asked in a tiny voice. Her phone *pinged* again, and she checked the latest message. George stood motionless, feeling like a fifth wheel. She let out a guttural snort of laughter, muttering something as she tapped away at her keypad. George remained still, watching her finish. Finally, she put the mobile down.

She stretched out a hand. George observed that her nails were painted a brilliant vermillion. For some reason he thought of Elspeth. "Holly Lucas. Tomorrow it's my birthday." She stared at him with piercing azure eyes as he took her hand and nervously started pumping it with suspicious eagerness. "If you don't get your wing-wang out right now I will *crush* you. If you don't get your honkey-doodle out right now and I get my birthday treat tomorrow, I will personally come round to your home and I will crush your testicles under my heels like overripe plums. I will fucking *end* you."

She let his hand go.

She's a dragger. She's blackmailing people. She's blackmailing you.

"And I get a picture," she chirped, indicating the pink mobile phone on the bench. "My friend and I have our birthday on the same day, so we're trying to get the most amount of dick pics." She said all this without any humour in her voice.

George took a moment to absorb all this information. He opened his mouth to say something, anything, but his throat simply emitted a small clicking noise. He didn't dare look down at her heels.

Softly, almost purring, Holly said, "Listen...just whip it out. It'll be over in a moment. Then I get to make an ass out of another suit."

Another *ping* and Holly retrieved her phone. That mobile announcement sounded like a death knell. He stood there, indecisive. Reflexively, his hand wavered towards his zipper, but then his brain kicked into gear and he started thinking: *She might not get her birthday treat tomorrow. She's young...it may be another twenty years until she gets her treat. She's just dragging. Enjoying the power.*

Fear crept into the pit of his stomach, churning and coagulating like thick, spoiled stew. Holly's smile was wide, almost voluptuous as she replied to the text. She looked at the canteen entrance, as if she were already planning her next target.

But what if you defy her? What if she gets her treat and comes in tomorrow, in her bright orange boiler suit and stabs your testicles with those sharp, pointy heels? No one will stop her, and she'll be well within her means to do it. She'll kill you and come in the next day all smiles and red nails. What then?

"C'mon, just let the birdy fly." She said, getting the camera ready on her mobile.

George felt his chest tighten again. Terror as black as midnight swept through him. His brain raced with all different scenarios. In some of them, he simply ran away from Holly Lucas and fled from the building, running the entire way home, curling up into a small ball under his duvet. In another scenario he simply fell to the floor and violently convulsed, flailing his arms and legs like an expert contortionist drag queen attempting a death drop. His pulse thudded steadily in his throat.

What a day. First, the girl on the platform. He replayed the way that she flew from the platform straight into the front carriage of the train. The sickening, crunching sounds as it rolled over her. George's hands curled into fists. The utter humiliation of Parker taking over the Mitchell case, with that sniveling, conniving weasel Faulkner *yuk-yuk-yukking*. He felt his eyes roll wildly in their sockets. Then...then there was the mysterious letter telling him about his daughter.

Something inside George snapped. He held up the hand that a moment earlier was so near to unzipping his flies, allowing his flaccid penis to escape into the wild.

"Let me stop you there, Holly, just for a second. Where do you actually work?" He asked this in a voice that was not his own. Without even realising it, his arms started to fold in front of his chest in a defiant gesture, his whole posture changing from fearful wretch into business power-point mode.

"What?" Holly asked hoarsely, surprised at this sudden dynamic shift.

"What. Department. Do. You. Work. In?" George asked, in an eager voice that had lain dormant for years. A voice that made George Bryant somehow taller.

Holly's venomous expression retreated in on itself, her brow creasing into a puzzled look. "Audio Visual," she meekly responded.

"Uh-huh," George said vaguely, authority swelling within him, "do you know that I saw a caretaker throw a schoolgirl in front of a train this morning?"

This stumped Holly. George could see that she was looking for a witty retort, but he didn't give her the opportunity to answer. "It doesn't matter now, Holly. You know why it doesn't matter? Because she's dead, Holly. That's right. Dead. They'll likely be scraping her brains off from the track for the next couple of days."

George was unaware that his own voice was rising, shifting a few octaves higher with each word.

"Yeah, that's right, Holly," he pressed on, "threw her out on the track like rubbish. You think it's a coincidence that the lower waged workers get their Birthday Treats before their thirties and the '*suits*,' as you call them, don't seem to get them at all?"

Holly's eyes darted left to right, her face screwed up in bewilderment and disbelief as her brain processed this information. George found himself leering now, arching in towards her, hunched like a rapacious animal stalking an elk, lowered on its hind legs, readying itself for the kill.

"You don't have a grievance with me, Holly. Not really. You have a gripe with what this place means to you, how it holds you back. Hell, maybe you've been pissed off with your boyfriend for so many years that you take pleasure in this kind of shit now, isn't that right?"

He could see tears welling up in her eyes, so knew he was reaching the heart of the matter. He pushed on. "Is that it? You fucking idiot? Is there a guy involved? A fucking fuckturd? Holly, you cretin...are you *that* fucking transparent that you project all your insecurities onto the people you work with, rather than direct them at the bastard buggery dipshit boyfriend that's causing all this?" George didn't grasp it but found himself screeching. "You shithead. You fucking idiot shithead. He doesn't treat you right? He doesn't appreciate you, Holly? Is that it?"

Another *ping*.

George dove forward and grabbed the phone from her hand roughly. The raw power generated by his massive bulk and momentum astonished them both, inadvertently sending Holly crashing back so that her ass bumped against the table, sending her sprawling. But George didn't stop there – something buried deep in his psyche had been awakened and he'd be damned if he didn't follow through on this animalistic impulse. He dashed the mobile hard against the far wall, where it impacted with a severe and satisfying crack.

"How does it feel, Holly?" he screamed, flailing his arms in the air, "how does it feel to be useless? Put that on your next AV feed!"

Something flashed in his peripheral vision and he managed to blurt out a feeble, "what are yooooooou-" before the security guard with the buzz-cut leapt and knocked the wind out of him, hurling them both to the floor. Before he knew what was happening, the burly guard sat on top of him, applying some skillful pressure to his arm, causing a sharp pain to jolt through his entire body. He heard a noise that dubiously sounded like plastic ties being wrapped around his wrists and then he was pulled to his feet. For the second time in the last ten minutes after being so close to the floor, he felt breathless and dizzy.

Before George was escorted to the security room, he saw Holly kneeling over her broken phone, cradling the smashed pieces of plastic, sobbing pitifully.

⊕

The reprimand was swift. Faulkner stood by the doorway, eager to leave. Any mention of Holly's name during the debrief generated a spasmodic twitch to his face and any mention of George's upcoming birthday made his body practically dance. He'd rather be anywhere else than in a cramped, sweaty security office filled with beige-coloured pullout filing units, but procedure dictated that George's Line Manager should be present for an official warning.

George sat languidly, nodding his head at all the right moments where a gap came up in the conversation, muttering affirmations in all the right places when he was expected to confirm that he understood everything being said to him, but he wasn't really listening as the head of security reeled off all The Network terms and conditions frequented with prior birthday treat offences. After an hour, they wrapped up and Faulkner bolted out of the room quicker than a coked-up party reveler. George managed to give him a final stare of maximum contempt before he left, though. It was the small victories that mattered.

He left early that day. On his way home he thought about the girl on the platform, the way her legs danced swiftly in the air before her skull smashed against the driver's window. He wondered if her headphones were still on the platform or if a staff member had retrieved them. And then he thought about the Boiler, the way he sat down after he had received his treat and looked correctly drunk. He wondered whether Holly would come into work the next day wearing a brightly coloured Boiler suit, armed with a Kalashnikov, spraying bullets in all directions. *Don't be stupid,* he chided himself. *Where would she get a Russian rifle? A snub-nosed Uzi though...*

George thought all these things and much more as he continued to walk home. Another rebellious thought broke out of the miasma whirlwind spiraling through his mind as he glanced over at pub on the corner, The Crown and Anchor.

I could do with a drink. A nice, refreshing beer. Followed by a whiskey. Or several. Before he knew he was doing it, George Bryant found himself pushing through the smokers standing outside the pub on the corner, going through the doors.

Department of Information public poll:

82% in favour of Agents retiring contestant Alice Paige before 5-day goal

12% in favour of Alice Paige surviving

6% Undecided

- From The Department of Information website

@minstry_info

7

ALICE

MONDAY

103 HOURS REMAIN...

Just going to get you snug as a bug in a rug, that's right. Slippery Jim knows keep his friends close, yes he does...

Alice had been through the ringer of foster homes during her childhood (*she's too excitable, she breaks things, we were looking for someone a little less loud*) but her last foster parents before she turned eighteen had been sweet enough. Mr. and Mrs. Ambrose had been a hippy couple that couldn't conceive their own children, so had a few unruly teenagers in their home. It had been bliss.

Not like with Janet and Eugene. Not like them at all.

Slippery Jim wants you to bend over, princess. Slippery Jim just wants to be sweet to you...

Alice couldn't remember the first time she picked up a guitar.

She had no memory experiencing that eureka moment when she picked up the Gibson Les Paul for the first time.

Memories of a little box room in the Ambrose house were hazy, but she recollected with vivid clarity the heavy wood and how it felt satisfying in her small hands. Mr. Ambrose had played for most of his life, but his arthritic fingers had rendered the use of them useless on the guitar, and she remembered the day he gave the Les Paul to her. Fragments of pictures were coming together, like a decidedly slow jigsaw puzzle...she sat cross-legged on her bed, with a small notebook lying in front of her. As she strummed her fingers across the strings its tones were rich and full. As far as Alice was concerned it was the best guitar in the world.

Just tell me you'll practise, Mr. Ambrose had said, with a wan smile on his face.

Every day, Alice had replied.

That's great princess. Just don't turn around. Let me be sweet to you. Let Slippery Jim be sweet to you.

No, that wasn't right...

Mr. and Mrs. Ambrose had been caring. They had been gentle.

I can be gentle to you, Eugene whispered in the darkness.

His blurred face danced in her mind like a light bulb swaying in a dark room – flashes of a study...ornate furniture and shelves lined with leather bound books.

Look what you've done, silly. It's okay, I'm not mad...

Had Janet been upstairs, 'putting her face on' as she used to say?

No. Janet had been out.

Slippery Jim knows how to keep his friends close, yes he does...

Alice tried to play the guitar for Mrs. Ambrose but after a few minutes she would put her liver-spotted hand up to signal for quiet. Alice had felt rejected.

Did I do something wrong?

Mrs. Ambrose shook her head. This made Alice angry. Why did she stop her? She'd been practising for weeks. Even back then the rebellious streak was beginning to coagulate – sharp comments from the young girl about reducing her rights to freedom of expression, only to hear her foster mother's response, *'I'm not seeking to reduce your rights, love, just your volume.'*

Had they argued about that? Was it even her foster mother that had said that? Old memories were like wood in the rain, they warped after time.

It didn't matter to her though, she possessed something in the world that no-one could take away from her. She wanted to learn all the riffs of her favourite rock songs, with dreams of performing onstage, thrashing her head manically to the beat of the music. Alice wanted to get to the stage where her music would fill the air without effort, like waves crashing against rocks on a beach. All the notes were inside her ears, waiting to be heard live.

She would twist her fingers in all sorts of odd shapes to form chords around the maple wood fret board and once or twice, would slide her hand up across the higher frets. *Smoke on The Water* was a favourite that she wanted to master, but at the young age of eleven her wrists were bony and weak. The strings sliced her soft fingertips open on more than one occasion, and when she messed up, she would shout and have a tantrum, beating her stupid hands on the bed like a toddler. In those early days she would vent, letting out all the frustration in profanity and shrieks.

That's great princess. Just don't turn around.

Another image: Janet in the study, arms laden with shopping bags.

Eugene. What are you doing?

She remembered a lot of shouting, back then. Janet and Eugene were not good foster parents. She had been with them for a year. Janet and Eugene were nothing like the Ambrose couple.

The kind foster parents, the hippies - would tell her to calm down, to breathe – but that just frustrated her even more. She had been a tumultuous child back then. How had they put up with her tantrums? The screams, kicking her feet against the wall in wild frustration?

She counted frets, made notes in her little book, started to learn the order of the strings, trying to remember which fingers went on which string order. The first time she mastered the intro riff of *Smoke on The Water* was a revelation. It was an achievement. She would pump her fists in the air, kick her legs out and squeal with delight and then go right back into it until the chords became muscle memory.

Oooh, Slippery Jim's hit the jackpot alright...

Time slipped by. She was sixteen when she formed The VamPyrates, a four-piece prog-metal band. When they first started out, bathed in the dim lights of whatever back-alley club they managed to talk their way into, she would clutch tightly to her modified cherry red Gibson onstage, inhaling deeply. Nerves were trying to shred her body, but it only improved the energy of her performance. Alice would look over the crowd, dark eyeliner and crimson lips pursed.

Why don't you wear that lipstick your mother has? You'd like that, wouldn't you?

She's not my mother, Eugene.

You know what I mean, princess. And that lovely summer dress. It's so hot out today.

Quiet, deep inhales. That lovely moment of silence – of anticipation – before the drumsticks clacked together cueing her in. Then would come the onrush of adrenaline as the first deep bass tones thundered from the amps. It would always reliably raise the hairs on the back of her neck and the thrumming sound of her guitar had a hypnotic soothing quality that she craved. To lose herself to the melody of the guitar was her idea of a heaven. Her heart kept time with the drums, pumping the music through her veins as she lost herself in the routine. Eventually, she lost all sense of everything except for the music. By then, she didn't just play the electric guitar, she was symbiotically infused with it.

She spent her teenage years in the lowliest of dingy establishments around the city, playing to disillusioned ex-pats, or regulars that didn't care about music. She played in halls to spoilt brat kiddies and she played corporate gigs with men in expensive suits that would leer at her on stage, and she'd perform in the background whilst wedding cakes were cut. Everything vibrated when she turned up that amp and whatever building they performed in would be treated to her solo renditions, whether they liked it or not. Dave Lazer, the front man of the band, would pierce the air with his vocals - some reacted to the beat, others continued to chatter, but for Alice she felt like the music spoke to them in some manner.

It wasn't long before she and Dave were a couple. Her passion up until this point had been about music. It was a source of great friendships, great loves, new romances. She smoked cigarettes, ran with the wrong crowd, left home when her grades dramatically dropped, but she'd never really indulged boys before forming the band. Alice knew when Dave Lazer auditioned for frontman that they would sleep together. It was his cautious smile. It was the way he stared at her in an enticing way.

Look what you've done, silly. It's okay, I'm not mad...

Did I do something wrong?

It was the way he literally reflected the lights from the stage. When they played, they'd almost melt together in the vibe – moving around the stage as easy as smoke. After years of covering the songs she adored as a child, they started writing their own lyrics, performing their own sound. And it was wonderful. She was particularly proud of their first demo, seven of the eight songs she had written herself. *Snotgrass City* had a mean tempo – kicking in straightaway with manic energy that always got the crowds pumped.

Alice would pluck, strum and twang with animalistic rage and Dave would shriek, screech and bellow as if it were their last night on earth. Somewhere along the line Alice had picked up a black leather Bircham jacket, the kind where the zipper ran down from the collar bone to the naval, adding studs to the back to spell out DWN (Down With Network). It was the kind of jacket that she'd keep forever, moulding into the shape of her body like they were interdependent of one another. Where before Alice had been spending her teenage years angrily playing with her guitar, Dave showed her a new way to channel her bitterness and antipathy – they joined protest groups rallying against the inhumane treatment of the people that entered the games on The Network, joining public speakers as they waved their placards at the faceless corporation that valued statistics above human life.

Slippery Jim wants you to be his friend...I've got lots of friends...

A recent memory surfaced in the gloom. Alice pushed her way through the crowd into the bar, dark and barely lit. Hundreds of conversations told in loud voices, all of them competing with the music that dominated the atmosphere. Usually, she would soak in the laughter and the smiles, but tonight something was different. The VamPyrate's were not playing, but they had an understanding with the manager of The Pit. They got to play every other night and Dave worked behind the bar. They got free booze, or they took whatever they wanted at any rate. The crowd was young, students from the neighbouring University. The Pit was one of the few remaining places where Degenerates and Social Credit elitists could hang together without too much friction. Most pubs and clubs had been shut down years before, but The Pit languished in a fetid state of debauchery, alcoholism and despair. Along the wall was every hue of amber liquid in their inverted bottles. The smell of stale beer and body odour clung to furniture and skin alike. A hint of sick tainted the air. Just another Friday night. Alice felt flushed, the news she'd received hanging over her like a guillotine.

"Dave!" She shouted over laughter and conversations.

Bodies throbbed and undulated as one in the main room, as ERD lights pulsated all different colours. The music on tonight wasn't her favourite, it was a new type of synthwave dub that the masses were clamouring more and more for these days. Several Free-Vees in the establishment were playing *Wheel of Misfortune*, and a contestant was talking amiably to the show's host. He wore spectacles and was looking out to audience members to decide his next move – if he spun the wheel, he'd have a one in six chance of claiming the next tiered prize. Poor bastard, Alice thought to herself. Even if he somehow managed to miss all the forfeits, he wouldn't be the same person again. Not after The Network got their claws into you.

That's great princess. Just don't turn around.

"'Ello sweetheart," Dave said, already handing her a whiskey.

"I need to talk to you." Alice replied with eyes that were black and featureless as the bottom of a well. Dave had seen that look before, usually just before a gig started. It was the look of the lone warrior, strapped with C4 and their thumb on the detonator button. He waved her over to the backroom.

Alice nimbly jumped over the bar. Everyone was too drunk to care.

Smoke permeated the pungent smell of the green room, creating a heavy, stifling and nauseous effect on Alice. Graffiti-ridden cork boards covered the walls and ceiling. Half open guitar cases, backpacks, and cans of beer littered the floor like discarded clothes in a brothel. No-one came here with anything wholesome in mind, Alice absently thought.

"What's going on?" Dave asked, peeling open a beer can.

The muffled music droned in the background; the bass still sharp enough to shudder in her chest.

"I'm getting my Birthday Treat on Monday."

Dave froze as he lifted the beer to his lips and his eyes bulged out, too far out, like a cartoon character just realising the ACME anvil was about to fall on his head. He opened his mouth slowly and was about to speak when the door opened. Some of the groupies from the band onstage were about to pile in but Dave launched at them, flailing his hands in the air and screaming at them to get out. He slammed the door shut and locked it. Alice could see a vein throbbing from his neck as if he were about to explode.

Eugene. What are you doing?

"Well, you're just going to have to take it then, aren't you?" he said with a trembling hand on the door.

"We've spoken about this Dave..."

"No! No, Alice...*you've* spoken about this. You've said what would happen if we ever got chosen. But that was all a *joke*. That wasn't real then. You *were* joking, right?"

On the TV, the bespectacled contestant fist pumped the air, before grabbing the wheel to spin it. To the crowd's disbelief, the marker landed on a cash prize. The studio erupted into applause before the host with teeth whiter than Alice's porcelain toilet turned to him and offered even more for a second spin. Alice sighed. She expected this would be Dave's knee jerk reaction and wanted nothing more than to skip a few stages down the line to the planning period.

She wondered then if she was going to end things with Dave. They'd been playing together for a while, but the band wasn't going anywhere. She knew it. Secretly, she felt that Dave knew it too, but it was an unspoken topic never discussed.

That's great princess. Just don't turn around.

As much as she felt anxious when she received the email about her Birthday Treat, there was also an exhilaration she hadn't experienced in a long time. This was important. She could do something with this.

"I found out this morning. The Network emailed me. Now, I can stand here and blather on about the fact that I'm not going to abide by The Network's rules until I'm blue in the face but we both know what I'm going to do."

Dave turned and his eyes were bulging out of his head again – his colour alabaster white and his cheeks hollow as if some magnanimous force had sucked all the marrow out of him. "Not true. There are loopholes. You don't have to...kill anyone. You could set a dog on fire or crash a car into a shop...I dunno, you could rob a bank if you wanted." He gulped down some beer. Wiping his mouth with the back of his hand he started pacing in the room. "Yeah...there are loopholes. You could...you could beat someone up! You could beat me up. Like, badly. Actual bodily harm. That's a law. That's a law you could break."

Alice politely grabbed his arm, guiding him towards her. "You know that's not how it works." He had a giddiness about him, an excited high of a drunken gambler down to his last chip. She wondered if telling him had been the right idea...she should have done this alone, not put anyone else in danger. And although she hated to admit it, Dave wasn't the most sensible of people that she knew. He was too fidgety. His mind often became distracted and it was another reason why she was thinking of ending things.

But mostly, it was the look he had in his eyes now. He was scared. A scared boy.

"But I mean, bad, like. You could beat me up to an inch of my life." He unhooked her fingers from his arm, downing more beer. She didn't want to deal with the drunk version just now.

Alice came forward and cupped his face in her hands. "You know I'm not going to do that, Dave."

"Then we'll find something else you can do. Yeah, yeah...maybe you can wreck an important piece of art or something –"

She brought his face level with hers. "Dave. Listen to me." His eyeballs darted from left to right. When he got flustered, he reminded her of that marine from the film *Aliens*, when he started bugging out over the deaths of his comrades. But she didn't need him stressed out right now. She needed him level-headed.

"I made my choice long ago. I'm not going to take my Birthday Treat."

"But that means...that means..." He couldn't finish the sentence.

"Yes. I'll enter the *Hunted* TV Show."

He let out a stifled sob. "No-one's survived that."

"Freddy Henshaw survived it."

"That was five years ago, Alice! Do you know how many people go on the run? They have like, a contestant every week. The odds are forever *not* in your favour."

"Which doesn't give me long to plan something. Now, I need you to focus."

Dave nodded and for a fleeting moment she thought he might cry. He let out a heavy breath and ran his hand through his hair. She kissed him then. A long, hard kiss, one that she wanted to laugh and swim and bathe in. Then she told him her plan.

◉

She was alone in the green room while Dave went off to find the man that would put her in contact with the back-alley SCOOP suit modifier. She watched the Free-Vee. The man with spectacles on *Wheel of Misfortune* decided to go for broke and span the wheel for the ultimate jackpot prize. A lot of close ups on the contestant – furrowed brow and slick sweat glistening from his forehead. They cut to audience reactions as the wheel started to slow, passing forfeit after forfeit in agonising anticipation. The game show host was blithely telling the contestant about all the money he could win in this single swipe, and the camera pans back to the contestant's exasperated face as it finally lands on a forfeit and the crowd gasp in horror. The contestant seemed to crumple inwards, and the audience collectively held their breaths as the host announced what forfeit was in store for the pitiful loser.

You'll get to meet Slippery Jim's friends real soon...

Alice watched the TV screen, her nails digging half-moons into the flesh of her palms as the show smash cut to a small arena in the studio – filled with Styrofoam pillars and sand. The spectacled man has changed from his normal clothes to a mock costume of a gladiatorial warrior. He was armed with a spoon. A cage door opened, and the camera zoomed straight at the opening. The bear on its hind legs was taller than any man Alice has seen, and it exposed its teeth in an angry fashion. From its blood red eyes Alice wondered what drugs they'd injected into it to have the animal worked up. Its teeth were like daggers and the bear roared at the small, tiny man waving the spoon in front of him like a priest attempting to banish a ghoul.

The beast charged at the screaming contestant, swinging its enormous paws wildly and with no sanctuary it wasn't long before the animal struck the man across the chest, literally cutting him in half.

The camera pulled back to the host who made a glib comment about the man writhing in pain in the arena floor as the bear tore into him.

What do you call a bear with no teeth? A gummy bear. Geddit?

Eugene, that's such a dad joke.

That's the point, princess. I can be your dad if you like. If you really want me to be. Janet and I have been talking, and we'd really like you to stay with us.

Dave opened the door and looked at her with a serious, steadfast look on his face. His shoulders, broad and unburdened with the information half an hour ago, slumped into a downward-facing V.

"Okay, it's sorted." He said in a tight voice, cracking open another beer. "Good and bad news scenario, love. Good news is there's a guy called Mitchum who'll be able to deactivate any trackers in the SCOOP suit and get the suit off you. Bit of a sleaze, but I've got word that he's good at what he does. The bad news is that you'll need to be in central London just as your 24-hour Birthday Treat expires. He's squirrely and doesn't do call outs. It's also going to be £250."

Alice leaned forward, contemplating this information. "This could be good. Most people try to head to the country...but hiding in plain sight might be easier."

Slippery Jim sees your eyes...what beautiful eyes you have...

"What did you say?" She asked.

This isn't how she remembered the moment.

Dave smiled at her. It's a horrible, raggedy smile, like slits in a mouth made by a knife. "A wicked man hides behind his beard, like the devil."

Alice felt strange.

Eugene, what are you doing?

Did I do something wrong?

I'm not seeking to reduce your rights, love, just your volume.

When she looked at Dave it was from a different angle. She should be on the sofa during this memory, going over their plans... but she's on the floor instead...no, not the floor. It's too spongy to be the green room at The Pit.

This is different. She's on a mattress. One of her hands is cuffed to a railing, but the corkboards are gone now. The walls are different – mildew and damp cover every surface. There's also a terrible stench of decay and spoilt meat.

"Dave. What's happening?"

That's great princess. Just don't turn around.

Dave leered down at her with his hot, reeking breath. His face shifted imperceptibly, and that's when Alice realises...she's been dreaming.

The following is a phone exchange between Action News journalist Patricia O'Neil and Vice President of The Network, Cassandra Rey

PATRICIA O'NEIL: Thank you for taking the time to speak with us, Miss. Rey – I understand your schedule…

CASSANDRA REY: You've got five minutes. How can I be of assistance Ms. O'Neil?

PATRICIA O'NEIL: Well, as I'm sure you're aware, the CEO blogs that have been circulating from The Network have been quite provocative in their candid nature about Mr. –

CASSANDRA REY: I don't hear a question.

PATRICIA O'NEIL: Yes. Well, let me get straight to it. Certain representatives feel that the blogs may be…how to put this delicately, indicative of a mind that may not have all the mental faculties of a person in such a prestigious position.

CASSANDRA REY: Our CEO is dying. He's made that perfectly clear. But his psychological and intellectual state is perfectly normal. It's facetious to think he wouldn't be able to carry out his duties. Next question.

PATRICIA O'NEIL: Has there been a third-party source to confirm that? We only have a report by The Network's physicians to confirm this.

CASSANDRA REY: Your line of questioning is impertinent, Ms. O'Neil. We have a highly trained staff of doctors, psychologists and surgeons that are working around the clock to give the best treatment to our CEO.

PATRICIA O'NEIL: Has he chosen his successor yet?

CASSANDRA REY: That's neither here nor there. Whatever choice he makes will be the right one.

PATRICIA O'NEIL: But it's highly likely that he'll name you as the new CEO?

CASSANDRA REY: I have no further comments on the matter.

PATRICIA O'NEIL: Okay, sure. As it's coming up to the five-year anniversary of Frederick Henshaw's successful run on the *Hunted* TV show, are there plans to bring back our favourite contestant to give an interview about his experiences? It seemed awfully strange at the time that once he won, he seemed to vanish without a trace.

CASSANDRA REY: When a contestant manages to last the five-day period, they are given a substantial cash reward and an abundant Social Credit uprate. I couldn't possibly fathom where Mr. Henshaw is now, but I imagine it would on a beach somewhere sipping on cocktails.

PATRICIA O'NEIL: There's been speculations and rumours from various factions that his disappearance after his legendary win is in fact, a hoax. That he was caught early and doctored images and videos have been used to fabricate his win.

CASSANADRA REY: Once again, I'm not hearing a question.

PATRICIA O'NEIL: Are you aware of The Movement, Miss. Rey?

CASSANDRA REY: Our five minutes is up.

PATRICIA O'NEIL: Can you confirm that Birthday Treats and certain shows aired by The Network are just a way of slowly eradicating the impoverished and Degenerates of this country, Miss. Rey?

CASSANDRA O'NEIL: The people voted in The Network. Remember that. The people wanted this. Good bye.

There is an audible click and the line goes dead.

PATRICIA O'NEIL: Jesus, what a cunt. Did you get all that, Steve?

8

KAVANAGH

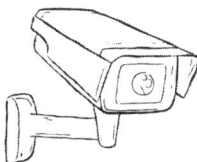

MONDAY

103 HOURS REMAIN...

The interrogation room was a hollow cube of concrete, one way in with no windows. Kavanagh dropped the manila envelope on the desk, scrutinising the punk singer in front of him with narrow eyes. In here, you would have no idea how much time had passed or even if it was night or day. By the time he'd finished his meeting with Cassandra Rey, David Lazer had already been waiting in this room for several hours. Kavanagh requested that he should wait a couple more before he was ready to be interviewed. The isolation was total, and the equipment he'd ordered had already been placed.

The reason for that was simple: he wanted to scare David Lazer. He wanted to scare him so bad that by the end of this interrogation the Degenerate looking bastard with the leather jacket and ripped T-shirt would forget his own name.

Working at The Network had taught him a thing or two about liars. Lying and deception were common human behaviours he came across daily. People liked to believe that they were fairly good at detecting lies and would use some of the most common nonverbal cues as red flags, such as observing fidgeting and squirming, or that the suspect wouldn't look you in the eye. Or that their eyes would lull to the right when they spoke, accessing the right-side hemisphere of the brain, the area known for performing tasks that have to do with creativity. But Kavanagh knew most of those notions were simply old wives' tales. He regarded Dave Lazer with a cold and cynical enthusiasm. Getting the truth out of someone was like cracking a safe: given the right tools and time, any box could be opened.

Any *person* could be opened.

But time was against him, and he needed answers. Fast.

So far, the kid had been resilient. The Agents had roughed him up a little, as he was sporting a swollen eye and split lip, and there was a thin pencil mark of blood coming down from his nose. He'd only offer monosyllabic answers to questions fired at him. But then Kavanagh had asked for the equipment to be brought in. On a wheeled trolley by the side of the desk sat a small surgical tray with a pencil.

Just a normal pencil.

There were also some surgical gloves. He had to contain his excitement every time Lazer's eyes glanced to them. It was these moments that he desired, the way he could lightly see the cogs starting to turn in the suspect's head. What must they be thinking of the innocuous item on the tray? He stifled a razor blade grin by clearing his throat.

"What's in a name, David? That's the question I want to address today. Do you know why you're here?" Kavanagh asked, running his fingers along the manila envelope in front of him.

David stared at his captor with glimmering, feverish eyes.

"Absolutely not. This is totally absurd. I demand to see someone in authority. I know my rights, innit? I literally know my rights."

Kavanagh nodded compliantly, easing himself back into the plastic chair, the type that was designed for maximum awkward posture and could have been stolen from an inner-city pre-school. The kid was good at keeping a poker face, but his use of unnecessary superlatives in his first reply were damning. Yes, there were times when these words were appropriate, but not when you've just been asked a simple question. In Kavanagh's experience, people who insisted on peppering their speech with them might be trying to bolster their argument or use them as a distraction technique. In this case, Kavanagh assumed it was the latter.

"Mr Lazer," Kavanagh said, "the Agents that have...mistreated you have been reprimanded. I don't tolerate that sort of tomfoolery."

David seemed to straighten up at this. Kavanagh wanted to placate the boyfriend, to come across as comforting and someone that he could trust. He'd try it out, at least. Kavanagh knew that he was anything but comforting, and he had little time for theatrics.

"Can I get you anything? Some water perhaps?"

David shook his head.

"Well, how about some cigarettes? Under the circumstances, I can't offer you opiates but how about the regular kind?"

David shuffled in his seat, crossing and uncrossing his legs. He certainly didn't trust Kavanagh yet, but he detected a small catalyst of conflict.

"Yeah, sure."

Kavanagh retrieved an Amber Leaf pack and a lighter from his jacket pocket. He didn't smoke himself and found it a vile addiction but had read up on Lazer's file. Front man of The VamPyrates. He slid the olive-green pack towards him. With trembling hands, the rocker shook one out. Kavanagh leaned forward as David put the cigarette between his lips and snapped back the cover of a zippo lighter. There was intimate silence as he flicked the wheel. David went to slide the packet back, but Kavanagh gestured a dismissive hand.

"Keep them," he said, beaming a wide smile. David drew deep, the glowing ember of the cigarette pulsing like a cherry red traffic light. The moment caused a sudden memory to surface in Kavanagh's mind, something he hadn't thought of in years: an eleven-year-old boy shivering in his bed, with tears rolling down his cheeks. The boy rocking his forehead back and forth against the bedroom wall, silently weeping. The hot needle sting on his forearm from his father's cigarette throbbing with pain.

He shuttered the memory away. Unconsciously he scratched his forehead, an old habit from when he was young. He noticed David looking at him questioningly.

Back to the matter at hand.

"I've only got a couple of questions for you, David. Mainly though, I want to know what's in a name, hmm?"

The rocker blew out some smoke. "No-one calls me David, matey."

"My apologies, Dave."

"Only my friends call me Dave." He jabbed a finger at Kavanagh. "You call me Mr. Lazer."

Good, thought Kavanagh. He's becoming loquacious again. Kavanagh leaned forward, looking serious. "Where is Alice Paige, Mr. Lazer?"

David chuckled, ragged and hearty. He shrugged, ash falling from his cigarette onto the table. He brushed it off with the back of his hand onto the floor. "Don't know who you're talking about, mate."

Kavanagh sighed. Usually, he would enjoy playing along to this cadence, like a master fencer parrying the half-truths, riposting the lies and feinting the rebukes, but he simply didn't have time for such frivolities. Alice Paige was out there somewhere, and no sightings had been reported. It would be dark soon and the chances of her escaping doubled. He couldn't let that happen. She had to be stopped.

"It's a shame the band had to end this way."

David let out a derisive snort. Kavanagh opened the manila envelope and took out a glossy black and white photo. "This was your drummer, Mr. Cheddar."

David peered at the full-face photo. It wasn't quite a mug shot. It had more in common with those old history photos of gangsters sprawled out on roads, ridden with bullets. There would usually be a puddle of blood beneath their bodies. And fedora hats. David knew that their drummer, Nigel Cheddar, was dead by the way his eyes looked back at him from the photo. They had a hollow quality to them, like doll's eyes. There was something wrong with his head, as if the photo had been rolled in on itself to fit in a tube and hadn't completely straightened out yet.

"We were questioning Mr. Cheddar over an hour ago," Kavanagh said, nonplussed at David's reaction to the photo, but exuding a faint impression of menace. "Most Agents prefer a certain appendage when they torture suspects, Mr. Lazer. Some like to focus on the soles of the feet, whilst others go for pulling out teeth and so on. In some instances, the genitals are the area of the body some Agents like to focus on. It appears that your drummer's head was the area in question for this interrogation. I believe an apparatus was attached to his skull and for every wrong answer he gave the Agent, a screw would be tightened. Perhaps the participating Agent had a hankering for melons."

"You...killed him." It wasn't quite a statement. More of a bemused, wondrous confirmation. Kavanagh always delighted in those moments. When the penny dropped.

"Technically, it was the seizure that killed him." Kavanagh replied dryly.

The colour drained from David's face as if someone had pulled an internal toilet chain. A deep, guttural moan escaped from the lead singer's throat and he slid sideways, tumbling from the chair. He made retching noises, but nothing came up. Kavanagh remained seated, tilting his head to look upon the punk rocker on all fours, groaning an anguished, inhuman sound. Kavanagh always felt slightly embarrassed by other people's distress. He felt an insatiable disingenuous notion towards David Lazer in that instant, a repulsion for the man that he couldn't quite put his finger on.

Was it disappointment at his turgid reaction to the photograph? Or perhaps he expected more resistance from him? For the second time in the interrogation room a recollection surfaced to the shoreline of his mind – a report card from school. A-. The cold voice of his father that would not entirely leave him: *You must do better, son. You don't want to find yourself down there. Down there with the rest of them.*

Kavanagh's arm itched. He would have to check his bandage later.

David Lazer was on his knees, fumbling with the knob of the door. "I demand to see my lawyer! I know my rights!"

Ah, the same old tunes. How utterly predictable.

The door suddenly flung outward, causing David to stumble backwards. Confused and alarmed, the front man attempted to get up and move forward, out of the room, barging the man who had opened the door.

Agent Valentine had other plans for the scrawny young rocker. Valentine was broad and tall, extremely grubby looking and was as bald as a stone. Kavanagh thought he looked ghostly pale, but what was startling was the emaciation of his face. It was like a skull. Valentine's face was serene and strangely child-like. But Kavanagh knew better than to be duped by appearances. The thing with Valentine was that when you were around him you had the horrific feeling like you were sitting on the edge of a bad smell, that wouldn't fully reveal its source. And the man was psychopathic, Kavanagh was sure of that. It was the eyes. His eyes seemed filled with a murderous, unappeasable hatred.

David tried to squeeze past the man mountain, but Valentine simply stood immobile and watched with disinterest as the singer thrashed around him, pummelling the agent with profanity and feeble pushes.

"Agent Valentine, would you please restrain Mr. Lazer?"

Valentine moved so fast that Kavanagh barely saw what happened. One moment David was yelling blue murder in his face, screaming about lawyers and rights, and then the next his ear was caught firmly between the first and second fingers of Valentine's right hand. David recoiled, trying to pull away but Valentine simply applied pressure to his grip, turning his hand slightly. The effect was immediate. David let out a startled yelp of pain, visibly shrinking in the agent's hand. He beat his hands ineffectively on Valentine's arm.

"Do you want me to tear it off?" Valentine asked. His voice was deep and grating, as if his vocal cords had been scrubbed down with sandpaper. Kavanagh wasn't sure if he was addressing David or himself, but for dramatic effect he considered the statement for a moment.

"No, Agent Valentine. Just sit him down, please."

Valentine shrugged, as if pulling the man's ear off would be as simple as pulling the wing off a fly. He frogmarched David back to his chair.

"Now," Kavanagh said softly, "I hope we don't have to experience anything like that again, Mr. Lazer. Sit down."

Valentine released his grip from David's ear, but remained behind him, crossing his arms over his chest like a bouncer at a night club. David clutched his ear and tentatively rubbed it, sitting down before Kavanagh. David's face was drawn and pinched, and he looked down, maybe from exhaustion or hunger or maybe some of all of it. His shoulders sagged and hot tears cascaded down his cheeks. Valentine produced a few zip-ties from his jacket and secured Dave's arms and legs to the chair.

"Now, Mr. Lazer...I want to draw your attention to the equipment on the trolley to your left." As Dave's eyes slowly scanned the surgical tray, Agent Valentine moved effortlessly round to the trolley and began stretching the latex surgical gloves. "I said to you before that Agents typically prefer a specific part of the body to work on. The feet, the genitals, so on and so forth. Agent Valentine here prefers the *eyes* when it comes to questioning our suspects. I must admit, I share his sentiment. I truly do believe the eyes are the windows to the soul. Before you on the tray is a normal, household pencil. Do you know what he'll do with the pencil if you fail to answer my questions?"

The front man of The VamPyrates started shaking like an old man with palsy. A bubble of snot formed at his left nostril, and Kavanagh looked on with a mild sense of amusement as it expanded and retracted with each sobbing breath.

"Please…" Dave said in a small voice. "Please…I don't know…anything."

Agent Valentine snapped on the gloves, interlocking his fingers. Kavanagh smiled at David, and the smile was as genuine as a car salesman greeting a potential buyer. Valentine held out one of the gloved hands and plucked the pencil from the silver tray.

"Where is Alice Paige?" Kavanagh asked.

David was shaking his head, tears streaming down his face.

Kavanagh nodded to Valentine. The agent moved fast, his free hand gripping the crown of David's skull and clutching a fistful of hair. David screamed in defiance, shutting his eyes tightly. Valentine brought his other palm with reassuring steady hands to Dave's head, pulling his hair down, forcing the singer's head to snap back.

"No! No! Nooooo!"

Kavanagh stared at David's throat, the way the Adam's apple undulated wildly within the trachea. "There comes a time Mr. Lazer when we finally realise the core of our failings. That we're making the wrong choices in our lives day after day…"

Valentine bent over the young singer, like a deranged dentist about to start work on a patient. The hand that gripped Dave's hair snaked its way to his forehead and a gloved finger started peeling open his right eyelid.

"Most of us think we want happiness and love," Kavanagh continued, as Valentine inserted the sharp lead tip under his open eyeball, "but we hear misleading messages every single day."

David crowed, an anguished and surprised noise. Valentine continued pushing the pencil in further. David began screaming then, a gargled, braying clamour. "We're told all the wrong things, don't you think? Commercial notions of beauty, power and wealth. But they're so wrong. So…so wrong. To achieve happiness and love all you need to do is make them your focus."

David uttered a choked gasp, a noise so alien to the human brain that only tattered snippets could escape his mouth. "Everything else," Kavanagh continued, waving Valentine away, "is highly dangerous. It's no wonder we're all so confused, don't you think Mr. Lazer? When we achieved what society told us we wanted...the result was just more emptiness. A hunger."

David's head flopped down as Valentine went back to the trolley. The singer made short, rasping gulps. His eye had swollen into a shapeless cherry-coloured mass with a black hole in the middle of it.

"I imagine you feel a little disorientated." Kavanagh said. "Are you aware of any rebellious groups committed towards harming The Network, Mr. Lazer?"

David shook his head. The table in front of him began to be polka-dotted with dark spots of blood, contrasting sharply with the beige wood colour.

"My father used to be a philosopher, did you know that, Mr. Lazer?"

David retched.

"He told me a story once, a story I'm going to tell you now. It's an old Zen Buddhist fable. It will help the disorientation you're feeling. I want you at peak optimum consciousness when I ask you my next question."

David muttered something, spat on the industrial grey floor tile.

"A long time ago," Kavanagh said, "two old men visited a market in a big city. The village they belonged to was poor. Food was scarce and hungry mouths were plentiful. These two men, aged but wise, had been asked by the villagers to buy food. None of the other villagers wanted to go to the market themselves, you see; they were afraid of being tricked by nefarious traders. So, the two men went to the market with the money and returned the next day. As they approached the village, late in the evening, the villagers ran out of their homes to greet the men. Cheers rose from the crowd. Hungry mouths salivated. There would be food tonight!"

Kavanagh took a seat opposite David.

"But the two men had come back empty-handed, and the joy of the crowd quickly turned to anger. Why hadn't they brought any food? Now the villagers would go to sleep hungry. Now the children would be famished. This was unacceptable! This was outrageous! The men waited for the crowd to tire itself out. When the villagers fell silent, the elder of the two men spoke. 'You placed your faith and your money in our hands. Both are gone. When you lose faith in yourself, you lose everything.'"

Kavanagh waited for a response from David but didn't get one. He sighed.

"Let's be frank. Those two old men were bastards. But they had a point, don't you think?"

David's head lolled to the side, and he finally looked up then, with a kind of horrid, obscene glee. He flashed a smile at Kavanagh.

Kavanagh found himself smirking.

"What's in a name, eh? Tell me where Alice is, Mr. Lazer."

David shook his head.

"I must warn you," Kavanagh said, "that once the pencil tip penetrates the pupil, the reaction will be immediate. Valentine usually prefers bleach but we were on low supplies today. I've sometimes heard an eyeball fizzing. Isn't that extraordinary? The smell is atrocious, however."

A sort of premonitory tremor passed through Dave as soon as he felt Valentine walk back to his chair. He attempted to slither away from Valentine, as if he were mustering every fibre of his body to transform into a liquid, so that he could simply slip away from the chair and pool into the cracks and crevices of the room. To Kavanagh he looked like a small, inconsequential rodent.

"Wait! Waitwaitwaitwait..." Dave cried out in a cracked, high pitched voice. "I don't know where she is! I'm telling you the truth! She didn't want me knowing any details!"

Kavanagh raised a hand. Valentine stopped in mid-stride; a seething animosity spread across his face. The thug wanted to have his fun; Kavanagh noted. The dystopia of the average person is the utopia of the psychopath, he thought to himself mildly.

"But you have helped her?" asked Kavanagh thoughtfully.

Dave looked between the colossal agent to his left and then back at Kavanagh, as if this short reprieve would benefit him somehow. Valentine was craned over Dave again. His face looked mammoth because of its nearness, and hideously ugly. Moreover, it was filled with a sort of exhilaration, a lunatic intensity. He made a violent effort to raise himself into a sitting position, and merely succeeded in wrenching his body painfully. He started thrashing again, swinging his head left and right. The veins bulged from his neck as if he were about to explode.

"You fucking fascists! You cunts! You'll never get her! You hear me? YOU'LL NEVER-"

His shouts turned into strangled screams as Valentine jabbed the pencil straight into his eye.

"There is a way you can save yourself," Kavanagh said, over the agonised howling. "You think there's no other way, and perhaps you're trying to negate the pain – wishing it on someone else. In the end, it always happens. Everyone has their threshold, but you can still be happy, Mr. Lazer. You can still walk out of this room with a future." Kavanagh looked across at the pitiful creature in front of him. The room stank and Kavanagh grimaced as he realised Dave had soiled himself. More than ever, he had the air of a teacher taking pains with a wayward child.

"You do have a future ahead of you," Kavanagh repeated as Valentine stepped away from the chair. The singer's head lulled from side to side, his right eye a black hole of utter destruction. The pencil protruded from the socket. Blood dripped from the hole that used to be his eye in thick gloopy tendrils, down onto his shirt. When Kavanagh spoke next his voice was gentle and patient. He embellished the role of a priest or a teacher, ready to persuade and explain rather than to punish.

"We could be harsher, Mr. Lazer. There are medieval devices, abysmal things...that we could strap to your head to make it feel like we were taking pieces out of your brain. By the end of it, you'd be a gibbering wreck, with no recollection of who you are. But I want to help you, Mr. Lazer. Will you let me help you?"

David warbled incoherently. His remaining good eye rolled white to the top of his skull as though stunned, with dark blood oozing down his face. Kavanagh listened as a very faint whimpering came out of him.

"Don't give into the pain, David," Kavanagh said, as didactically as ever. He slid out from his chair and in a moment was next to David's ear. "We can save your eye," he whispered. "We know that Alice is out of her SCOOP suit. All we need from you is the name of the person that helped her out of it. She's an intelligent girl, we know that. She'll be long gone by now, David. So, what's in a name, eh? Just think...we can stop this pain for you now. We can inflict this pain on someone else. Someone else who deserves it. Wouldn't you like that, David? Wouldn't you like someone else to receive this pain?"

Slowly, David began to nod his head.

Good. So very good.

Valentine grunted.

"I shouldn't have to describe what would happen if Agent Valentine applied a slightly persistent pressure on the end of this pencil," Kavanagh said. He let David refocus. Amid a stream of blood and saliva, David squeaked an affirmation. "Tell us the name of the person who helped Alice out of her SCOOP suit, and you can go home. That's all I ever needed, David. After all, what's in a name, eh?"

David opened his mouth and told Kavanagh what he needed to know.

I love how #HuntedTV can take you to another place. For example, @ryanlando is on at this café now so I'm going to a different café. #burn #hatehunted

@Jordanslater

856 replies 7450 RTs 6208 Likes

Has anyone seen any footage of @alicepaige online? Girl's gone toground. I heard they're interrogating all members of #VamPyrates. And you know what that means. #gulag #POW #neverseenagain

@lifer_4_lyfe

457 replies 4331 RTs 2597 Likes

@lifer_4_lyfe have you heard their album? I'll be honest. Not bad. Not bad at all.

@Leahsummers

548 replies 2244 RTs 999 Likes

What I wouldn't give for some nude pics of @alicepaige to appear 'suddenly' online.

@HotPikachusex

697 replies 4435 RTs 566 Likes

What I wouldn't give to have not read your username.

@hannah_vintage

1969 replies 7217 RTs 4116 Likes

I heard she's still in London #goinghunting

¬

Who's coming out to play tonight? Gunna head to da Old Mount.

¬

Bringing my Lucille bat out. Awww yeeaaa

@CRicoh

44 replies 120 RTs 520 Likes

Old Mount soudzs gd. got a free houze now that Gran's been retyred.

@Brian_Bowerman

2 replies 5 RTs 7 Likes

THEY TRACK YOU IN YOUR SCOOP SUIT. EVERYTHING ABOUT THE NETWORK

IS A LIE #thenetworklies

@For_The_Movement

567 replies 1248 RTs 2421 Likes

Case #337

NetworkID: 8716367 Bryant, G.

Time: 15:43

8716367: You realise that you'll be penalised?

#337: (sigh) It doesn't matter.

8716367: According to rule number five of The Network Terms and conditions, if a Self-Contained Ordinance and Optimum Paragon Suit wearer breaches, violates or fails to follow, or act inconsistently with the rules -

#337: I know the rules. I followed them.

8716367: That's currently under review. Not my area, but what I'm interested in is why you crashed your car into a shop you knew didn't have anyone inside.

#337: Property damage. Breaking and entering. Do I need to go on?

8716367: But your vid shows you approaching the house of a...(rustling of papers) Mr. Delano on the morning of your Birthday Treat. I've gone through the vid, looks like you waited outside the house for more than three hours. You were armed with a knife.

#337: Yes.

8716367: What were your original intentions? Before you changed your mind and crashed your car into the shop?

#337: Who said anything about intentions?

8716367: I've looked through your file. Seems like you and Mr. Delano have been friends for several years?

#337: We went to school together.

8716367: He's got a family, two kids.

#337: Yes.

8716367: And you've been single for the past five years.

#337: So?

8716367: I've also looked at your social media. You both seem to be quite close.

#337: There a law against that?

8716367: I don't want to sound like I'm prying, [REDACTED] – I just want to get the full picture. I want to help you…help you with your breach of contract. Were you in love with Mr. Delano?

#337: …

8716367: It's okay. Take your time.

#337: I wasn't in love with him.

8716367: No?

#337: I'm *in* love with him. Always have been.

8716367: You were there to kill the family.

#337: There was a time…just after we graduated. It lasted a few months, but we both agreed that it would ruin our friendship. That's what he said, anyway.

8716367: You didn't believe that?

#337: Have you ever felt so close to someone…so in sync with them, that it just makes sense? Things made sense with us. It all clicked. He was just afraid to open those feelings.

8716367: But he's been married for four years now.

#337: Not happily. He's always complaining about her. About the children. Always.

8716367: But you didn't go through with it?

#337: I went through all the scenarios in my head. In the happiest one, they're out of the picture and we get back together. I knew it would take some time…some forgiveness. But in the end, it would be my happily ever after.

8716367: What ultimately changed your mind?

#337: There's no such thing as a happy ever after.

9

GEORGE

MONDAY

101 HOURS REMAIN...

George Bryant's Social Credit Score limit was one hundred and thirty-six. It wasn't the best social credit score, but it also wasn't the worst. He would be able to purchase things that other, less fortunate civilians of the country couldn't. According to the monthly mandate, he was allowed fourteen units of alcohol a week. That equated to six large glasses of wine, or six pints of lager or ale. Or, George thought devilishly as he finished off his fourth whiskey, fourteen 25ml glasses of the good stuff.

George didn't usually drink, so every now and then he'd treat himself by getting completely and utterly shitfaced. *Today,* he mused ruefully to himself, *has been one of those days.*

The Crown and Anchor was a bright place. He marked that down in its favour. There was nothing worse than a dingy, dark pub where you could hardly see yourself eat or drink. He ordered the barman over and requested another whiskey. He was starting to feel good. Starting to feel *limber*, as his old University chums used to say, just before they went out on an evening and painted the town seven shades of beige. The barman was tall and slim, sporting a pencil thin moustache. He reminded George of one of those 1940's style boxers, with chiselled chin and hairy arms.

"Whiskey, please. Make it a double."

The barman gave a non-committal nod and started making his drink. George felt inside his coat pocket and felt the edge of the piece of paper with words so innocuous and damning all at the same time. He couldn't force himself to look at the carefully etched lettering now. Couldn't force himself to ask the question that had been plaguing him all day.

How do they know about my daughter?

Like a gap created by an extracted tooth, George tongued and probed that question. There could be no way that anyone in his department would have access to that information. None at all.

A friend.

Who was this mysterious friend that informed him of his upcoming Birthday Treat? George didn't have many friends these days. All his old school mates had slowly ebbed away from the area, marrying into the contract with a house, car and white picket fencing. George thought about his own marriage to Elspeth. As the barman returned to the counter with his drink and the Social Credit reader, he thought that his marriage was a lot like the feeling he had with his parents when he was a child. He never worried about them; he just expected them to be there when he returned from school, with dinner on the table and a warm house to sleep in. He found with a despondent sort of apathy that he felt the same way about Elspeth. They were just roommates now.

I still have a few good years left in me; George hollowly concurred as he swiped his Social Credit Card across the pin reader. There were no children to be maimed in the car wreck of his marriage, and if

Elspeth wanted a divorce, he would give it to her, no questions asked. He looked at his phone. There were no messages. She didn't even care that he was late, probably too consumed with her stories on the Free-Vee.

Even worse, he thought miserably, *she simply doesn't care.* George often thought about divorce, but the whole process seemed too protracted and left a bitter taste in his mouth. Then there was the flat to think about, who would get what in the settlement and the whole process just gave him a headache.

But she'll never ask for one, he thought. *She's too consumed with the whole generic setting of life, watching her stories and going about things with no conviction. No passion. And she takes out whatever grievances she has on me.*

The small digital read-out claimed that he had eight units of alcohol left to consume for the month. That was likely a few more glasses. George's face, already starting to darken with whiskey, darkened more. He should have just purchased a bottle from the supermarket and would still have leftover credit. But he didn't want a bottle. A bottle meant going home and being grilled over why he was drinking in the first place. And he didn't want to do that just yet.

It was dark outside now, and the whiskey was doing its job.

A commotion in the far corner of the pub drew his attention. A knot of six teenagers were gathered around a table. George observed the gangly group dressed mostly in black from the pub counter, listening as they laughed loud and swore at one another. A couple of them had ERD's, but they all spoke at a frantic pace, as if they'd taken uppers with their booze. It wasn't until George had surveyed the whole table that he realised that most of the party were trying to get the attention of a slim-shouldered girl with her back to him. They gesticulated and spoke like youngsters gaining a sense of surety in themselves and perhaps that was the most dangerous phase of all - physically competent without the experience to know when to show restraint.

George gulped down his whiskey and was about to call it quits when the girl everyone on the table had been clamouring for suddenly tilted her head back and burst out in laughter, and it was then George realised it was Carina, the coffee shop girl.

George shivered and for a moment was conscious of his body beneath his clothes and a feeling of fingers lightly tracing over his skin. He swayed from the counter with sudden light-headedness. He was sure it wasn't just the whiskey causing the effect. Anxiously, he checked his phone again but there were no messages. He'd been in the pub for over an hour and wondered suddenly if he should remove his coat, as he was feeling warm. He absently ordered another whiskey from the pencil-thin moustache barman, who lifted his eyebrows in affirmation and went to get another tumbler from behind the bar. The sounds of the pub, the voices and the laughter all sort of blended in a big, echoey stew.

What was it about this girl that made him feel so uncomfortable? She was probably half his age.

But she's mature – you've spoken to her a couple of times in the coffee shop, she carries herself with a certain...distinguished attitude.

They would likely have nothing in common. Then there was the fact that he was a married man, and she likely had a boyfriend.

Look at the table. All the guys there are practically climbing over themselves to get her attention.

Then there was the last irrefutable piece of information he'd discarded to the back of his mind. She didn't even know his name. She thought he was called Gary. He found himself grimacing. *To her, you're the fat kid at school no-one liked.* But there was something else. Some deep, desperate reptilian part of George that wanted to impress the girl from the coffee shop. He'd been like that at school, when he'd stood before Jordy Mitchell with his guitar, just a gangly, awkward kid with scruffy hair and faded jeans, and all he wanted in the world at that time was to get into the band *The Four Horsemen*. He remembered the way the other band members looked him over, as if to say 'what, this retard?' and scoffed when he'd asked to join.

"Yeah Daffy, but we need someone on bass, otherwise we can't play The Garage on Saturday night."

Dressed in an old, checked shirt with two buttons missing and baggy jeans that had seen better days, Daffy, the drummer clasped his hands together and let out a low whistle.

"So, you wanna be in the band, then?" Jordy had said. And that's all she wrote. George wasn't a great musician, and his shredding days were short-lived, but for that moment, for that insane, gargantuan moment – he had stepped up the nerve to ask to be in The Four Horsemen and he'd been repaid in kind.

His illusion of years gone by was interrupted when he saw Carina starting to leave the table. Crestfallen at having missed his opportunity to do something...anything, he downed the last of his glass of whiskey.

The pub was low on drinkers, typical for a Monday, he suspected. George wasn't a big fan of company and preferred the quiet nights, but now the lack of patrons made him feel like he stood out. He surreptitiously observed Carina pick up her bag, make a comment to the group, at which they chuckled heartily, and then she left the table, walking down the hallway. Was she leaving? He placed his glass down on the chipped wooden table in front of him and picked up the nearest beer mat. There was a picture of an anchor on it, along with the slogan Premium Ale, Premium Quality. Without pause, George began to peel the printed face away from the cardboard. It was a habit that Elspeth scolded him for whenever they went out for a drink.

When was the last time that had happened?

It seemed to halt the sombre thoughts that tended to wander through the dark, insidious alleyways of his mind. After the last piece had fluttered to the bar, George made up his mind. He wasn't going to entertain the thoughts of attempting to speak to the coffee girl. It had been one of those deluded contemplations that one often has after a few drinks. Like saying drunkenly that you'll agree to put up a shed in a neighbour's back garden and then spend the next hung-over morning sporadically uttering 'fuck' to yourself for agreeing to do such a stupid thing. He chuckled to himself and felt his mood lighten a little. It wasn't often he had such moments of levity. Not when the mirror showed him a man that looked closer to fifty than his actual age.

Misery had been hard on his face.

In a move that seemed both causal and urgent at the same time, George stepped back from the bar and slinked past his stool. A quick trip to the loo and then he'd be on his way home, shaking his head with the embarrassing bullet he'd managed to dodge.

As he walked down the hallway, he looked up to see Carina about to brush past him. A knot tightened in his stomach. *You're doing a dumb thing*, he thought, before opening his mouth.

"Carina?"

They stood looking at each for a moment. There was something unapologetic about the way she regarded him that made him break eye contact first.

"Don't I know you from somewhere?" She finally said. George's heart leapt inside his chest. She did remember him!

"Yes...I'm George. You serve me coffee every morning."

Her brow furrowed and for a second something flickered across her face, and the closet word he had for it was fear, but the expression was gone in an instant so he thought it may have been a trick of the light. Or the whiskey coursing through his veins. She looked at him with eyes so dark they looked almost expressionless. Unreadable. Her hair was a tangle of curls and fell about her shoulders. He wondered with a curious wonderment how it would feel to run his hands through her hair, to feel the coarseness between his fingers.

Stop it, George. You're old enough to be her father.

"I thought your name was Gary?" She said.

He felt all the blood rushing to his face and realised that his head likely resembled a beetroot. "No," he mumbled, "it's George."

Carina slapped her hands to her mouth in horror. "Oh my God! Are you saying I've been calling you Gary all this time?"

George's head was thrumming like a fuse box. Why had he even said anything in the first place? The coffee shop waitress lent forward and deferentially put her hand on his. Her flesh was warm and he felt an invasion shudder through his body, an unwanted intimacy. George knew that if she asked him to do anything in that moment he wouldn't hesitate. He hated that she made him feel like ice-cream on a warm porcelain bowl. A poor yogurt of a man.

"That's okay," he stammered, pulling his hand away.

"It certainly is not! Let me buy you a drink, as a way of apology. Please, it's the least I could do."

George began to wave her away in protest, but Carina folded her arm round his and began leading him back to the table. She smelt like strawberries. Before he knew what was happening, he was sat down in the middle of the bench and Carina was introducing him to all her friends. The three boys at the table all looked as if they were auditioning for some unwarranted KISS reunion, and George felt a tipsy giddiness when he realised that the teenagers in front of him probably didn't even know who KISS were. He stifled a laugh as Carina volleyed off the names of the people in front of him that he would instantly forget.

"How do you all know each other?" George said politely, anxiety starting to pull ahead in the race between drunkenness and apprehension.

One of the boys who had a nose piercing and a ratty face gesticulated at one of the other kids at the end of the table. "We knew each other through Kaleb at first, but then like, came the performance. The performance. Carina knocked it out of the park, and we hung out and got to know each other, and I'm not sure if that night was when it happened, but by the next time I saw her, we all kind of just started hanging out together, you know?"

The kid was like a machine gun spitting out verbal bullets. George's head started to swim. Nose piercing kid was nodding his head energetically, and George wondered if he was on something. His pupils were saucers. The guy in the middle of the bench had applied severe eyeliner and looked like a panda. He nodded in agreement.

"Yeah, that performance was off the hook. When are you going to do something else, Carina?"

George had no idea what they were talking about but ascertained that perhaps they were part of some performance art troupe. The third kid who had a hooked nose (Kaleb?) sat with a scowl on his face, looking menacingly at him. The anxiety he felt was starting to flourish. Carina tilted her head back and laughed. For George it was a sound he felt he hadn't heard in a thousand years. He instantly felt at ease around her.

"I don't think I'm ready for the West End just yet," she said, lifting herself from the bench. "But maybe in a few years...who knows? What did you want to drink, George?"

George mumbled that a pint would be fine and watched her saunter towards the bar. Watched those slender, athletic legs walk away. When he turned, he felt Kaleb's eyes on him.

"And how do you know Carina?" Kaleb asked. It wasn't particularly unfriendly, but the question wasn't filled with mirth, either. Even in his tipsy state, George knew he would have to be careful.

"She serves me coffee in the mornings." George replied, trying not to slur his words.

The boy scoffed. "She's not, like, your slave, man. She doesn't serve you coffee. It's people like you that are crippled by a forced dissociation of the mind. Y'see, we believe we stopped slavery, but *we* know that we didn't, we simply exported it." George noted the boy's lit eyes as he chattered on excitably. "We are the beneficiaries of slaves within industries from the pub we're sitting in right now to the coffee shop Carina works in. Our civilization is built on the bones of these angels and I am here to tell you–"

"To be quiet and let George drink his pint," Carina interrupted, planting George's glass on the table. "Quit with the lectures, Kaleb. They're proper cringe."

The other two boys started cackling with laughter, but Kaleb looked like a puppy who had just been caught fouling on its master's carpet. Carina embedded herself next to George again, brushing up against him as she tucked her legs under the bench. He felt hot again.

"Listen Kaleb," she continued, taking a sip from her glass, "we know our world is dying and we buy hundreds of products we don't need, fuelling the wanton global destruction with our purchases, but it's like as it always was. The rich get richer, the poor get poorer. The elites laugh and The Network steal from us and control us with fear and distraction. If you want to truly save the planet, if you want to live a noble life, get away from The Network. Or join up with The Movement and make some real-life changes."

George glanced over his shoulder to ensure no one in the pub was listening. He'd heard stories of underground rebellions; everyone had. A group called The Movement that rallied against The Network. There'd been articles about skirmishes in South East London and of colleagues that had disappeared from The Network building after having one too many drinks and saying things they shouldn't. Black vans pulling up outside houses and dragging people away, never to be seen again.

"Okay, okay," Kaleb hissed, his eyes darting from one side of the pub to the other. "You've made your point, Carina."

She looked at him with the incredulity of a man who had just pulled a pin on a grenade and was trying to put it back into its catch. Kaleb didn't make eye contact with her. "You're right. I totally understand that you're upset, but we need to watch what we're saying in public..."

"Oh, for the love of - you know what you are? All of you? Children. Kids playing make believe. You want to know why I won't perform in front of an audience again. Because it's bullshit, that's why. People are being killed every day and we slap a sticker on it and give it a name and that makes everything alright? Going into the bathroom and scribbling graffiti on the toilet walls of anti-fascist statements, well doesn't that make us dangerous? But that doesn't really do anything, does it? Marching down the road one day a year against The Network never really accomplishes anything, does it?"

George didn't know how to react to this sudden change in atmosphere. He sat as still as a mouse, in the futile hope that the conversation would be over, and they could talk about pleasant things, like the weather or what was on the Free-Vee last night. Because that's what kids talked about these days, wasn't it? Kaleb looked down at his pint.

"We're suffering in a system of greed in which the most corrupted and debased humans win power over us and make hell on earth. Yet we do nothing. We play along. We've played along for so long that it's desensitised us. We put these people in power, for crying out loud! Change is simple – but we need radical change. We can't just tweak their politics, we need a whole new system and it starts with you and me."

Silence descended over the table. George cast a half-apprehensive glance over Carina before he took his pint and let the cold nectar slip voluptuously down his throat. In that moment he realised that Carina would never be the mysterious girl from the coffee shop anymore and she never would be again. In a way it depressed him. She had voiced deeply repressed opinions of his own, and in such a nonchalant and public way. To some respect he thought her show was a little put on, and he felt that she was determined to be as different as possible, regurgitating articles and thought pieces from novels that she may have recited for a play. The thought irked him. His fantasy about her hadn't included politics and The Network.

"I get what you're saying, Cay – I really do, but..."

Carina slammed her fist down on the table. Perhaps they'd all had too much to drink, George thought sourly. There was a sort of calculating ferocity in her eyes, a desire to hit or kick Kaleb in the testicles with the boot of her heel and continue talking as if nothing had ever happened. He took another gulp of beer, thinking of an excuse that wouldn't sound too flimsy to pardon him from this situation. Carina pointed a finger at Kaleb and opened her mouth to say something, but George beat her to it.

George said it very quietly, almost casually: "I saw a girl thrown on the train tracks by a boiler today."

Kaleb's eyes flittered nervously from Carina to George. He took the interruption as a form of escape.

"Sometimes," George continued, "I want to shut my eyes and empty my head from all the Birthday Treats I've seen over the years. I'm not just terrified of it all...I'm angry too. There was a dragger at work today that threatened me with using her potential Birthday Treat this week as a way of getting what she wanted. Can you imagine that? We all get on with it but we're always aware of eyes watching us. It's getting to the point where nothing is our own except the few cubic centimetres inside our skulls."

Another pause of silence shrouded the table.

"You're pretty dark, George." Carina finally said, looking at him with large, watchful eyes. When George looked up, she was smiling. "But we're a dark bunch, so I guess that makes you okay."

The other three guys started snickering. As Carina lifted her drink for a toast, she was laughing too.

"To the bastard future!"

George found himself lifting his own glass. They all clinked.

"Now...who wants to go to a party?"

Curiously, George found himself grinning and nodding.

It was odd for George to make a connection so fast, to give his trust so easily, tentative though it was. It wasn't that she was easy to talk to, he felt like he could tell her anything and she'd absorb his words, not simply let him prattle on and then change the subject when a gap appeared in the conversation. Whenever he tried to speak to Elspeth about something happening in his life, she would offer monosyllabic grunts, not even looking at him. There was something in the way Carina smiled, a warmth, a genuineness, a softness that was alien to him.

Rat faced piercing guy (who he found out was called James) was talking energetically throughout the train ride, babbling on about everything from the latest TV show he was watching to deep philosophical queries about the practical applications of face cream. Eyeliner guy (his name was Nigel) seemed a tad more laid back, nodding and smiling when James was talking, but Kaleb seemed to be sulking, preferring to stay close to Carina than any of the others.

Soon they were tumbling out of Thornton Hill station and George found himself sobering up. The sky was dark and foreboding. *You're doing a dumb thing and every moment you stay longer is going to get worse*, said that curt little voice inside his head. George was about to stop and tell the group that he had made a mistake, that he had things to do and would get back on the train but somehow it seemed that Carina sensed his apprehension and took his arm, guiding him down the street. George remained silent.

The music in the house was so loud that it made George's skin tingle. The bass thumped in time with his heartbeat as though they were one, filling his body with an inward shudder. George liked the music but felt a little overwhelmed by the amount of people in the flat. Strobe lights flickered in some of the rooms, but he was aware that the place look dilapidated, with wooden struts protruding from the walls like an exposed ribcage. The smell of urine, sawdust and stale beer pervaded his nostrils. He didn't know who owned the place, and although Carina waved at a few people they didn't seem to talk to anyone, as if this was a routinely meeting place for everyone and no one. They had been let into the flat after a few attempts ringing the bell, but George couldn't shake the feeling that he felt out of place, as though he was the oldest one in any of the rooms they walked through. The sober part of his brain was starting to awaken, and it was telling every orifice of his body to leave. He also hoped no-one thought he was someone's father. Thick plumes of blue smoke hovered in the air wherever he went, and they found themselves huddled in a circle amongst dancers in what appeared to be a living room. It wasn't long until a plastic cup was handed to him by Carina.

"What is it?" George found himself shouting over the roar of music.

Carina winked at him. "Does it matter?"

George noticed through the manic strobe lighting that Kaleb was studying him in hostile silence as he drank from the cup. It wasn't aggressive, exactly; merely a kind of belligerent wariness, a momentary stiffening of a scientist as they analysed their most cherished lab rat ingest a possible lethal overdose. The liquid was warm and burnt the back of his throat. It tasted like liquorice, but there was something metallic in there too, like copper. Or blood. He wanted to gag as it scorched his oesophagus, but he held firm.

Through watery eyes, he wanted to pinpoint something in the room that he could focus on, to prevent him from hacking up whatever vile substance he'd just swallowed. He noticed that the windows in the flat appeared to be frosted over but were merely coated with dust. Once again, he wondered to himself what he was doing in such a place. *Too late now*, said the voice inside his head. *You've gone too far now. I can't help you, dummy.*

Kaleb turned away, muttering to himself and was soon lost within the crowd. George discerned that the song currently playing got louder, pulling him into the throb and rhythm of the crowd, moving and swaying like a multi-headed beast sharing one brain. Another cup appeared in his hands and he drank it gladly. In his lean throat, his sharp-pointed Adam's apple made a surprisingly rapid bopping movement, and the liquid vanished. This time it seemed to go down with much more ease. He felt warm all over, as if someone had put a cosy blanket over his shoulders.

Nigel and James were talking, but George couldn't hear them over the music. He smiled and gave nods of affirmations in gaps where it would be expected, but he suddenly realised that Carina had disappeared from the circle. He glanced over the crowd of people in the room but couldn't make her out, so he slipped away from the room.

"Hey, let me get you another drink."

George turned. It was Kaleb. The boy with the hooked nose was smiling, but in George's swaying vision it seemed humourless.

"I'm okay, thanks."

"No worries, *George*." Kaleb turned and made his way to the kitchen. It appeared that the cacophony of whooping in the densely thick room started to mingle with the music, creating a sound that was outlandish to George's brain. He stumbled past a few people and felt as though a fire was burning in his belly. He looked down at his half empty cup. The liquid looked black and unsettling. He let it drop to the floor, pushing past the dancing people as they flailed their arms in the air wildly. He needed to get out...he needed air.

In the hallway, at the bottom of the stairs he could make out two figures, talking. He drunkenly bumped against the wall and Carina spun her head round. She had a weary smile on her face, but George looked at her eyes. There was a frightened animal skittishness to them. Carina looked worried.

"You okay?" He said, trying not to slur his words again. His head was starting to feel like a one-man band, clashing symbols and all.

In an instant the frightened look was gone, replaced with her resplendent smile. She came forward, her hand felt for his and gave it a fleeting squeeze.

"Yeah, I was just talking to-"

The other figure peered his head around from her shoulder.

"Hey, fuck-knuckles!"

George's heart turned to ice and his bowels to water. For a few seconds he was too paralysed to move.

Parker.

Parker from work.

From his department.

From The Network.

"Well, well, well...fancy seeing you here, old sport!" He nudged past Carina, eying up George in an amused and surprised way. George felt his legs start to turn rubbery. Perhaps it was a combination of whatever he'd been drinking, the pumping music and now seeing one of his colleagues, but everything seemed to start crashing inward. Parker's silly pug face beamed into his. George had a vivid hallucination in that moment of smashing a sledgehammer right into the middle of it.

"What are you doing here?" George stammered; brow furrowed. He couldn't handle this right now – not now. He grasped one of the stair spindles, more to keep himself upright than anything else. In a sober state of mind, he might have been able to come up with an excuse, something plausible. Right now, his brain was adjusting to the shock of seeing Parker standing right in front of him. He felt like he'd been caught rummaging through the old man's liquor cabinet.

Parker clapped a hand on his shoulder. "I could say the same thing for you, fella! Well, you gotta lead your life your way, right? If you ain't losing your mind, you ain't partying. Am I right?" He burst out laughing, a wild, maniacal sound that seemed to reverberate throughout George's bones. He wondered if Parker had been drinking the same vile concoction he'd been given or had been smoking an abundance of opium cigarettes. Perhaps there would be a way out for him still. George looked on helplessly as Carina slid away from them, going up the stairs. Parker followed his gaze and leaned into him. "I'd steer clear of that one," he whispered. "She's trouble."

George felt himself blush.

Parker leaned back; his eyes narrowed. "I don't know why you're here, George. But I'm glad. I was starting to think you were like all the other stiffs. But there's something different about you." He eyed George with curious intent. "But we're friends, right? Not just colleagues. Let me get you a drink!"

Parker sauntered off, down the hall. "Wait here! I'll be right back!"

George did a quick arithmetic in his head. If he left now, there wouldn't be anything too incriminating about his presence at this place. Parker would make a few jokes tomorrow at work, (Christ, he would have such a hangover) but he'd put it down to reckless abandonment – he just wanted to cut loose for an evening. There was no way that Parker would mention this to anyone else of consequence. Would he mention anything to Faulkner? When did Faulkner listen to anything that Parker had to say? After the stunt he pulled today, he couldn't afford another reprimand. There was no one else he could think of that would lead the trail back to Elspeth. Damn, his thoughts were all over the place. He felt like his head was on another planet.

But why are you thinking like a man that's committed adultery? The snide voice from the back of his mind said, smugly. *Only guilty men have that kind of logic, that kind of thinking. And you're not guilty, are you Georgey-boy?*

Not guilty. Not yet.

George looked at his hand. She had squeezed it just before going up the stairs. And the way she'd wrapped her arm around his, earlier. *Those were all signs, right? Why did she go upstairs?* She wanted him to follow, didn't she? He may have been out of the game for a long time, but he knew what the signs were. Didn't he?

Grimly conscious of the poor decision he was making, he slapped a hand on the finial of the bannisters and ascended the stairs. As he went higher, the music from the rooms below started to subdue. He felt a little better for that. Several doors looked closed on the landing. He chose one at random and knocked on the door. It jerked open, and Carina pulled him into the room.

It was cramped, dim and cave-like, with a cheap looking pine framed bed in the corner. There was a small window looking out into the darkened street, covered by twenty-something year old net curtains. Dirt encrusted beige wallpaper was peeling off the wall.

"I'm not sure what's going on here. How do you know Par-"

The next moment she was in his arms and kissed him almost violently. At the beginning he had no feeling except sheer disbelief. It could not have been more than five seconds, and yet it seemed like an eternity that their mouths clung together. He could feel her firm breasts through her clothes, her youthful body strained against his own, the mass of her dark tangled hair against his face. He savoured the taste of her lips upon his own. He clasped his hands around her neck, and they kissed again, passionately. Then he felt her shoulder give a wriggle of dissent and he pulled away. They were both breathing fast, but the smile had reappeared round the corners of her mouth.

What are you doing? The tiny voice in his head screamed. *This is madness!*

"This is wrong," he finally said, looking down at his shoes. "You're too young for me. You're-"

"Tell me about the girl on the train tracks." She said.

An image of headphones floated in his head. The discarded headphones that lay on the platform. He looked up.

"I'm good at spotting people who don't belong, George." She said, taking his hands in hers. "When we met at the pub tonight, there was something about you that seemed...different. No one talks about the boilers in a real sense anymore, no one talks about the finality of it all. They've become an inconvenience to people, nothing more. And what happens to the victims, George? What happens to the families of the girl you saw this morning? Will her name be remembered?"

George knew the answer. Feeling slightly ashamed, he pulled away from Carina and ran a hand through his hair. Below them, he could hear the muffled drumming of music and howling of revellers.

"I'm...sorry," he said meekly. "You're probably fifteen years younger than I am. I shouldn't have-"

"You haven't done anything I didn't want, George. I know you're married."

The words stung. His stomach contracted so hard that his legs buckled and he almost fell to his knees. He managed to sit on the bed.

"You know what I've just noticed?" He said, flustered. "I've just this minute noticed that there's no Free-Vee monitors in this place. Not in one room. Isn't that crazy?"

Carina sat next to him on the bed. She placed her hand on his shoulder. "It's hard to find places like this. Every month we try to throw a party where there's no Social Credit rating system, no Free-Vees, no Network. It's a reminder to let us know that we're not controlled by them. That's why I asked you to come tonight. I could see it in your face when you spoke about...what happened this morning. I felt like you needed this. You needed to be reminded that you're not controlled by them."

George put his head in his hands. A feeling of hopelessness cascaded over him. He knew that it was all useless. He thought of the note in his coat pocket, the one that reminded him that at the end of the week he would be getting his Birthday Treat. Whether he put on a SCOOP suit and committed his treat, or whether he refrained from wearing it, it made no difference. The Network would get him just the same. When he turned sixty a Retirement Agent would arrive at his house and put a bolt gun to his head. He envied Carina's optimism, her resilience. He had purchased a garage, a few years back – a refuge from Elspeth and work and everything else in between. No one knew of the garage. It was his fortress of solitude. He wanted to take Carina there now, away from all of this. But there was still that part of him that thought all of this was a fantasy.

Only through the years of drudgery and monotonous repetition had he finally accepted the universal truth: that no matter how successfully you dodged The Network, sooner or later they were bound to get you one way or another.

"I don't have much time before Kaleb tries to find me like the lost puppy that he is, but would you be able to meet me tomorrow?"

George was suddenly aware of Carina's face a few centimetres from his own. His heart stirred painfully. "After work?" He asked.

"No," she replied promptly. "Take the day off. Call in sick if you like, but meet me at twelve o'clock at the Park, just beyond the bandstand at Chiswick. There's a cluster of funny looking trees past the bandstand, you know the ones?"

He did.

"I trust you, George," she continued, "I know we don't know each other that well, but I need to ask you something before anything else."

Carina looked him straight in the eyes. "Are you happy?"

George blew out some air. He hadn't expected to hear that. With just three little words the world slipped out from beneath his feet. He realised that Carina was staring at him. She hadn't blinked.

"No." He said slowly. "I haven't been happy for a long time."

She took his head in her hands and leaned in, kissing him again. This time it was tender, affectionate.

"I'm with The Movement," she said, standing up.

Before George could say anything, the door burst open and Parker sauntered in, carrying two cups. "Hello, hello, hello. What have we here then?"

George, slack jawed with open mouth, had no idea. No idea at all.

Brad Swanson is nervous, as if he's waiting to hear bad news from a doctor's office. We meet in a restaurant filled with men in suits and leather jackets the colour of chocolate milk with a rotation of colourful polyester turtlenecks. It's a fancy, rich-people part of north London. The setting is appropriate, given what we're here to talk about: *I Am Freddie*. It's the new film that tells the story of Frederick Henshaw, the only known survivor of the **Hunted TV** programme. His meteorite rise to fame and then… nothing. Henshaw mysteriously disappeared out of the spotlight following his now infamous 5th day win. Some news sources affirm that Henshaw took his prize money and fled the country, whilst others stipulate that The Network ushered him away and have given him a new identity.

"I mean, God. It's a gargantuan role when you think about it." He inhales sharply. "Yeah. It's weird. Here's the only guy that decided to give up his Birthday Treat and went on the run for five days. Against the whole country. And he got away with it." He clams up, as if he's said something he shouldn't. "Sorry, I don't have anything to add to that."

It takes a while for his nerves to ease. "People don't believe it," he says, "but I'm naturally quite shy. I've had to work hard to mask that, not appear anxious or nervous. In character I feel like I can do anything, really. That's part of what attracted me to acting. And this role poses many questions about what it is to be human. If you have considered how different the human condition might be if we were to abandon learned behaviour then Freddie's story will provide something that piques your interest…I hate my own birthday, I hate being the centre of attention."

Given the level of Swanson's recent success, he may have to start getting used to it. After slowly beginning his career in British television, he's hit Hollywood with a bang, playing the villainous lead alien T'Saarg in *The Night They Came*, which required being at work before 3am for four hours of hair and makeup, as his character was entirely green. And had several testicles.

For someone who is so reticent in interviews, so reluctant to give anything away, Swanson hints at a rebellious side that doesn't come out much in public. He's "quite lazy," he says and "couldn't tie his shoelaces without someone telling me to do so." He was not always well behaved at school, he claims, and she has never liked authority. Although I'm not sure about this, as his eyes continually flicker to two Agents posing as his PR team at the far end of the bar.

I ask Swanson what attracted him to the role of Freddie Henshaw, and the potential controversy surrounding the material (in one scene, Henshaw references the public mass shooting of twenty-one bankers by Erik Volt, during the early years of Birthday Treats before stricter regulations were Governed). "Erm," he says. "I think the script deals with some good elements about the regularity of man and the dominance of our settled personality over our impulsive desires. I mean when Birthday Treats started, no-one wanted to partake, did they? It's kind of like re-training your brain not to do something. You remember when smoking was banned in pubs? Everyone kicked up a fuss at the time, or so we're told...things like that happen in History all the time. It's evolution." Swanson looks over at the bar, with the two PR men. "I mean, when the tragic loss of a mass shooting happens, what scared many even so today; it was a sobering dark look at the dark side of human nature. That pivotal moment when Volt took more than one life was a real loss of innocence, and that's what the film addresses. It's a look back at how things were...but how they can be."

"The ideal place would be for it to be completely normalised and not a big deal. And I feel like we're working towards that, in all different kinds of areas, not just to do with consequences with what happens after, the way families are impacted, everything. I feel like we've made huge strides in the last couple of years." He laughs. "But I'm really looking forward to the time when I no longer have to answer questions about it!"

It's late and the bar is filling. Swanson can't talk about the films he's doing next. I ask him if they have anything to do with the enigmatic Network CEO but he just smiles. "I don't want to say, because everything's in development at the moment." Tonight, he's going to meet some friends for a drink. "And take it easy, and just relax," he says, looking relaxed when the PR guys move away, at last.

- Patricia O'Neil, Action News Journalist

10

ALICE

MONDAY

100 HOURS REMAIN...

Wrenched from the depths of some convoluted, troubling dream, Alice awoke with a start and lay on her back looking into the darkness. A menacing jolt of pain shuddered from her head down through her body and she grunted with fatigue, clenching her teeth as the pain throbbed at the back of her skull. Attempting to rub her neck, she was surprised to find that her hands were constrained from doing so. Blood pounded in her ears. Alice felt an overwhelming sense of dread then, descending on her like a curtain, smothering her in claustrophobia. Fear was wrapping itself around her neck, stifling her breathing. Her hands had been shackled. She closed her eyes, focusing on her breathing. She realised that there wasn't a sound in the room at all – she could only hear the hastened rasps of her own breath. So much had happened in the last twenty-four hours... rejecting her Birthday Treat...getting her SCOOP Suit removed.

Oh God...that creep Mitchum. That sonofabitch. That sonofabitch.

She let out a stifled sob, feeling pinpricks of tears forming over that memory, but told herself to pull it together. The black-market creep got what he deserved.

Still makes me a killer though, doesn't it?

The memory of what happened in the chop shop still worried her, but only because it reinforced a suspicion she'd been harbouring after the attack. That she didn't feel any guilt over the murder. She struggled, collected her thoughts, uttered mechanically the opening stanza of a VamPyrates song; but they were useless, meaningless - nothing but the dead shells of words. What she would do to take it all back now...to just engage her Birthday Treat and have done with the whole torrid situation. She could be back at The Pit, drinking. She could be with David.

Could've, should've, would've.

No. She couldn't dawdle on the past, or what could have been. That would only lead to mistakes. After a couple of exhalations, she remembered where she was and the moments leading up to her unconsciousness. Slowly, she opened her eyes and let them adjust to the darkness. She could make out silhouettes of shapes, but nothing concrete. She had no way of knowing how long she'd been out for and didn't know whether it was still daytime. There didn't appear to be any windows in the room, so she supposed she could be in a prison cell, or perhaps a basement or cellar. There was an overwhelming smell of dust, damp plaster and something else... something sickly sweet and cloying. Like gone-off meat.

Ok, Alice. How are we getting out of here?

Her mask had been taken off. Where it was now, was anyone's guess. A sudden, tremulous thought occurred to her. *If that hobo had taken off my mask and chained me up here, what other things has he done with me?*

Her trousers were still on. She didn't feel any pain or discomfort in her lower regions. It still didn't improve her situation, but at least there was a slither of relief.

She was lying prone and wriggled to rest on her elbows. She flexed her wrists, but the shackles were secured tightly. Not much she could do escaping that way. She felt with her fingertips along the chains along to their anchor; smooth steel plates bolted to the ground. She tried to jerk her hips so her hands could retrieve something, anything from her pockets that might assist her, but it was of no use. A door opened, sending a blinding swathe of light into the room.

Squinting her eyes, the blackness began to lighten into dim and indistinct shapes – the figure that entered the room was short of stature and engulfed in an insidious cloth hood and cape that reached to its ankles. The shape padded into the room in the most disturbing fashion. Alice's eyesight was drawn mechanically to those ankles and feet, which appeared gnarled and wasted as they pattered horribly into the room. A thin hand emerged from the folds of the cloak and pulled down on a chain. The room was illuminated by a single bulb hanging from the ceiling. Alice could make out the features of the hooded man – his face was gaunt, deeply lined and haggard with what looked like a life lived on the most meagre and poor food sources. It was the face of the man who had knocked her out. He flashed a black-toothed smile at her, remaining still as the light bulb created dancing shadows around the walled-off room. The man exhaled forcefully from his mouth so that his lips were trembling. Alice couldn't tell if it was amusement or anger or something far more sinister.

"Your hair wants cutting," said the hooded individual. He had been looking at Alice for some time with great curiosity. In the brightened surroundings, she noticed the curve of the man's spine, almost like a drooped flower. Her first reaction was that he must be a Degenerate, and she had invaded his personal space. There may be a small possibility that he didn't watch any of the Free-Vees and didn't know that she was on the run. It was a small possibility, but at this stage of being imprisoned against her will, it was all she could hope for. He pulled back his hood, revealing long silver hair that fell forwards, obscuring every part of his face. As he approached Alice, he muttered something to himself. His progress was slow and halting. Alice could smell him now, a foul smell of hot rubbish, stale alcohol and cigarettes. His face tilted up alarmingly, into the light and his features appeared more heavily lined than a walnut. Alice noted with grim realisation that there was a slight indent on his forehead, accompanied with crisscrossed scars and angry tissue damage. He'd once had an ERD disc. She'd heard stories of Degenerates that had illegally removed their forehead discs, with the aid of backstreet vendors. However, the risk of removing them without inflicting some type of permanent brain damage was as likely as successfully removing a kidney with nothing more than a blunt spoon and some Benadryl.

His lips stretched over toothless gums and when he spoke it was as if his throat was made of sandpaper.

"You broke into slippery Jim's house," he said. "Broke in without even offering slippery Jim butter. That's rude."

Alice said nothing. She looked at the cloaked man and blinked several times. "I was just...I'm sorry. Is this your home?" She finally replied.

"What day of the month is it?" He asked. He had taken a watch out of his pocket, and was looking at it uneasily, shaking it every now and then, and holding it to his ear. When he manoeuvred it in a certain angle, Alice noticed with unnerving trepidation that the face was missing. There were no hands and no dials. She considered a little and then said: "The twenty-fifth."

There was a faint, mad gleam in Slippery Jim's eyes. "No, no, no. That won't do. That won't do at all. That would mean I'm two days in the past. The butter didn't work, don't you see?" He anxiously showed Alice the watch. "Some crumbs must have got in there as well. Yes, yes!" his face looked yellow and waxy in the light. "Slippery Jim needs more butter. Better butter!"

Alice wondered whether she'd been expected to answer. The last thing she wanted to do was offend the deranged man. Her whole life,

Alice rarely cried, and if she did it was never in front of people. As a small girl, she'd once helped her foster mother bake a cake in the kitchen. She burnt her hand and as the pain travelled from the scolded appendage to her eyes, she swallowed it back and calmly went to her room before she allowed a whimper to escape. She turned away from Slippery Jim so that he couldn't see her face properly. She didn't want him to see the tears forming in her eyes, or that she was stifling them back with quivering lips.

There was a flash of a scowl from Slippery Jim but it may have been directed at the watch.

The man brayed loud enough that each guttural cry bounced around in the confines of the room. The sudden noise startled Alice and she flinched backwards on her elbows. The man's final cry dissolved into choked laughter and Alice laughed this time as well in a kind of anxious release.

"Slippery Jim knew you were special." He sighed, wiping tears from his eyes.

Slippery Jim smacked his lips and wiped his mouth with the back of his hand. Alice could see that he looked tired – his face looked fleshy and brutal, and behind those crazed eyes there was intelligence and a sort of controlled passion; but he also looked like a man who had been beaten by life. There were pouches under the eyes and the skin sagged from the cheekbones.

Alice had encountered a few Degenerate revellers in The Pit, and most of the experiences had usually been in her favour. When The VamPyrates had played a show, she had been filled with an eclectic mix of emotions as she strummed her guitar onstage, occasionally seeing the bright colours of ERD discs pulsate in the gloomy atmosphere of the club. But then there had also been times when empty bottles had been thrown onstage by Degenerates in a temper. She knew their moods could switch at the drop of a hat. She'd need to keep this one happy.

"Would it be possible to get me out of these chains?"

Slippery Jim looked blankly at her. He didn't answer immediately, and for a moment Alice thought he'd slipped into a fugue-like state.

It wasn't uncommon for Degenerates. For a second, she saw his expression unguarded and unintended; he had the look of someone in a deep state of confusion. But then he blinked several times and looked at her again.

"Of course." He said. He moved forward and Alice was assaulted with another wave of noxious scents as he produced a key from under his cloak and began unlocking the shackles. Once free, she stood up and instantly felt lightheaded. Slippery Jim had whacked her harder than she initially thought.

"Would it be possible for a glass of water?" she asked, rubbing the back of her neck.

Slippery Jim clapped his hands together, beaming a wide smile. Some drool trickled down the corner of his lips. "Sure!" he exclaimed, heading to the door. As he opened it, he looked over his shoulder.

"Well...follow me, silly beans!"

Alice smiled, her eyes quickly scanning the room for a blunt instrument or any type of weapon she could wield. She grimaced when she found nothing that would aid her through this unexpected turn of events.

I don't know how long I've been out. The original idea was to be in and out of the chop shop and make my way to the country.

She followed Slippery Jim through the door and down a narrow, dark corridor.

"Do you live here?" She asked.

"Oh, yeah sure. Slippery Jim's fortress of solitude." He giggled like a schoolboy that had let slip a secret. She brushed against a set of bamboo wind chimes that created a hollow clacking. They made her think of bones knocking together.

"So I know when the invasion happens."

Alice thought back to the cans attached to string when she broke in. They passed through a bead curtain that opened into a large room, or more accurately, a chamber. Alice readied herself and stepped inside, as if expecting the skeletal remains of Slippery Jim's previous victims to be scattered on the floor. The room was colder than her cell, and smelled mustier, but there didn't appear to be any long bags made of rope netting filled with dissected limbs hanging from the ceiling, so she felt moderately better. Alice walked around, looking at some of the pictures on the wall. A few frames were broken, sticking out like rib bones. She caught a reflection of herself in a cracked mirror. It had a lot of those peculiar diseased-looking spots that mirrors get when the silver mercury was tarnished. She could see multiple versions of herself in that cracked mirror. She didn't like the look of any of them.

There was a small coffee table littered with bric-a-brac and a threadbare sofa that smelled of nicotine. Slippery Jim motioned for Alice to sit down. She gingerly lowered herself into the sagging remains and placed her hands on her lap. He kneeled next to the table and picked up a small metallic figurine. It looked like a stick man but made of loose pieces of copper wire and plastic.

"This is you. Alison Paige."

He handed her the haphazardly made effigy. A wave of dizziness hit her. "You know who I am?"

"Sure. You're everywhere. On all the Free-Vees." He smiled warmly enough, but Alice felt desperation behind that smile. His eyes glittered like glass. She turned the metallic figurine of herself in her hands while he examined some of the other materials on his table until he found what he was looking for: a greasy and dirty looking tub of butter. From underneath his cloak, he brought out the watch again and laid it on the table. He sat cross-legged and scraped out some of the butter with his finger. He began cautiously applying it to the inside of the watch with no face. Alice could tell that he was concentrating, as his tongue had slipped out of his mouth at an upward angle.

"I'm going to need better butter. This lot's gone bad."

Perhaps she had been wrong about him. Maybe he was just a lonely Degenerate that made friends with wire to compensate for his solitude in this gloomy place. She put the figurine down and leaned forward.

"Slippery Jim...could I leave now?"

"Leave?" He said absently, probing a finger at the timepiece. "Why would you want to leave? Everyone's looking for you. Slippery Jim can hide you. Slippery Jim has lots of hiding places."

"I can't stay in London," she said, but noticed a certain hollowness to her own voice.

Slippery Jim folded his knotty hands together and winced, as if she'd slapped him. "No, no, no..." he said absently, turning pensive as he looked at the far wall. Through the wall. He began rocking slightly on the balls of his feet, unwringing his hands and scratching his forehead where his phantom ERD would have been. Alice wondered to herself what kind of life Slippery Jim had led up until this point, and how he had survived for so long without any Agents picking him up and putting him back into the system. He began moaning softly, like a querulous child that had its favourite toy taken away from him. Once again, Alice speculated on how long it had been since he'd spoken to anyone...or had anyone in his domain.

"How long have you lived here?" She inquired.

Slippery Jim stopped rocking, leaving the tinkering of his junk and looked up at the ceiling. He remained motionless for several moments.

"Long time." He said.

Alice nodded her head. "How long was I unconscious for?"

"Unconscious?"

She was about to say 'when you hit me over the head,' but bit her tongue. She would need to try a different tact. "When I was asleep."

"Oh...few hours. I made your little person in that time."

"That's great. Feels like I was out longer. Thanks, Slippery Jim." Alice got to her feet and rolled her shoulders, cracking her neck. As nonchalantly as possible, she tried to keep the quiver from her voice. "Say, if I wanted to visit the little girl's room, where would I go?"

Slippery Jim peered over the table inquiringly at her. Then he motioned his head to the bucket in the corner of the room. *So that's the awful smell.*

"But I'm a girl, Slippery Jim. Girls can't go in front of boys. Don't you know that?"

Slippery Jim seemed to weigh this up in his mind, looking at her with that expression of deadly disconnected curiosity.

"Yeah...makes sense. Okay, if you go down the hallway and up the stairs, you can find girly room there. But don't touch any of Slippery Jim's stuff. I'm going to get a good price on my little people when I sell them!"

Alice forced a smile and gave him a thumbs up. *See, we're friends now. Good 'ol friends. Best buds. BFF's till the end.* She hurried out of the room, crashing into the hanging tin cans placed in the darkened hallway. Slippery Jim guffawed and shouted after her that she was being a silly bean for not remembering the cans, and she shouted back that yes, she was indeed a silly bean. When she got to the end of the tunnel she turned right through a narrow passageway and found herself back in the main atrium, where she had been when she first entered the house. *I never even noticed there was another passageway. And that was in the light. I wonder how many secret little nooks this place has.*

She was back in The Pit, talking to Dave before his face melted into the bulbous potato-like caricature of Slippery Jim. She looked directly into those eyes in her dream and saw...nothing. Dead eyes. Insanely, *We've Got To Get Out Of This Place* by The Animals popped into her head. Her foster mother had often remarked that Alice would start whistling tunes when she was completing her chores, and now she thought about it, music would often distract her when she was trying to work certain things out. It was like having an inbuilt jukebox, playing songs that befit the mood.

The air was cool and moist, like a musty cellar. She could barely see the remains of the staircase in the main walkway now and clenched her fists by her side. She couldn't find the passage she'd originally walked through into this mad house. Mentally, she calculated how long it had taken her to get into the place. She had been walking slowly though, making sure no-one was home. If she made a mad dash for the opening, it may take her a few minutes to wriggle out from the hole she'd created. It would only need a few minutes for Slippery Jim to catch up with me. *And a few minutes is something I'm sorely lacking now.*

She descended into the narrow passage, assuming the way to the exit. She groped around in the dark to find purchase on the walls. There was one of the fucking dangling noise traps down this corridor, she remembered. She pressed herself as close to the slimy wall as much as she could. Alice stepped on something that shifted beneath her feet, then gave way with a sickening crunch. Lowering to her knees, she blindly put out a hand to the ground and felt a long and spindly item. Her hand moved its way up the notched edges. It's just one of the bamboo shoots, she told herself. It's just one of the – her hand found a bulbous, hard end. Her fingers probed in the darkness and she hooked her fingers into two sockets. It was a skull. She brought up a length of spinal column and a skull. She flung it away in disgust and pushed on.

The air seemed fetid in this restricted passage with the pungent press of something irretrievably decayed. Alice felt her breathing becoming rapid. The vile odour was more repulsive than anything else she'd smelt in the building. Alice brought up her hand and held it over her nose, but it was a fruitless gesture. She wished she still had her mask with her. She cursed under her breath when she found herself in yet another room, not the end of the corridor where she assumed to be. Alice swept her eyes across a row of heaped debris. Upon closer inspection, she saw what looked like filthy rags. But her eyes had become accustomed enough to the darkness to see what they were. What lay before Alice was mostly bones, many of them long past purification, but there were more recent bodies stacked in the room too, in all manners of decomposition. For once, Alice was thankful that the blackness obscured the exact details. Their arrangement was too orderly to be anything but deliberate.

It's okay, it's alright. I'll just go back the way I came and look for another hallway. That's all there is to it. That's all I need to-

"Look at you, silly sausage! You've found my other friends."

Alice swirled on the balls of her feet just in time to see the leering face of Slippery Jim.

HAPPY HORGAN: Thank you for joining us, Dr. Prakash

DR. CHANDRA PRAKASH: Thank you for having me.

HAPPY HORGAN: So let's dive right into it. Last year there were 200,000 referrals of children and young people into mental health services – an 85% increase in two years. What questions should we be asking about such a sharp rise? Can it really be that this generation's teens are inherently more anxious, sad, or vulnerable than those of the past?

DR. PRAKASH: (laughs) Well, we're encouraging young people to talk about mental health, but when they do, the support is not always there. The Network are striving to bring together critical voices in psychiatry and psychology to look towards social change as a means of preventing mental distress, rather than always seeing people as fundamentally disordered or damaged.

HAPPY HORGAN: So, who came up with the term Degenerate then?

DR. PRAKASH: It's not a term we use in the profession – but unfortunately it has become synonymous with disaffected youths in areas of deprivation and poverty.

HAPPY HORGAN: But isn't that the problem, doctor? The proportion of children living in relative poverty in the UK risks hitting a record high by the Network's end of fiscal year. Pledges to funnel millions of pounds into improving mental health provisions are farcical considering the number of shows actively seeking participants dealing with such illnesses, exploiting them, in fact. With such endemic suffering caused by continued austerity measures – including further cuts to already buckling services, are we not putting a band aid over a larger problem?

DR. PRAKESH: Listen Happy, we could sit here all day and talk about the abundance of anti-stigma campaigns geared towards young people, or how the system has changed in the last decade with non-prescriptive drugs-

HAPPY HORGAN: You're referring to ERD's?

DR. PRAKESH: They work. It's as simple as that. The discs have neural dopamine receptors that are triggered when the user feels depressed or sad. They also serve as a great way to signal what they're feeling to other people. We're promoting the idea that we should talk about things more often and it's OK to have a mental health problem, but it's made us afraid of emotions. Since ERD's have been introduced, it's combated this stigma.

HAPPY HORGAN: But one could argue that by simply not having a high social credit limit and having an ERD fitted does little to encourage emotional resilience. Let me give you a hypothetical, doc. Maybe I lose my job and after weeks on the sofa, masturbating and eating Quavers, my wife leaves me. This sends me into a spiral and because I'm not contributing to society, my SCS slips. And by the next month it slips again. It slips so much that I get a visit by some Network Agents and they give me an ERD.

DR. PRAKESH: I see what you're doing, Happy – but I'm not going rise to it. You're referring to a recent article stating that some youths have been too readily diagnosed with mental illness, when many will be responding reasonably to the difficult business of growing up. ERD's are not issued 'willy nilly.' For example, a common Network medical approach for borderline personality disorder is dialectical behaviour therapy, which often requires patients to attend "pre-commitment sessions" to establish that they are "owning their diagnosis."

HAPPY HORGAN: Do you think we were better as a country with the NHS?

DR. PRAKESH: I couldn't possibly fathom. It's been over-

HAPPY HORGAN: Do you believe The Network are methodically choosing people with lower Social Credit Ratings, particularly youths with ERD's for Birthday Treats?

DR. PRAKESH: I couldn't possibly comment on that. It sounds preposterous to assume that –

HAPPY HORGAN: The implication is that we are, potentially, creating a huge group of people who believe they have perennial mental illness; creating long-term contestants for the future of The Network.

DR. PRAKESH: I don't think that's the case, Happy.

Birthday Treat

HAPPY HORGAN: Unfortunately, Doc – I disagree. Up next: The Third Child Law – a report of several families that have foregone the Universal Credit tax by having a third child in the home. But before that, here's The Bangles with '*Just Another Manic Monday*.'

- From The Happy Horgan Live Show

@Happyhorgan

11

KAVANAGH

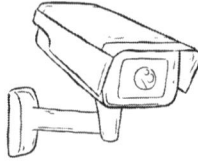

MONDAY

100 HOURS REMAIN...

"Bit of a mess, isn't it?"

Kavanagh and Valentine had entered through the backyard into the basement kitchen. Under the cover of darkness, it had been easy for Valentine to bust the lock without too much disruption. Kavanagh had thought to himself that the bald headed, monosyllabic thug was proving to be a far greater asset than he had originally imagined. Cracked, dirty mugs sat discarded on the filthy looking counter. There was a sickly-sweet, butcher-shop odour in the air. Kavanagh's eyes glanced over last year's calendar hanging askew on a nail in the wall, to the noisy refrigerator humming with the intensity of a motor that was dead but didn't know it. He shuddered at the thought of what kind of food was inside. Kavanagh motioned to Valentine that he was going to explore the rest of the house as he approached the kitchen door.

The rusted hinges squealed in defiance. A haze of dust permeated the hallway, settling on any free surface it could find. The boarded over windows allowed vestiges of the streetlights to seep through, lending the chop-shop a ghoulish effervescence. Kavanagh continued down the hallway and passed through plastic flaps into what he perceived to be the workshop area. It was a large square room, looking all the larger from the absence of most of the furniture. A tawdry splaying paper adorned the walls, but it was blotched in places with mildew, and here and there great strips had become detached and hung down, exposing the yellow plaster beneath. There was a small desk against the wall littered with empty phials and bottles. There was also an old radio that was playing an LP, but the needle had reached the end of the record and was only emitting static. The main source of light in the dimly lit room emanated from a free-standing lamp, the kind that ended in a circular head that were commonly used in hospitals and surgeries. These were the only items that looked sanitary or used in a way that warranted cleanliness. The rest of the derelict chop-shop blended right in with the rest of the street. Kavanagh gave some credit to Mitchum for being able to brazenly go about this type of work, removing SCOOP Suits under the scrutinising eyes of The Network, just a few feet away from the busy high street and cameras. There was a dentists' chair in the middle of the room, bolted to the ground. Crowded around the floor of the chair were many gas canisters. A small jib arm extended from the struts and Kavanagh made out an assortment of operating equipment and machinery. It looked like some type of medieval surgery. Kavanagh reached down and cautiously scratched his arm. It had begun itching again.

"Mr. Mitchum. A pleasure to make your acquaintance."

The back-street specialist wore overalls and sat in front of the dentist-like chair, lifeless. His body was slumped over, half-sitting, half-lying. His face was directed upwards, as if he were in the middle of some ritualistic appreciation of the Gods and had finished by staring at the ceiling, his mouth agape in reverence. A small screwdriver-like device protruded from his left eyeball and remained wedged in the socket. A pool of blood stained the floor beneath him. On his rigid face there stood an expression of surprised horror. Kavanagh considered the malignant and terrible contortion of the body, combined with the low forehead and prognathous jaw that gave the dead man a singularly ape-like appearance, which was increased by his writhing, unnatural posture. Kavanagh brought the overhead lamp down and inspected the SCOOP Suit remover. His remaining emerald green eye was wide open, but his iris held a sudden sadness. It was blatant by the smell that his bowels had released its contents. Kavanagh detected another odour. He reeked of whiskey. It seemed to breathe out of his skin in place of sweat and blood, but the mingled aroma was unpleasant.

"Got yourself involved in a little mischief, hmm?"

Kavanagh scanned the lamp across the floor. Nitrous Oxide canisters were on their sides, as if they had been spilled purposefully. An orange crumpled SCOOP Suit lay abandoned amongst some other clothes. What caught Kavanagh's eye however was the backpack.

Valentine walked into the room, his head rotating mechanically and taking everything in like an automated turret.

"Anything?" Kavanagh asked. The enormous Agent shook his head. "So, Mr. Mitchum. Care to tell me what happened here?"

The lifeless body of Robert Mitchum remained silent.

"Aha, I see what you're saying, Mr. Mitchum. Then let me hypothesise a...scenario, if you would be so kind. I think, Mr. Mitchum...that a young girl by the name of Alice Paige visited you to have her SCOOP Suit removed. Is that not so?"

Kavanagh walked over to the small table and carefully raised the needle of the record player, letting it drop just at the beginning of the vinyl. A bluesy type song danced out of the instrument. Kavanagh's foot began to tap and his head nodded and swayed.

"Man I love that sax!" he said, twirling on his heels. "Deep as the soul and as sweet and soothing as honey pie. You like Jazz, Valentine?"

The burly Agent shrugged.

"Tsk, Tsk, Valentine. Come now, man...music gets the blood pumping, gets the electrolytes fizzing in the old brain stem. You might be wondering why I'm a little excited at the current moment, Valentine. The answer is simple: we have ourselves a genuine crime scene here. A murder. You know we haven't had one of these little beauties for..." Kavanagh looked at the floor, as if in deep thought. "Well, in all honesty I can't remember the last time. There are no crimes and no criminals these days," he said, querulously. "The Birthday Treats have really done their job with the main populace, haven't they?"

Valentine opened his mouth as if he were about to say something.

"It was a rhetorical question. Now...let's see what we have here."

Kavanagh walked around the room, examining every surface in the workshop, studying each item with an intensity he'd never experienced with retiring aged pensioners. He felt alive. Alice Paige was his mission now, finding her was of paramount importance. It was like a game, a hideously exciting game that could only have one outcome for the poor creature he was tracking. The anticipation of finding her...tracking her down like an animal gave him a nervous kind of energy he'd rarely experienced before. It tingled through him like electrical sparks on their way to the ground, gathering in his toes. It was more profound than cutting himself, he realised with shuddering clarity. His flesh tingled apprehensively, and he found his arm itching again. He made it a rule, whenever he caught himself not focusing, to prick his arm hard enough to draw blood. It was his chosen form of self-discipline, his guard against irreverence and distracted thoughts. His eyes flickered towards the corpse, his voice gravely and low.

"You've been a naughty boy, haven't you Mr. Mitchum? Our records show that you've been arrested a few years ago for exposing yourself in public. But your social credit limit has usually wavered around the one hundred mark. Kept yourself in the middle band, although you have a bit of an impulse control problem. Like our intrepid little bird, Ms. Paige, you've been trying to keep under the radar and not cause any trouble, haven't you?"

Valentine sighed, as if the drama being performed before him wasn't quite bothersome yet, but a chore he had to endure. Kavanagh paid him no mind as he took a few confident strides towards the dentist-like chair. He bent down and picked up one of the Nitrous Oxide cylinders. "You've been a busy little bee, haven't you? How many SCOOP Suits do you remove a month, I wonder? How many desperate faces do you look at as you use your little tools to cut and free these people? And along comes Alice Paige...she's different, isn't she, Mr. Mitchum? Not like all the others...with their missing teeth and their ERD discs attached to their foreheads. There's something about her. Something special."

He brought the opened container to his thin, hawk-like nose and sniffed. A lingering chemical smell was still present. His expression changed to an air of alertness and decision. He dropped the canister and looked at the body of Mr. Mitchum.

"You told her she'd need to be anaesthetised, didn't you? SCOOP Suits are made of intricate polymer weaves, something that normal knives can't cut through. They're burn proof and have the armour of Kevlar, so you made up some sort of story that the only way to get it off would cause her some pain, therefore being put under would be the way to go. I'd hazard a bet that you stressed the importance of the pain element, didn't you Mr. Mitchum? So, what happened...did you put her under and have your way with her, hmm? Or did she awake mid-way through?"

Kavanagh got down on all fours and studied the floor. Agent Valentine remained still, but his eyes assumed a vacant, lack-lustre expression which may have been mistaken for mental abstraction.

"No, that doesn't sound like our girl," Kavanagh continued, skimming over the cracks in the floor. "You would have dosed her up. No way she would have been able to wake from that toxic stuff. No... our girl's smarter than that. She would have been prepared, wouldn't she? If I'm right..." he padded forward on his hands and knees, "she would have done her homework. She would have known the type of character you were, isn't that correct Mr. Mitchum?"

He finally stopped crawling when he detected something on the floor. Something small. He plucked it up with great care and stood, brushing himself off. He opened his hand to Valentine.

"Plugs, Agent Valentine. Discreet, imperceptible plugs that she inserted up her nose."

Valentine nodded his head in agreement.

"Cassandra was right about one thing. She certainly is different from all the others. So, what does that tell us Agent Valentine?"

"I'm hungry."

"Yes, quite. Now I know what you're thinking Valentine: 'Agent Kavanagh, this is making my nipples all hard, but why did she have the foresight to prepare herself for being anaesthetised in the first place?' That is the question, isn't it? Maybe she argued with Mr. Mitchum. That tells us she can be quite persuasive, doesn't it? And, having the laborious and tedious task of interrogating Mr. Lazer earlier, it's quite apparent that she has a firm controlling grasp over him..." Kavanagh walked the floor again, a finger to his lip. "She likes to be in control. But there's something else." He squatted down next to the corpse and studied the screwdriver pointing upward at the ceiling. "She knew you were up to something. Some nefarious deed... she panicked, lashed out. I don't think it was her intention to kill you at all, Mr. Mitchum...she just wanted to get away. A struggle ensued... she grasped whatever was nearest to her-" his eyes flicked to the surgery table with the other apparatus, "and thrashed out wildly. Poor Mr. Mitchum...you never stood a chance, did you?"

Kavanagh stood up, motioning Valentine at the backpack on the floor. A continuous hiss had indicated that the vinyl had finished its song. There was something about the slight crackle that enhanced the situation for him, making everything clear.

"Okay, let's wrap this up. Panicked, she left her extra clothes and assorted goodies on the floor there. Agent Valentine, if you would be so kind as to search the contents to ensure we haven't missed anything, I would be forever gratified. Let's also get this on the news, showcasing that Alice Paige has fatally wounded a poor member of the public in a vicious attack in the heart of London. Should get a few more people revved up at the notion of catching her."

Valentine slowly lumbered across the room and rifled through the backpack. An extra set of jeans, various tops, some high-quality rubber prosthetics (nose, forehead and chin) and food rations revealed much of what Kavanagh was expecting. There was also a Taser-gun and a few fake ID's also stashed away. Kavanagh didn't assume that they'd find her passport; with her Social Credit score she qualified for one, but he didn't think she would be stupid enough to try and leave the country. Her first mistake had been to travel into London to get rid of her SCOOP Suit. Now out in public, without her disguises, she wouldn't get far. No doubt she'd try to hunker down somewhere, burrow herself in like a tick. With the fake ID's in their possession, trying to find a hotel would be nigh-on impossible. There was always the chance that some back-alley sleaze pit would welcome her in for the right amount of cash, but after this unfortunate situation...

She wouldn't trust anyone now. She'd try to find somewhere secluded...out of the way from all the nasty people. She'll bundle in somewhere warm and safe and hide until nightfall.

Kavanagh checked his watch. It was already dark.

"Valentine, with me!" he barked, heading for the back door. Valentine rummaged around and found other food supplies and let out a small grunt when he found a sandwich bag. The back door was open. In the dim light he could make out a greasy handprint stain on the door frame. That wasn't grease. That was blood.

Outside, a small garden led to an alley way by Hopkins Street. Turning the corner onto Peter Street, Kavanagh looked up and down the narrow alleyway. One end lay towards the market stalls, which were closing for the evening. At the other end was a decrepit-looking building and some closed shutters.

"Valentine!" Kavanagh shouted. The graceless Agent lurched out from the back door with the sandwich in his hand. "When you've managed to unpretzel your stomach Agent, I could use you over here."

Valentine took a gargantuan chomp from the sandwich and shrugged.

"I want to know if any drones were flying around this vicinity today. And get some CCTV of this area. Ms. Paige came out of this exit. Which means she's either blended in with the crowd or is holed up somewhere nearby."

"Social media is spiking exponentially," Cassandra chuckled through the speakers of the tablet. "Alice Paige is the most hash-tagged event in the last couple of weeks. You are dead centre of the eye of the storm. Do you have a fix on her location yet?"

Kavanagh clenched his fists under the scrutiny of the camera lens.

"We've just been scrubbing through the last few hours of CCTV and drone footage from the area."

"And?"

"We're still collating information."

Cassandra's sharp eyes studied him through the tablet monitor. "We're nearly into the second day, Agent Kavanagh. Must I remind you that not one contestant in the history of the *Hunted* TV programme has made it past day three?"

Kavanagh smiled. It was the only thing he could do without letting out a short, sharp snort. "The matter is in hand."

Cassandra didn't say anything else. The tablet simply cut to black and Kavanagh looked at his own reflection. Valentine moved it out of his eye line and started scrubbing through the CCTV footage again.

"Now look at this," Kavanagh said, holding out his hands briefly and letting them drop back to his sides with a soft clap. "What's the word, Valentine?"

The other Agent held the tablet in front of him at arm's length as if it were an alien piece of technology newly discovered. His brow furrowed in grim concentration. Kavanagh sighed and looked over the burly man's shoulder. It was a drone feed, from earlier that day. There was nothing of noticeable interest; the market stall holders continued to sell their fruits, and people milled around and then – someone ran into the picture frame and stopped suddenly. It caught Kavanagh's eye and he stared at the pixelated person for a moment.

Valentine moved his hand like a meat pendulum to swipe the footage forward, but Kavanagh stopped him.

"What do we have here?" Kavanagh said as he flicked his chin in the direction of the tablet footage.

The bald Agent squinted at the screen, looking for something he may have missed. The person with the short cropped blonde hair was still standing in the same position, looking over at the comic book shop on the corner of the street. Kavanagh wondered what her line of sight was, and what she was gazing at. People walked past the figure without any thought, just like the sheep they were, wandering aimlessly in the crowd. Kavanagh saw the figure's chest rising and falling rapidly, as if the person onscreen had just run a short distance and was out of breath. He knew it was the girl. Valentine grunted in a low, testy way. Just a faint irritation in his voice, but Kavanagh knew he hadn't spotted it yet, and was feeling frustrated.

"What's the odd thing in the picture, Valentine?"

The figure now looked straight ahead, breathing rapidly. The camera was quite far away, but it was 8k optimised and even from this distance he could swear that she had closed her eyes, as if in meditation.

She's just killed someone. For the first time. Now she's the most wanted woman in the country.

Valentine huffed again, becoming agitated.

"What stands out to you?" Kavanagh said and smiled, but it wasn't a question, just like it wasn't a smile.

"Girl. Not moving."

"Good." Kavanagh nodded, looking pleased. Looking like a teacher who had coaxed a difficult answer from a slow pupil. The blonde-haired individual with ripped jeans and white top turned suddenly and ran back the way she came. Which meant she returned to Hopkins Street. It felt like someone had ignited a box of fireworks in his head. Kavanagh felt a mental chess piece move strategically in his favour. He waved at Valentine to put the tablet away.

A paroxysm of elation shuddered through Kavanagh, and he rubbed his hands in a pompous and self-satisfied manner. "Now," Kavanagh said, speaking with the air of someone who had finished with the boring procedures and may get down to what they like, "the rat scuttled off to find a temporary home," he smirked. He pointed down towards Hopkins Street. Pointed at the dilapidated building where a couple of hours previously, Alice had entered.

"We're going to squash some vermin, Valentine."

Valentine turned and looked at Kavanagh. Those eyes looked hungry. Ravenous.

It didn't take them long to find the makeshift entrance Alice had made. With little effort, Valentine wrenched the corrugated fencing to make a gap big enough for them to both slide into. More of a chasm really, Kavanagh joked to himself, but instantly put the thought to the back of his mind. The adrenaline was starting to pump through his veins, with the thought of catching Alice Paige. Just this morning he'd been promoted and this time tomorrow there was a likelihood he would be promoted again. He'd show Cassandra Rey. He'd show his father. He'd show them all what he was made of.

He felt more alive than he had in years. He realised this and was grateful to Alice Paige. He was starting to feel an ethereal connection to the girl - the scene in the chop shop was sloppy, but he knew a survivor when he saw one. It made him think of himself.

Under instruction, Valentine ventured into the dark recess of the hallway first. The towering Agent bent forward like some old, rusty piece of machinery whirred into life by a jolt of electricity. Whatever was hiding in there, Kavanagh wanted him to find out first. Against the dark night sky all Kavanagh could see was the crumbling walls of the entrance. It looked like a black hole into oblivion. With a mirthless grin, he slipped through the gap and into the entrance of the building.

He passed by cracked windows and mouldy, browned wooden walls. There was a palatable charge in the air, and Kavanagh had to stop himself from giggling like an idiot. He was feeling the kind of tension a person experiences just before the jump scare of a horror movie. He knew that something tangible was coming but had to suppress the excitement he felt under a cool exterior. Debris and broken glass crunched under his boots, and he wondered what expression Alice would pull before he retired her. In all his years working for The Network, he'd become accustomed to the different faces just before the captive bolt penetrated their skull, entering the cranium and catastrophically damaging the cerebrum. Most people closed their eyes beforehand, muttering a prayer or some other indecipherable nonsense, which disappointed Kavanagh. He wanted to see the spark go from their eyes.

This new role created a type of longing he didn't know he'd been missing until now. He doubted that Alice Paige would close her eyes, no sir – she would put up a fight. She would fight with all the teeth and all the nails to get herself out from the corner she'd painted herself into, and Kavanagh knew it. Maybe, just for the first time, when her window closed, he'd be able to see where her soul went.

There was a hollow clattering noise, and the dark silhouette of Valentine rocked sideways.

Kavanagh snapped out of his reverie. "Valentine?" His voice seemed to come from far away, like an echo from the reverberating walls of a cavern.

With self-discipline almost anything is possible.

He hadn't been concentrating. His mind had wandered and now something bad had happened.

Let's have a chat, son. The icy voice of his father. *Let's have a little chinwag, you and I.* It was the voice he was never able to refuse or shut out.

He could make out dark shapes swinging in the darkness in front of him. The noise they made was unmistakable. Tin cans on strings. The kind of thing a kid would think to place in a fort to make noise if any intruders entered. Sound traps.

"You idiot," Kavanagh hissed in the darkened hallway. Valentine didn't say anything, didn't need to. He knew he'd fucked up. They paused in silence for a moment. "Be ready." Kavanagh finally uttered.

Slowly, they started moving again.

Kavanagh had never wanted to be a police officer. The thought of sitting behind a desk and writing up reports never appealed to him. He vaguely remembered when he was young, and the Metropolitan Police had been taken over and had essentially become a private security company. But he had sharp intuition, a kind of sixth sense that the likes of police officers developed over years working on the force. A kind of instinct when something was about to happen. *It's a feeling you get in the pit of the stomach, a kind of churning...but not uncomfortable.* He felt it now, and just as Valentine stepped out of the narrow hallway into the main vestibule, he was about to shout out a warning to the broad-shouldered Agent.

A shadow lunged across his field of vision and collided with Valentine. Taken by surprise, the burly Agent staggered to the side and his shoulder hit the wall.

"This is Slippery Jim's house!" screeched the shadow, leaning into the stunned Valentine. Kavanagh rushed forward just in time to see a man dressed in a cloak clamp his teeth down on Valentine's shoulder, fixing like a vampire, tearing through Valentine's shirt and drinking his blood when it burst through his skin. The scruffy man's beard was thick and tousled. Kavanagh laced his fingers together to make his hands into a cudgel and raised them above his head to get as much velocity as possible. Just before he had a chance to bring his hands down on the man's skull, he wheeled out of the way of the blow and Kavanagh slipped, crashing to the ground.

Slippery indeed, Kavanagh thought, chiding himself for being so clumsy. He put his hands out to protect himself from the fall and was rewarded with scratches and cuts. He shuddered to think what had been left down here with all the pigeon shit and dirty needles. He'd need a shot when he came out of this place.

"Slippery Jim's not going to give her up. No sir-eeee!"

The dishevelled man with scars on his forehead produced

something from his coat. For one stomach freezing moment, Kavanagh thought it might be a gun. Being shot at point blank range inside a dilapidated building would not be the way he imagined himself going out. The object he pulled out thankfully wasn't a pistol, although the distinct glisten of a switch-blade knife wasn't welcoming, either.

"I'll cut you up like little fish!" The man screamed, with bright malevolence in his eyes. He lunged at Kavanagh with whip-like speed.

Before the blade could imbed itself in Kavanagh's chest, Valentine's hand jerked forward and clamped down on the Destitute man's wrist. The man let out a gasp, whether from the immense pressure of Valentine's grip or the sheer shock of being caught unaware, he didn't know. Kavanagh stumble-staggered to his feet and watched with great delight as Valentine twisted his hand. The sound of bone snapping was surprisingly sharp, like a twig being broken in a reverb chamber. The man squealed out in pain, looking at Kavanagh with wide eyes. Crazy eyes.

With his free hand, Valentine hooked his thumb into the bearded man's left eye socket. More cries of pain as the soft gelatinous membrane pushed inwards, and Kavanagh thought he heard the faintest wet popping sound – the sound of someone stepping on a plump grape. Kavanagh allowed his partner to have his fun. The bearded man flailed his non-broken arm to try and push Valentine away, screaming as he did. Kavanagh likened the effort to a dandelion trying to fight off a hurricane. A moment passed and then Valentine's thumb disappeared into the eye socket, all the way up to the knuckle.

"You do have an obsession with eyes, don't you?" Kavanagh said. Valentine grunted, and the lifeless body of Slippery Jim dropped to the floor. Valentine dabbed his enormous hand to his neck, wincing at the blood from his wound.

"We'll get you patched up once we've secured the building. And we can use our torches now, as the element of surprise didn't really work in our favour, did it?"

Valentine looked at his shoes, like a schoolboy being reprimanded by the headmaster.

"You check out the first floor. I'll see if our intrepid guest is hiding somewhere down here." Kavanagh squatted and picked up the knife the Degenerate had kindly donated to their cause.

"Are you here, little Alice?" Kavanagh called, clicking on his little flashlight as he walked down the atrium to the first room. Silence replied, which was what he expected, but that little ping was starting to swell in his stomach again. That sixth sense telling him that someone was here…hiding in the shadows. "If you surrender yourself to us know, that'll be the end of it. We'll take you in…and *process* you." He scanned the first room with the torch, which was devoid of any furniture. Just more bird shit and rubbish. His nostrils flared slightly and the frown on his face deepened. There was a smell all right, something he'd been accustomed to from all the years of retiring people. It was the smell of death.

"My name is Agent Kavanagh," he said aloud, silently striding to the next room. He skimmed the light of the torch around, revealing broken furniture and damp surfaces. The smell was stronger around here. He kept the knife out of view, with the blade pressing against the underside of his arm. If he found her down here, he'd make it linger. He would look into her eyes because he wanted to see. He wanted to see the difference between this tough girl and all the others. He also wanted to report back to Cassandra with good news.

"If you come with me now Alice, we'll have you back with your boyfriend in no time at all. We're not here to hurt you. Don't believe everything you see on the Free-Vees."

One last room at the end of the atrium. As he approached the door, he tried the handle. The door creaked open. The pungent odour of putrefaction overwhelmed him. He stood there for a moment, casting the light across the room. There was a beaten-up sofa to the left and various broken cabinets scattered on the floor. The back wall was lined with shelves stacked with what looked like metallic toys of various kinds. There were also dozens of little figurines hanging by threads from the ceiling. It reminded Kavanagh of air fresheners in cars. At the far wall seemed to be a pile of bodies, haphazardly piled on top of one another.

A clever girl...a tough girl, could bury herself underneath all of that. A clever girl may try to use that as camouflage.

"You know Alice," Kavanagh said into the darkness, "my father used to be a toy maker. He would make all these wonderful things from wood with his own hands."

He stepped into the room, blinking in the gloom as he slowly inched towards the pile of corpses. He could hear the faint sound of buzzing flies. "Once, he made me this exquisite toy doll when I was young. Made it just for me. It was life size, so very tall."

He was halfway in the room. The noxious stench from the bodies reeked and Kavanagh put the back of his hand holding the knife to his nose.

"The thing was," he continued, creeping closer to the pile, "I hated that thing. Loathed it. It had these eyes that made your flesh crawl. I had to keep it in my room and I couldn't sleep at night because it was just...looking at me. Always staring."

He was looming over the pile. The flies were plentiful, the intensity of the buzzing like static on a radio. From this distance, he could make out the tell-tell wriggling of larvae infesting the decayed meat below him.

"So you know what I did, Alice? I burnt the thing. I burnt it so it wouldn't look at me anymore."

Kavanagh stepped forward and struck at the pile of bodies with the knife.

Something flew out of darkness behind him. Kavanagh was quick, and with a deft swipe of his arm buried the knife fist-deep into the nape of the attacker's neck. He'd left himself vulnerable though and the dark shape crashed straight into him, delivering a hard blow to his chin. The body seemed big, too big for a girl and his first thought was that another Degenerate was in the building. The momentum of its trajectory sent them both crashing to the floor. For the second time in the last ten minutes, he was on his ass. In any other circumstance he would have been embarrassed if Valentine were here. The torch slipped from his hand and went skittering to the floor, causing a small light show display that made shadows dance in the old building. It was only then that Kavanagh smelt the rankness of the thing on top of him. Whatever had come at him was not alive. Hadn't been for a while. He pulled the knife out of the rotting body and grunted as he rearranged himself.

"Fuck you," cried a small voice from behind the sofa. He could just barely make out the gaunt face of Alice Paige in the gloom.

Stupid, stupid, stupid! He swore, scolding his own ignorance. She'd been hiding behind the sofa the whole time.

She turned on her heels to run, but Kavanagh was faster. He deftly pushed the thing off him and leapt towards the exit. Her plan of distracting him with...whatever she had lobbed in his direction had worked, but his interaction with the bearded hobo had heightened his senses and reflexes. Without thought, he kicked out at the dark shape in front of him and caught Alice's ankle. They both went crashing to the floor. She wailed in agony as he heard a hard, toneless crunch beside him. He could hear Alice already scrabbling, so he manically brought the knife down in an arc and felt immense satisfaction when he felt it bury itself in something fleshy and malleable, followed by a guttural shriek of pain.

"I hope I hit something important," Kavanagh giggled, retracting the blade for another blow. There was a blur in the darkness before something solid met the bridge of his nose with a substantial crunch.

Kavanagh howled with agony and dropped the knife. His hands went to his face and he rolled on the floor. Blood from his broken nose gushed between his fingers like water from a busted mains pipe.

Let's have a chat son. Let's have a little chinwag, you and I.

"You little -"

Another blur in the darkness and something heavy hit his chest. *Third time's the charm!* He heard his father say, as the warm blood poured down his chin in rivulets and into his mouth. For a moment he lay stunned, not quite accepting the damage that the girl had inflicted upon him. The receptors in his brain hadn't caught up to signify the pain yet, that would come in a few seconds. It was the shock of all the blood flowing from his nose that snapped him from his dazed state.

Kavanagh was quick to get on his knees and he fumbled in the darkness for the blade. He felt a warm swoop of air towards his face as Alice kicked out at him, which caused him to stumble. A moment later, he heard the patter of Alice's feet as she ran down the atrium towards the hallway.

"Valentine! She's down here! She's on the ground floor!"

He gingerly probed his nose, the swelling already in full effect. Now he felt the pain. Now he felt it.

"She's-" but before he could finish his sentence, he knew she'd already gone.

He'd let her escape.

Cassandra would not be pleased.

(Page extract from The Network's Terms and Conditions 'Birthday Treat' instruction sheet – emailed and signed by the user before commencement of their Birthday Treat.)

FAQ's

What can you do on the day of your Birthday Treat?

The wearer of the aforementioned SCOOP Suit will be permitted to commit an act of lawlessness deemed appropriate by the governing state of The Network. This includes ABH (Actual Bodily Harm), GBH (Grievous Bodily Harm), RTC (Road Traffic Collison) MDK (Murder Death Kill) Please refer to page 45 for more information.

Can I blow up a school bus with my Birthday Treat?

No. Following the tragedy of the public mass shooting of twenty-one bankers by Erik Volt during the first year of Birthday Treat roll out, stipulations have been ushered in to avoid mass murders by Birthday Treat participants (or genocidal tendencies. Please refer to page 87 for more information.) This includes using any vehicular transportation (including planes, trains, farmyard machinery or automobiles) to be used against public/private buildings, the use of bombs that may extinguish more than one soul, and incendiary devices. More details stipulating these infringements can be found on the main Network website.

What if I just littered? That's a criminal offence, right?

Wrong. Not in the eyes of The Network. ANY ATTEMPT TO OTHERWISE UNDERMINE THE OPERATION OF THE NETWORK, MAY BE A VIOLATION OF CRIMINAL AND CIVIL LAW and you could find yourself with a fine and deduction of Social Credits. Littering is considered a LOW-LEVEL OFFENCE and would be treated as such.

I'm a pacifist and don't believe in harming a fellow human being. What can I do?

It is entirely your right not to participate with your Birthday Treat. If after 24 hours you do not comply however, you'll be automatically entered into the *Hunted* TV show. You will then have five days to remain undetected by the public and **Network Agents** in accordance with The Network's protocol. Good luck, pacifist citizen!

I'm religious and my beliefs forbid violence of any kind. What can I do?

185

It is entirely your right not to participate with your Birthday Treat. If after 24 hours you do not comply however, you'll be automatically entered into the *Hunted* TV show. You will then have five days to remain undetected by the public and **Network Agents** in accordance with The Network's protocol. Good luck, religious citizen!

I'm worried about the consequences of my Birthday Treat. I live next door to a neighbour who keeps playing loud music at night. If I acted against this person with my Birthday Treat, could their family come after me?
All members of the UK entered a treaty once the coalition of The Network came into power. Under no circumstances can a family member of a citizen that has had a Birthday Treat performed on them can retaliate without total forfeiture of their Social Credits and family's assets, unless they have received their own Birthday Treat. One of the main reasons by introducing the law of Birthday Treat was mainly as a deterrent – if you act as a compliant citizen of the country then most likely another person won't be looking for you on their Birthday treat, and vice versa. In the first year alone, crime was reported on a downward curve of 82%. More details can be found on The Network's website.

12

ALICE

MONDAY

99 HOURS REMAIN...

Through the dark back alleys, through several chain linked fences and past an eerily quiet construction site, Alice paused underneath a shop alcove and measured her wounds. Her heart was thumping in her ears and she knew she had to calm herself.

How did they find me so fast? How did they know where I was?

She saw a party of drunken winos huddled round a fiery rubbish bin, but no Agents. No wailing sirens. No drones.

What to do now?

She didn't know the answer to that. She was tired and scared and all the running had made everything hard to think. Pain flared from her side and all she wanted to do was sit down on the curb and cry out in frustration and anger.

Time was against her. It wouldn't be long before they had assessed the CCTV cameras in the area and triangulated the route she had taken.

But she hadn't known what route she'd taken herself. She had stumbled out of Slippery Jim's emporium of dead things and had made sure she couldn't see any cameras before taking unexpected turns and jumped over fences to ensure her escape from the building was random. It was highly likely she'd been picked up on one or two – you couldn't move in the city without Big Brother watching you with its sentient eye.

They'll find me. That's what they do. That's their job.

She closed off that train of thought as she lifted her shirt. Panicking wouldn't get her anything but dead. That weird fucker talking about dolls had stuck her good. An open gash about three centimetres wide yawned at her. She was lucky that the knife hadn't severed anything important.

You don't know that, though. You could be internally bleeding and wouldn't know anything about it until you dropped dead. You need a doctor. You need medical treatment.

She didn't feel like any vital organs had been lanced through. She hadn't been the most astute student of biology, but if her pancreas or liver had been speared, she wouldn't have made it as far as she had. All the poisonous shit in her bowels and liver would have seeped into her blood and sepsis would kick in.

But how long did that take? Was it a few minutes or a few days?

She'd need to stitch it closed. The blood had blossomed around her mid-section, and she felt warm-like treacle run down her legs. Why had she decided to wear a white shirt, of all things? She zipped up her leather jacket. That would hide the wound for a while, but she'd bleed out and fall unconscious unless she staunched it. Where to run now?

She tried to think of past contestants that had decided to forego their Birthday Treat. What was their first impulse? Like animals, they would usually go to ground. Hide away in a little dingy flat or hotel away from seeing eyes. But they were always found.

But you have an advantage. You've got rid of your SCOOP Suit.

That was something. They wouldn't be able to track her with whatever inbuilt device they had stitched underneath the gaudy orange boiler suit. But now she was bleeding, and it wouldn't be long before it started seeping through her jeans. Not many people are observant, but there were always some.

Can't take the trains now. They'll be updating the Free-Vees soon enough with where I was last sighted. There's always going to be gangs sniffing around to try and get their prize fund for catching me. Dead or alive. But probably dead.

Think.

I'm in central London. It's late. I can't contact Dave, otherwise I'll be putting him in danger...if they haven't already got to him. Did he tell them where I'd be? Most likely...he was the only one who knew about Mitchum. He was the only one who knew that I'd be getting the SCOOP Suit removed. Oh God, what if they've done something horrible to him. Oh sweet Jesus, what if they've –

Think. Calm down.

Okay. Okay. My disguise has been left behind. I have about £300 to my name and I need to stitch myself up. I could try and break into a pharmacy, but that would likely set of an alarm. Hospital's out of the question.

Think.

Stick to my people. That was the advice. Original plan is pretty much out the window now. I've got to last five days. I've nearly been killed on day one. I've nearly been –

Stop it. You're not going to spiral. Not now. Think.

Clubs. Clubs will still be open. Dark places, where the blood won't show. Where Degenerates will be dancing and drunk and looking for a good time. Looking for a good time girl.

Alice nodded to herself. She was around Tottenham Court Road. They played this area before. There was a place...Dave brought a pig's head as a prop for the show, thought there would be a talent agent in the audience. Thought it would be good for their brand to throw the pig's head out into the audience. What was it he said? Just like Ozzy biting the head off a bat. People may not remember the songs, but they'll remember that. Oh *they* remembered all right. Nearly got them thrown in the cubes when they launched it during the crescendo of their last song. What was that place called? *Just need to find somewhere out of the way, off the streets.*

Fuck, what was the name of the place? It couldn't have been less than a year when they played there. It had a pub's name...The Old... something or other. If she had her phone with her, she would have been able to find it in under ten seconds. But they could trace phones, they could pinpoint her exact location within milliseconds. That was the first thing she told Dave when he told her some of her ingenious plan. The first thing she ditched was the phone. No communication, that was the only way she'd be able to survive.

But it looked like they'd already gotten to Dave. Insidious thoughts crept back into her mind, like talons scratching at her brain, demanding to be let in. She tended to think of the worst-case scenario – it was the only way she could avoid them. *The Old Horse and Hound?* No, that wasn't right.

She remembered the way Dave looked at her before she left, that night in The Pit. He had a way of making himself look like a dishelleved Droopy from the old Loony Tunes cartoons. He'd move slowly and lethargically, just like the dog. That was her nickname for him. Droopy Dave.

The Old Mount.

That was it.

She carefully hobbled out of the shadows.

The fear sat quietly, a small knot of contortion in her stomach becoming more of a feeling of being smothered by an invisible hand. Alice controlled her breathing, from erratic ragged inhales to long, deep gulps of air. Each step felt like a bolt of lightning down her side.

I'll fight it. I'll fight the feeling as my body writhes to be free or shut down entirely.

Alice balled her hands into fists and held them like that until her knuckles turned white. The adrenaline was starting to wear. That Kavanagh Agent had tripped her up when she'd flung one of the dead bodies at him. She couldn't believe that she'd picked up a corpse to use as a shield. She'd thought about hiding amongst Slippery Jim's victims, but she just couldn't bring herself to do it. To burrow underneath those cold things that were once human. They would have found her, at any rate.

I'm sure before the five days are up, you'll be doing a lot more things you never thought you could do. Boss Bitch was back, telling her what to do. She turned it over in her head, the last day. Coming into London with a disguise in bag and baggy clothes to hide her SCOOP Suit. That creep Mitchum telling her that he'd need to administer a sedative to get the suit off her. Having the nose plugs already inserted as he lowered the mask on her face. Feeling his hands on her body as she pretended to be unconscious as he cut away the boiler suit. Feeling his hands grope and squeeze when the Suit was finally off. Feeling his fingers move down...kicking out, not pretending to be asleep anymore. His startled reaction, soon turning to violence. Lashing out with whatever came to hand. And then a wet squelch as he tumbled back into the chair.

Alice walked past the group of winos who were paying more attention to the bottle being passed amongst them than to her. She stifled a nervous snicker as she thought about the irony of it all. Just last week she would have loved the attention, playing onstage with the band. The way people looked at her when she shredded was something she couldn't describe; it was almost otherworldly. Her nerves were trying to take over her body, but it only improved her performance. Her heart kept time with the drums, pumping the music through her veins as she lost herself in the performance. Eventually, she lost all sense of everything except for the music.

She started humming the tune of their latest song, '*Death Stare*,' as she rounded the corner and saw the club up ahead.

Each time something bad happens, part of you gets stronger, Boss Bitch said. *To survive this, this new version of fear needs a name and I crown it fear of failure. This is how you keep moving forward. Fear is shackles, fear is a knife in the gut slowly twisting. Fear is a constant hammer on the head.*

She wouldn't succumb to it.

She could hear muffled electronic music drumming from inside the club. The Old Mount was one of the few establishments around Tottenham Court Road that remained as a testament to one of the remnants of the old world, but they were becoming less and less every year. Everywhere now was baristas or cafes or generic bars with no identity - all clean with waiting staff. Not here. It was the great unwashed of the city.

A man behind a cart was selling caramelised peanuts. The rich, sweet aroma made her stomach gurgle. When had she last eaten? Any provisional rations had been left behind in her bag. But she couldn't think about that.

Alice dipped her head as she came up to the Club entrance. Across the road, an 8K electronic billboard screen flashed an announcement that she'd been sighted in London. They were still using the old photo of her with her Joan Jett black hair, so she clung to the small hope that they hadn't caught any new feeds from her escape from the dilapidated building. The bouncer on the door gave her a small uncommitted nod, not really taking her in. Just another girl looking for some booze and a dance. As she slipped through the doors she grimaced, feeling the wound on her side rub against her leather jacket. It was a small mercy that the guard hadn't frisked her, otherwise she might have crumpled into a ball and asked for the Agents to take her away there and then. She caught her reflection on one of the glass panels of the door. She looked pale with dark circles under her eyes. Hopefully, the darkness of the club would hide how she looked. She quickly paid her entrance fee and made her way to the stairs leading down. She'd taken out a wad of cash before the SCOOP suit had been fitted and had hidden it about her person. She had about £280 left, and that was to last for the next several days.

If I make it that long.

Pain flared up her leg as she strode towards the stairs, but she willed it away, trying to act normal as the darkness of the club swallowed her whole.

An old anxiety resurfaced in her as she descended to the main dance floor. It went all the way back to secondary school before she'd mastered the shreds and found the short leather jacket she'd wear almost every time she went anywhere. Before she was a part of The VamPyrates. Before she found her identity. It was the feeling of going into a crowded room and not knowing anyone. There was no control, no power. There were groups that knew other people, friends and acquaintances – all laughing and shouting to one another over the blare of the music. Alice felt like an outsider (not for the first time since she'd foregone her Birthday Treat) but she'd been mostly alone leading up to now. She felt outside of her own skin. She felt like an intruder, an imposter.

This area was like the aurora borealis; beneath the dry-ice smoke swirled an array of blues, acid greens, hot pinks and gold. Alice couldn't see the main dance floor, for the wall-to-wall people twisting and gyrating to the beats. A sharp smell of drink wafted towards Alice as she made her way to the bar. A sea of ERD lights pulsed different colours and Alice scanned the large room, looking from one leering face to the other.

All grinning idiots, she thought. *I just need one grinning idiot that doesn't watch too much TV.* Chance was going to be a fine thing, but she had to hope.

It was the only thing she had left.

Alice pushed her way to the bar, imagining that it was just sweat causing her shirt to stick to her stomach. She leaned on the bar, more out of necessity than anything else. A momentary reprieve of pain as she lifted her leg onto the golden rod at the bottom of the bar and she lolled her head to one side, pushing out her lips just a little. The barman was there to take her order, his eyes dropping only momentarily to give her a once over. She twiddled her hair in a seemingly absent-minded way and slurred slightly as she gave her order, to give the impression she was a little drunk. She watched him fetch her drink and took in the other revellers squeezed in to order their drinks. She needed to find someone who wasn't in a big group, preferably someone who was on their own. It was unlikely, as Degenerates tended to pack together like hyenas.

These are my people, she tried to reason. When I have the power

– when I play onstage...there's nothing that can touch me. Nothing at all.

But. There was that deep absurd fear gurgling at the bottom of her stomach again.

The bartender returned and Alice slipped him a note from her leather jacket. A stab of pain wrenched her side and she held her arm by the wound. She'd need to be more careful unless she wanted to bleed out all over the club. Then she saw him.

He was standing awkwardly by one of the columns, nodding his head along to the beat of the music. His ERD pulsated a dull sepia. He looked gangly and his clothes looked a little too small for him. Alice reckoned he was maybe sixteen or seventeen. All pimples. He looked like he was by himself, or that his friends were on the main dance floor. She wouldn't have long. Taking her bottle, she sauntered over towards him. She bit her lip, slowing down her pace. All she needed was for him to look in her direction...just a glance...just a small look her way...

He turned and caught her eye and before she could mock shyness a genuine grin spread across his face. His ERD throbbed a dark maroon and in that moment, she felt her body flush warm. This was a person she wanted to know more than she'd ever felt before. This guy would be her saviour. If only for the night.

If she'd had more time, she would have played it casual, but she reckoned if the Agents weren't already scouring the area they soon would be. The direct approach it was, then.

"You like the music here?" Alice asked.

The boy didn't look at her, instead he grinned in his teenager way, part love and part mischief, and spoke to the bottom of his empty drink. "I like the cows," he said loudly, over the music.

Alice blinked. At first, she thought this was some type of Degenerate street lingo, a password game that the gangs cooked up to make sure they weren't being busted by undercover Agents. But then she saw the walls were painted with all red mooing cows, perhaps some type of homage to *A Clockwork Orange*.

"They're very nice." Was all she could think of to say.

His laughter didn't build slowly but instead exploded as good as TNT. It was a sound she hadn't heard recently and it felt alien. Alice laughed too, remembering that the best way to earn someone's trust was to laugh at their jokes, mirror their movements. *Just two idiots laughing,* she thought to herself. *Two stupid people, having a beer and laughing like there's nothing else going on in the world.*

"I'm Roxanne," She said, putting out her hand. The boy's lips almost moved to say something then his eyes darted back to his drink. Alice wanted to know what he was going to say but knew that he needed to be coaxed out of his embarrassment, gently. If she pushed too hard, he'd likely rabbit. He started to pick at the label of his bottle, balling up little tears with his thumb and forefinger and flicking them to the floor.

"Brian. My name's Brian." He said, looking at the band playing.

Alice's side was throbbing. She suppressed a grimace and said through clenched teeth, "I don't suppose we could go somewhere more private so we could talk? You like me, don't you?"

Brian's ERD flashed a brilliant vermillion. *I think he wants to do more than talk,* Alice told herself, but she could deal with hormonal Degenerate Brian when they were somewhere a little safer. In her peripheral vision she could see the mounted Free-Vee playing security footage of her escape from the building. The crawling ticker text beneath the footage was stating that she was in or around Soho. She didn't like the way the pain in her side was increasing, and she could see that the band playing were fixing to finish their set. Once that happened, the main lights would come on and people would start to look more closely at the stragglers. She needed to act now.

She pitched forward and pressed her lips against his, feeling his body loosen. Just a peck. Something to get the ball rolling, a way of getting out of this place in a hurry, and she wasn't proud of it. She was about to pull away before Brian held her head in his hands and slammed his lips into hers, nearly knocking the wind from her lungs. Alice granted access, and Brian's tongue delved inside her mouth. It was a sloppy kiss with the strong scent of stale beer being exchanged in the intermingling of their billowing breaths. She likened it to a muscular eel worming around looking for food and when they pulled apart, she had to fight the urge to wipe his thick saliva from around her lips. His hands fumbled and worked their way around her body, feeling each crevasse, but when he placed a heavy hand on her side, she felt an explosion of agony and nearly slapped him across the face. Instead, she forced a smile as he took shaky, shallow breaths.

"Roxanne" he whispered slowly, prolonging each syllable as if to savour them. Alice took his hand and started leading him towards the exit.

"Could we go back to your place? Do you live with anyone?"

He followed her as if stupefied, and she could almost see the swirls of emotion ricocheting through his brain. Lust and desire. His ERD pulsated all the colours of yearning.

They slipped out onto the streets and Alice turned to Brian.

"Do you have a taxi app on your phone?"

"I used to have Uber."

"Uber went bust years ago. What about CabHail or -"

"Hey!"

Alice turned her head to the doors of the club. A group of four young lads were at the top of the stairs, lighting cigarettes. The one who had shouted had his hair slicked back. He wavered unsteadily on his feet, but he was looking directly at Alice with a look of concentration on his face.

"Do I know you?" he asked. His eyes were trying to focus as his mind connected the dots where he'd seen her face before. "I swear I know you..."

Shit. Shit. Shit.

The bouncer on the door had been vaguely watching the group with indifference, just wanting them to leave without any fuss, but now his attention turned to Alice. He too was staring in a way that made her feel uncomfortable.

Alice took Brian by the arm and started marching down the street. The flame in her knee was starting to go nuclear, but she couldn't afford to be noticed now. Not now.

"Hey! Wait a second. How do I-"

Alice searched for a cab. Black Taxi, private – it didn't matter. Nothing mattered right now apart from getting away. Alice looked over her shoulder and slick hair guy was at the bottom of the steps, shouting after her. Her heart was thumping in her ears and she couldn't hear what he was saying but hoped that he wouldn't look across the road at the electronic billboard where her face was being broadcast out to the world. Her side felt like it was exploding with all the bombs in the world detonating at once.

The bouncer tapped slick back guy on the shoulder, and they were talking, and as Alice turned her head to look for a taxi she felt nausea swirl around inside her head like foul water emptying from a drain.

"There's a cab," Brian said sluggishly.

Alice locked on to the black taxi as a few passengers disembarked and she started flagging madly with her free hand. A whip-like sting scorched her side, but she pushed it away, pushed it deep down. Blood was already seeping through her jeans and anyone could see it now if they looked properly. She opened the taxi's back door and pushed Brian in.

She took one last look back before she jumped in, just in time to see the bouncer and slick back guy look up at the billboard, then back at her, then back at the billboard again.

"Brian, where do you live?" She asked, anxiously.

"Hammersmith."

The driver grunted something in affirmation and began fiddling with his controls.

"I'll give you double if you can just go now, please." Alice said.

"*That's her! That's fucking Alice Paige!*" came a strangled voice from across the road.

Oh please God, oh please…just get me out of here. Just let me live through this evening.

"Okey-dokey," said the driver, oblivious to the commotion happening across the street. As the taxi pulled serenely away from the curb, Alice glanced out of the rear window to see a group of people running towards them. Slick back guy and the bouncer looked like jackals, with the tops of their lips pulled back in predatory rage. Thankfully, there was no traffic on the road and they soon became small dots as they left the main streets and turned off onto the motorway.

Had they been able to get the registration of the taxi? Alice doubted that the drunk group would have had the foresight, but the bouncer. The bouncer, maybe.

"On second thoughts, can you take us to Chiswick instead?"

"It's your dime, lady." The driver said, nonplussed.

"But I don't live- " Brian began to say, but Alice put a finger to his lips and hushed him with a suggestive pout.

Half an hour later, he was already beginning to doze in the backseat. Alice was relieved, there was only so much small talk and idle chit-chat she could muster without contorting in pain with each judder the cab made. She was feeling lightheaded and dizzy, but she willed herself to stay awake. In her mind she was already planning the next step forward. Where would she go after leaving Brian's flat? How would she get out of London? She could only hope that Brian owned a needle and thread – to look at him he didn't seem the type, and instead pictured a small room stinking of Lynx body spray and four day worn pants.

Jesus, what if he lives with his parents?

As if reading her mind, Brian slowly murmured: "My Nan told me to tell a girl she looked pretty when she did."

"You live with your Gran?"

He mumbled something and yawned, his head resting against the window.

"Whereabouts in Chiswick you want dropped off, love?"

"Just by the station."

"Sure."

Soon they were at Turnham Green. Alice scanned the area outside. It was early morning, and the streets were darkly quiet. She'd need to walk to Hammersmith, which was about twenty minutes away. She thumped Brian on the arm and he stirred awake, wiping away some drool with the back of his hand.

"Thanks," she said, handing over several notes to the driver.

"'ere, listen love," the driver said, "I don't need your money."

A look of confusion swiftly altered to alertness. Flight or fight mode switched on like a light bulb. The driver saw the panic in her eyes and put his hands up in a placating gesture. "I know who you are, love." His eyes flicked to Brian. "You'd be an idiot not to."

Alice shuffled involuntarily back in her seat. She was guarded and wary. Brian leaned off to the side with the door open, pressed one finger to his nostril and blew a snot-dart out of his other nose-hole.

"Listen, love – I'm not one of those vultures out there. My daughter...Charlie...she had her Birthday Treat a couple of years ago. Didn't want to go through with it, see? She wanted to do what you're doing. But couldn't go through with it." The driver looked away from Alice, and she could see tears brimming in his eyes. "Anyway, that's not important anymore. What's important is that you get through the next five days. Here," he fumbled with something and for a split-second Alice thought he was going to bring out a weapon and shoot her, but a wave of relief washed over her when he simply produced a card. "Here's my number. Personal, like. Just to let you know that you've got friends in the right places. The Movement are about. They're watching, right?"

Reluctantly, she moved forward and snatched the card. There was a mobile number scrawled in spidery handwriting. Brian stretched beside her, oblivious to the conversation.

"They might track you down to find me," she said.

"Ask no questions, tell no lies." The driver replied, with a soft, sad smile. "I just picked up a fare. I pick up a lot of fares during the day. They all blur into one, really. Anyway, better go. You going to be alright, love?"

Alice hastily nodded, suddenly aware of potential cameras in the vicinity. She took Brian by the arm, shoved him out and they started off on a quick trot towards Hammersmith.

It took longer than she anticipated to arrive at Brian's flat. She would have to stop occasionally to catch her breath, and at one-point Brian noted that her jeans were turning crimson. Finally though, they both stumbled into the flat. The first thing that Alice noticed was a large coffee-coloured stain in the living room.

"You okay? You're looking a bit peaky."

Alice lurched against the wall; her muscles too drained to keep her upright anymore. It was like she'd spent the last hour willing the pain away, and now that there was some semblance of safety everything came crashing down around her. She grunted, clutching at the skirting as she waited for the dizziness to subside. The wall felt cool against her cheek. She took a few deep breaths and used it to ground herself as she focused on the texture of the wallpaper between her fingers.

"Brian...do you have a needle and thread. And some vodka?"

Brian stood in the middle of the living room, looking up at the ceiling, deep in thought.

His gaze slowly descended, and he looked at her with level eyes. "Are we going to have sex?"

"Get me...those things...and I'll think about it." She said.

Brian seemed to calculate this in his mind before he padded through the hallway into a room. Alice bit down on a moan. She didn't want to be here anymore; she didn't want to be part of the *Hunted* TV programme. Why hadn't she just performed her Birthday Treat?

She licked her dry, cracked lips as Brian came back with a small sewing box and a bottle of vodka. Alice forced herself to her feet, gasping as searing pain lanced through her side and knee, then staggered forward to the bathroom, slamming the door behind her.

Alice perched herself on the sink and peeled her leather jacket off over aching arms. She caught herself in the bathroom mirror. She couldn't believe how pale she looked in the reflection and hoped against hope that it was just bad lighting. Her white shirt was sopping wet with blood. Her jeans were bloody. It seemed like there was blood everywhere. Even now, in a stranger's flat and with Agents hunting her, she tried to direct any new flow of blood into the sink and prevent any spillage onto the floor.

Mum and Dad brought up a good girl, she thought meekly to herself. Janice and Eugene.

She'd never known her real parents. Just the orphanage for the first couple of years of her life that she barely remembered and then Janice and Eugene. Two real salt of the earth types. Mass on Sunday. Following whatever dredge the Free-Vees regurgitated at their dinner table.

Eugene.

She hadn't thought of her foster father in a while. Perhaps the events of the day were some sort of psychological link. What a nightmare. Alice pulled down her jeans and as she moved the fire in her knee raged hotter. She scrunched up her face as she inspected the wound in the mirror. She'd torn it wider. Through gritted teeth, she turned on the taps and then unscrewed the bottle of Vodka and poured a generous amount onto the injury. A new kind of pain jolted through her body, bringing her to the edge of oblivion. She knew she'd need antibiotics, but that was for later Alice to worry about. Right now, she needed to stitch. Her hands were trembling.

"Are you okay in there?" Brian's wavering voice floated through the door.

"Uh-huh," Alice replied, as black dots swirled in front of her eyes.

She clamped the two pieces of flesh together, but not so tightly that it would tear at the slightest pivot. Her fingers were slippery with water and blood, but she held her breath as she dipped the needle into some vodka and then proceeded to staunch the open hole in her midsection.

"Do you want some beans? Grandma always made me beans for dinner. I know how to make 'em!"

The words escaped through clenched teeth: "Sure thing, Brian. Beans sounds great right about now."

"Okay."

Alice heard him move away from the door and she carried on with the task at hand. What the hell to do with Brian?

You've already killed a person today, a snide voice crept through the roller-coaster of thoughts clanging around. It wasn't Boss Bitch. This was a new one. This was an insidious voice brought on by blood less and fatigue. *If only it had been a few hours earlier, you would've got your Birthday Treat done and dusted. Now look at the mess you're in. Just stab Brian like you did with the creep Mitchum. Yeah, remember him? The stinking pervert that was trying to rape you?* She shook her head. Mitchum was self-defence. She hadn't meant to do what she did. *But you brought the plugs for your nose, just in case, didn't you? Because you know what kind of scum there is around here. You've been dealing with scum your entire, miserable life. Brian's the same, isn't he? Just looking to get his rocks off. Dip his beak. Just like all the others.*

He was just a Degenerate. A simpleton. Nothing more.

Mitchum wasn't though, was he? He knew exactly what he was doing. Just like Eugene.

"Shut up," she hissed, passing the needle through her flesh. The pain would cancel out the sinister voice. She would board up those thoughts like a survivor in a zombie film. She was thinking crazy because she'd lost blood, that was all. She could deal with Brian later. *Future* Alice could deal with all of that later. *Now* Alice just wanted to sleep. Just to close her eyes and forget this whole day had ever happened. Forget everything that happened.

She hoped so, at any rate. But hope was in short supply these days.

When she was finished with the needle and thread, she cleaned up the bathroom as best she could. It probably wouldn't pass any sanitary awards anytime soon, but it would do. She could clean it thoroughly tomorrow, to leave no trace she was ever there.

She discarded red, raggedy clumps of wadded tissue paper down the toilet and flushed. She rotated her body, and even though every muscle screamed at her, she felt like the stitching would hold. She dumped the soggy, vermillion shirt in the bath and took a towel, wrapping it round her.

When she came out of the toilet, she saw Brian in the kitchen, fussing over a can he hadn't opened yet.

"Oh. I thought we were having beans." She said.

Brian frowned, his ERD pulsing a canary yellow. "I know how to make beans!" he snapped.

Alice raised her eyebrows and made her way to the sofa. Every ligament screamed in her body and she just wanted to close her eyes. Just for a few minutes. She slumped onto the sofa and everything seemed to sing at her, an orchestra that had spent the last few hours building to a crescendo that now was finally coming to its climax. The tiredness inside her made her hang limp like wet laundry on a cold still day.

"Do you have a shirt I could borrow?" She asked.

Brian seemed to think about this for a moment. Alice had never seen someone think so visibly before.

"Sure." He padded away into another room.

"What's the stain on the carpet?" she said, not caring whether she was thinking or saying things aloud.

"Ah. Yeah...that's my Nan," Brian replied, from the other room. "She was recycled. Over retirement age, innit?"

Alice blinked heavy eyes; her forehead creased. "You mean your Gran was...killed here?"

He came back into the room and threw a crumpled shirt at the sofa. "We're meant to say 'retired.'" Brian said with a smile, focusing back on the tin in the kitchen.

"Jesus."

"She was smart. I think she was older than the retirement age. I get half her social credits, so that's good."

Alice quickly put on the shirt out of Brian's vision and let the damp towel cover her like a warm blanket. She closed her eyes.

"I have some friends around the estate. They give me special missions sometimes. I deliver secret packages – I shouldn't really be telling you this, but I think I can trust you, what with us about to have sex and everything. My friend, Charlie? He showed me the best way to make beans. He says most people use a can opener, but you can stab it with a knife, too! I can never remember where Nan used to keep the can opener, you see. I'm going to use a knife. Sure."

Brian opened the drawer and brought out his Gran's kitchen knife. For a moment he turned it slowly in his hand, getting the glint from the ceiling light reflecting off the blade. He really liked the way it made it look all shiny. After he'd pierced the can several times, he used a spoon to bend the metal and he was able to gloop the beans into a pot. He'd only done this a few times, but it gave him a certain satisfaction. A certain power.

"Shouldn't be too long," he said, glancing over his shoulder.

Roxanne was asleep. Her mouth slightly open, head rested against the arm of the sofa.

"Ah crap," he mumbled. "I'm never going to have sex."

What does The Network know about you? Download Flappy Flap privacy app to find out what The Network Knows about you today.

@FlappyFlapPrivacyApp

519 replies 983 RTs 3,272 Likes

Has anyone seen any footage of @alicepaige this morning? Homegirl spotted in Soho. Apparently people running after her in the streets. Check out the vid – huntedmyth.com/soho/London…

@lifer_4_lyfe

786 replies 14,320 RTs 19,735 Likes

@lifer_4_lyfe is this real? Who's the guy she's with? Love interest?

@Leahsummers

432 replies 1,764 RTs 345 Likes

She's doing some of dat naughty online cam girl shit – bow-chick-a Wow-wow #camgirl #hotsex #naughty #alicepaigesex

@HotPikachusex

345 replies 435 RTs 324 Likes

Still looking for that leather jacket. What's a girl got to do to get some Feedback here?

@hannah_vintage

2456 replies 3217 RTs 116 Likes

I was there! Saw her leaving in a cab!

¬

Soho. Boys. BATTER UP! #goinghunting

@CRicoh

57 replies 345 RTs 650 Likes

Beans in the microwave and a hot girl on the sofa! Yay!

@Brian_Bowerman

2 replies 5 RTs 9 Likes

WE NEED TO HELP ALICE PAIGE. SIGN THE PETITON. END THE NETWORK.

#thenetworklies

@For_The_Movement

.

13

THE OLD MAN

TUESDAY

86 HOURS REMAIN...

My wonderful assistant Cassandra told me that my last blog post may have been too dour, what with the news of my condition and reflecting on mistakes of the past. My mother used to tell me that to know where we're going in life, one must remember where we've been. She was always coming up with little nuggets of juicy catchphrases, and I've always tried to remember them.

Anyway, enough with the depressing stuff – a memory came to me the other day and I wanted to share it with you. It's the first recollection of an important lesson when I was young and has forever stayed with me since. Do you ever find that's the way with memories sometimes? You can forget what you ate for dinner a week ago, but some memories from our childhoods stick with us with such clarity that it seems like it was only yesterday that it happened?

Isn't that strange? Well, I wanted to share this memory with you as I believe it was one of the starting blocks of how I began to perceive people, and how I would use this valuable lesson later in life with other business situations.

When I was a kid, say about eleven or twelve, there was a Youth Club that all the young reprobates would hang out at. I use that term endearingly, of course. We weren't reprobates at all – it was just that we were of an age where we still had the innocence and naivety of youth and hadn't yet discovered the follies of adulthood. Too young to be in the pubs, too old to be playing on the streets. So, there was this place, which was a marvel for us. I could be looking through rose-tinted glasses here, but the place was huge. It was the longest room I'd ever seen, filled with pool tables and arcade machines, and at the back there was an even bigger room, much like a hall that they used as an inside football pitch. I think it used to be a gentleman's social club, because there was a bar alongside the wall too, but instead of serving beer to us, it would literally be like a tuck shop, selling everything from gobstoppers, fizzy cola bottles, to crisps and curly wurleys. They had blue neon lights fitted on the shelves where they would normally have bottles of liquor, so the place always looked like it was Christmas.

Anyway, it was easy to spend a whole day in that place – there were no windows, and the interior was dimly lit, so hours could trickle by and you wouldn't even know what time it was until they shouted over the raucous that they were closing. Whilst some kids would leave late and get the bus home, my mother was the worrying kind of parent and would always ensure that either herself or my Dad would pick me up.

"A worried mother does better research than MI5," she would say to me sometimes. Another little quote from mother dearest. On one occasion, I can't remember why, both my dad and mum were tied up, so they phoned me to say that my Uncle Tommy would be coming to pick me up.

Now, the thing you must know about my uncle Tommy was that he was from my mother's side of the family and enjoyed the odd bet now and then. I was playing a game of pool when I felt a heavy calloused hand prod me on the shoulder.

"Playing a wee game of pool, are ye?" He said in a rough, Irish voice.

I was just finishing up and having won the last round had the rights to play the next challenger. Without any hesitation, my uncle Tommy fished in his pockets and brought out his wallet. He slapped a ten-pound note on the table and picked up a cue.

"Let's see how good the wain is, then."

"We don't bet for money, Uncle Tommy."

"Ah, for God's sake, boy. Smooth seas do not make skilful sailors, you hear me?"

I didn't really, not then. The thing you must realise, dear reader, is that back in those days, ten pounds was an awful lot of money to an eleven-year-old. I got pocket money, sure – and I earned some extra coinage on the weekends from doing a paper round and washing people's cars, but I wasn't entirely comfortable with the possibility of losing the only money I had, especially as I was planning to spend a lot at the comic bookstore the next day. Uncle Tommy was already racking up the balls, and I didn't want to seem like a spoil sport in front of an authoritative figure, so I matched the money with all the coins in my pocket and we got to playing.

Uncle Tommy would tut and mumble things under his breath as I pocketed balls, and slowly I started to feel confident that I might win the game and walk away with twenty pounds. What I could buy with Twenty pounds! My eleven-year-old mind raced with possibilities. My hubris got the better of me however, and I clumsily made a shot that didn't connect with any of my balls.

"Two shots to me then, eh?" Uncle Tommy guffawed, taking a considerable amount of time to chalk his cue. With his first shot he was able to pocket two balls, and when he missed the second shot, he took his forfeited turn to pocket two more. He only had the blackball left, and I held my breath as he took the shot. He missed.

"Ah to feck with ya," he cursed, shaking his head. The white ball had landed nicely square in the middle of the table. It was an easy shot, but there was a lot riding on the line. I'd seen people crumble under the pressure of the last shot and I didn't want to give my uncle the satisfaction of seeing me squirm. I got into position, squinting with one eye as I mentally projected the angle of the shot. The tip of my tongue jutted from the corner of my mouth as I carefully powered the cue.

It was textbook. I could feel myself grinning ear to ear as the satisfying sound of the blackball plunged into the corner pocket.

Uncle Tommy gave me a slow clap of appreciation, saying that yeah, okay, I had some skill. Just as I went to retrieve my winnings, he slapped a twenty-pound note on the table.

"How about this, boyo? Double or quits. Maybe you can show this old dog some of those tricks you've been practising, eh?"

My mind reeled at the prospect. There was potential here for me to walk away with forty pounds! I'd never see that kind of money in my life before. I could buy hundreds of comics with that kind of dosh.

"I don't have any more money though," I said.

"Ach, don't worry about it. We'll put it down as an IOU if you lose, eh?"

At that moment I felt like a visitor inside my own body. The sensible thing to have done at that precise moment would have been to politely decline the offer of another game, take my winnings and go home with Uncle Tommy. But it was like that twenty-pound note was calling to me, like a siren song luring the unfortunate sailor from the ship. It seemed like every nerve below the surface of my skin had suddenly gone dead, and this aberrant whisper inside my head told me with an absolute confidence that I should take the bet. That I would win.

So I did.

"You're on," I said to Uncle Tommy.

He racked up the balls, but there was something imperceptibly different about his posture. It was as if in the last game he had been hunched over and slow, now he seemed to stand straight and moved with a gait that belied his age.

"You want to break?" He asked.

"Nah, you go ahead." I said. Those were the last words I uttered during the game.

Uncle Tommy broke the V-shaped pyramid with a mighty crack and scattered them, pocketing two striped balls immediately. Without hesitating, he lined up the next shot and one after the other they fell. It was almost as if he held some magnetic power over the white ball, making it curve and twist to his design.

I hoped and prayed that he would miss his next shot. When that didn't happen, I hoped and prayed that he would inadvertently knock one of my balls into the pocket. When that didn't happen, I noticed that my knuckles were white, wrapped tightly around my cue. All the sounds and smells inside the youth club seemed to magnify for me in that instant. Maybe that's why I remember it all so vividly.

Within minutes he was on the eight ball. He even had the audacity to give me a wink as he hit that straight into the corner pocket. It was over.

"C'mon kid, let's get back to your ma," he said, scooping up the winnings from the table.

My uncle had hustled me.

He taught me two important lessons that day. Firstly, to use a quote from my mother – a fool and his money are soon parted. From that moment on, nothing I did where the only reason for doing it was the money was ever worth it, except as a bitter experience. I had gambled money I didn't have, thinking it would procure me material items that at the time I thought were important. I've made my fair share of mistakes since then, but money has never been one of them. Uncle Tommy taught me the value of money in that youth club all those years ago. When I started The Network, it was never about profit, or ratings, or bonuses, or percentages.

It was about the people.

That memory I've just shared with you was a catalyst for me – it was the branch in the road that put me on track to be where I am today. Now, I could have been sore about the fact that my own blood had hustled me out of money. I could have been thin skinned about it and cried until the cows came home about the unfairness of his overwhelmingly superior pool skills, but I took it for what it was.

A lesson.

A harsh lesson, no less, but one that stayed with me.

The second thing my uncle taught me was to practise. I thought I had decent enough skills to beat him, but really, he let me win that first game to give me buoyancy, to give me the elation of the win, only to capitalise on that. Every day for the rest of that summer I would watch people play pool, I would get tips from the greatest players on the scene and I would practise, practise, practise. By the end of that summer, I got so good that I thought I'd try out my uncle's trick on one of the other boys at the youth club. There was this kid, Mark Albrecht. Lanky kind of guy, but nice. Quiet.

I challenged him to a game, and just like my uncle did a few months earlier, I slapped some change down on the table and we bet money on the game. I threw it, of course. Made it look close though, just like my uncle had done. And then the money shot - if you'll pardon the pun. I leaned in, with more money that I'd been saving up that summer and challenged him for double bubble. I could see the glint in Mark's eyes, just as my uncle had seen in mine.

It was a slaughter.

Poor Mark was near tears as I potted the eight ball. I wasn't callous enough to give him a wink, but I thought about it. And this was the second epiphany I had, if you will. This was the moment that I learnt how manipulating people could hurt them. I looked at Mark as I shovelled my winnings into my pocket, and I could see the unequivocal and pure deflation in his face. It was almost as if I'd throttled his dog in front of him.

It was my greed and pride that let me down that day with my uncle. Just like greed and pride had let Mark down. But I didn't have to be like my uncle. That was the moment I realised that I could change things around, for the better.

I could do something about that.

"Here," I said, giving him half of the money back.

"But...you won," Mark replied, bemused.

"It's what we do with the winnings that matter, right?" I said. I'd like to think that I was cool like Tom Cruise in *The Colour of Money* at that point, but maybe I was overreaching.

Those were the two lessons that my uncle taught me that summer.

And that's why I never took anything at face value ever again. It's been a good tool to use in the business world – a lot of people are looking at the net profit growth and the quarterly figures. I was looking the other way, at the people that I would be able to work with.

Mark and I became good friends that day. We left the youth club and got some ice cream. He became my business partner years later. I like to think that our friendship was formed on that day during a game of pool, because instead of taking something away from a person, I gave back.

And that's what I've been trying to do ever since.

(Self Contained Ordinance and Optimum Paragon) Suit

Our high-quality ballistic panels are available in a wide range of covert carriers!
Level II or IIIa ballistic protection is available unobtrusively, comfortably and discreetly.

In line with The Network's privatised security forces (You know them as AGENTS – KNOW YOUR
ROLE!) we at SureGuard Safety Clothing (SGSC) have full confidence in all our SCOOP Suits – and
their proven ability to meet ballistic threats with confidence!

The SCOOP Suit material uses alternating layers of extraordinarily strong Winchester Synthefill VII
fibres, along with ArcticGuard polyester – which means it can absorb the energy from a knife or bullet
and distort it, making you one effective Birthday Treater! Also, our suits can deflect over five thousand
degrees Fahrenheit, so you could be in the eye of nuclear fallout and all you'd get is a sunburn!

Because our SCOOP Suits are interlayered with fibrosteel mesh, it can withstand the dynamic pressures
of up to eighty-five pounds per square inch, which means you'd be padded and secure for your exciting
adventures!

Under no circumstances should you try to remove your SCOOP Suit once an Agent has secured it to
your person. In no way do we monitor your GPS location. So rest assured, you can carry on with your
Treat!

Although the standardised SCOOP Suit comes in Orange, we at SureGuard Safety Clothing (SGSC)
have a variety of different coloured Suits to befit ALL your needs!

Ladies! For a limited time only, SGSC have a special offer JUST FOR YOU!
Whether you're petite or carry a sub-compact, the Can-Can Concealment Garter Micro is your answer
for thigh carry comfort! Sophisticated and timeless, it's the premier choice of concealed connoisseurs.
Keeping your weapon under cover and within reach puts confidence in your hands and a spring in your
step!

So what are you waiting for? Order your personalised SCOOP Suit today and get ready for your
Birthday Treat of a lifetime!

- An extract from the SGSC website - **www.SGSC.MOI.org**

#401: You know how many people are in this world, man?

8716367: Tell me.

#401: 9.9 billion.

8716367: That's a lot.

#401: Fuck yeah, it is. You know my apartment block has people crammed in there, bursting at the seams, man. It's like, overflowing. Like rats. Can't move without those fucking *things* slithering about. I fuckin' love The Network, man. They've got it right...They *know*, y'know? You get to whack those fuckin' little shits when they pop out of their holes. You ever play that game, where you have the mallet and you jus' POP them on their little stupid heads?

8716367: You seem quite animated about it.

#401: I just...I just never thought I'd get my Birthday Treat, y'know? I'm forty-three. Been dealt a hard hand in life, y'know what I'm sayin'? Not that I'm complaining, like. Made me into the man I am today. A rod for The Network. A broadsword. Those fucking little bitches...thought they could laugh at me all the time. Calling me names.

8716367: You'll have to excuse me, I'm running behind on some of the latest cases, so I'm only watching your Birthday Treat vid now...you refer to yourself as The Pied Piper. You have a thing for rats?

#401: That's my handle, man. That's my avatar, y'know? I'm a paladin cleansing the world of the infestation. Of the rats.

8716367: Says you're a janitor at a school...

#401: Those fuckin' bitches. I can hear 'em talking about me, y'know. Every day. Calling me names. That fucking bitch got what she deserved.

8716367: Wait a minute…

#401: Think they're better than me. Better social score. Better way of life. Y'know what they call me? At the school?

8716367: You were at Chiswick Park station the other day…

#401: They call me The Trashman. Say I smell like rubbish. Do you know what it's like to have some snot-nosed princess calling you that, day in and day out? I can't help it, it's the job, y'know? I wash every day but the stink…the stink of that place…

8716367: You. You threw her on the track.

#401: Oh baby, I didn't throw her. She flew. You think a princess can't fly? I made her fly that day. I made her fuckin' soar.

8716367: I was there. I was there and I didn't do anything.

#401: Like Icarus, man. Y'know, I almost saw her wings -

8716367: You're a fucking monster.

#401: What?

8716367: You heard me. What kind of person does that to an innocent child? What kind of sick, deranged lunatic does that?

#401: Hey, woah – what's going on here? This is my -

8716367: You SICK bastard. You EVIL MOTHERFU -

[Call Terminated by Network Central]

14

GEORGE

TUESDAY

85 HOURS REMAIN...

George blinked his crusted eyes awake, regretting every decision he'd made in his life that led him to this point.

A dull *whump whump whump* drummed behind his left eye, as if a miniature person were inside his head, tugging on his optic nerve. He slowly arched his back and stretched, feeling the balloon under his cranium slowly inflating with mounting pressure. He sat up and the room swirled around him like a kaleidoscope of shapes. He squinted and moaned before retreating under the duvet. He felt safe, wrapped up in a cocoon. He dared to open one eye to view the digital clock read out.

Doesn't matter what time it is. I'm not going into work today.

But he'd have to call work. He'd have to speak to Faulkner. The idea did not sit well with him.

He allowed a small growl to escape his cracked lips and he mentally counted to twenty in his head. After twenty seconds he would get up and go to the bathroom. That was the plan. After the time had elapsed, he counted another twenty seconds. Waves of nausea added to his misery. He'd lost count of the number of whiskies he'd consumed the night before. And whatever was in the plastic cups at the house party. *I do not go to illegal house parties on a Monday evening. I go home on Monday evenings, have dinner and watch the Free-Vee. That is my life. It is boring and mundane. I lead a trivial life. I do not get drunk on Monday evenings. I do not cheat on my wife. I do not lead a double life.*

But then a dull thought came to him. Something that sat uneasy and made him swallow hard.

I'm with the movement.

That's what Carina had said before Parker had stumbled through the door.

I'm with the movement. The words mingled with the twanging in his skull in a way that rhythmically sung with one another.

I'm. Whump. With. Whump. The. Whump. Movement. Whump.

What had he gotten himself into? His brain felt like it would swell beyond the capacity of his skull and his dehydration was too obvious to ignore. He counted another twenty seconds before sliding off the bed. If he'd have to, he'd wriggle on his belly to the bathroom. Like a slithering snake.

Not a snake, he thought pitifully. *A worm. I'll worm my way to the bathroom like the maggot that I am.*

His stomach lurched.

Perhaps some painkillers would help. He stopped squirming on the bedroom carpet. He could hear the Free-Vee in the living room, so Elspeth was watching her stories again. He'd tried to be as quiet as possible coming in last night but had the feeling he'd woken her. Had he fallen up the stairs? It was possible. George deduced that there was simply no easy way to slide into a bed without the mattresses creaking and the reverberation eddying out to someone else sleeping on it. He gently pulled himself to his feet. The room swayed, almost causing him to lose balance and he reached out for the wall. He waited until the rocky room became stationary again. He smacked his lips and his stomach turned in an unfriendly way. A fry up was probably the last thing he needed but he was going to have one anyway.

Meet me in the park tomorrow, Carina had said, slipping past him as Parker offered more drinks. *At the bandstand on the green.*

He padded towards the bathroom. He splashed cold water on his face just to feel something refreshing and took a large breath. The mirror showed his eyes, a latticework of pink over white.

He took his finger and pulled down an eyelid.

Conjunctival lymphoma.

Conjunctival hemorrhage.

Conjunctival hemangioma.

Conjunctival nevus.

Conjunctival melanoma.

George blinked several times. He inspected his white tongue. He'd watched a documentary once of an alcohol addict, going to get a scan of his liver. The doctor ruminated that every time the addict took a drink, it was like burning his hand on an oven grill. The burn would heal over time, but it would leave a scar. And every time he took a drink after that, he'd burn himself in the exact same space. At some point, the doctor gravely assessed, the skin won't be able to take all the burning.

George shuddered at the thought.

When had he become so scared at everything in life? Inspecting calories on almost everything he ate, umming and ahhhing about the fat concentrate on meals.

It's because you're getting older, a voice chirped over the pneumatic drill jolting through his skull. He'd been noticing things in the last five years, a small cluster of burst blood vessels on his left calf. Thinning hair. Shortness of breath after walking up a flight of stairs. These things had never bothered him before. Elspeth had once proactively ensured they ate well – they'd gone vegetarian for a couple of weeks a few years ago.

Back when she was actively doing...anything. Now, she just watched the Free-Vee. She used to love going to exhibitions in the city, meeting up with friends and *doing* things. Anything.

Now, it seemed like a tiredness had wrapped around her like a comfortable blanket and had remained there over her skin, grey and cold. There used to be a time when George would have called some friends, asking for a meet up to shove them out of their apathy. But it was strange how easy it was to just slip into the routine of monotony. And George knew, with absolute certainty, that he had at some point unwillingly wrapped himself in that same blanket. The blanket of cold, comfortably numb nothingness.

Jesus, George thought. *Once you pass thirty, is this it? Every day just becomes a game of 'am I sick, or is this just how I am now?'*

He opened the bathroom cabinet and rifled through the abundant pill bottles, phials and other elixirs promising vibrant youth and vitality. This one would make your hair thicker and fuller. That one would give you mobility and help your bones. He found the ibuprofen and dry swallowed two, almost retching in the process. He had a shower which made him feel better, but his thoughts kept on drifting back to Carina and The Movement. As he towelled himself dry, he had a curious thought that perhaps this was the nudge he needed in his life right now. He'd been fantasising about something like this for a while now, hadn't he?

But at what cost?

Then there was the letter. The letter from the anonymous source telling him he'd be getting his Birthday Treat soon. Who had sent the letter? How had they hand delivered it to his desk in the building. Had Carina been given access? She was part of The Movement, so maybe the chance encounter at the pub last night hadn't been so serendipitous, as he'd first thought. Could Faulkner be behind it? He had been waiting for him at work the other day, hadn't he? Waiting to talk to him about taking away his responsibilities and giving them to Parker. What if the whole shitty boss routine was just that?

A routine.

And what about Parker? The village idiot who had a care-free smile to everything presented to him. His brain hurt thinking about such conspiracy theories. Yes, he decided that he was going to work. Another normal day, just with a hangover to deal with.

Life was okay, wasn't it? He and Elspeth had a roof over their heads, he had an okay job. So what if the last couple of years had been a continual habitual process? They were trying to save money, right? He was aiming to better their lives in the long run, so what if they were in a slump. Things would change soon – and he didn't need to involve himself in some tin pot anarchic group to get a rush. His social credit score was above average. If he kept his head down and continued down this path, in the next five to ten years they'd be sorted. He'd get himself something to eat, get dressed and go into work. Because that was the right thing to do.

And what if he got his Birthday Treat? What would he do with it? The thought of ending someone's life was just too barbaric to comprehend, no matter how much propaganda was shoved down their throats day in and day out from The Network. He closed his eyes and a red image ballooned at the back of his mind – the girl on the platform yesterday morning. The pin-wheeling of her arms and the half second realisation that she was going under the train. The wrap-around headphones lying prone on the station platform.

He could never do something like that. Rob a jewellery store? Bludgeon someone over the head with a stick?

Dump your baby in a rubbish bin?

He found himself hyperventilating in the bathroom. Just the thought of it set him on edge.

I didn't give her away. Not me.

"George!" Elspeth shrilled from the living room. "Are you done in the bathroom? I've been waiting to go for ages!"

He looked at himself in the mirror.

Not me.

⊕

After George had brushed his teeth, he dressed like he normally did for work and went into the living room. He picked up his briefcase and had a short conversation with Elspeth about the latest on *Hunted* TV (The Alice Paige girl was still on the run, she'd gone to ground, and it was all extremely exciting as people on social media were saying that she was still in London.)

After a perfunctory kiss on the cheek (she hadn't mentioned anything about arriving home late or drunk, so he assumed she'd either passed out on the sofa and had come to bed after him, or that she had passed out on the sofa and had woken up in the morning, to continue her binge watching) he picked up his briefcase and mumbled something about what they would eat for dinner that evening. Elspeth started rattling off some dishes she'd seen on the cooking channel yesterday, so he nodded affably and left the house.

He had been so close to telling her everything. About the letter, about meeting the group in the pub, about the house party and about Carina.

So what stopped you?

He felt a dull embarrassment creep over and take hold. He could have put it down to the hangover. He could have put it down that he wanted to leave the house as urgently as possible. But the real reason was far more transparent. He was a coward.

The air was crisp, and he breathed in a lungful as he started walking towards the station with the intention of going to work. But from somewhere at the bottom of a road the smell of roasting coffee – real, pure coffee, the type that Carina sold, came floating out and invaded his nostrils. George paused involuntarily. He found his hand slipping into his jacket pocket and before he knew what he was doing the call connected through to Faulkner.

"I don't think I'll be in today," he said, although he felt untethered from it – like he was outside of his body listening to a stranger talking on the phone.

"Oh?" Faulkner replied. George detected a hint of relief in his voice.

"Yeah...I think with...what happened yesterday, it's probably best to take a few days off. Get my head in the right frame of mind."

Faulkner agreed. He hung up on his manager just as he was about to slip into HR mode, talking about mental wellbeing. He found himself standing by the entrance of the park in Turnham Green. He didn't remember the short journey there, or what he'd been thinking about.

And then she was there. His heart seemed to turn to ice and his bowels to water. Was that sweat trickling down the side of his face?

Whump. Whump. Whump.

The headache was back with a vengeance. Carina casually walked down the road and entered the park. He noticed that her tights were ripped in several places and he was ashamed to admit that his eyes lingered on the fleshy parts of her legs that were displayed. She was at the bandstand, a small hexagonal place where Degenerates could plug in their guitars and busk for money. The amps were shot and it always crackled loudly when people played. George enjoyed it was there. Gave him a modicum of hope.

For a moment he thought she hadn't seen him at all, but then she glanced across and looked him straight in the face. He felt his breathing stop. With a smirk, she walked quickly on as though she had not seen him at all.

Follow me little fly, that smirk seemed to say, *follow me for a little while longer. I'll show you glorious things.*

He was too paralysed to move. The memories of last night flooded back to him in an instant. The kiss...her lips against his, so different than Elspeth's fleeting and dutiful pecks. The caressing, the way her hands probed and stroked. There was a need in that kiss, a desire he hadn't felt for a long time. He hadn't imagined it, had he? Was this simply the foolhardy imagination of a man on the precipice of a mid-life crisis?

Or worse yet, he moaned internally, *have I gone full tilt over the edge and haven't realised I've been freefalling into oblivion?*

It was an effort to walk. His stomach gurgled and a cramping pain seared through his belly. He should have eaten something before he left.

But you knew what you were going to do, didn't you Georgie boy? You were never going into work. You've fallen under her spell, you little insignificant fly. You've fallen straight into her web and you don't even care what it will cost you.

For a couple of minutes, he had the feeling that his bowels would empty right there unless he visited a lavatory soon. He started walking, keeping a safe distance between himself and Carina. The spasm soon passed, leaving a dull ache behind.

George halted when he saw Carina walk past the bandstand and take a left under the bridge. He wondered vaguely what to do, then followed her down the dark tunnel. A dark thought crossed his mind –wearing the orange boiler suit and running up behind Carina, pushing her down into the wet ground. Running his hands over her body and ripping at those tights, ripping them away and tearing off the rest of her clothes. She would defend herself, but that would make it far more delectable. He felt a stirring below and involuntary blushed. He abandoned the idea immediately, not wanting to progress with that train of thought. He felt miserable then, tailing a member of a party that could have you imprisoned just through association. This had been a bad idea, a monumental mistake. He should have just walked on past her at the park, walked to the station and carried on until he was at work. All he wanted to do right now was to trudge home quickly and then sit down and be quiet.

Carina threw a cursory glance over her shoulder to see if George was still following and then crossed the road at the end of the tunnel, leading to quiet town suburbia Chiswick. Rows upon rows of Edwardian and terraced houses lined the streets, and George wondered where she was leading him. Compared to the decrepit house party yesterday evening, he couldn't imagine that anywhere in this part of town would house Movement renegades. The streets began to narrow and there were odd brick-a-back shops that were scattered amongst hamlets like Chiswick. George couldn't fathom how these shops still sold things: everyone ordered everything online now. He was surprised that the main retail outlets closed some years ago – he thought that ordering clothes online would be counterproductive, what if they didn't fit? They would need to send them back and then order a different size. And even that may not have fitted. It just seemed illogical to him. Not that he ordered many clothes online these days.

The lane widened and soon he was on another footpath. Funnily enough, George had never really walked down this way before. He'd lived in Chiswick for more than five years and had never taken this path. The notion struck him as strange, but not in an uncomfortable way. More that he hadn't taken the time to know the area he lived in. He was walking down a cobbled street of little two-storey houses with battered doorways which gave straight on the pavement and made him think he was in a different country, somehow.

They traversed dark doorways and narrow alleyways that branched off on either side. It seemed to George that they had been walking for about twenty minutes, but time seemed inconsequential to him when he saw Carina's form a meagre twenty yards from him. They strolled over a pass and then soon the traffic and din of Chiswick was behind them, a static white noise. George walked slowly, looking for movement, any sign of life, but it was like they were both cut out from the real world and were wandering through a diorama of the street.

Carina crossed the street and entered the shade of a shop awning. George looked both ways – deserted. He found this odd at first, but then remembered why no one came down to this area: everything was closed or in the process of being closed.

Carina winked and then walked into one of the shops. George regarded this; the door didn't seem locked, but it couldn't have been open either, could it? He crossed the road and had a look at the shop. The windows were coated with dust. A hand-painted sign taped to the inside of the window revealed: CHARLOTTE'S ANTIQUES AND SECOND-HAND SHOP. OPEN MON-FRI MORNINGS. George examined some of the items adorning the window display. There was a long, elegant cocktail dress and a tweed jacket decorating a couple of mannequins, a few shoes of varying shapes and sizes and a bin with a collection of discarded umbrellas. With the feeling that he would be less conspicuous inside than hanging about on the pavement, he stepped through the doorway.

Inside, the shop looked gloomy and deserted. A ceiling fan above was barely rotating. In the middle of the room were slouching armchairs with a battered looking coffee table centre stage. There were four or five ranks of bookshelves, brimming with paperbacks with an aisle up the middle and aisles on either side. The tiny interior of the shop was in fact uncomfortably full, but George thought there was almost nothing in it of the slightest value. He thought that back in the day, when Elspeth and he used to go out on occasion, she would like this place. The dusty picture frames stacked along the floor in a haphazard but calculated line, trays of nondescript items littered on any surface available to the eye, tarnished watches that did not even pretend to be in working order, and other miscellaneous rubbish. George would have perused the books available and then left without purchasing anything, as was his way. There was a counter in there, too – where a tubby black cat sat perched, watching him with disinterest.

George turned down the central aisle and flinched involuntarily when he saw a woman standing there, looking at him.

"Can I help you with something, love?" She said. She was an old woman, frail and bowed. George was startled at how old she looked; she couldn't be more than sixty – she would have been retired. Her hair was almost white, and she made small, fussy movements. George noted that the tips of her fingers were swathed in paint and she wore an aged jacket of black velvet, which gave her a vague air of creativity, as though she was a painter, or perhaps a musician.

They stood there looking at each other for a moment.

"They're upstairs, waiting for you." She said.

More than one.

"Oh." George smiled politely as people do when the joke is in but they're out.

"I'll make some tea," she said softly, turning and walking to the end of the shop. George followed her until the far wall, and then she held up a soft palmed hand and indicated a narrow doorway, leading upstairs. George nodded and followed towards the doorway. He walked slowly up the steep and rickety staircase to a tiny passage, where he reached a single door.

Do I knock?

He balled his fist up tightly but the door swung inwards just as his arc came down. Carina stood with a mischievous smile on her face.

"Howdy," she said. "Thought you'd never show. Kept us waiting a while."

Us. Them.

"Come on in, fuck knuckles."

"Parker?" George said, incredulously.

"The one and only, baby cakes."

Carina slid to the side of the door, gesturing her arm like a magician's assistant about to demonstrate a trick. George entered the small room. He noticed that the furniture was still arranged as though the room were meant to be lived in. And then realised that the old lady downstairs probably did live up here. The floorboards were bare, and George felt them groan under his weight as he ventured further into the middle of the room. A slatternly armchair was drawn up to a small fireplace. Parker sat there, with his fingers arched into a steeple. There was one small window in the room, and underneath it occupying nearly a quarter of the room, was an enormous bed with the mattress still on it.

"You wouldn't have come if I'd just asked you, buddy."

"What's going on here?" George asked. He wanted to sound assertive, but the end of his question ended on a high note.

Parker thought for a moment, the way he often did, before answering. He looked directly at George, unblinking. When he spoke, his words fell a beat slower than average speaking pace.

"You followed us down the rabbit hole, George."

George felt hot. Magma level heat, radiating up through his body. Why was Parker talking about rabbit holes? What was going on? He wanted to scream at them both, for upsetting his daily routine. He could see Parker's neck snapping in his mind and it felt good. He wanted to pick up the chair Parker was sitting on and smash him in the face with it, splattering red blood on the dirty walls. What an improvement that would be.

"You're with The Movement?"

There was a small pause for dramatic effect, and then a nod of the head.

"And you've known about this?" George addressed Carina, with a sour little twist of his mouth. He felt betrayed by Carina, for duping him in the first place and leading him to this sketchy shop in a part of town he'd never been before.

"It's not her fault, George," Parker said. "I needed to know you were on board."

George felt flustered and idiotic. "*On board?*" He turned sharply at Parker, sitting contently on the armchair, as if nothing could rattle him. "On board for what, exactly?"

"Why, bringing down The Network of course."

George stared at Parker.

Carina grinned broadly. "We're fooling ourselves if we think top-down change will happen, George. We've been blindly watching stupid reality shows and playing video games while the Earth has gone past the tipping point and into an all-consuming oblivion. When The Network became the governing force of this country, we thought it was all over. The poverty. The suffering. The anarchy. But of course, one corruption simply took over another."

"You're both crazy," George replied carefully. "This is nonsense. You're talking about treason...about things outside of our control. To try and topple The Network would be like trying to heat a house by burning the furniture. It can't be done."

Parker and Carina shared a look – the kind of look, George summarised, of dog owners that had just witnessed their prize poodle defecating on the carpet. Parker stood up; his hands palmed in a conciliatory fashion.

"George...look around you. People are frightened by the Boilers out there, frightened by the lifestyle we've been groomed to accept.

Do you think its chance that most people who receive their Birthday Treats live in abject poverty? Do you look at the numbers, George? The Network will excrete statistics about fair percentages, but we know what it's always been about. It's a cull, George. When was the last time you saw an executive who earned more than six figures in a boiler suit? When was the last time you saw a fat old banker waddling down the street in bright orange? The Network preys on the fearful. They know that the Degenerates will gladly take out their frustrations and swelling anger on each other."

George studied the man in front of him. Who was this person? He no longer had the cadence that Parker from work exuded. It was as if the person he had known for the last few years was an imposter. He felt a mixture of emotions but bubbling above the surface of all of them was betrayal.

"You're mad." George said simply.

Parker snorted. It was the first action that reminded George of the Parker of old.

"What's madness, George? Repeating the same routine day in and day out for years and expecting different results? Frederick Henshaw never made it to the fifth day, did you know that?"

"Nonsense. It's documented. I've seen the videos."

"All doctored," Carina interjected. She had been quiet during this time, but George could see something behind her eyes. It was the same look she had when admonishing Kaleb in the pub the night before. "They used deep fake technology. The Movement have been able to secure the real footage of what happened to Freddy Henshaw. He made it to the third day, and it would have been close...but Agents gunned him down in sewers below East London."

Now it was George's turn to snort derisively.

"Show me the tapes then."

Carina sighed, looking at Parker. He simply shrugged.

"We don't have them with us, George."

"Well...that's convenient, isn't it?" George realised that he was sounding more and more like an impudent child. "You don't have it on your phone, no?"

Carina crossed her arms. "That footage is highly inflammatory material, George. Do you know what would happen if any member was caught with it on their phone?"

Parker made a small movement of his thumb across his neck.

"Well..." began George, feeling the ground opening before him. He should have just gone to work. Everything would have been fine if he'd just gone into work.

"It's been happening for years and with no change we'll continue to sacrifice the people we love to a fundamentally flawed system," Parker said. "We've been watching you for some time. That's what The Movement is all about. We-"

"What do you mean, you've been *watching* me?" George asked, curtly.

Parker raised his eyebrows. "You didn't think I worked in your department by accident, did you?"

George took an involuntary step back.

"And *you* of all people know about the dangers of Birthday Treats, George."

The letter. His daughter.

George hesitated, suddenly aware that a significant amount of time had elapsed and the air in the room seemed to have changed. Had become denser.

"You left the letter on my desk." It wasn't a question.

Parker slowly nodded. "Came in earlier and made sure no one saw me. Then simply waited for you to arrive and made my entrance a few minutes later."

The heat was pulsating from his face again. His head was splitting, like a burst marrow. Questions rattled around like pebbles in a shoe. How did he know about his daughter? How did he know he was going to get his Birthday Treat? Why him? He felt blood pumping through his neck.

Carina walked over to George, her shrewd eyes watching him unobtrusively as she rested her hand on his shoulder. "It's okay, George. What you've gone through...what you've endured – it's not your fault. You've cocooned yourself away for so long that you've swallowed the 'I don't care,' or 'I'm too busy to care,' party line for so long that it's your morning, afternoon, evening meals. This may all come as a shock to the system, but you know if you're being honest with yourself that you can't live with that anymore. Why did you come out with us, last night?"

George pulled away from her. "You don't know anything about me," George remarked quietly.

Carina sighed softly. As if she'd been here a hundred times before. "You came with us because you're not happy, George. You saw me and you saw some other fantasy life. And I perpetrated that imaginary world for you because you so desperately needed it. If we'd have more time then maybe, I don't know...maybe we could have carried on with that for a while. But time is against us." She took his hands in hers. It could not have been more than ten seconds, and yet it seemed an eternity that their hands were clasped together. He glanced down and took a mental snapshot of her long fingers, the smooth alabaster flesh under the wrist.

A whirring noise made Parker pat his pockets and take out his phone.

"How did you get mixed up in all of this?" George asked, as Parker conferred with someone on the other line.

Carina tilted her head to the side. "Just like you, I had a traumatic experience with someone close to me. A Birthday Treat."

George untangled his hand from hers. The exit was close. He could turn around, walk away and pretend this morning had never happened. Retreat into the shallow carapace of a life he'd created for himself.

Parker nodded enthusiastically on the phone and eyed George.

"That's great, Samson. We're at the antique shop. See you in five." He thumbed the phone off and turned to George. "As Carina mentioned, time is against us, George. The Movement is a system of like-minded individuals, people who were frightened by the daily news but wanted to escape the placation set upon them by The Network. There are people in The Movement from all walks of life and each person has a specific role to play. When we figured out how to make a revolution work, we diligently got to work. True revolution, the kind that sticks and makes the world safe for everyone is like evolution. But we know that like a deep-rooted weed, we'd need to be careful as we tried to extract it."

George shook his head. "You're living in a bloody fantasy world. Both of you. You can't beat them. What makes you think you can?"

Parker smiled. "Every positive change in history that I can think of began with peaceful protest. We've had those protests, George. But no-one ever gets heard. We just become a statistic for them, just a huddled mass of people bleating about how unfair everything is. We need something else that'll wake people up in the softest way possible but waking up is hard to do as you know. You're getting your Birthday Treat, George. I know you won't do anything with it. Nothing substantial at any rate."

"How do you know I'm getting mine? You can't be sure. You can't."

Carina eyed George softly. "As Parker said, The Movement have a lot of people involved in its infrastructure. It's not just a rag-tag bunch of idealists. We've been slowly building our army for years, now. Some of these people have invaluable skills. Some of these people can get access into their mainframe."

"Bullshit."

"It's true, George." Carina pulled out a folded piece of paper and handed it to him, before slowly walking to the small window in the room. "The Network pick the most vulnerable. The weakest. Those who have large families and not enough income to maintain them. They do this so that the lower classes will tear themselves apart. There's usually a couple of Birthday Treats per week. Sure, most people pick ABH or GBH, but there's a lot of people who enjoy their treats, that can't wait for them. They kill and they act out every sadomasochist fantasy they could ever conceive."

George thought about the girl at the train station again. The look on the boiler's face after he had committed to his act. Like he had unburdened himself. He opened the folded paper. It was a list of names. Hundreds.

"What is this?"

Carina stared out of the window, the grey ominous skies looking set to spill and pour open. "These are the people receiving their Treats. Your name is near the bottom, George. We've been planning this for a while."

George scanned the page. "You said that they target people with lower incomes. So why-?"

"Why you, Georgie boy?" Parker slapped his hands together. "Because they must throw in the odd anomaly now and then, to throw people off the scent. Imagine it, George – if it was just Destitute getting their Treats every week. There would be outrage. Sometimes, the middle men in the offices need to let off some steam, too. And unfortunately, you're a level seven drone worker bee. You're not important to them. Just a mundane person going about their life with no real aspirations or goals. You're expendable."

George sat down on the bed before his legs gave out. The mattress was old, as it caved in easily against his weight. "Why don't you just ask one of these other people on your list? Why me?"

Parker shot finger guns at George. "How long have I been working for you, George?"

George shrugged. "Six months?"

"And what do you think I've been doing in those six months?"

George didn't have a clue. All he'd known was that Parker was an underachiever, someone who he'd thought had been coasting through life on a wave of idleness, seeking nothing but the vast expanse of lethargy and gluttony.

"I was watching you, of course," he continued, reading George's reaction. "You have to realise, that we're taking a massive risk by approaching you like we're doing now. We don't reach out to just anyone, Georgie boy. I can see you've been distant over the last couple of weeks...getting nearer to your birthday. I can see the conflict inside you. And then the incident at work yesterday. You've accepted the way things for so long that the kettle finally boiled over."

Parker turned to Carina. "You should have seen our boy, Carina. Wow...it was marvellous. The way you threw that phone at the wall!"

George looked up from the list of names he'd been absently reading.

"You've been manipulating me this whole time. Saying things... treacherous things...pulling my guard down."

Parker swivelled and looked at George sternly. "I never manipulated anybody, George. I knew it was time. We can't live with that way of life anymore, and if you're being honest with yourself, instead of swallowing the bull they feed you day in and day out then you'll know you can't either."

George sat silently on the bed for a moment. Carina turned her gaze from the window.

"He's here," she said.

Parker nodded. He shouted down the stairs to the old lady who ran the antique shop to let the next guest up to the room.

"What do you know about my daughter?" George whispered.

"That's what's really going to bake your noodle."

Carina and Parker loomed over George. "And that's why I know you're going to help us."

There were some heavy steps and then a man appeared at the doorway. He was a large man, with a larger nose. The tip of it was bulbous and red, the capillaries burst. Likely a heavy drinker. George's stomach turned again, but this time he wasn't sure it was because he was hungry. He felt like he was going to be sick. This was all too much.

"Hey," the man said, eyeing George with caution.

"It's okay Samson. He's with us."

"The large man stood at the doorway, as if he were afraid to step into the room. "I picked her up last night from a club," he said. "Dropped her off in Chiswick but knew it was to throw off any Agents that would be asking questions. Double backed and followed at a distance to a house in Hammersmith."

"You know where she is now?"

"Well, if she stayed round the place. She was limping, so not sure what state she was in. Very cagey. As can be expected."

Parker assessed this information carefully.

"Who are you talking about?" George asked slowly. Saliva was building in his throat. He felt bile rising.

Parker was standing at his side and looked down at him intently. "The lass that's been running around for the last twenty-four hours. Alice Paige. *She's* your daughter, George."

George opened his mouth to say something, but no sound escaped. His face began to redden, and all the energy left his body. He had the impression of swimming up into this room from a ghostly plain, a sort of underwater world far beneath the old floorboards of the antique shop. How long he had been down there he did not know.

His stomach lurched again and this time he did vomit.

Then his phone pinged.

Hello Mr. Bryant!

Congratulations!

You've been successfully chosen for a BIRTHDAY TREAT! Your Network ID is: 2359876

Now it's time to activate your account so that we can prepare the next steps for your once in a lifetime opportunity to commit any infraction without ANY consequences!

Before you get started, we would STRONGLY recommend that you keep this information to yourself. Sign into your account at https://birthday.network.com/startnewlogin

1. Click the 'create your avatar' button on the dashboard menu
2. Choose your profile name and fill out any prerequisite questions on the screen. Please note that we have online psychiatrists that can answer any queries you may have.
3. Every SCOOP SUIT is fitted with an 8k GoPro camera – if you have a smartphone or tablet you can sync up with the instructions included!
4. Your Birthday is on the - - 29th - - of this month. Please select a morning slot between 6am and 9am when Network Agents will come round to deliver your SCOOP SUIT and answer any questions you may have.
5. You can choose a pre-selected SCOOP SUIT colour, but please note that there may be a fee included. Orange is the standardised colour.

Once you complete these steps, your account will be activated. You'll be able to join our online forums where past BIRTHDAY TREATERS can share their experiences with you!

Ready to get started? Check out our resources for new TREATERS at: https://support. network.com/getstarted

Our step-by-step guide will help you learn:
• Lacerations and cauterisations – know your wounds and how to treat them!
• A Navy Seal's Go-To Gear

- One-Bag BIRTHDAY TREAT essentials for your day of adventure!
- The Bold and The Beautiful: Hydrochloric acid and where you can find it
- Hit Them With The Pointy End: Your Guide to blades

We hope you have a great day tomorrow!

Yours,

The Network Team

- -

Important note: The Network periodically review accounts for security purposes and to verify billing information. We use cookies/share your information to customize ads. you can accept their use but you can disable them if you wish, See Privacy Policy & Terms Of Use.

15

KAVANAGH

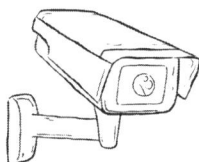

TUESDAY

83 HOURS REMAIN...

Kavanagh's nose was the star of his face, and not in a good way.

He lightly pinched the strip of white bandage across the bridge and a paroxysm of pain jolted through his skull as if a nail bomb had exploded inside it.

But pain was good.

Pain was helpful.

It kept him focused. Having spent all night and morning looking through CCTV footage, he'd need it.

One of the younger Agents rapped his knuckles against the window of the SUV. "They're ready for you," he said.

Kavanagh exhaled. He'd changed the dressing of the deep wound sliced in the flesh of his upper right arm. It had been heavily oozing blood and there was a bluish-purple bruise forming around it. He'd ordered one of the Agent underlings to get him a fresh shirt and had changed inside the back of the mud-splashed SUV, welcoming the small respite of sitting on soft leather.

Kavanagh lightly pressed his index finger against the centre of the cut and sucked in a sharp breath as the pain spiralled across his body. Colourful spots contoured the sides of his eyes and he had to bite his lip from the agony of it all. When it waned, he could move, and he breathed slow and deep until it had all passed.

He'd underestimated Alice Paige.

Whupped by a girl, eh? His father's voice cackled at the back of his mind. *Can't say I'm surprised. You remember that time when little Joni Cassidy from down the road beat your little skinny ass because you didn't give her a ride on your bike? Blubberin' like a little pussy. Oh, she gave you a good chat son, didn't she? You had yourselves quite a little chinwag, yes sir.*

"Shut up." Kavanagh muttered.

Dealing death had always been his business and it was the only trade he excelled at. He wasn't interested in the form of how people died, that was something Valentine looked forward to, no...Kavanagh was intrigued about the exhalation of the soul. The exit from the body. The way a lifeforce would simply slip away into the ether. Or the cosmos.

It had been something that had enthralled him as a child, and as far back as he could remember, Kavanagh had always taken great pains to find the moment of when a life stopped. It had begun with small insects, pulling the wings off flies, trapping a spider and piercing it with a knife, but they were too small, too insignificant to catch the moment.

They'd had a cat, once. Its name had been Petra. One unmemorable afternoon he walked down to his father's shed at the bottom of the garden and rummaged around until he found what he was looking for – a pair of thick garden gloves. Then he found Petra nuzzled by the garden fence, picked her up with the gloves and strangled her.

As expected, the cat hissed and clawed, gyrating and flailing its limbs to escape. But Kavanagh held on. It would be too quick to snap the creature's neck...he had to *squeeze* the life out of the feline. He wanted to see Petra's eyes glaze over just before the moment.

Ever since then he'd been trying to recapture that feeling. That instant of eventuality.

Something had awoken within him during his encounter with Alice Paige in the dilapidated building. She was resourceful and tough, not like any of the docile, complacent sheep that had given him nothing but apathy over the years.

He had been foolish to misjudge her. Perhaps it was his excitement of the chase itself that had overwhelmed his sensibilities, but after having a curt phone call with Cassandra Rey his focus had become laser sharp.

Alice Paige was a real challenge.

A challenge he would conquer.

He would make sure her death was not swift. Just like his cat, he would like to see her eyes blink out of existence. Maybe then he would be fulfilled. Maybe then his purpose would be complete.

The first thing he had done after receiving medical treatment for his nose (he was told that it wasn't broken but would likely swell in the coming hours) was put out a widespread bulletin stating that Alice Paige had been sighted in London. His attempt at containing the situation between himself and Valentine had been thwarted, which irked him greatly, but he was practical enough to realise that he may not be so lucky in the future. The hours were sweeping by rapidly and he was already late playing catch up.

He'd hurt her. Whenever his nose throbbed, he thought back to the satisfying moment of plunging the knife deep into her flesh. It was dark in the building, but he surmised that he'd cut her in the thigh. It had excited him. Not in a sexual way, but in a profoundly personal way. It had stirred him spiritually.

Unfortunately, it looked like he hadn't nicked any major arteries, otherwise they would have found her body by now. He and Valentine had followed the trail of blood for a couple of yards outside the building, but it became apparent that she had staunched the wound or had wrapped something around it to prevent any further leakage.

He admired her ingenuity.

The second thing he had remedied was obtaining a firearm. Now that he had been promoted to a hunting Agent it was standard issue, but in his haste to find Alice Paige he hadn't even thought about procuring it from HQ. Running into the abandoned building without a weapon had been a mistake. Kavanagh had thought that the brutish hulk of Valentine would have been enough, but he had been brash. He'd radioed in and the same junior Agent that had given him a new shirt also supplied the holster and weapon.

A Glock 17. Kavanagh knew all about that tough little weapon. Seven and a half inches long from firing pin to muzzle tip. It delivered quarter-ounce bullets at nearly eight hundred miles an hour. Seventeen rounds to a magazine, hence the name. It was light and compact. Snugging the holster over his shirt, he winced as he put on his jacket. He'd cut too deep on his arm, but he'd cut Alice Paige even deeper. He'd make sure of it.

Ryan Lando, the presenter of *Hunted* TV, was fluttering around outside the SUV, with his camera crew.

Mr. Square jaw and cheekbones. Just in time for the afternoon show.

Kavanagh knew the sort – the kind with a practised casual arrogance. It was a contrived kind of casual. A forced, albeit polished attitude. His smile was like the flicker of light across a razor's edge, a used car salesman brand. Part of the downside of putting out a bulletin was that the vultures came to peck at the crumbs. Kavanagh was aware of gangs – mostly Degenerates that tried to track down contestants of the show, armed with baseball bats, knives – whatever they could get their hands on, really. They were mostly unsuccessful with their attempts however, using the excuse to stalk people like Alice to get high and get wasted. He could only think of one occasion a few years back where a group cornered a contestant and had beaten them to death. Each member of the gang was given fifty Social Credit points and some cash for their reward.

He straightened and took a moment to compose himself. Ryan Lando would interview him about the progress of their hunt, and their little chat would be broadcast across the country. He was representing The Network. Every micro expression on his face would be scrutinised by so-called professionals to prattle on their own podcasts and media shows, so he'd need to be in control. He took another glance in the little mirror of the sun visor and smoothed down his slicked-back raven-black hair. It was shiny and perfect and could have been mistaken for one of those plastic wigs you snap down onto a Lego character. It was just a pity about the plaster across his nose. He considered taking it off but that would have looked worse on the high-def feed.

Stepping out of the SUV, he pinned Lando with a stare. It was appropriate to show an authoritative demeanour straight out the gate. Lando was wearing a burgundy suit – looking like an archaic relic from the disco era. The camera guy who was all jowls and belly hastily adjusted the camera on his shoulder and they came hurrying up to where Kavanagh stood. He felt better with the Glock 17 by his side now. Even took a moment to imagine whipping it out and firing several shots at the stupid reporter's face.

Show time.

"Agent Kavanagh!" Lando bellowed, all teeth and grins. "Would it be possible to have a moment of your invaluable time? We've got an audience simply biting at the bits to find out more about the search for Alice Paige."

Although he would never admit it, Kavanagh was secretly biting at the bits too. The CCTV footage they'd scrubbed through mainly showed drunkards and revellers in the heart of the city, but not much in the way of wounded young contestants trying to escape with their lives. Which meant that Alice knew where the blind spots were. Once again, even though his frustration levels were cranking higher with each hour wasted looking painstakingly through the footage, Kavanagh had to respect her tenacity.

"Of course," he said, patting his jacket down.

"Okay, let's roll in three...two..." Lando mouthed one and then paused briefly at the camera lens to perfect that charlatan beam of a smile.

"Things are developing with rapid speed in central London folks, as a confirmed sighting of contestant Alice Paige has everyone in a frenzy. I'm joined live with Agent Kavanagh of The Network. Agent Kavanagh, can you give us more insight into what happened here during the early hours of the morning?"

Kavanagh cleared his throat, adopting a stolid demeanour.

"Sure, Ryan. We were alerted that Alice Paige had removed her SCOOP suit and investigated the scene, and by using CCTV we were able to track her down to a decrepit building close by."

He failed to mention the dead boy of Mitchum. He wanted to keep that little chunk of information under wraps for the moment.

"Is it possible that we could investigate the building? There may be clues that *Hunted* viewers may find helpful in the investigation."

Kavanagh bristled at that. Like some fat couch potato at home would have all the answers by looking at a decaying mess of a hobo's filth home.

"Unfortunately not, Ryan. We're currently sweeping the area for forensic data and any encroachment by the public would endanger any potential information that could prove useful."

It was complete nonsense, of course. There were no Agents apart from the clean-up crew taking away the lifeless body of the hobo that attacked them, as well as several other bodies that the Degenerate had killed over the years, but Kavanagh felt Ryan Lando's wings needed to be clipped a little. He felt a small surge of delight as Lando's jawline clenched.

Thought you could get a few more episodes out of me, did ya buddy boy?

Ever the professional, Lando suddenly changed tact. "So how did she escape? I see the bandage on your nose, does that have anything to do with what happened in the building?" The lilt of Ryan's voice and the shit-eating grin that went with his words told Kavanagh that was a joke, so he laughed. It was a hollow, empty laugh.

Officious prick.

"The building homed several Destitute reprobates, and a skirmish ensued. Unfortunately, during this skirmish and with the little resources at our disposal at the time, Alison Paige managed to flee the area. Sometimes Ryan, when you get into the *real* action, you take a few blows."

Ryan Lando nodded his head, but he wasn't agreeing with Kavanagh.

"Uh-huh. Uh-huh. I see. So, Agent Kavanagh, where is Alice Paige right now?"

Kavanagh didn't appreciate Lando's tone, and where this thread was going. He needed to shut this down.

"We're collating with various tech departments, as she's been spotted on several cameras after her escape. Now if you'll excuse me-"

"So you haven't seen the latest footage?" Lando said, whipping out a tablet. Before Kavanagh could respond he was playing a vid. Like a shark smelling the appetising whiff of chum, the cameraman immediately turned to Kavanagh as Lando thrust the tablet toward him.

The film appeared to be taken from a mobile phone. Three young guys hanging around outside a club. One with a slick back hairdo was rapping at the camera, some nonsensical words about baby powder and where he'd apply it to a certain celebrity's undercarriage. Kavanagh could see a bouncer at the door, watching the drunken tomfoolery unfold with disinterest. Behind the ponytailed rapper, the door of the club opened and a couple walk by, but they're not in the shot long enough to make out. The soon-to-be viral rapper continues to wax lyrical but turns his head and stops suddenly.

"Hey!" He shouts to someone off screen. Kavanagh could tell he's had a few drinks, as he staggered a little when he yells this.

"Do I know you?"

The fourth guy, the one with the camera phone, pans towards where slick back rapper is hollering, and Kavanagh sees her then. Alice Paige. She has her arm around someone, and she's trying to hide her face, but Kavanagh knows.

"I swear I know you..." Slick back rapper exclaims, his brow furrowed in determination. The bouncer that had been impartially involved so far, turns his head and looks at something else off camera.

"Hey! Wait a second. How do I-"

The bouncer seems to put two and two together.

"Shit," the bouncer says, almost a whisper. He points to the thing he's looking at off screen, and all eyes of the group follow his finger. Camera phone boy snaps to what they're all looking at. It's a digital billboard of Alice Paige's *Hunted* TV profile. She had jet black hair, but the leather jacket is unmistakable. The camera comes back to the group and there's a moment where everyone looks at each other with wide eyes.

"Are you telling me that's Alice Paige?" Slick back rapper says, almost in disbelief.

"There's no way..." the bouncer replies. They do a comical double take at the girl, and camera phone sweeping back just as Alice and the guy she's with get into a car.

"*That's her! That's fucking Alice Paige!*"

Suddenly the group of boys and the bouncer are running towards the car. The camera whips up and down with the motion of the sprint. Out of breath, the feed focuses on the car as it pulls away, leaving them behind.

"Bruv! That was Alice Paige. Ohmygosh!"

Slick back rapper starts to screech into the camera where you can find him on social media, as Lando turned off the tablet.

He looked at Kavanagh with a *two can play this game* smile. In that moment Kavanagh hated Ryan Lando with every fibre of his being.

He couldn't let this spiral.

"Yes, we're aware of the footage," Kavanagh replied, in the coolest voice he could muster. "As I told you, we're collating with our tech departments. Now, if you'll excuse me Mr. Lando, we have a participant to catch."

Kavanagh walked away from Lando and the cameraman then. He didn't care if they decided to chase his back, calling out other questions. The seething anger boiling inside would have to be released somehow. He went calmly back to the SUV and opened the back door. With the tinted windows, no one would be able to see him plunge his face into the cushioned leather seating and let out a silent scream.

Half an hour later, Valentine sauntered over to the SUV with a tablet in one hand and a burrito in the other.

Kavanagh scowled at the colossal Agent as he opened the door and awkwardly arranged himself into the back seat.

"Where do you even find the time?" Kavanagh asked, snatching the tablet from him.

Valentine shrugged as he chomped half the burrito in one mouthful.

"And you couldn't even get me one?"

Valentine looked up. After a pause he shook his head.

Kavanagh's fingers danced an arpeggio on the display and various windowed feeds came online. He examined the screens carefully.

"The footage from the camera phone was too far away to ascertain the car license plate," he explained to Valentine, "I've gone over it again and again but there's nothing to tell us about the car. However, I can pull up other feeds in that area."

He tapped a few more times on the console and brought up one main screen.

"This," he lamented, "is the closet camera to the car. It's a taxi, which is good – that narrows down the field. But it'll take time we don't have to find the right one. Let's see if we can get the number plate..."

He punched in a few more keys. This image was taken far away, likely from a camera positioned high on a tower block. But it was at an angle that showed the front of the cab. He could make out the small ant-like figures of the boys and bouncer chasing after the car as it sped away. He focused the picture to the license plate of the cab. With a few more commands on the tablet the image bloomed, and he waited patiently as the screen buffered to load the extremely zoomed image.

He slapped the tablet on his lap when the image finally came through. "Fuck!" The image was too pixelated to discern the numbers.

Kavanagh rubbed his forehead. He could hear his father's shrill cackle at his misfortune. *Whupped again by the same girl, eh?* His father mocked. *Can't say I'm surprised. Never had the stomach for taking care of business. Real busines, I mean. Your mother coddled ya too much. Made you soft. Like a limp dick at an orgy. Sucked on that teat for too long. But you and I son, we're going to have a little chat. Yes sir, we're going to have ourselves a nice little chinwag, aren't we?*

"Okay Valentine, we're going to need to contact all the various taxi and private cabs in the area that were working this morning. Get some other Agents to-"

He stopped.

Kavanagh reached out and brought the tablet up close. He needed to be sure. From this angle he could clearly make out the cab driver with a snub nose, Alice's pained expression...but more importantly, he could make out with clear definition the person sitting next to her. There was no mistake.

He had retired his grandmother, after all.

"Well...what a small world. Hello Brian."

Statement of informer [REDACTED] (10.30pm)
Interview Conducted by Cassandra Rey
Informant codename: J

CASSANDRA REY: I understand you have some information for us?

J: Nah, nah, that's not how this is gonna work.

CASSANDRA REY: Oh?

J: First, I want immunity. Second, I want enough Social Credits to keep me happy for a lifetime.

CASSANDRA REY: You think you're bargaining with us [REDACTED]?

J: Bargaining? Lady, I'm giving you The Movement on a fucking silver platter. I think that deserves a little quid pro quo, y'know what I mean?

CASSANDRA REY: [REDACTED], what makes you think anything you have to say will be relevant to us?

J: Well, I'm sitting in this little cushy office, ain't I? Must mean something if I'm talking to you, right? Do I have your attention now, lady?
[Silence for ten seconds.]

CASSANDRA REY: Let's say…hypothetically, that you did have something worthwhile that The Network could use as part of its anti-social legislation to combat those against us. How did you come by this information?

J: Because I used to one of 'em.

CASSANDRA REY: You're admitting that you once used to be involved in a terrorist party movement group?

J: Hey, y'know what? I just had a thought…there's a third stipulation. My ma turns sixty in a few years. You can take her off the recycling list, right?

[CASSANDRA motions with her hands. Two uniformed Agents approach the desk.]

CASSANDRA REY: You find yourself in a perilous situation, [REDACTED] I'd think very carefully about your next words.

J: I rolled the dice. Figure I'm better off being a Network stooge than a flunky for those arseholes.

CASSANDRA REY: You're very bold, aren't you?

J: Fortune favours 'em, I guess.

[CASSANDRA REY clicks her fingers. There is scuffling noise, followed by strained gurgling.]

CASSANDRA REY: You do realise that I could end you right now and no-one would none the wiser. No-one saw you enter, and no-one will certainly see you leave. Do you have *my* attention now, [REDACTED]?

J: *Yesssh.*

CASSANDRA REY: Good.

[CASSANDRA REY clicks her fingers. There is audible wheezing and spluttering.]

J: Fuckssake…

CASSANDRA REY: Let's play a game, you and I. You're so enamoured with quid pro quo, so let's get down to it. You give me something that we can use and then I will generously give you something you can use. Let's start with a few names of your 'ex' party members, shall we?

J: Sure…sure…but because of that little stunt I have a fourth request.

CASSANDRA REY: My…we are full of beans today, are we not?

J: One of the members…you don't touch 'em. You don't go near 'em. Understand?

CASSANDRA REY: Names first.

J: One of the main guys…calls himself Parker. Don't think that's his real name but he's got connections. Knows how to get things, where to 'hide' people, if you get my drift?

CASSANDRA REY: Oh, don't worry [REDACTED] – I'm drifting, all right.

[To one of the Agents]

CASSANDRA REY: Get this information to our people on the ground. Right now.

16

ALICE

TUESDAY

82 HOURS REMAIN...

Alice awoke with a start.

It took her a moment to come to her senses. The walls were different, she wasn't familiar with the room she was in.

How did I get here?

She was on someone's sofa and she was about to call out but there was no strength in her voice, just a whisper. Her forehead was damp with sweat. She felt everything was damp with sweat. Even under a light cotton sheet she was radiating heat like a brick right out of the oven. She put the nightmare of Eugene and Janet to one side of her sweltering brain – she hadn't thought about her time under their 'care' for some time now.

You're burning up girl, Boss Bitch voice told her matter-of-factly.

When that Agent pig stuck you with his knife. You're gonna need antibiotics. Somewhere to rest. Somewhere to chill.

She couldn't rest. She couldn't chill. She needed to get out of London, go where no one would be able to find her. She'd already spent far too long in the belly of the beast, and she'd nearly been caught twice now.

The club. The cab. The guy.

She was in the guy's house. Tentatively, she leaned back against the arm of the sofa, her body aching, cheeks flushing. A momentary chill tremored from the tip of her head to the bottom of her toes and she realised she was shivering.

Not good, Boss Bitch noted. *Not good at all.*

Alice closed her eyes for a few moments, felt the world around her sway like a swing so opened them again. She felt dehydrated.

She tried to stand and found it extremely difficult.

"Oh, you're awake Roxanne."

Lifting her heavy head, she saw the boy from last night. His ERD throbbed a

Brendan? Bernard? Shit, what was his name? Her brain felt it was stuffed with a thousand cotton balls. She'd have to pay attention to the small details like someone's name, if she wanted to survive the next few days.

"It's me, Brian."

That answers that, then.

She cleared her throat that seemed clogged up like her bathroom plughole and asked for a glass of water.

Brain pointed at the sink.

Nice to know chivalry isn't dead, she thought, as she shuffled over to the kitchen. Her side seared with pain with every step, and she remembered the Agent in the abandoned building giggling like a schoolboy as he stuck her with the blade.

Kavanagh. That's what he called himself.

There was a name she wouldn't be forgetting in a hurry.

She ran the tap and just lapped at the cold stream. The water felt good, and she started inhaling gulps.

Brian looked on with an impassive face.

Maybe she could stay here for the next couple of days? *Too risky. By now they would have found the cab I travelled in last night.*

That made her think.

"Brian," she said, turning off the tap and wiping her mouth, "how long was I out for?"

Brian smiled as she mentioned his name. His ERD flashed and she could see his face turn red. He fidgeted uncomfortably, like a child catching a glimpse of a porno mag for the first time.

"Oh, you've been sleeping for most of the day." He said idly.

Shit.

She looked at the clock on the far wall. It was early evening. Looking out the window, the sky was the colour of fading denim. She had wanted a few hours to think about her next step, but the couple of hours would have cost her.

They could be on their way right now, the Insidious Voice whispered, *it wouldn't have taken them long to find the cab you were in.*

But she made him drop them off in Chiswick. That was a couple of miles from where she was now.

Could she take the risk?

The doorbell rang.

"I'll get it," Brian said, cheerfully.

Her head felt gummy, but in that instant things started to click into place. Like the way a cold, hard slap could sober a drunk person. She couldn't be seen with Brian; she couldn't be seen at all.

"No, Brian, wait…"

It was too late.

Brian was already opening the door as Alice bolted down the hallway.

"Oh. It's you again. Hi Agent Kavanagh."

HAPPY HORGAN: You've joining us live in the studio, folks – The Happy Horgan show is proud to announce that we have with us Dave Lazer, front man of The VamPyrates and long-term squeeze of current contestant in *Hunted TV*, Alice Paige!

DAVE LAZER: Yeah, alright Happy?

HAPPY HORGAN: Well, I think a lot of our listeners would like to know…are *you* okay, Dave? Our sources tell us that you were being interrogated for most of yesterday.

DAVE LAZER: It was nuffin', innit?

HAPPY HORGAN: And I can't help but notice you're sporting a new piece of eyewear.

DAVE LAZER: The patch? Ah mate, that's just…like, you know…fashion. Innit? It brings me to the reason why I'm on your show.

HAPPY HORGAN: Oh?

DAVE LAZER: Yeah, yeah. We're, like…taking the band in a new direction.

HAPPY HORGAN: Is that so? That's interesting, Dave. Since Alice Paige has become a contestant on *Hunted TV*, sales on your debut album '*Snot Grass City*,' have skyrocketed in the charts. Some critics are calling it incendiary - a throwback to the haughty primitive thrash of early punk with a dash of political sneering from the side-lines. It's resonating with a lot of the younger crowd, Dave. Lyrics like: 'Down with The Network/They're feeding you bullocks/but we're all mindless jerks/gulping down their rubbish…' is getting quite the attention. We can't play it here on the show for obvious reasons, but some of the clubs are jumping back on the punk bandwagon.

DAVE LAZER: Yeah…well…you gotta roll with the times, Happy, y'know?

HAPPY HORGAN: A rolling stone gathers no moss, eh?

DAVE LAZER: You what, mate?

HAPPY HORGAN: Never mind. So new line up? What happened to the other members of the band?

DAVE LAZER: Err…yeah. Yeah, as I said, we're going in a new direction.

HAPPY HORGAN: Is it true that the new bassist comes from The Network manufactured band, Up With Production?

DAVE LAZER: Where you gettin' your info?

HAPPY HORGAN: We've got some great researchers working for us.

DAVE LAZER: Listen, right…we're just trying new sounds…less…

HAPPY HORGAN: Political?

DAVE LAZER: Yeah…well, we'll always have politics in the background, like…just not in yer face.

HAPPY HORGAN: Sounds a little convenient don't you think? Being in The Network's building for more than twelve hours and then suddenly announcing a new band member. And a new fashion accessory?

DAVE LAZER: Think what you like, Happy. Think what you like, mate. I'm only here to plug the new album we'll be releasing in a few months. If our fans are digging the tunes now, wait till they hear our second album. Follow us on -

HAPPY HORGAN: Can you tell us if you've been in contact with Alice?

DAVE LAZER: Uhh..no.

HAPPY HORGAN: Do you have a message for her, if she's listening?

DAVE LAZER: [coughs] Well…what with the new member of the band, Yoko…joining us….umm…y'know…well, I'd like to tell her in person, like…but we may not get that chance, will we?

HAPPY HORGAN: You're telling your girlfriend –

DAVE LAZER: Ex-girlfriend, Happy. Ex. Just want to make it perfectly clear that we broke up before she got her Birthday Treat. I told her she should have taken it, Happy. Trust me on that.

HAPPY HORGAN: We've got to break for commercials but stay tuned to find out more about Dave Lazer's new autobiography in the works, which chronicles the early days of The VamPyrates, as well as meeting Alice Paige and their journey together.

DAVE LAZER: Yeah…yeah thanks Happy.

- From The Happy Horgan Live Show
@Happyhorgan

Case #403

NetworkID: 8716367 Bryant, G.

Time: 09:27am

8716367: It's okay…take your time. It's important not to withhold.

#403: …they don't tell you that the screaming will be so…intense. Y'know?

8716367: Who's screaming [REDACTED]?

#403: The kid…the fucking kid. Every day. Every fucking day. They say at the hospital that it's, like, a phase? But this was over six months. Constant. Gripper…my old man…he said that there's two types of screaming for babies…there's wailers and there's the ones that shriek. I had one that fucking blew the decibels off the scale. Grabber…he's part of a gang, y'know? But I'm his old lady, so when I got pregnant, it was like, this is it, okay? Time to settle down. Time to become a family. Get out of that business, I said.

8716367: And what business was that?

#403: Fuck you, asshole. I'm not talking about that. This is all confidential, right? Like that priest, confessional thing, yeah?

8716367: Of course. I was just trying to paint a picture of –

#403: Well Bob fucking Ross, paint a fucking mountain, y'hear? This 'aint about Gripper's biz. It was the lifestyle. Needed to change. We thought the baby would do that for us.

8716367: But it didn't?

#403: Fuck no. Made it worse. You think Gripper wants to be in a house with a crying baby all the time? Red puffy face and snot all over everything? That's another thing they don't tell you at the hospital. The amount of shit and piss and snot. Gave Gripper all the excuse to leave and go off running with some fucking whore. Could smell the cheap perfume every time he came back. But then the baby would start crying again and we'd get into it.

261

8716367: It sounds like you may have experienced some post-natal depression. Did you ever feel -

#403: I don't get fucking depressed about anything, asshole. You're not listening to me. Why does no-one ever listen to me?

8716367: I'm sorry [REDACTED]. I'm listening. Go ahead.

#403: This goes on for a while, y'see? Now I realise that I'm the OLD lady holding the fucking baby. Not just his old lady, y'see what I'm sayin'? Nah…fuck that. Fuck that shit right out of Kansas.

8716367: And then you got your Birthday Treat.

#403: …and then I got my Treat.

8716367: [REDACTED]…it tells me here…it tells me…you suffocated your baby. Is that right?

#403: It was the only way.

8716367: …what about Gripper?

#403: What about him? Was the best…best fucking decision I ever made. Now…we're back, just like old times. No more running around with whores, no more excuses late at night on the phone. No more –

8716367: How did he feel about it?

#403: We're good. We're real…good, y'know. Feels like old times.
First couple of weeks were rough, y'know? But in the end –

8716367: Is that what he told you?

#403: Yeah…I mean…we haven't really spoken about it, y'know? It's something we both said from day one…if we get a Treat, it is what it is. Like old times. We can smoke and drink and party again. Just like…old times.

8716367: [REDACTED]?

#403: Just like…old times. That's what we wanted, y'know? It's what we both wanted.

8716367: You know what I think? I think it's the worst decision you've ever made.

#403: I…I…FUCK YOU, ASSHOLE!

[Call Terminated. The Network has noted second Terminated Call within 24 hours for subject BRYANT, G. Noted in Log. Prep for full evaluation of caller's behavioural patterns.]

17

GEORGE

TUESDAY

83 HOURS REMAIN...

The cab peeled away from the curb and shot down the street like a bullet.

George didn't feel any better, and glumly sat wedged in-between Carina and Parker. Her knee lightly brushed against his thigh when they turned a corner or hit a pothole, which made him feel hot and flustered. But Parker's knee also did the same thing on the other side, which made him flustered, just in a different way. Parker hadn't been quiet since they entered the cab. George just wanted solitude and peace now.

"What is fascism, George?"

George shrugged. If his shoulders could sloop any further, he'd be able to touch his toes.

"Fascism is a by-product of a society without imagination. Look outside these windows, George. What do you see out there?"

George assumed his question was rhetorical, so remained silent.

Alice Paige couldn't be his daughter.

It was impossible.

These people were lying to him.

Parker continued his diatribe. George could see the shining eyes of someone possessed. A fanatic.

"What is the opposite of Freedom? Fear. I see fearful people on the streets every day. I see the same look on their faces and it sickens me to the core. For years, these people have let fear control them. They've let The Network slowly eradicate any kind of free-thinking and have replaced old rulings with barbaric showboat gameshows. They say our world is a paradise of draconian laws enforced by unthinking executioners. I say freedom is a state of mind. A man with imagination has no borders, no laws, no restrictions."

George wondered if he should ask the cabman to stop.

"Parker, I don't think George wants to hear this at the moment."

Parker craned his neck round and pointed a finger at Carina. George could smell the cheap scent of aftershave, and in his heart a feeling of defeat and resentment encapsulated inside him a shell of despair and hopelessness.

"He needs to hear it, Carina. Our schedule has been changed and we don't have much time."

"Time for what?" George croaked. It was the first time he had spoken inside the cab. His voice seemed distant and far away.

Parker smiled. "Why, revolution of course, Georgy boy."

"I'm not one of your revolutionists," he moaned, closing his eyes. Perhaps if he kept them closed, all of this would go away. He would wake up in his bed and the last couple of days would have been a dream. Perhaps he would have a nice cup of warm cocoa.

Carina placed a hand on his knee. It was at the same time exhilarating and pathetic and brought him back to reality.

"George, that's exactly why we need you." She looked at him with those pleading eyes and George couldn't help but feel a pang of lust again. "Our people get rounded up like cattle and are never seen again," she continued. "We've been waiting for...*I've* been waiting for, praying for, top-down change, but I know it won't happen that way. We're fooling ourselves if we think it will. We'll claw at each other like animals just like we did before The Network came into power. With you on our side, we can do that. We can make change."

Parker nodded. "And it's change in one building that we need you for when you get your Treat."

The cab lurched to the side as Samson turned violently down one of London's sprawling streets. George felt his guts heave again.

"What building? What is this all about?"

Parker straightened himself upright.

"Here's a scenario for you George. Remember when the vaccinations came out for COVID-19?"

George vaguely did. It was such a long time ago. He nodded anyway.

"Look what happened to our young and bright years later. Seventy per cent of children under the age of ten have ERD discs and the mental capacity of a dim lightbulb. You think that's coincidence?"

George remained silent. He'd heard the conspiracy theories. He'd read the articles.

"Our environment determines our social evolution," Parker continued, and in turn our social evolution determines our biological evolution. And it's all rotten, Georgy boy. Rotten to the core. We don't even stop to dwell on the fact that the number one cause of death of our minors is suicide - yes, children killing themselves. And for the record, that means our culture - the one we accept so passively - killed them. I can't live with that. Not anymore."

Carina applied pressure to his knee. He turned and looked at her then – what Parker had said had touched a nerve. In that instant, he knew the reason why Carina had joined The Movement.

"And it's about to happen again," she said.

"What do you mean?"

"That tipping point I mentioned earlier," Parker said, "we're already way past it, George. The Network thought that by dulling the population and keeping them indoors with Free-Vees, that would sort out the problem. That by keeping them entertained with vicious shows that would quell the rioting and the looting and the general unrest. And it did, for a while. I'll give them that. But with the vaccinations that corrupted the generation after COVID-19, they still weren't able to sort out the real problem."

Samson barked at them that they were a few minutes away from their destination.

"Which is?"

"The real problem," Parker sighed, "is overpopulation. Always has been. We have it on good authority that The Old man of The Network will be announcing something special over his blog today or tomorrow. Whether it's the imminent danger of a new virus, or some fucking energy drink that will make you smarter, be sure that he'll proclaim some type of new drug that will be mandatory for the population to take."

George furrowed his brow. The cab came to a stop and Parker looked out the window, assessing the area.

"I don't get it," George said.

"Sterilisation, Georgy boy. The Network is going to neuter half the world."

Parker and Carina's doors opened at the same time and they shot out. George shuffled over to follow but Carina closed the door on him. Samson opened the window a crack.

"You should stay here, George." Parker said.

"Why?"

"There could be Agents around looking for Alice. You'll be compromised if you're caught with us as you have your Birthday Treat in a few days. We'll evaluate the situation, but we may need to leave in a hurry. Listen, we'll grab her, come back and then I'll direct us to the safehouse."

Samson grunted an affirmation.

"Safehouse?" George asked.

Parker looked around him nervously, as if by being at the window of the cab was enough to get caught by Agents.

"I'll explain everything later. Let's just get out of the open, okay?

Samson's got some good jokes to tide you over until we get back. Tell him that one about Cambodia. You'll love it Georgy boy."

George locked eyes with the cab man in the rear-view mirror. By the stare he received back it appeared he wanted to do anything else but share jokes.

"Great." George said flatly.

Carina looked at the massive high-rise against the ragged skyline. The apartment building seemed like a red-brick behemoth. The walls were defaced with graffiti and it looked like anything that broke stayed broken. Perhaps sitting in the car with Samson was the better option after all.

"What floor?" Carina asked.

The cab driver shook his hand from side to side. "I reckon fifty-third. I waited and counted the levels when I saw the motion light turn. It's the last flat on that level."

"Have you got it?" She asked.

Samson lifted a small duffel bag that he'd been keeping under his seat.

"Not sure the clothes will fit, but there's some sunglasses, a few masks, overnight provisions. Won't be great under scrutiny but should do the job in a tight fix. Also got that other thing, too." He tapped his nose as he passed the bag through his open window.

Carina shouldered the duffel bag and nodded her head. With that, Parker and Carina scurried away and became enveloped in the building's lower atrium. Shortly they were out of his eyesight.

George sighed, sitting back in his seat. Now that Carina and Parker were gone, he had time to think. How had the morning degraded so fast in such a short time? If he'd gone to work none of this would be his problem. He could sit idly by and just let things sort themselves out. *Things* always sorted themselves out.

But that's what you do all the time, isn't it Georgy boy?

Let things resolve themselves. Don't disrupt the flow and everything would turn out okay in the end. It's how he had stayed married to Elspeth for such a long time, even though he was desperately unhappy. Because the routine dictates. It's how he took his morning protein pills for all the vitamins in the alphabet even though secretly he knew they didn't do anything for him. Because the routine dictates. It's why he ate his greens and tried to stay healthy.

Because the routine dictates.

Did he really believe what Parker and Carina told him? Why was he still with them if he didn't?

Because you're a coward. Because if you tried to leave, they would have stopped you. And you hate confrontation, don't you? You'd rather go along with it even though every fibre of your being wants to be somewhere else right about now.

George the coward. Pathetic George. George the lowly. One of those titles would be emblazoned on his tombstone when he died. He knew it.

"So, I'm in Cambodia, chilling at the beach and meeting people, as you do, chatting away and drinking," Samson said suddenly, breaking George from his meddling thoughts. "One of the guys I meet is Jurgen. He's as wide as he is tall, and he has this fantastic big belly that sticks out like a barrel. But that's not what stands out about Jurgen. No, what stands out, is the enormous tattoo that he has written across his torso, over his belly. Five letters. One word. PIZZA."

George blinked, and nodded his head.

"We're drinking and getting to know each other; y'know, the way things go...but my mind keeps wandering back to the tattoo. What's the significance of it? What does it mean? Does it represent his social commentary on the state of the world? Is it a pet name? And the longer we sit there drinking, the more determined I am to work it out. So eventually, after a lot of beers, I pipe up with the question.

'Hey, Jurgen'

'Yes, Samson'

'Can I ask a question?'

''Course you can Samson.'

'What does the Pizza tattoo mean... Is it a childhood nickname? Does it have a symbolic or deeper meaning?'

And Jurgen puts down his beer and looks me square in the eye and says:

269

'No, I just love Pizza.'

Samson burst into laughter at the memory. George kindly chortled along too, but it was hollow and short. Samson's booming laughter quickly ceased, and he stared out the window.

"That was a good one," George said, as if he needed to validate the cab driver's ego. Samson gave a shrug, as if he had a whole stand-up show prepared. George didn't feel in the mood to listen to anymore.

"I'm just going to stretch the legs," he said.

"Okay, but don't go too far. You heard Carina."

George truly didn't know if that was a threat. The cab man was big, and his belly touched the steering wheel of the car. He wondered briefly if he had a tattoo of the word pizza inscribed across it but felt queasy again.

Fresh air, that was what he needed.

The cab was parked in an almost empty parking lot surrounded by a concrete basin and construction equipment. Looking over his shoulder George noted a playground that was brimming with young children, mothers and buggies. The playful din of infants wailing in the background soothed him a little, as if the sound anchored him to reality. Looking at some of the kids running around, George felt happy and melancholy at the same time.

He took in a large gulp of air and started walking towards the high- rise. He glanced back at the cab and exchanged a look with Samson to indicate he wasn't wondering far. Leaning against the high-rise wall covered with graffiti, he felt an urge to have a cigarette. He couldn't remember the last time he had smoked, but it must have been at least fifteen years.

Probably around the same time that you thought everything in this world would kill you, he mused to himself. The routine had weighed him down for years now: check his eyes in the morning. Take his protein pills. Eat three pieces of fruit a day. Don't sit in a seat for more than an hour. Light exercises in the afternoon and evening. Eat vegetables. When had he become so formulaic in his routines?

There were a lot of questions floating around in his head. Parker had mentioned a safehouse, and a building that he could walk into. What had The Movement planned for him? He thought again about Carina, the kiss at the party. Had it all been simply to lure him over to their cause? He shuddered at the ridiculousness of it all. He'd acted like a fool, like a giddy schoolboy that had been told by the prettiest girl in the class that he was attractive. But George Bryant knew the truth – he'd never been the popular boy at school. None of the girls looked at him that way. So why would things change years later? He sighed, looking upward at the layers of concrete and blue sky above him.

If only he'd gone to work that morning.

He glanced over at Samson, who was now talking animatedly on the phone as he jabbed a finger at something. George pushed himself off the wall, following the trajectory of where Samson was pointing. He looked up again, but this time could see someone dangling off a balcony.

You don't see that every day.

George ran to the cab.

"She's on the fucking balcony Carina!" Samson cried, his cheeks scarlet. "Get to the flat below and hook her in, for Christ's sake. She's literally holding on to the ledge with her fingertips!"

George opened his mouth and stared at the cab driver for a moment.

"Should I...should I do something?" he said.

Samson cradled the phone on his shoulder and thrust his gesticulating finger at George.

"Get up there, help them," he said, before returning to the conversation with Carina.

Okay, George. Time to man up. Time to do something with your life.

George turned, started half-running, half jogging to the tenement block.

Time to see your daughter.

And then he saw something that made him stop.

George frowned. He understood what he was seeing, it was a simple shape above him, and he knew what the shape looked like, but the meaning of the event eluded him. Why would this form be falling from such a height? The silhouette above him was becoming larger, and George realised with unnerving clarity that the arms of the body were pinwheeling, like a comical Wile E. Coyote.

As if in a trance, George followed the shape as it descended now at zero velocity, watching in awe as the body turned and barrelled like a circus performer within a mammoth tent. But he knew there were no safety nets in this circus performance. George had half a second to realise the placement of where the shape would fall.

He wanted to shout out at Samson to burn rubber, to drive away from the parked area, to leave the car, to dash out of the door, to do anything – but he only had time to open his mouth and utter:

"Shit."

There was an explosion of broken glass with a bone crushing metallic collision. It seemed like a million fragments of glass burst away from the cab like knives through the air. The roof crumpled like paper. A short but unbroken silence followed, the first true quiet, George observed, that he had known for days.

Embedded in the crushed roof of the cab, was the body of Parker.

George had never been the type of boy to throw a pumpkin from a great height on Halloween as a trick on some poor, unsuspecting neighbour, but he imagined what he saw in front of him was how the pumpkin would look like afterwards.

Parker's innards littered the rooftop of the cab, and Parker himself was bent at unnatural angles. His arms flopped stupidly to the side, as if they were trying to grope something in the air.

George thought about the girl that had been thrown on the tracks when the Boiler had his Birthday Treat.

He wondered why Parker hadn't screamed.

Department of Information public poll:

65% in favour of Agents retiring contestant Alice Paige before 5-day goal

28% in favour of Alice Paige surviving

7% Undecided

- From The Department of Information website

@minstry_info

18

KAVANAGH

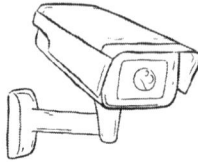

TUESDAY

82 HOURS REMAIN...

"...Agent Kavanagh?"

The ERD on Brian Bowerman's forehead pulsated a canary yellow.

"Hello, Brian." Kavanagh said, smiling. If Alice Paige was in the flat under an alias, which he believed she was, he didn't want to spook Brian and cause a scene. If she wasn't sleeping or in the shower or toilet, then she would have heard his name when Brian opened the door. Fortune favoured him in this instance though, as they were on the fifty-third floor and there was no way that she would be able to jump out of the window or hide in a basement or attic space.

No, he would play this smart. Just as smart as the girl. He would say they were here for their inspection, have a little look around and if needed wait for the calvary. He had her trapped (*If she* was *still here*) and he wouldn't let her escape again. Not a second time.

"I thought the inspection wasn't due until a few weeks?" Brian asked nervously.

Kavanagh considered this. He gazed at Brian for a moment, the look of a Headmaster who would brook no nonsense. He would treat nonsense harshly. Just as his father had.

"It's procedure, Brian. Now, be a good lad and let me have a look around, yes?"

Brian shrugged, as if it didn't bother him, and stepped back from the door, allowing Kavanagh to walk past.

"You can close the door, Brian." Kavanagh said this loud enough so that anyone else in the flat would hear. "In fact, better safe than sorry. Bolt it shut."

Brian obeyed, fiddling with the latch on the door.

Kavanagh's hand lightly unfastened the safety strap of his sidearm. It was a deft move and fast enough that Brian wouldn't be able to see if he decided to turn around at that moment. He needed to be careful here, as Alice could spring out at him like a cornered animal. He already had underestimated the girl once. But he always learnt from his lessons.

"Do you want anything to eat? I can make you some beans if you like?" Brian asked.

Kavanagh slowly walked down the hallway, peering into the bathroom as he made his way to the living room. He noticed something in the bath but would come back to that once he had conducted a full sweep. So far, nothing out of the ordinary. The Free-Vee was on, and that damned reporter Ryan Lando was gibbering on about the latest *Hunted* TV news.

"Or I can get you a squash. I think we have Apple and Blackcurrant, but Nan used to get those for me, and I'm not sure if I've drunk it all…"

Brian was babbling. Kavanagh was undecided if it was because of the boy's simple ways, or if he felt intimidated. He sometimes forgot that being in the presence of an Agent was like being interrogated by a police officer. It was weird how they could get you running your mouth off, as if you had a decomposing body in the boot of your car... or if you were hiding a well-known fugitive in your flat. Kavanagh said nothing, panning his eyeline around the living room, moving methodically and deliberately.

"You seem nervous, Brian," Kavanagh said, as he nudged one sofa with his knee, before checking behind it. There wasn't any cupboards or wardrobes in the living room, just a single double-glazed door leading out onto a small stone balcony wide enough to accommodate two chairs, which gave a panoramic view of Hammersmith. It had a geometric railing like those on low-income apartment buildings of yesteryear, and the floor was poured concrete, already beginning to erode. There was no one out there.

"Me? Oh no, I'm not nervous." Brian's ERD flamed from an orange hue back to canary yellow.

"Your disc says otherwise," Kavanagh said.

Brian padded into the kitchen and ran the tap. Perhaps he wanted to be facing away, Kavanagh thought. Doesn't want me to see the colours of his disc and give the game away.

"Brian...did you come home with anyone last night?"

The tap stopped running.

Brian turned with an absolute petrified look on his face. Kavanagh couldn't help but smirk at that. The girl wasn't hiding in the living room.

"What did she tell you, Brian?" Kavanagh said from outside the bathroom door. "What name did she give you?"

Brian sauntered to the hallway. "She said...she said her name was Roxanne. We didn't have sex, I swear! I made her beans...and...and... am I in trouble, Agent Kavanagh?"

Kavanagh peered into the bath. He found a crumpled, balled-up shirt. He picked it up. Correction: a blood stained balled-up shirt. The fact that it was mostly a dark brown shirt now and not its original white made Kavanagh smile. He knew back in the dilapidated building with the hobo that he'd stuck her good, but he never thought she had lost this amount of blood. That was good. That meant that she wouldn't be running far.

Kavanagh exited the bathroom and slung the shirt on the hardwood floor for Brian to see.

"Naughty, naughty Brian." He teased.

There were only two rooms left. His grandmother's bedroom, and Brian's bedroom. The door to Brian's room was ajar, casting a trapezoid of light on the floor. Kavanagh put his index finger to his lips and brought out the Glock 17. He moved quickly towards Brian and clamped his free hand over his mouth. He was so close to him that he could smell beans and garlic emanating from the young Degenerate.

"Don't say a word. Don't even breathe. Do you understand me? Shake your head if you do. That's good. Now, just wait here and soon this will all be over, okay? Just like with your Grandmother."

Kavanagh spun and made his way quietly down the hallway to Brian's bedroom.

Inching the door open, the muzzle of the Glock 17 was the first inside the room. Kavanagh noted the blue wallpaper, posters haphazardly taped to the walls and a small bureau with trinkets and items on it. Brian's bed was in the far corner and a large wardrobe to the side of it. There were no windows in here, and Kavanagh recoiled as the smell of teenager engulfed his nostrils.

Only two hiding spots for you, my dear, he lamented, switching his sights from the wardrobe to the bed and back again. *Something tells me you're not the sort to scurry under the bed...but you have been surprising me these last few days.*

Kavanagh dropped to one knee, gripping the handle of the Glock tightly. *No dead bodies to throw at me this time,* he thought, as he craned his neck and looked under the bed.

Nothing but wadded, crusty tissues.

Swivelling, he pointed the gun at the wardrobe.

Come now, Ms. Paige. I hope I get to see the life burn out of your eyes. Let me see when the soul leaves the body. I want to see that in you. Yes...I want to see that very much.

Kavanagh stood, took a step forward and reached the handle of the wardrobe with his free hand. His gun finger curled round the trigger.

I hope you don't disappoint me like all the others...

He turned the handle.

HOW CAN YOU HELP?

London is one of the most exciting and diverse cities in the world – and policing it is no easy task, but it's a truly rewarding one. It takes a huge number of people from all sorts of different backgrounds with a wide range of skills and experience. Do you have what it takes to be one of them? Find out if a career with The Network is just the change you're looking for, and what kind of challenges, experiences and rewards you could have in store…

Working for The Network doesn't have to mean retiring the over 60's or becoming a referee of one of our thousands of live online shows. Just as important as our uniformed officers is our 20,000-strong team of professional and support staff working behind the scenes. It's these skilled people who provide the organisational capability to keep London safe and entertained. Click the buttons below and find out which staff roles are currently available, the responsibilities, pay, benefits and training you'll receive and how to apply.

What qualifications do you need?

Qualifications are no longer a requirement for all posts. The exception will be where there's a specific qualification attached to the role. For example, a SCOOP Suit registrar examiner would need to be a registrar expert and a member of the Council for the Registration of Birthday Treat Practitioners. Maybe you can help determine who will be next to get their Birthday Treat?
Instead, all posts advertised externally should list the competencies or skills required to undertake the role. You'll then need to show in your application how you meet those requirements.

Also, we're constantly on the lookout for pickers and packers. Since 90% of retail shops have been liquidated in London, The Network has become the number one resource for all your goods and services. Remember Amazon? The Network bought majority of stocks during the pandemic and we're the No. 1 service for quick and efficient deliverable goods. So get on the line (literally) and help the people of this great country!

Or perhaps you want to become an Agent? Field work, working with Ryan Lando on Hunted TV – you will literally have a license to retire! Subject to intense psychological evaluation, these roles are typically suited for people that have a military background, or for an Agent working within the retirement field that wants to broaden their horizons. At The Network, anything is possible!

Skills and personal qualities

Again, these will vary depending on the role. But it's fair to say that good communication and teamworking skills will always be welcomed, together with resilience, customer focus and respect for race and diversity!

Subject to approval, if you are an unfortunate owner of an ERD, it will be highly unlikely you will be considered for a role within The Network. We're looking for bright sparks, not dummies, dummy!

- Apply for a Role with The Network

TheNetwork.org

19

ALICE

TUESDAY

82 HOURS REMAIN...

"Oh. It's you again. Hi Agent Kavanagh."

Alice dived to her right before Brian opened the door. On hands and knees, she scrabbled frantically to Brian's room. She managed to close the door with her heel just before she heard the Agent step inside the flat. It didn't shut fully, but she wouldn't have time to go back without being seen, so she left it and hugged the wall, hoping that her pursuer didn't decide to come this way first. She feverishly looked for an exit, an escape, a window, something, anything to get her out of this situation. But there were no windows in Brian's room. Just posters of girls and cars and shitty carpet. She'd been stupid to sleep so late in the flat, but the way her hair clung to her clammy skin and the prickly heat she felt, she knew there was more to worry about if she made it outside the flat.

You got yourself a damn fever, Boss Bitch said. *Muscles are cramping, sweating like a pig – you need some antibiotics.*

It was a wonder she'd woken up at all. She felt tired, more tired than she'd ever felt in her life. How much blood had she lost when that prick had shanked her?

Maybe she could wait it out. Brian was going to be the deciding factor in this, she knew that. The whole thing could end here based on what the horny teenager decided to say. But he was a Degenerate with an IQ lower than her foot size. Of course he'd tell the Agent everything he wanted to hear.

Hide under the bed?

No...too obvious. All he'd have to do is peek under there and the game was up. *Game?* Boss Bitch snapped, *This 'aint no game, girly. This is your life we're talking about here. There are no continues, no re-runs and no second chances. You fucked up the minute you walked into that place to get your Boiler Suit off.*

It was true. She'd had a plan. But the best laid plans of mice and men often go awry.

English lessons paid off then, huh? Guess Robert Burns will help you out here, right? Oh yeah, let's just wait for old Burnsy to arrive, waxing lyrical. That'll get you out of this pinch. Maybe he'll talk the guy to death. Sure.

"In fact, better safe than sorry. Bolt it shut."

That was the Agent. The same one from the dilapidated building. He was talking loudly, loud enough for her to hear. That meant he knew she was here.

Alice bit her knuckles to stifle a scream.

He's a sneaky one, that Kavanagh. Doesn't mean he knows you're here though...

The wardrobe. An insane thought crossed her mind. In those old cartoons she used to watch, the burglar or the villain would always go on tippy toes when they were trying to ensnare the wascally wabbit or the running bird or whatever fuck animal they were trying to catch. But forcing all the weight and pressure onto the tips of your toes was a bad move. One squeaky floorboard and she'd be dead.

Alice took two long strides over to it.

Luck still seemed to be on her side.

She turned the handle and slowly opened the wardrobe, hoping with all her might and will that it didn't make a sound.

It swung out fully without so much as a squeak. Making herself as small as she possibly could, she slipped in without disturbing any clothes hangers and lay down, closing the door.

The smell was terrible in the wardrobe.

There were some loose jumpers, trousers and shirts on the bottom and she meticulously covered these on top of her, so even if the door opened, she hoped she could camouflage herself to look like a bundle of unwashed clothes.

It was a small hope, but one she desperately clung to.

"What did she tell you, Brian?" Kavanagh said from outside the bathroom door. "What name did she give you?"

Jesus, he's close. He's so close now...

Alice calmed herself. Just like when she felt a panic attack coming on, she went through her internal countdowns and eased her breathing. Through a slither in the door, she could make out a fragmented part of the room by the bed.

How did he find me?

Alice retraced her steps from the night before. Okay, it was likely that they had cameras on the cab she used as they left the club. But she had purposefully routed the cab to Chiswick, a few miles away. Although her side had been stinging like a sonofabitch, she'd been careful to avoid any CCTV or drones. She'd slipped down narrow alleyways and had even gone through a darkened park to avoid the main streets. All with Brian in tow.

Alice, Boss Bitch said, in a special leading-up-to-it careful voice. *Maybe Brian isn't as dumb as he looks. Maybe...he realised who you really were and called it in.*

No. If Brian had ratted her out, then there would helicopters, reporters and everyone surrounding this place. And he seemed sweet, in a simple kind of way. No, there was something else.

Maybe this Agent is simply good at what he does. Maybe he's a hunter. And you, my darling...are the prey.

Alice heard Brian's door open and all thoughts shattered. That burst of adrenaline was thumping through her again. She raised her palm and scissored two of her knuckles together in a nose pinching gesture. She didn't breathe.

Through the crack in the wardrobe, she could make out the Agent slowly scan the room. Now in the daylight she could see him properly. His features were sharp and hard. She wouldn't call him good looking, but he had the kind of face you would see on the bust of a roman emperor: the high, arched eyebrows, the firm, slightly cruel thin-lipped mouth. She assumed he had a hooked nose but it was covered with a bandage, and his eyes were rimmed with bruising. But the main thing Alice was concerned about was the gun in the Agent's hands.

She studied the Agent as he went down on one knee. His face was unpleasantly long, and colourless. His black hair was slicked back tight against his skull and Alice believed for a moment that he could well have been the incarceration of Death itself.

The notion made her want to burst out giggling.

It's just nerves girl, Boss Bitch warned, *remember that time when you were playing in that plinky plonkey jazz band and halfway through the set your guitar string broke?*

Alice remembered.

And what was it you said, full blown into the microphone?

Alice had said, *Oh, you dirty cunt.*

And what happened next?

The next day, when she went into band practise, she found all the other members of the jazz group sitting in the studio with faces like curdled milk. All women know the feeling of realising that in their absence something has taken place amongst a room full of men. There was an awkward atmosphere and Jesse, the lead singer, cleared his throat to speak.

"Save it," Alice had said at the time, not even bothering to put down her guitar case. "You want to throw me out, fine. Do it for a good reason, not because I swore onstage. Fucking cowards."

And with that, you went off into the sunset, didn't ya girly?

And then a few weeks later The VamPyrates were formed. And she was the boss.

The sniggering sensation had eroded away just as fast as it had blossomed within her.

None of that mattered now.

The Agent looked under the bed and scowled. Alice squeezed her nose harder as his attention turned to the wardrobe. His arm lifted to turn the handle.

Alice coiled herself like a spring. Either two things would happen: he would see straight through the crappy mound of clothes and shoot her until she was dead, or she would leap out and hope that she could get in a few good licks before he shot her dead.

Either way, Alice Paige contemplated the fact that in a few seconds, she would no longer be alive.

Agent Kavanagh's fist curled round the door handle.

"Hey!" A voice called from the hallway.

It was the short universal sound of surprise, anger and challenge. The sort of sharp instinctive sound of a concerned citizen when they see something wrong happening in front of them.

It was a single syllable that saved Alice's life.

The Agent spun on his heels, clicking back the hammer of the black automatic weapon in his hands.

"Woah, woah...easy there, fuck knuckles. You might slip and do something dangerous with that thing."

Alice had to release the grip on her nose. She hadn't exhaled for more than a minute. She clenched her fist to stop it from shaking. From the crack in the door, she watched intently as the Agent slowly walked towards the door, pointing the gun at the person she couldn't see.

"Who are you? What are you doing here?" said the Agent.

Alice slowly let out the breath she had been containing. She felt a wave of dizziness cascade over her. She willed herself not to pass out.

The voice from the hallway seemed jovial, mocking even.

"Just a concerned neighbour. Checking up on...my boy over here."

The Agent left the room, and Alice could only hear their voices now.

"This is a crime scene. You're going to leave. Now." The Agent's voice was stern, but Alice detected something underneath it. An urgency...no, more like a defensive tone of someone who's just been caught doing something they shouldn't.

"On who's authority?" The new voice questioned.

"On authority of The Network. Leave. Now."

"Well, I'm sure you have the proper paperwork, right? I mean, I may not be the sharpest tool in the shed, but even I know that you need a writ or papers to barge into someone's house, right?"

There was a small beat of silence.

"Brian," the Agent said, "who is this?"

Alice could hear Brian stuttering.

"It's okay Brian, I can speak for myself," the new voice chimed. "Name's Parker. Pleasure to make your acquaintance."

There was another moment of silence. Alice could practically envision the gears churning around within the Agent's head.

"Parker...well, let's step outside for a moment, shall we? I can explain everything that's occurring here."

Alice heard their shuffling footsteps fade away.

Move now, Alice thought to herself. *That Parker guy, whoever he is, has brought you nothing but time. That Agent will be back here in a few minutes and will open the door. You. Need. To. Move.*

Opening the door, she pulled herself out and nearly screamed as a piercing sting shot through her side. She quickly checked her wound and was thankful that her slapdash stitching hadn't ripped open. She would have to be careful how she manoeuvred for the foreseeable future.

If you have a future, an ominous voice whispered.

She peered out of the door of Brian's room. The hallway was deserted, but she could hear voices just outside the main front door. It seemed that Parker was protesting and going into a tirade about his rights. She weighed out her options.

One: Use the element of surprise and bolt out the front door. I could knock that Agent to the ground and flee. But in her condition, she didn't know how far she would make it. And didn't he have a partner? Where was he during all of this? Not the best idea.

Two: He's already searched most of the flat. Just choose another spot to hide and wait it out. That was risky, but a better possibility. She could hide in the living room, but who was to say that more Agents weren't already closing in on this area? Something else also perturbed her about that line of reasoning, the way the Agent had seemed almost defensive when confronted by that Parker character. Almost as if he were playing a hunch by coming to Brian's flat in the first place and maybe he hadn't called it in. Almost like he was personally involved in finding her and taking her down by himself.

The thought sent an icy, bony finger down her neck.

She couldn't worry about that now. With her back against the wall, she shimmied down until she was at the T-junction of the flat. Now she could hear Agent Kavanagh and Parker clearly through the door. They were a few feet away from her. The thundering of her heart beating against her chest made her feel dizzy again. Her legs felt elastic and she propelled herself to the living room to keep momentum going.

Don't lose it now, Alice.

She scouted around the living room. Nothing. She could try the other bedroom, but she couldn't be sure that Agent Kavanagh had already searched there yet.

The balcony.

Alice stared at the double-glazed door leading out to the small concrete slab with a couple of deck chairs. The surrounding blanket view of Hammersmith's treetops and buildings gave her a moment to calibrate what she was thinking.

Just hook yourself over the railing and drop down to the flat below. Simple.

Yeah, she mused. Just as simple as that.

Whatever choice do you have?

"Shit," she whispered, trying the handles. The door opened inward, and she stepped out onto the balcony. The cold air slapped her clammy face like an open hand. Stupidly she looked over the railing. They must have been up at least fifty storeys. From this height the street below looked no wider than a child's squiggly drawing of a train track.

Don't think about it, just get it done, Alice said to herself.

She twisted, hauling one leg over the railing, and felt a tight pull on her side again. Brian's flat was the last one on the row in the tenement block, and the balcony was at the corner of the building. She sat her ass on the railing, one leg dangling into air and the other firmly anchored to the balcony cement.

What am I doing? What am I doing?

The front door to the flat was a few feet away, but at this angle Alice was hidden by the corner. Deliberately not thinking about the horrifying drop below her feet, Alice gripped the railing with both hands, as if she were now riding a mechanical bull. All she would need to do is swing the other leg over the railing, ease her position forty-five degrees and start to lower herself. That's all she would need to do.

"You've no right to be here. I don't care what you say," Parker said, his voice defiant in the face of the authoritative Agent.

"You think this is all a joke, don't you Mr. Parker?"

"Do you see me laughing?"

"Hey guys," Brian said, "I think we should all get some squash and talk about-"

"No." Parker snapped.

Alice closed her eyes briefly, took two sharp intakes of breath and swung her other leg over the railing. Her heels found purchase on the ledge of the balcony, but whilst her torso was facing outward into oblivion, she would need to turn around fully to lower herself.

"My father was a comedian, did you know that?" The Agent's voice had taken on a chilling calm. Alice tried to blot it out of her mind as she prepared herself to twist. "He wasn't famous or anything like that...he wasn't even that good. I think he started doing comedy just to get away from the family. Travelling all the time, in different parts of the country. He'd be away for about six months of the year. Do you know what that's like for a young boy growing up? A young boy needs a fatherly figure. It puts pressure on the wife. On the mother."

"What the hell is this? Family therapy time?" Parker said, incredulous.

Alice's right foot slipped.

For a strange, timeless moment she felt herself fall, all her weight from the neck down becoming like an anchor submerging into an invisible sea. Her arms clamped down hard on the railing and she stifled a scream as her body snaked in the air. Her legs flailed madly for balance, and then she found herself clutching the railing in a lover's embrace, the hard metallic steel pressing razorlike into her chest.

"Anyway, one night he's playing a gig in this real shit-kicker of a place," Kavanagh continued, ignorant that his target was just an arm's stretch away from him. "Calling it a dive bar would be too generous. But the place is packed. My dad's backstage, going over his lines, making sure he gets the timing and pauses exactly right. Gotta make 'em laugh, right?"

Alice noticed that there was no witty comeback from Parker this time.

And now he's realised what I already knew...this guy in unstable. He's dangerous.

"He finally gets called on, and just as he's about to go onstage he notices smoke billowing from the green room. A fire had broken out backstage. He comes out to applause, and the first thing he says is that there's a fire and warns the audience. They think it's a joke, like it's a routine or something and they start applauding more. He repeats it, waving his arms in the air – the fire has caught on now and starting to tear through everything. But the acclaim he gets is even greater. I think that's how the world is going to come to an end, Mr. Parker: to general applause from dumbfucks who believe it's all a joke."

Now, the real tricky part.

Alice would have to do something she really didn't want to. She would need to look down.

With her breath sliding in and out of her lungs with shallow force, Alice slowly extended her arms until she could see directly below her. Just as she assumed, the balcony for the flat down was in perfect unison dimension wise. This presented the problem she feared: she would have to shimmy down and find purchase on the railing below with her feet.

If the Agent simply looked over his shoulder, he would see the girl in the leather jacket perched over the balcony. He would take out his gun and shoot her and she would fall to her doom.

Breathe, Alice...one step at a time.

Alice lowered herself into a squatting position, her hands sliding down the railings.

Now or never.

She let one of her legs slide out from the balcony ledge. She drummed her foot like a manic tap dancer to find the railing below, but only found air. She would need to close the gap. She allowed her other leg to drop off the balcony edge and now all her weight was being carried by her arms. She could slide her hands down to the base of the railing, but even then, her feet were still groping to find purchase.

"You should never have come here, Mr. Parker." The Agent said. His voice was quiet and secure. Confident. Alice's abdomen throbbed with the strain. She could almost feel the stiches tearing.

"And as a member of The Movement, you put me in a perilous position."

Even swinging from a fiftieth storey balcony, gasping and sweating and shaking, this line made her stop for a moment.

"Oh yes, Mr. Parker. Your surprised expression just confirms it for me. We know all about your little plans with the militia group. What were you planning to do, round up Ms. Paige and take her back to your secret lair?"

"This is absurd," Parker said, Alice noted a tremor in his voice. The assurance that radiated from before, when they were inside the flat, was gone. "This is slander...this is totalitarian bullshit...this is..."

"My partner, Mr. Valentine."

Alice heard a squark and some scuffling noises. Her arms were burning with pain, but she still hadn't found the railing beneath her.

I'm too short. I need to close the gap even more.

She would have to take her coiled hands off the railing and hang from the cement. It was the only way. A sudden flash entered her mind: free falling in the air as she plummeted to the ground. But in her vision, she landed on her feet. Her shin bones struck upward and exploded through her thighs – her spinal column would implode in on itself and her neck would snap like a twig. She saw all of this in an instant.

Spreading her fingers, she slowly moved her left hand down from the railing and gripped the edge of the balcony. A single tear streamed down her cheek and she realised with terrifying acuity that she was silently sobbing.

"You...can't...do this," Parker spluttered.

"True, it probably would be more advantageous for us to let you live, Mr. Parker – I would enjoy torturing you...but quite simply, one of your friends has given us all the information we need. And we're out of time."

Alice forced herself to glance at the corner of the building.

Just in time to see Parker hauled over the balcony.

She opened her mouth to scream, but no sound came out. She watched Parker cartwheel and as he plunged. He completed a revolution as he tumbled and she stared at him with wide eyes.

He stared back at her.

And then he was gone.

All energy left her body and her right hand slipped from the base of the railing. She would fall to the ground with Parker and then all of this would be over. The nightmare would finally be over.

Alice closed her eyes as she let go.

But she didn't feel weightlessness. She felt a different sensation. Arms wrapped round her midriff pulling her in. She fell inwards, scraping her head against the very ledge she had been clutching onto moments earlier. And then she was rolling. She opened her eyes.

A woman was on the balcony floor, panting. Alice saw that she was quite striking, as if she could be in a band herself. She was staring at Alice with a half-smile. She stretched and used the weary, twisted motion of someone easing a sore back.

"I guess I don't have to say come with me if you want to live, right?" The girl asked.

Alice blinked.

The girl got on her knees and held out her hand.

"Fuck it. Come with me if you want to live."

Join our membership scheme today and you can save £££ and Social Credits in the future.

Flappy Flap – the privacy app that works for you.

@FlappyFlapPrivacyApp

345 replies 872 RTs 2,456 Likes

Day 2 and @alicepaige is still going! At this rate she'll be giving Freddie Henshaw a run for his money! What do we say? Think she'll Go the distance?

@lifer_4_lyfe

1,345 replies 18,967 RTs 19,005 Likes

@lifer_4_lyfe YES! YES 100% Can you imagine?

@Leahsummers

547 replies 1,544 RTs 657 Likes

I've found some nude pics of @alicepaige – subscribe to my channel And I'll DM them…
#camgirl #hotsex #naughty #alicepaigesex

@HotPikachusex

754 replies 677 RTs 432 Likes

FOUND A VERSION OF HER JACKET! May have to get the 'ol Sewing kit out and make some adjustments, but gonna get my Paige MOOD ON.

@hannah_vintage

4,567 replies 4,3127 RTs 756 Likes

Some Agents talked to me and the boys – she's in Chiswick

¬

Boys. BATTER UP! #goinghunting

@CRicoh

439 replies 542 RTs 886 Likes

I nevar knew peeple cud fly. Can't find Roxanne tho.

Secund thyme this week Agents hav been at my gaff.

@Brian_Bowerman

5 replies 7 RTs 10 Likes

WE NEED TO HELP ALICE PAIGE. SIGN THE PETITON. END THE
NETWORK.#thenetworklies

@For_The_Movement

867 replies 3678 RTs 5979 Likes

NETWORK ADMIN: It has been brought to our attention that your last couple of calls have been irregular with the ITC protocols dictated by The Network.

8716367: I've been meeting my quota.

NETWORK ADMIN: We're not referring to your quota levels. Two calls were terminated in the last 24 hours. This is unacceptable. We've just received word that you have received disciplinary action for assaulting a member of staff. Holly Lucas. Audio Visual Department. B-Level. NetworkID: 9762902

8716367: She was dragging.

NETWORK ADMIN: Dragging?

8716367: Yes. Dragging. She had her birthday due this week. Demanding things from people under the veiled threat that if she didn't get what she wanted she would use her Birthday Treat on them.

NETWORK ADMIN: With any breach of Network rules, you should have brought this to your line manager.

8716367: Yeah. I'm sure he would have resolved the matter.

NETWORK ADMIN: In a moment you will see several sequential images in front of you. Please look ahead.

8716367: A Rorschach test?

NETWORK ADMIN: Please look ahead 8716367.

8716367: Fine.

NETWORK ADMIN: Please state the first image that comes to mind when you see the images.

8716367: Bat. Two people clapping. Human face. Animal Hide. Bat. Mother. Human face. Lobster.

NETWORK ADMIN: Calibrating. Please face forward and tell us the next sequence.

8716367: Is this necessary? I've been given my slap on the wrist. I'having a bad day, that's all.

NETWORK ADMIN: Please look ahead 8716367

8716367: Bat. Two people clapping. A woman's face. Animal hide. Bat. Daughter. Daughter's face. Lobster.

NETWORK ADMIN: Thank you, 8716367. We'll collate.

8716367: You do that.

NETWORK ADMIN: You were a psychologist previously.

8716367: I was.

NETWORK ADMIN: It's conceivable that you could alter the result of the behavioural pattern test from your prior knowledge and experience.

8716367: It's conceivable. But I wouldn't.

NETWORK ADMIN: Thank you, 8736367.

8716367: Can I leave now? It's been a long day.

NETWORK ADMIN: One more thing, before you go.

8716367: Sure.

NETWORK ADMIN: You were present when Case #401 conducted their Birthday Treat. Your heart rate and blood pressure rose substantially during this call. You were present when the Birthday Treat was conducted.

8716367: …yes.

NETWORK ADMIN: You may want to call one of our operators to discuss this. Your sanity is valuable to us.

8716367: I'll do that.

[8716367 will undergo further evaluation once test results have been collated. Please note abnormality in answers 14 and 15.]

20

GEORGE

TUESDAY

82 HOURS REMAIN...

George, who had never had a premonition in his life, was suddenly filled with a clear certainty that was both eerie and nauseating.

I'm not going to be alive at the end of the week. Agents will enter my house and retire me for being part of The Movement. They'll take Elspeth away in a strait jacket and they'll recycle my organs.

George stood without moving for five seconds. His eyes were wide, staring at the grotesquely mishappen body of Parker. A flap of skin that used to be attached to his skull fluttered slightly, like a plastic bag caught in a bush. George was fleetingly aware of a coppery taste pooling in his mouth. He must have clamped down on his tongue when the body pulverised the roof of the cab.

George looked for Samson, but saw and heard nothing. The twisted metalwork and shattered glass didn't give him much hope for the driver. A warped notion filled his mind – that he would see Samson's belly protruding from the wreckage and etched on it would be an exquisitely detailed tattoo of a pizza.

George sucked in cramped air, feeling his lungs caving in on themselves. He heard a buzzing noise, filling his ears. He felt like he was standing there for hours, but as he turned to walk away, he heard someone calling his name.

He stumbled towards the noise in a fugue state, only seeing Carina and the girl when they were directly in front of him. Carina was panting, out of breath. She had her arm around the girl, who looked haggard and was barely standing. Carina unshouldered the duffel bag and gave it to George.

"We have to go. Now." Carina said sharply.

George glanced over his shoulder, pointed at what remained of the crumpled cab.

"But...we can't leave Parker."

Carina inclined her head towards George. It was a gesture which said: are you serious?

This is what shock feels like, he said to himself. *Lack of blood flow means the cells and organs don't get enough oxygen and nutrients to function properly. Many organs can be damaged as a result.* He'd read that. Maybe if he just laid down on the ground and closed his eyes for a few moments, it would pass.

Carina was already making her way past the tenement block, dragging the girl along with her. To the untrained eye, it looked like two girls coming back from a night on the town.

The girl. Alice Paige. His daughter.

"Okay. Yeah. We have to leave." George's voice was supplicant and miserable. The voice of a man who knew he was far too deep in the shit without really understanding exactly why. He caught up to them as they crossed the road. Carina was looking for cameras, zigzagging down different roads. She put the palm of her hand on Alice's forehead.

"She's burning up," she said, "and the neighbour wasn't particularly impressed with me barging into her house the way I did.

She may have recognised Alice as we ran out of there, so we put as much distance from this place as possible. The two Agents up there won't take long to find us out in the open like this."

Thoughts swirled round George's head. He'd lived in Chiswick for most of his life and realised that he didn't come into Hammersmith that often. It was late afternoon, and people would be congested on the high street. Public transport would be out of the question. They could call another cab, but that could draw attention. He looked down and noticed that his knuckles were white. He was clenching the duffel bag as if it were a bomb.

"I don't live that far away," he spluttered. "And I have antibiotics. We could try to lay low there for a while." He was surprised that the sentence came out of his mouth.

Why am I doing this?

If they were caught now, he wouldn't be able to talk his way out of it. The time for backing out had escaped him this morning when he was in an antique shop liaising with members of a guerrilla group. He should have walked away then. He should have gone about his normal life with his normal routine and everything would have been fine.

Carina nodded as they carried on down a residential street.

"Can't you call one of your friends to pick us up?" George asked.

"No...you can't call anyone," Alice said. George looked at the deathly pale girl who had been on the run for three days. Her eyes rolled to the back of her head like marbles and her forehead was slick with sweat. "I heard them...the Agents. If you're with The Movement, then you've been compromised. There's a mole. That's how they... how they knew-"

"How they knew Parker was involved. That's why they killed him." Carina said, finishing her sentence.

"I have to stop." Alice murmured.

Carina shook her head.

"I'm going to throw up," Alice added, unclasping herself from Carina. George spotted a small alley and herded the others there. After a quick glance over his shoulder, they left the street and he felt his heart quicken. If anyone saw them here it would be suspicious. Two girls and a grown man chatting merrily in a garbage ridden alley? He felt dirty and unclean, as if he were brokering some type of sexual deal with them. That's what people would see, at any rate. He remembered something Parker used to say to him when they were working together in the office.

It's all about the optics, Georgy boy. You think people want to see a bloated, puffy faced geriatric take out their Birthday treat on someone on the Free-Vee? No, no, no...that wouldn't be entertainment, George. That's why they always pick young people. Stupid people. Malleable people.

Poor bastard.

The alleyway was straight like a drinking straw and almost as narrow. The sounds of the roads bounced from one side to the other and light from the flat windows reflected from the dark brick walls.

Alice staggered to the wall as she tried to force down the bile, but it was too late. Her stomach contracted so violently that she had no time to reach the bin bags. Hot liquid spewed out of her coughing, choking mouth. Her stomach kept on contracting violently and forcing everything up and out, but it was mostly fluid. George wondered how long it had been since she'd eaten. Her face was white and dripping bile, sweat, and tears. She lurched forward and sunk to her knees. The pungent stench invaded his nostrils and she heaved one more time even though there was nothing left.

George felt bad that he couldn't offer her a glass of water or offer to clean up the mess. He deferentially patted her on the back, but she flinched from his touch and moved away. The stomach-acid stench of vomit filled the entrance of the alleyway. She surveyed the mess with watery eyes and her stomach dry-heaved again.

"We have to keep moving," Carina said, her eyes darting from Alice to George. "You hear those sirens? That's the whole Network coming down here to cordon off this place. They'll have perimeters set up in no time and they'll find us. George, how much further to yours?"

George estimated the walking distance in his head. "Probably a mile, mile and a half?"

Carina clenched her teeth. "Open the bag," she finally said.

George looked dumbly down at the bag he had been carrying since they left the apartment block. He unzipped it in a stupor, bringing out some clothes, sunglasses, a mobile and wig.

"Put that on," Carina commanded.

Alice wiped her mouth with the back of her hand. "Listen," she said, "I appreciate what you did for me back there, but I don't know you guys. I've been fine on my own for the last couple of days. I'll be fine for the next couple."

Carina let out a derisive snort. "The way I see it, you've been lucky. But luck only gets you so far. You can trust us. We're with The Movement."

Alice smiled a lipless smile. "With all due respect, you and your movement can go fuck yourselves."

Carina sighed and leaned forward. Spoke quietly.

"We're serious here, Alice. You saw what they did to Parker. They did the same thing to my brother. And they'll be doing it to countless other families until someone stands up to them. Can't you see what's happening here? You're igniting a spark. We've got a plan to help you do that." Carina stared at the wall for a moment. "We...had a plan. Parker wasn't supposed to...I mean..."

George heard a couple walk by the mouth of the alley. He glanced over his shoulder as they walked past. Luckily, they hadn't been too bothered to look in their direction. He wanted to go over to Carina and hug her in that instant. He knew that a family member had been involved in a Birthday Treat the moment she clamped her hand down on his knee back in Samson's cab, but now she had confirmed it. Her brother. What horrible act had The Network performed on him? He could see her envisioning him now, as her eyes welled with tears.

Or it could all be an act, a warning voice whispered, *she could be saying exactly what Alice wants to hear. What you want to hear. She's good at that, isn't she?*

George shelved the thought.

"My name's George," he said softly, breaking the silence that had descended in the narrow alley. "Pleased to meet you, Alice."

He held out the duffel bag. Smiled. The friend. The ally. The protector.

He hoped it would garner the oldest response in the book.

Alice shrugged unhappily. Made a listen-up gesture.

"Let me say this once...just to be clear. I don't know you, *George*. I don't trust you. I don't trust anyone. So trying the good 'ol Uncle routine won't fly with me. And you," she tilted her head at Carina, "I don't do the whole girls united front act. Girls don't seem to like me, so I don't like them."

"That why you always play in a band with all guys?" Carina asked. Her moment of thoughtful reflection had vanished. Now it seemed to George that these two were sizing each other up for the first time.

"What, you've seen my mugshot on the Free-Vee and you think you know me?"

"Yes, Alice. I know you. We do our research." She looked at George, a pointed expression on her face. George felt his cheeks redden.

Carina was about to say more but her eyes caught a group of Degenerate teens milling around the entrance of the alley. They hadn't paid them any attention yet, but it wouldn't be long. She motioned to George and Alice and they started walking the other way.

"You said we'd been compromised," Carina said urgently, "did they say any names? Do we know who the mole is?"

Alice shook her head.

"No names."

Carina made a small huffing sound. They came to the other end of the alleyway, leading into another residential street. She looked both ways up and down the path before waving George and Alice to join her.

"Here's what we're going to do," Carina said, matter-of-factly. "Alice...I don't have time to argue with you but trust me when I say we're here to help you. Change into these clothes, give me your jacket, and go with George. You'll be able to rest and lie low for the day." She grabbed the duffel bag from George and thrust it towards Alice. She turned to George. "Agents will be swarming the area, and I can't risk what the neighbour may have said to them. They'll be looking for two girls, but they won't be looking for a middle-aged man and a girl."

George felt a barbed sting at the remark but remained silent. Alice shrugged off her jacket and handed it to Carina, but George observed a hesitation. As is the jacket meant more to her than just keeping out the cold. Carina swapped hers and grimaced slightly as she flexed her arms. Alice had a smaller frame and the jacket was too tight for Carina.

"You think you'll be able to get home without being detected?"

George looked at Carina. "I'll get her to mine."

"Okay, great," She handed him the mobile. "It's a burner. Only receives incoming calls. I'll be in contact when it's safe. I need to get some information. And something else. Something important."

She took out a small USB from her pocket. Held it in her hand for a moment.

"This is important, George. This is where I give you absolute complete trust. Do you understand that?"

George nodded.

"Do you understand that?" She asked again.

George said he did.

Carina handed him the USB. Let out a breath of air.

"Don't lose that," she said as she turned and started walking up the street, the opposite way to where George lived. "I'll be in contact soon. Get her some antibiotics and stay inside. If I hear anything I'll reach out."

George frowned as Alice put on the sunglasses and wig.

"You don't know where I live."

Carina turned and flashed a smile. It was the same one that George had been accustomed to seeing every day when he picked up his coffee in the morning. That seemed like a lifetime ago.

"Of course I do." She said, and then she was gone.

⊕

George and Alice had been walking for half an hour. They had remained silent for the duration.

How do I explain this to Elspeth?

He knew she devoutly watched *Hunted* TV, and would freak out as he arrived back home with Alice Paige in tow. He would need to speak to her, tell her everything. Lay it all out like a desperate poker player bluffing with a bad hand. How would she react? Would she scream and shout, like he thought she might? Or would she call Agents immediately? He couldn't let that happen. He would have to tell her that she was their daughter. That might stop her. It would have to stop her.

But is she really? You know there's only one real way to find out.

George grimaced and kept his head down, looking at the pavement in front of him.

George had surreptitiously glanced at Alice at intervals during their silent walk back to Chiswick, and the young girl seemed to be moving ahead by sheer willpower alone. At times she would clutch her side and frown, as if she had a pain in her stomach. She stumbled frequently, as if she had dozed off and woken up just as she was about to fall. Her face was ashen, sweat glistened from her forehead.

"Have you eaten?" George finally said, as they took another corner down a quiet street. He would be sure to stick to side roads and avoid the main ones at all costs.

Alice remained quiet. He remembered the alleyway and the vomit. There hadn't been any chunks at all, just fluid.

"Want to tell me the last time you ate?" He asked calmy. "We're going to be spending some time together, we can be civilised about it, right?"

Alice looked at him as they walked. But her eyes didn't focus on him. She made no reply.

"Listen Alice...I know all of this is bizarre, but there are people out there that want to help you. I'll rustle something up for you when we get to my place. We might as well try to get along, okay?"

Alice nodded. It seemed mechanical.

She'll keel over at any minute. Then people will start looking.

"This thing is itchy as hell," she croaked, scratching the obsidian wig Samson had picked for her.

George smirked. "Better than the Pompadour look, right?" He enacted a little hip shake and pretended to have a microphone in his hand. "Thankyouverymuch."

Alice continued walking. Her breath quivered in short, quick gasps every time she inhaled, her lungs having no choice but to painfully take in the chilled air around her.

"Let's be clear," she said. "Civilised is not the same thing as friendly."

George felt a little embarrassed for trying the Elvis impersonation. But she was talking to him at least. Progress.

A small pang of fear swelled in his stomach each time they passed someone on the streets. He felt like he was transporting drugs or some other illegal contraband, and everyone was looking at him. As if they knew he was hiding a secret. He didn't understand how Alice had been doing this for the last couple of days. He knew that his nerves wouldn't have survived.

They came down a familiar road, and George felt a little less restless knowing that his house wasn't far away. The evening was drawing in, and the blue skies from earlier had mottled into a grey, darkened sky.

George cleared his throat. "Can I ask you something?"

Alice shrugged. She dragged herself along the road, as if she would fall over at the slightest breeze.

"Why did you do it? Why didn't you just take your Birthday Treat?"

For the first time since they had left Carina, Alice stopped walking.

George turned. Alice opened her mouth to say something and then hesitated. "If I have to tell you that," she finally said, "then you don't get it at all." She carried on walking.

They remained quiet until they reached George's road. Once she stumbled and George went to help her, but she batted him away. He felt fatigued, the day's events wearing heavy on his shoulders. Conspiracies. Death. Agents.

Apprehensively, he fished for his keys.

"Listen...my wife, she doesn't know anything about this."

Alice looked at George. Her eyelids drooped heavily and she wavered in the pathway. "Is she going to be trouble?" She murmured. Direct.

George moved cautiously to the front door.

"She'll be fine," he said.

Just like the washing up and the clothes. Fine always takes care of everything. He sighed heavily and opened the door.

PART II

WHY BE YOU? CONFESSIONS OF A VR FREE-VEE ADDICT

Do you want to be you?

I'm being serious here. Take a moment for that question to sink in.

I'll wait.

Do you wake up in the morning and feel content with the job you have? Do you like your friends and family? Do you feel comfortable in your own skin? If you answered 'yes' to all the questions above, put down this book and stop wasting your valuable time. But…if you answered 'no' to just one of the above, let me tell you friend…you're not alone. I understand just how you feel.

There used to be a phrase at the turn of the century that the world belonged to the 'one percent.' Today however, one thousandth of a percent seems closer to the truth. And unless you're already working for The Network, your chances of joining this elite class are even less than that. How long have you been just struggling to get by with your cheap ass Social Credits that only allows you one bottle of wine a week? How many hours have you slaved away at that desk, just to get a paltry pay slip at the end of the month that gets devoured by your debt? How many times have you looked out from your crappy tenement block apartment and though to yourself, 'one day, I'll be able to leave all of this and ascend to greatness. One day.'

I have the solution.

With VR on your Free-Vee, you can be anyone.

A secret agent that fights an interstellar war on Mars. A rocker that gets all the groupies at the end of the night and parties until the break of dawn. Or maybe you want something a little different? Maybe you want to play as an Agent tracking down the latest contestant on *Hunted* TV. You can do all of this in

VR – and with the technology available nowadays you'll feel every shot, every punch, every electric shiver down your spine.

So, I'll ask you again: Of the billions upon billons of people in this overpopulated planet, do you want to be you?

The answer for me was always 'no.'

And so my story begins…

- Prologue of Michael Mink's autobiography, WHY BE YOU?

21

THE OLD MAN

WEDNESDAY

62 HOURS REMAIN...

Everyone remembers their first day at work.

At least, I like to think they do. There should be a nervous energy bubbling underneath the surface, a can-do attitude to take on anything...everything. That's how I felt on the first day when I founded The Network. People thought I was crazy to start this venture. Even Bea had her doubts. As someone who's been married for over thirty years, I can tell you with an honest hand on my heart that every couple goes through some rough patches. When I had first started batting round the idea of The Network, that time wasn't just a rough patch for us. That was a threadbare, pull the loose thread and everything will unravel type of patch.

But we persevered.

Bea believed in me. And I trusted her. I always used to tell people that she was the head of the relationship and I was the heart. We worked together as a good team and in most ways, that's what gets you through the rollercoaster ride of a long relationship.

So we persevered. I had to sell the pharmaceutical company that my folks established for the start-up capital investment required to get The Network up and running, and let me tell you, that was an emotional decision to make. Imagine being trusted with your parent's life-long work and company and being in the position to gamble it away on a dream. You hear so many stories of people throwing all their eggs in one basket and coming up short, but there was something special about The Network...I could feel it in my bones, as my old man used to say. I don't think he would begrudge me too much now, seeing where we are and what we've achieved, but in those early days...

It all came about in a strange roundabout way, you see...certain alignment of events transpired for The Network to begin. Some would say divine intervention, but I've never been a spiritual kind of person. I would just say that I lucked out and a series of incidents transpired at the right time. And I was at the right place.

You guys wanted to know about the history of The Network and how it was founded, right? As I said before, I don't have time for memoirs – I had a check-up today and the quacks say that I've probably got about seven months left in the 'ol human odometer, so unfortunately I lack the hours to put everything down in finer details...but at the very least I hope these blogs help paint the picture.

So.

My mother and father started the pharmaceutical together waaaay back in the day. A small corner shop to begin with, they worked effortlessly morning, afternoon and evening for seven days a week. They taught me that to get things done in life, you graft. And graft they did, dear reader – for the small shop on the corner turned into a larger shop, and then a warehouse. The warehouse turned into a building and so on and so forth. When my father died, he entrusted the family business to me – producing and manufacturing medicines, cures, tonics and everything else for distribution to hospitals, private companies and health care services. There were other companies that did some of the same stuff we did, but their problem was their interests were too earth bound and they were only invested in capital. My father was the same. The plan was for me to continue running things the way he had, and Bea and I would be comfortable in life.

But then the pandemic hit.

It's crazy to think about it now, but for over a year the world effectively stopped. Some of the older generations will remember it like it was yesterday, but I figure that most people want to forget that time. I was unhappy, Bea was unhappy. I decided to turn the catastrophe into an opportunity. A way out for all of us.

With the help of some good folk within the company, we were the first to come up with the vaccine. The UN were working on inoculation treatments too, but their versions were only ninety-four per cent effective. What we came up with was one hundred per cent full proof. No side effects. It took a while, bidding wars can have that effect, and when the fat cats see money in their eyes everything seems to slow to a crawl. We finally managed to strike a deal with the Government and our vaccine rolled out for the masses. At first, we thought it was just going to be the UK, but eventually it ended up being the whole world. I won't insult your intelligence dear reader, but my company made a tidy nest egg from that deal. Very tidy. I could have retired there and then, bought several islands in the Bahamas. But that's not the way my mind is set, you see. Never has been. As I mentioned before, it was simply a means to create a new opportunity, to help the people of this country. To heal. Yes, that once in a lifetime golden ticket deal gave me enough capital to start putting the wheels in motion to start up The Network. That was step one.

Now, I know there's been speculation running rampant recently with children with mental defects. The colloquial term used for these people - *Degenerates*, is something I've never been fond of. Arguments have been made that their parents, the people who received the initial inoculation years ago, passed down a genetic mutation to their offspring, but I can categorically deny these false accusations here and now. I've attached a link to the bottom of this blog with the hard evidence: facts by the medical association with all details to the immunisation serum we produced and manufactured at the time of distribution. It hurts me sometimes to read these false accusations, but I realise that with great power comes great responsibility. Not even sorry for stealing Spidey's quote. Because it's true.

Do you really think we would roll out millions of phials to the world, knowing that there was even a shred of doubt it would cause some defect in a person's DNA? What do you think I am, some crazy moustache twirling villain, laughing manically in his evil lair?

I know there are people out there that believe the earth is flat... that secret radio waves are being transmitted into your homes and into your heads from a secret bunker, that we're building a robotic army that will render the human meat bags currently working on factory lines obsolete...but you know what? That's fine. Believe *all* those things if you like. Who am I to tell you different? I can only give you the facts of what The Network have been doing over the last several years to provide this country a stable and safe landscape for years to come.

Step two was coming into play. You remember my friend, Mark? The boy I swindled at pool from my last blog post? Well, we became firm friends as we grew up, and Mark and I became business partners. He used to be something of a technical marvel, you see. I named him my VP of The Network when it was all up and running.

Well, after the deal with the immunisation jabs went through, I realised that the potential to create my dream was there. It would still be a long way off to rival the big-name firms you used to see, but I could feel it coming ever so much closer. But the future wasn't in medicine anymore – it was technology. Mark was the shining light for the way forward. He had these ideas, these phenomenal ideas...the way I saw it, I was fortunate enough to be in an industry at the time that helped the world...but it wouldn't *heal* the world. And Mark was key to that.

So, I had to make the tough decision to sell the family business that had been bestowed upon me by my parents. As I mentioned before, it wasn't an easy choice to make. Bea had her doubts, and secretly I think she wanted one of those islands in the Bahamas...but once I relayed my plan...my vision...she could see the good it would do for people.

So Mark and I started up a tech business, after the deal with the immunisation jabs. Nothing fancy, small potatoes considered to what we've built now, but we were trying to solve all the little problems that had become big problems.

Baby steps.

According to the Institute for Economics and Business research, traffic costs were a problem years ago. I know right, with the country in turmoil and people losing their jobs and homes and everything else, why am I bringing up something as paltry as traffic costs?

It's the classic woods through the tree scenario. £610 billion pounds were being wasted with people sitting in traffic, fuel costs, impact on the environment – the list goes on and on. Even when I was young, a lot of our mass transit infrastructure was falling part, and the cost to fix it was astronomical. Mark had the solution.

Drones in the sky.

When you thought of the early prototype drones, they were merely used for fun or for recording panoramic shots for documentaries and films. Mark was a massive geek head, and he realised that the way forward was by configuring drones to become bigger and bulkier. We developed new mechanics with our new firm, experimenting with new materials and lighter composites. We were working on world changing stuff.

A lot of people have attributed the drones as my brainchild but believe when I say that Mark Albrecht was the man who accomplished this. When you see those little critters flying in the air delivering groceries, when you buy something online and you receive it an hour later, he's the man to thank. Although I started out a tech company that would later evolve into The Network, I don't really have the head for technology.

Isn't that a strange thing to say?

Maybe it was the hours spent in my parent's corner shop, talking to people when they came in to pick up their prescriptions. Perhaps it was the need to communicate with people and find out their needs and wants that propelled me with the idea of making life better for people...

I'm the ideas man, you see. I had my work cut out for me trying to lobby with the Civil Aviation Authority to cohabit airspace with drones and planes and helicopters in the air at the same time, because although drones don't really go that high you don't want to mess around with take-off and landing procedures. And this wasn't something that happened overnight. We're talking years and years of red tape with the government. In the end, the only way forward was to take control of it. Literally. Privatisation can be considered a dirty word, but the real way to make change is to drop the dead wood.

So, instead of buying those islands in the Bahamas, we bought and privatised the CAA. This helped us tremendously. Fired the dead weight, brought in people who shared our vision, and the stamp of approval was set. In five years alone, we managed to reduce the traffic problem in this country once and for all.

But wait! I hear you cry, dear reader – wouldn't millions of people lose their jobs in the process? Well, the pandemic had already laid waste to that. The future, as the pamphlets said at the time, was digital. We set up schemes, sure. We helped the people when the government couldn't. And that was the final step – sharing my dream with the people of this country, informing them that their government was letting them down. That instead of stabilising the economy and galvanising sections that once made this beautiful country great, they were tearing it down, piece by piece with their greed and ego. And hubris. Don't forget that, dear reader...one of the prerequisite traits of a politician is hubris.

Oh, the controversary at the time. I remember it well.

There was a power in parliament once. A power that decided the destiny of millions. Now I must admit that there was a certain amount of political inexperience upon my part in those early days. But Mark, as well as being a tech whizz also conveyed a dogmatic and radical approach to appealed to all the disenfranchised parties at the time. Governmental efforts to raise taxes, undermine unions, and privatise and deregulate business in the United Kingdom contributed to an unstable economy and widespread worker dissatisfaction. The government met the resulting strikes and social unrest with absolutely no tolerance, and increasingly violent repression. This in turn spurred the militarisation of the police forces across the country, all of whom were given free rein on how they chose to deal with the growing and occasionally violent unrest.

We were growing in numbers and of influence. And in time we would control the power that parliament once had.

People demanded change. The beginning of The Network's regime came at a time of chaos and the collapse of governmental order and protection, saying that there was "no food" and that "the sewers were flooded and everybody got sick". The original government had fallen – though whether it collapsed because of the ensuing chaos in the country or because of its lack of direction, is still up for debate. There was a subsequent battle for control of the country that came to a head when our party finally emerged victorious, thanks in part to the assistance of the remaining economic and corporate institutions that I had managed to partner with. These years are a kind of blur to me, all in the name of returning order and safety to Britain.

And here we are.

Apologies for the abridged version of the timeline, but as I stated at the beginning of this blog, I think it's good to look back sometimes...really see where we came from. The Network brought back performing arts...we brought back the music venues and brought balance back to our crippled country. We gave *you* – the people, what you wanted. I see that Alice Paige has made it to the third day in *Hunted* TV. Perhaps we'll have another Frederick Henshaw on our hands, eh?

Ah, I almost forgot. Talking about our futures...I have a small announcement to make tomorrow. Stay tuned, dear readers.

DAY 3 UPDATE (Transcript to be approved before live commentary)

Morning folks, Ryan Lando here with some breaking news – alleged sightings of Alice Paige bring you closer to the action than you think! That's right hunters, we've got an exclusive just for you, where our investigation led us to an apartment complex in Hammersmith, West London.

"At first I didn't know what was happening," Deidre Barnes, 54, housewife and single mother of six said to us late yesterday evening. "I heard banging on the door and when I opened it this girl was babbling at me. Saying that someone was dangling off my balcony."

I question Deirdre for details of what the girl looked like. "Oh, it all happened so fast. She had a nose ring. Quite pretty. We went to the balcony and sure enough there's a girl there."

Deirdre was quite baffled by it all. "This young girl, she's out there like a shot. Grabs her just as she's about to fall. Well, I mean it's not something you see every day, is it?"

I asked Deirdre if she recognised the other girl.

"No…not at all. I was even going to offer them biscuits but they rushed right out of here. It wasn't until Agents swarmed the place and people started showing up here with baseball bats and the like. I never knew that gangs were after her on the streets. It's all quite –

Ryan: Hey Bob, can we change this?

Bob: What do you want chief?

Ryan: Uhh…this Deirdre woman. Tedious. Let's change the narrative a little. We know Alice is getting help from The Movement, right? Day fucking three and all we've got is this shite. Let's start by calling a spade a spade. She's not a housewife, she's unemployed. Let's get the masses to relate with her. Let's make her out to be vulnerable. People love that shit. Second…umm…lemme see here…make our mystery woman threatening, like Deirdre didn't have a choice by letting her in the house. Let's spice it up. These types of stories run better with the fans.

Bob: You want to say that our mystery surprise guest is part of the movement?

Ryan: Fuck sake Bob, you put 'alleged' in front of anything and you can say pretty much what you like. Look at the first line, do we know for fact Alice was there? No. But we *know* she was there, see what I'm saying?

Bob: Sure thing chief. Gimme a sec here. Okay, how's this?

Morning folks, Ryan Lando here with some breaking news – alleged sightings of Alice Paige might bring you closer to the action than you think! That's right hunters, we've got an exclusive just for you, where our investigation led us to an apartment complex in Hammersmith, West London.

A teary-eyed Deirdre Barnes, 54, unemployed mother of six, spoke with us to share her story. "At first I didn't know what was happening," she says, dabbing away a single tear. "I heard banging on the door and when I opened it this girl was shouting at me. She had these wild eyes, and she barged her way into my house. My home. I have six kids here, who knows what she could have done? She kept on saying that someone was dangling off my balcony."

I question Deirdre for details of what the girl looked like. "Oh, it all happened so fast. I thought she was going to kill me, you know? She had a nose ring. Rough sort or girl. She may have been Degenerate or with that guerrilla group. We went to the balcony and sure enough there's a girl there."

Deirdre was quite baffled by it all. "This young girl, she's out there like a shot. Grabs her just as she's about to fall. Well, I mean it's not something you see every day, is it?"

I asked Deirdre if she recognised the other girl. Could she have been an alleged member of The Movement?

"They rushed right out of here. It wasn't until Agents swarmed the place and people started showing up here with baseball bats and the like. I never knew that gangs were after her on the streets. It's all quite –

Ryan: Yeah, okay. That pops out a little bit more, don't ya think?

Bob: I just work here, chief. I don't get paid to think.

22

KAVANAGH

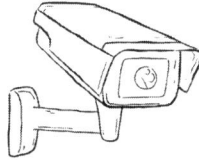

WEDNESDAY

61 HOURS REMAIN...

Kavanagh entered Cassandra Rey's office and was given his first instruction. It bristled him as it was a command issued to a dog.

"Sit." Cassandra said. She said it calm, but firm. Kavanagh couldn't help but notice the emphasis on the plosive consonant at the end of the word. As though she was saying it through gritted teeth. The part in her hair was exact, and her dark suit was sobering. You can come to me with any of your problems, that suit said to Joe public. To any of her underlings it curtly stated: Don't bother me with your issues.

Kavanagh sat down.

The Old Man's PA peered at him from across her desk, in a scrutinising way. She hadn't said anything to him, so he remained quiet. He knew what this was, he'd used it many times himself. A small power game, to see who would speak first. He wasn't going to give her the satisfaction of winning her little authoritative trip. He'd been awake for more than forty-eight hours straight and he was feeling agitated and fatigued. His nose throbbed.

Forty-eight hours of stress and mental exhaustion.

"Well?" She asked, after an uncomfortable silence. Kavanagh smirked inwardly to himself and then gave her a big wide PR beam.

"Seems like your source was correct. Mr. Parker was involved with The Movement, but not in the higher echelons of its structure. A middleman, so to speak. Someone who lubricated the gears for other cogs to turn."

There was no returning smile from Cassandra. "And you threw him off a balcony."

Kavanagh didn't like the way the prominence seemed to land on 'you'. Technically, Valentine had hurled him off the side of the building.

He cleared his throat. "It was unfortunate, but we were defending ourselves. His interference caused the target to escape."

Cassandra looked hard at Kavanagh. There was nothing on show. Her face and body betrayed nothing. But there was *something*. Her eyes burned with a kind of cruel energy. They sneered at Kavanagh out of her blank, bony face.

He wondered how she fucked.

He imagined she would be the one in control, on top. Her teeth gnashing as she bucked and gasped on top of whatever poor creature found themselves in that perilous situation. She didn't have much meat on her, and Kavanagh grimaced at the thought of her scrawny frame slamming down, grinding bone against flesh. He didn't think of sex often, as it was too much of a distraction.

With self-discipline almost anything is possible.

He imagined her face contorting into a paroxysm of ecstasy as she came. He had to clamp his tongue between his teeth from the sudden assault of laughter that threatened to escape.

"Yes," she said, "it's the second time she's evaded you. Perhaps I was wrong to promote you to this prestigious rank. It rarely happens, but even I make mistakes."

Force has no place where there is need of skill.

She opened a file and started scribbling some notes, as if to say her time with him was done. Kavanagh felt the tectonic plates of power shift from under his feet. Rey wasn't the kind of person to make idle threats. He knew that much about her. She couldn't dismiss him now, not when he was so close. Kavanagh's hands clenched in his lap, working against each other, sweating.

"I have a plan," he said briskly.

She stopped jotting notes. Started again.

He took the hesitation as a sign to continue. "What do you do if you want to catch a tiger? Or some other predator out in the jungle."

Cassandra looked up at him and stared.

"What?" she asked.

"You tether a goat to a stake...and lie in wait."

"What are you blathering on about, Kavanagh?"

Kavanagh unclenched his fists. The release felt good. "Can we make contact with your informer?"

Cassandra stiffened. "Out of the question. The informant will drip feed us intel when we need it. If we start barking at the door now, they'll likely get spooked. The Movement isn't our priority right now. Catching Alice Paige is. May I remind you, Agent Kavanagh, that not one contestant has made it to day four? The polls have just come in and people are starting to rally behind her. Do you know what kind of impact that has on The Network?"

"Until they become conscious, they will never rebel, and until after they have rebelled they cannot become conscious." Kavanagh said.

Cassandra looked at him for a long moment. "Excuse me?"

Kavanagh waved a dismissive hand. "Just a silly quote. Don't mind me. Am I right in thinking that this informant has made some...demands?"

Cassandra smiled at that. Kavanagh thought it was the hollowest smile he'd ever seen. He knew that the informant had, as he'd listened to the transcript an hour ago, but didn't want Cassandra to know that.

"There's a member of The Movement we can't touch." She said urgently, but quietly. As if she had bet money on a horse and found out it came last. There was bitterness in that voice.

"The girl with the pierced nose that helped Alice escape yesterday?" Kavanagh said.

Cassandra just stared at him, blankly.

"Yeah, I reckon that's the one." He sucked in air through his teeth, as if he were about to give an estimate for a car to a customer. "Well, here's your conundrum...Ms. Rey. If your priority is Alice Paige, then we need that girl. Think about it. Alice has been on the run for three days now. She's tired. She's drained. She's scared. But now she has help. Now she has someone to give her an inkling of hope. And hope can be a dangerous thing. Hope can be the catalyst for the end of things. If you want to catch Alice Paige before the close of play on Friday, then your only hope is to tether that girl with the pierced nose to the stake."

Cassandra leaned back in her chair, steepling her fingers in a pyramid.

"What makes you think this girl is the key?" Cassandra said.

"The only way she's managed to evade us so far has been luck. Now I'll put my hands up and say that Alice is a smart girl. Adaptable. Not like all the other...contestants you've had before. She doesn't stick to normal human traits like routines and patterns. But as I mentioned before, she's tired. Wounded. And right about now I'm figuring she'll take any help offered to her."

Cassandra nodded, slowly.

"But if she's so smart, surely she won't trust them?"

Kavanagh shrugged. "She probably won't. Not to start with anyway. Now, I've spent the last several hours going through all the feeds and drone cameras, but these guys are sharp. We've got the two girls coming out of the apartment complex heading west but it looks like they split up. If that's the case, you'll be damned sure that girl with the pierced nose gave her a way of communication. Or a safe house to meet up in. We could go the traditional route and sniff around, but that'll take time and resources we don't have. Or..."

Kavanagh raised his eyebrows, letting the sentence linger.

"Or we put our goat out for something to sniff." Cassandra said.

Kavanagh nodded.

You must submit to complete suffering to discover the completion of joy.

Cassandra leant forward with her head craned; arms crossed. An aggressive and defensive stance.

"This fucks up a lot of things for us, Kavanagh. You know that, right?"

Kavanagh knew then that he wouldn't be dismissed. Internally, she was battling with a lot of corporate deals and promises she had made, but they were *her* promises, not his. His job was to catch Alice. And he would. He would look her in the eyes just before the light went out. He would stand in awe as the cosmos shifted in those glittering orbs as they glazed over, and he would know total finality.

"Sure. But our main priority is to catch Alice Paige. This is the way we do it."

Cassandra looked at him again with those dark, scrutinising eyes.

"This is your last chance, Kavanagh. No more fuck ups. Do I make myself clear?"

Kavanagh smiled. His eyes flicked over to the gold-plated lifts, the only access to where The Old Man resided. He wondered if he was hobbled over an open jar with taloned fingernails, pissing into them. He'd been reading The Old Man's blog, the bullshit about helping people and making the world a better place. Kavanagh knew better. People this high up were only interested in one thing.

Control.

"Do we need to confirm this with..." Kavanagh pointed a finger at the ceiling.

Cassandra went back to her files, picking up her pen. "Any affairs concerning Alice Paige go through me, Agent Kavanagh. Our CEO is not to be distracted at this time."

"Uh-huh. Say, when this is all over, do you think I'd get to meet him? Like, when I bring in Alice?"

Cassandra looked at Kavanagh, with a weary look on her face. For the first time during their talk Kavanagh noticed something he hadn't previously. She looked tired. A shred of humanity breaking through the carapace. "He doesn't have long left. He has other pressing matters at hand."

She went back to her files.

"Anything else?" She asked.

Kavanagh took that as his sign to leave. He stood, glancing at the lifts again.

"No. Not at all."

Daedalus: Hey lady

WonderWoman99: Dom

WonderWoman99: what are you doing?

WonderWoman99: we're literally sitting across from each other.

Daedalus: it's about Kevin. We need to talk about Kevin.

WonderWoman99: ah, okay. Fair enough. Hang on, wasn't that a book?

Daedalus: what?

WonderWoman99: never mind. What's up?

Daedalus: don't get me wrong, I don't want to sound like one of THOSE guys, but

WonderWoman99: he's a massive cunt.

Daedalus: I mean…well, yeah there's that.

Daedalus: you know he's been given the Freddy Henshaw project?

WonderWoman99: serious?

Daedalus: heard from it from up top

Daedalus: they want to go over the footage. Polish it up.

WonderWoman99: FFS again?

Daedalus: particle effects. Apparently in the last version there's a slight discrepancy.

WonderWoman99: what discrepancy?

Daedalus: well, you know how they made it look like a race to the finish, some Agent fires off a round and the bullet ricochets off a pipe or some shit like that?

WonderWoman99: yeh

Daedalus: apparently the shading is off by 0.1%. Last time they showed the vid was years ago, so they want to make sure it all looks clean for the improved optics.

WonderWoman99: and Kevin's handling that?

Daedalus: yup

Daedalus: can you make sure he logs the original RAW file so we don't get f****d over?

Daedalus: you know that's tagged. Eyes only and all that biz.

WonderWoman99: UUUUUUUUUUuuuuugh. Yeah, couldn't let that nugget get out on a hardline. Has he done it before?

WonderWoman99: tagged and bagged, I mean?

Daedalus: what do you think?

xxSUPER_KEVxx signed in at 09:15

xxSUPER_KEVxx: HEY, ALL YOU CVOOL CATS AND KITTENS

xxSUPER_KEVxx: HOLA

xxSUPER_KEVxx: ANYONE THERE? YOU KNNOW I CAN SEE YOU, RIGHT? LOL

WonderWoman99: Hi Kevin

xxSUPER_KEVxx: JUST TO LET YOU KNOW I'VE BEEN ASSKED TO GO OVER FREDDIE

HENSHAW'S 'VICTORY' VID. MAY NEED A HAND WITH SOME SPECS IF THAT'S OKAY?

WonderWoman99: sure, Kevin. Just make sure you tag the original data file when you upload it to the

internal server, okay? It's important that the original data log doesn't get uploaded to a different server

file.

xxSUPER_KEVxx: YEAH SURE THING

WonderWoman99: because we can't have a breach. Not like last week, okay?

xxSUPER_KEVxx: ITS ALL GRAAAVY

xxSUPER_KEVxx signed out at 09:17

WonderWoman99: I hate him so much.

Daedalus: so much.

23

GEORGE

WEDNESDAY

60 HOURS REMAIN...

Elspeth took the news better than George expected.

She didn't scream at him, or pace the room listing all the ways that their lives would be ruined. In fact, George thought to himself, she seemed calm. Too calm.

That was when he noticed the wine bottle protruding from in between the cushions on the sofa. She had likely stashed it there when she heard him come in. She thought he had been at work, and now he realised why she'd looked so flushed when he came into the living room.

She hadn't been expecting me. Thought she would be able to get rid of the bottle before I came back home.

They'd had arguments over her day drinking before. On many occasions. But George, like always, had relented and walked away.

That always seemed to be the case. She would shout and throw up every little detail of what he was doing wrong, and then all the energy would leave him and he'd sit there, nodding his head and murmuring assent at all the appropriate moments.

But seeing the tip of that bottle nettled something within George. This time he would not bow his head like a puppy dog.

"So, I just want to get this straight," she said, with a moderate slur. George looked at her evenly. He didn't really know how much she put away each day, as she ditched the bottles somewhere. He figured she was a functioning alcoholic. But he wouldn't mention it just yet. He would save that for when she got really riled up. And he knew that countdown clock was moving closer each second. Elspeth sat cross legged on the sofa.

"I want to get this completely horizontal, because everything you've just told me seems a little farfetched, George. You're saying to me that Alice Paige...the girl who's been on the run for the last several days...the girl who is the most wanted contestant in *Hunted TV*...she's currently sleeping in our bed. And you're telling me...that she's..."

"Our daughter. Yes. Well, that's what I've been told."

Elspeth frowned, accentuating the long, vertical wrinkle that split the middle of her forehead. "Right. From a bunch of people... considered in the eyes of The Network as terrorists...that you've *just* met."

George shrugged. When it was relayed back him in such a prosaic fashion, it seemed implausible. He'd been so caught up in the last few days, with the note saying that he would get his Birthday Treat, then finding out about Carina and The Movement that he just got swept away with it all.

But the last couple of days had made him feel alive. The most energetic he'd felt in years. He knew how both pointless and fantastical it was at the same time. Knew it was merely a dream.

He slumped down on the sofa, next to his wife. Saying it aloud now, forming the words and letting them leave his mouth seemed to act as some sort of cathartic, soothing balm on a wound that had been festering for a while. It all seemed impossible. Crazy. He was a relatively smart man; he had a steady job and a house over his head. He and Elspeth had problems, sure, but every marriage did. How had he let this carry on for so long? People were dead. All because he had been a coward and had gone along with the flow. With the routine. Was this what a mid-life crisis felt like?

The way that Elspeth was staring at him, a half worried, half panic-stricken gaze, made him think that yes, this was indeed what a mid-life crisis felt like.

"They're using you. Don't you see that?" Elspeth said. He could smell the wine on her breath. Pinot Grigio if he wasn't mistaken. He wondered absently if she used mints usually to cover the scent.

George put his head in his hands. Everything had moved so fast to begin with. Yes of course they had used him. First, they had lured him in with the dangling bait of Carina (George had surreptitiously been vague about the details of how The Movement initially contacted him, and he completely left out the kissing scene) and then had manipulated him by using Parker as the man to seal the deal.

Poor Parker.

George tried not to think about his crushed body.

Tried and failed.

"You said she's sleeping?" Elspeth asked, chewing a nail.

"She was running on empty. Think she was running a fever, so I gave her some antibiotics and made her something to eat. When I came back into the bedroom, she was zonked out."

Elspeth nodded her head slowly.

"Alice Paige. In our house. In our bed." She looked at the Free-Vee where a contestant shot his arm in triumph after spinning in *Wheel of Misfortune*. She stood up, tightening the knot in her dressing gown. She patted him lightly on the shoulder, the way an adult would console a crying child. George felt a small sting of irritation fissuring beneath his surface.

"I'm just going to go in and check on her," she said. George opened his mouth to protest but closed it again. Elspeth padded out of the room.

George sucked in air. How had he been so stupid? Of course they were using him. It was so easy to see now. The way Carina's persona had changed after coming down from the flats, dragging Alice beside her.

She seemed hardened, like someone on a mission. Spoke to you the same way Elspeth natters at you. Lecturing. Admonishing. Like you're an imbecile that doesn't know what they're doing.

The worst thing for a man, George thought sourly, was to feel useless.

But at the party when she first told me she was with The Movement... she was different. She'd been flirting with me.

The same way Elspeth flirted when she wanted something. For a staggering moment George wanted to throttle both their necks for controlling him the way they had. Because it had been so *easy*.

George realised he'd been holding his breath and released it in one, long exhale. This was reality. This mundane, day to day existence. That's what he had to tell himself. The routine was real. Joining a band of terrorists was not. It was simple equation.

He pulled out the wine bottle from its haphazard concealment. There was nothing inside it. Elspeth had drunk the entire contents and it wasn't even the afternoon. He supposed he envied his wife in a way – being able to numb out everything, sitting around and watching Free-Vee channels all day. Not having to listen to tiresome people speak about their Birthday Treat experiences. Not having to listen to the vile horrors of what ordinary people could do when given exceptional circumstances.

George heard the bathroom tap run and wondered briefly if Elspeth had at least done the washing up since he'd been out. He picked himself up and went into the kitchen with the bottle in hand.

The plates were still stacked up in the sink.

George felt the hairs on his neck prickle. He tried to look at it rationally, to listen to the sensible voice in his head. *Listen buddy, it's fine,* the voice said. *You've been through a lot these last couple of days and now that reality is hitting home, the small things are starting to bug you. Just let it go.*

But that wasn't quite true. The small things that continually bothered George started a long time ago. An exceptionally long time ago.

George leaned against the kitchen counter and carefully placed the bottle down. Beneath his calm exterior a rage flushed through him, something so powerful that for a moment it frightened him. George clenched and unclenched his fists so hard he felt the nails puncture the flesh of his palms.

This isn't you, Georgy boy. This is someone possessed. What's happened to you?

Elspeth appeared at the kitchen door. Her face blank, expressionless. George realised she had splashed water on her face. She looked old. *How did we get so old?*

"It's not Mary." Elspeth said.

The name hit George like a freight train. A flash of an image emblazoned across his mind: the girl on the platform, with her headphones listening to a pop song. The way the boiler effortlessly flung her on the tracks. The panic stricken look on her face just before...

They hadn't mentioned her name in years. The name of their daughter. The daughter that had only been several months old when Elspeth discarded her like spoiled food. It all came back to him then, the shouting, the sobbing, running around the town, asking people, strangers for any advice. He'd shaken Elspeth by the shoulders, demanding to know where she had left their baby girl. But she couldn't remember. She said that she had been walking in a haze for hours. She was hysterical by then, howling like some wounded creature. George had searched everywhere, relentless in his pursuit.

They couldn't go to the police. The police were being disbanded. The Network were in power. They had bought out the entire nation, one politician, one lawsuit, one television studio and a piece of legislation at a time. The laws of new dictated that any crime would be met with severe retribution. Social credits had already been introduced and had essentially changed the way money was used in the western world. It didn't matter if you had a million pounds in the bank – if your social credit score was above a certain line, you were okay. The times of old went out the window with a click of the fingers. Birthday Treats had just been implemented, and if they went to the police George hadn't known then what their punishment would have been.

Because Elspeth had illegally abandoned their child.

Mary.

George gripped the countertop with both hands, the only thing keeping him standing.

"What?" he asked.

"It's not her," she glanced over her shoulder to make sure the door to the bedroom was still closed.

She leaned forward, "Mary had a birthmark just below the nape of her neck, on her back. This girl...Alice Paige, she doesn't." She whispered. A waft of wine hit him then, and George felt like the noxious smell would engulf him fully. Bring him into the zombie-like state of his wife. Bring him down to her level.

Elspeth smiled. It was an insipid smile that said they'd dodged a bullet. It was a lifeless smile that spoke to George and let him know everything about his wife but didn't have the guts to say out loud.

She never wanted their daughter back.

She had never wanted a child at all.

George knew this. He knew it after returning home, having spent a week trying to find his baby daughter around London, asking questions to the homeless, to Degenerates, all the while trying not to raise too much suspicion in case the police, or Agents as they were becoming to be known, got dragged into the situation.

After a week of tireless searching, he returned home for some rest. Elspeth had been there, still sobbing. She said that maybe it was for the best, that she couldn't look after a baby. She was going crazy, she had said. She was scared that she might have done something horrible to it.

To her.

George had slept then. Slept for an eternity. His bones felt weary.

The plan had been to wake up and start searching again. He would check every nook and cranny until he found her. He spoke to his wife again, calmer this time. Asked her again where she had left their child.

But then Elspeth broke down. Physically and mentally.

George took her to the hospital. Stayed with her while the doctors drip fed her and spoke about post-natal depression. Then they told him he would need to stay with her, look after her as she rested. He couldn't even look at her. He wanted to be out there, looking for his daughter.

But after weeks of constant apologies, promises and assurances that their daughter was in a better place, she wheedled him into submission.

And a part of George's soul died.

George would never say he hated anyone before. Not properly. Even when he lost his consulting job, and what The Network did to people with small businesses back then, he didn't hate them for it, because there was no real figure to focus it on.

But in that instant, looking at that smile, George *hated* Elspeth. She stood in the kitchen doorway, tickled as punch that the girl in the other room wasn't their daughter. The daughter she gave away so many years ago. Without telling him. Without consulting him.

George didn't know what to do with that feeling, the energy crackling through him. He felt as though his veins had been fed an electric current. He lifted a hand from the tabletop and saw his fingers trembling. He could take the bottle and smash it over on the counter and plunge the dog toothed shards into her neck. He could repeatedly stab away until the kitchen linoleum was covered in a crimson layer. He could bathe in the geyser of her blood and feel nothing.

It frightened and excited him all at the same time.

Elspeth clucked her tongue, as if she had made up her mind about something. "Well, there's only one logical option we can take here," she said, matter-of-factly.

George looked at his wife.

"What's that?" he asked through gritted teeth.

Elspeth tilted her head and looked at George inquisitively, as if he had just landed on the planet and was getting a banana confused with a telephone.

"There's a reward, dummy."

George's fist shot forward with lightning speed. In the half second before it would have smashed into his wife's face, he remembered where he was, who he was and pulled back, instead extending his index finger at her.

"Don't. Even. Think it." George hissed.

Elspeth's eyes went wide as she recoiled in horror from her husband. She didn't know who this man was, the strange, almost wild look on his face.

She had never seen such rage in George.

HAPPY HORGAN: What are you telling me, Pat?

PATRICIA O'NEIL: Happy, the evidence is irrefutable.

HAPPY HORGAN: Lemme just get this straight…let me take a second and get real close to the microphone here so all my listeners can hear with their own ears. You're saying -

PATRICIA O'NEIL: Yes.

HAPPY HORGAN: You're saying that Freddy Henshaw didn't make it out alive from Hunted TV all those years ago?

PATRICIA O'NEIL: It was fabricated by The Network. That's what I believe, yes.

HAPPY HORGAN: You know, you sound like one of my callers.

PATRICIA O'NEIL: I've spent the past year collecting the evidence. Interviews with people involved. Ex-employees of The Network. Cassandra Rey, vice president of The Network herself. We've had the vids analysed by professionals in their field. There are far too many inconsistencies for it to be true. And why haven't we heard from him since he won? Not even a congratulatory interview. Nothing. Nada. Zip.

HAPPY HORGAN: You're willing to wager your career…your Social Credit standing in society…you're willing to risk it all to say this live, on my show?

PATRICIA O'NEIL: My editor's afraid of what might happen if this gets published.

HAPPY HORGAN: Are you afraid of what might happen to you?

PATRICIA O'NEIL: People need to hear the truth, Happy. Not one single person has survived the show. The Network wants to keep a boot firmly on their necks. Keep them in line. Not anymore. I'm telling the people to revolt against their oppressors! I'm telling the people to –
[Audible Banging]

HAPPY HORGAN: What's going on?

PATRICIA O'NEIL: Agents are storming the building. People of London, this is what happens when you try to tell the truth in our day and age. You've been fed lies and corruption for years and you've become apathetic towards it all! You -
[Sound of crashing]

HAPPY HORGAN: Who the hell are you? Get out of my studio!

PATRICIA O'NEIL: People of London, you are being LIED to. They want to oppress you and CONTROL you! They –
[Microphone feedback. Sounds of struggling.]

- From The Happy Horgan Live Show
@Happyhorgan

24

ALICE

WEDNESDAY
59 HOURS REMAIN...

After George had given her antibiotics, she had wolfed down a sandwich and fallen into a deep sleep. She tossed and turned mentally. Dark and vile memories worked their way out of the shadows of her mind, like sewage seeping up beneath a city street. A form appeared before her, a silhouette of a skeletal man that sung to her. But whereas once before she would have strummed her fingers along her guitar in cadence to his voice, this version of the skeletal man rasped and bellowed notes that were unfamiliar to her. This wasn't a love song. These notes were jabs at her, telling her that she would never succeed. That she would die before the week ended.

The skeletal man was replaced with a room, a room she knew well. It was the study of her foster father, the one that had done the bad thing. The one who had been screamed at and set upon by the foster mother. The sweet jar lay shattered on the floor, but instead of lollipops strewn on the carpet there were a variety of decomposing heads, all looking up at her, staring intently. They were all heads of Mitchum, the man she had killed.

"Pick me up," said one of the heads. This one had a flap of skin dangling from its forehead, as if someone had left a tent opening unzipped. The peeled skin revealed white bone underneath. Alice bent down and cupped her hands below Mitchum's ears. She could smell the rankness of his breath as she pulled. It was the stench of spoilt food and mildew. The head didn't budge.

"Ow!" It said mournfully. Its mouth remained open, and Alice withdrew with a cry. Her hands were crawling with huge and sightless insects. With a convulsive grunt the Mitchum head winked at her and then the flap of skin dropped off, like a slab of finely cut meat. It plopped onto the carpet with a dull thud and Alice realised that the rest of Mitchum's skin was dissolving, blistering and fissuring as if something from inside the skull had activated.

"You little bitch," the Mitchum head gurgled as more bugs and beetles escaped from its mouth. The skin melted into globular folds, dripping off the skull onto the carpet. Alice looked around the floor and all the other heads started melting too, all of them staring at her and mouthing inaudible curses as the skin became a pool of liquid beneath her feet. Alice then felt she couldn't move. She was stuck.

And she was sinking. The carpet had opened and was swallowing her feet. She lost her balance and staggered backwards, but felt her other foot going further into the swamp of the carpet with a horrible slurp of suction. Within moments, the carpet seemed to be over the top of her boots and she was sinking further. The skulls of Mitchum dropped out of existence, and for a few seconds Alice felt stupid with surprise. She would need to act fast; because she knew something from the first day she had gone on the run, something that she had put to the back of her mind. She would need to rescue herself. No-one was going to save her. The cold void inched over Alice's knees, up to her lower thighs. Her disorientation gave way to survival as she started to flail her arms to grab something, anything for purchase.

"Don't turn around," A voice from behind whispered.

It stopped her dead. Frozen. It was something she heard such a long time ago. But the voice was different. Not her foster father.

It was him. Agent Kavanagh.

"But we both know that's not true, don't we princess? We both know I want you to turn around," the Agent said, "because I want to see those pretty eyes. I want to see them blink out. Will you show me, Alice? Will you show me your dead eyes?"

The carpet engulfed Alice up to her waist. She doesn't think about the cold, dead things that lurked underneath the carpet. The tendrils snaking their way up to touch her feet, to drag her down. She didn't want to join Mitchum down there, in the darkness.

"We both know it's only a matter of time," the voice said, closer. "Only a matter of time before I find you." Alice felt something brush against the nape of her neck.

The carpet had swallowed her up until only her head was poking out. Just like the head of Mitchum. She used all her strength to scrabble and haul herself upwards, snorting and growling with all the intensity of an animal. But it was worthless.

Alice closed her eyes. The one small victory she would be able to claim is that she hadn't screamed.

"I'm going to be late," said another voice.

Alice opened her eyes. Squatting on its hind legs sat a small, rabbit with long ears and a short fluffy tail. It was holding out a large pocket watch with one of its front paws.

"I'm going to be awfully late at this rate," it said, its brilliant white hide thumping on the carpet. It reared its head, its nose twitching as though it were smelling a potent flower before it hopped towards the study door. There seemed to be an emanating light from beyond the closed study door. As Alice sunk down to her mouth, it turned round and looked at her sullenly. "Too late for me, I'm afraid."

The door opened, and before Alice was consumed by the void, a brilliant, dazzling light filled the room.

◉

Alice opened her eyes.

The filigree wallpaper she stared at was not familiar to her. The duvet she was under, now soaked with sweat, was not hers. The bedroom was too clean. It was a chintz nightmare of flourishes and flowers – gaudy oranges and teal everywhere. On the bedside table sat a doily and a glass of water. The air had a pinecone fresh aroma and Alice knew that a potpourri dish lurked somewhere nearby.

Where the hell am I?

She scrabbled onto her elbows and darted her eyes around the room to find a weapon, or something to defend herself with. Then she remembered.

Dangling off the balcony. The girl with the pierced nose dragging her away from the flats. The man who brought her back to his place.

My wife, she doesn't know anything about this.

George. He said his name was George. She sat upright and wiped her brow with the back of her hand, which came away with a sheen of sweat. She'd been feverish, had collapsed on the bed when he brought her back. She felt like she'd just gone twelve rounds with a coked-up Orangutan, groggy and floaty, but she did feel a little better, rejuvenated. She rummaged under the duvet for her jacket, but then remembered she'd given it to the girl. Her security blanket. The one thing apart from her guitar that meant anything to her. And she'd given it away.

You had to, Boss Bitch said. *It was the only way to stay alive.*

There was a window in the bedroom, and through the threadbare curtains a purplish glow filtered the room.

Then she heard shouting.

She crept to the door and put her head against it. The panel felt cool against her warm cheek. Alice knew when she was being spoken about, the way that certain exclaimed points would be hushed by the other party. She remembered many times growing up and hearing those hushed arguments through walls.

She made out the words 'daughter,' 'reward' and 'a fine mess you've got us into.' Any other time she would have giggled into her hands, but there was an edge to the words, both parties venting some unspoken words that had been festering for some time. Alice knew that feeling, too.

She couldn't stay at this stranger's house. It may have not been the dilapidated building she found herself in a few days ago, but she knew she was in perpetual danger. She could creep out onto the hallway and slip out the house unnoticed. If they were busying themselves quarrelling, then it might be a while until they noticed she was gone.

The room swayed when she turned away from the door. Alice took a moment to compose herself, found her footing. She'd dreamt of something like this...didn't the carpet open like a gaping mouth and she found herself sinking? A vivid image of dissolving skulls and rabbits flashed in front of her.

She returned to the bed and lay down for a moment. She would count to one hundred in her head. She would count to that number, pick herself up and leave the house. That sounded like a solid plan.

Alice was asleep when she reached twenty.

The noise that woke her the second time was a door slamming shut.

The shapes in the room were now monochrome. She cursed herself for having slept again. Silently, she cracked the door open and surveyed the hallway. The lights were on, but the arguments from before had ceased. She stared at the stairs, leading down to the front door. She should just leave now, slip out under the cover of darkness. She'd take her chances outside, roaming the streets and finding somewhere to lay low.

Because that's been working out for you fine so far, Boss Bitch sniped. Alice sighed. Okay, she would talk to George, find out what he knew about The Movement, why they were trying to help her. *But what if George left? What if it's his wife in the living room?*

It was a chance she would have to take. On her toes, she crept down the hallway and peered into the living room.

George was sat on the sofa, his head in his hands. Alice let out a sigh of relief. If it had been the wife, she would have turned tail and ran.

"Hey," she said as she entered the living room.

George lifted his head slowly and gazed at Alice, with a dullen expression on his face. His eyes were red.

"She's gone," he said flatly. "Not in the 'just gone to the shops' way, either."

She sat down on the sofa next to him.

Alice frowned. She wasn't used to people opening their feelings to her. Whenever she felt depressed or unhappy about something, she would grab her guitar and play something to get out of her own headspace. Whenever people started crying or acting weird like George was now, she would normally head in the other direction.

"What way?" She asked.

"I don't feel anything at all," he said, looking blankly at the wall. "and that's what worried me. I guess after years of...just mindlessly going about our daily routine, whatever we used to have just slipped away. We haven't been happy for a while, you see."

Alice nodded her head, as if she understood. "Can't be as bad as my life. My boyfriend sold me out to The Agents. Useless fucker." She chortled after this, to lighten the mood.

"How are you feeling?" George asked.

"Well, after being punctured by an asshole Agent, left hanging from a balcony and generally feeling like shite, I'd say okay under the circumstances."

"You look better. You could hardly walk getting here."

"Yeah, where are we, anyway?"

George waved his hand dismissively. "Chiswick. Not that far away from Hammersmith where everyone's converging like a hornet's nest, but we should be okay here for an hour or two."

Alice turned her attention to the Free-Vee monitor, which was playing aerial shots of the flats in Hammersmith. An announcer was mumbling something about gangs of Degenerates roaming the area, armed with baseball bats and other household items. They were out there now, hunting her.

"What do you mean for an hour or two?"

He slouched back on the sofa and put his hands behind his head. "So, there's good news and bad news."

Alice was alert. "Okay. Give me the bad news."

"I don't trust my wife, Elspeth. She wants to hand you over to the authorities and claim the reward for doing so."

Alice leapt from the chair. She felt like she was about to explode. Whatever bleary sensations she'd been feeling suddenly evaporated. She felt a heat coursing through her. A pin from a grenade had been pulled.

"What?"

"She said she was going to her sisters place," he said, watching the Free-Vee, "but, she'll be looking for the nearest shop to buy some booze. She'll find a bench or a bus stop and drink, thinking about what to do. She'll stew for a while, but eventually she'll make the call."

Alice couldn't understand why he seemed so calm.

"She did something...something really bad years ago. The guilt, you see...the guilt has been eating away at her, I think. So, she started to drink, to numb herself from it. But the worst thing is I allowed it to happen. I allowed it to rot. Just because I thought that things could go back to normal. Because that's what I craved. Normality. In this fucked up world. Joke's on me, huh? I knew it back then, but I didn't want to admit it. Everything's far from normal."

George nodded, as if he were affirming this line of thinking. Alice started pacing the room.

"But you can't know that for sure, George. Maybe she's going off to blow off some steam."

He slowly shook his head, not making eye contact. "No. You... remind her of someone. Someone she let go a long time ago. She'll go for the reward because it means she'll get to be on TV. She watches this thing every hour of every day. It's consumed her. Like it consumes everything."

"Then we have to go *now*. We get in contact with the girl from the movement, we find out what their plan is and we move."

George laughed. It was hoarse and shallow. "They just use people,

Alice. Whatever agenda they have in store for you, it won't be in your favour." He looked at her then, eyes wide and unblinking. "They use everyone, just like The Network. We're chess pieces to them. Pawns. Don't you see that?"

"Then can't we hide at one of your friend's places?"

George laughed again, but there was no mirth in it. "Friends? I don't have any friends. Not any real ones, anyway. The last person I suppose you could consider a friend is being scraped off a cab roof as we speak."

Alice was starting to feel exhausted from his attitude.

"Listen, George. I'm sorry your marriage just went down the shitter, but I've got people after me. People that want to fucking *murder* me. Do you know what it's been like the past week? It's like there's something malign stalking me, at the very edge of my vision, but I can never get a proper glimpse. Do you know how that feels?"

George abruptly stood, towering over Alice's diminutive frame. His face blossomed red and she could see a thick vein cord throbbing in his neck. "And who's to blame for that, Alice? You're like all the other takers in this world, aren't you? Nothing's ever your fault. You're always pointing the finger at someone else, looking to justify the shitty hand life dealt."

"Fuck you!" Alice shrieked, a sound that tore a hole in the air.

Fire in the hole! Boss Bitch bellowed.

"Don't you dare think you know me. You want to talk about shitty hands, Mr. I-live-in-Chiswick hoity-toity la-la land? You sit here in your little fantasy life, your little suburban womb, like nothing's going on outside. You've trapped yourself in this make-believe bubble where you put a file in a tray every day and smile a fucking fake smile at your boss, but inside you're dead. I've seen your type. Walk past the buskers and the beggars with your nose turned up, thinking that their smell won't somehow infect you. But you know what? I'd take their place any day of the week over yours. Because at least they're *living*, George. They're survivors, and they're hustling every day just to get by. You're not a man. You're a boy. You think that tomorrow you'll get that promotion. Tomorrow you'll deal with the Agent asking for your birth certificate. Wake up and smell what's in front of you, George. Tomorrow came and went. People are dying, George. People are…"

She slumped back onto the sofa. Tears welled in her eyes and spilled over. She let them run freely down her cheeks. George stood motionless in the living room.

"Why didn't you just take your Birthday Treat like everyone else?" He muttered.

She looked at him. Saw through him.

"Because I don't want to *be* like everyone else." She said. "Do you understand?"

George nodded.

"Listen, I'm –"

"Save it. You don't owe me anything." She wiped the tears away. "Frankly, I don't know you or how you're involved with the movement, but at this precise moment, they're all I have finding a way out of this thing. I had a plan, but like everything in life that went out the window from day one. So, what can we do?"

George pulled out a mobile from his pocket. It looked ancient. "Carina said she'd call me when it was safe. I guess we can find somewhere else to lay low until then."

Alice didn't think it was a great plan, but then she heard Boss Bitch whisper, *but you don't really have anything else, do you?*

"Carina's wig and clothes will only get me so far without being recognised. Is there anything else in Samson's bag?"

George trudged out of the room and shortly returned with a horrified look on his face.

"What? What is it?"

George showed her.

Alice had seen enough action movies in her time to recognise C4 explosives.

We regret to inform our customers that FlappyFlapPrivacyApp can no longer be downloaded from your merchant vendor. From next week a subsidiary app can be downloaded. This will be called TheNetworkSafeGuard

@FlappyFlapPrivacyApp

467 replies 1,845 RTs 5,886 Likes

This is unreal – haven't seen anyone make it past day 3 before. Gangs outside my window – there's a buzz in the air. Calling it now: riots in London.

@lifer_4_lyfe

3,456 replies 24,957 RTs 23,065 Likes

@lifer_4_lyfe This is scary.

@Leahsummers

354 replies 875 RTs 876 Likes

Who dis goth girl @Alicepaige running with? Send over pics – pretty Sure dem lezbos scissoring all the way to the weekend! #camgirl #hotsex #naughty #alicepaigesex

@HotPikachusex

855 replies 362 RTs 637 Likes

Watch my vid on how I made the rocker look Alice Paige coat!

@hannah_vintage

7,661 replies 6,727 RTs 1,656 Likes

Gonna be LIVE Streaming as me and the boys hunt down the bitch!

¬

Boys. BATTER UP! #goinghunting

@CRicoh

3,653 replies 822 RTs 2,986 Likes

ALICE AND ROXEANNE ARE THE SAME PERSON? I HAD ALICE PAIGE IN MY HOUSE. OMG!

@Brian_Bowerman

765 replies 546 RTs 1,865 Likes

WE NEED TO HELP ALICE PAIGE. SIGN THE PETITON. END THE NETWORK.

#thenetworklies

@For_The_Movement

2,665 replies 5,778 RTs 7,649 Likes

25

KAVANAGH

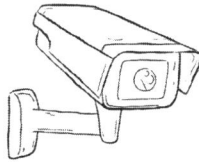

WEDNESDAY

52 HOURS REMAIN...

The inside of the small van swam woozily as Kavanagh's guts threatened to spill from his mouth.

"You couldn't have eaten that melted tuna sandwich outside?" He snapped. The dull hammer blows in his temple were dangerously raising to an apex of pain. Valentine's egg-shaped head gleamed in the interior light. The other Agent remained silent. Kavanagh had barked at him twice already during their stakeout, his irritability stemming from lack of sleep.

They were huddled round a small screen and a deck of monitoring equipment in the back of a van, no bigger than an ice-cream truck. The logo emblazoned on the outside was some florist company. Kavanagh absently wondered if anyone down the street would report the van. He hadn't known of any florist that would be parked for more than thirty minutes on a street. But they had been here for more than five hours. The windowless interior had seemed claustrophobic when they had first hauled themselves in, the enclosed metal space reminding Kavanagh of times he had been locked in the cupboard underneath the stairs when he had been a bad boy, but after several hours of sitting, waiting and assessing, the cramped space seemed to be closing in on him, as if the metal panels were indiscernibly folding inwards.

It made him feel weak.

The Movement's mole had been a complete pushover. *A real pansy,* his father would have said. He was a kid, playing the big man. Kavanagh had sized him up mere moments after speaking to him. His eyes had widened like saucers when he saw Valentine entering the rendezvous spot to set up the cameras and mic. The boy had practically pissed his pants as he questioned him about the target. That had been Kavanagh's small reprieve, at least. He had enjoyed the way the mole had stammered and spluttered as he answered their questions. The small, solitary line of sweat that had trickled down his brow.

It made him feel good.

He didn't trust the rat, but so far he'd proved worthwhile and the names he'd given Cassandra had checked out. Agents had already picked up three confirmed members of their little ragtag team of wannabe warriors, but Kavanagh had doubts. They were all low-level mules, just couriers with nothing valuable to share. The informant had given them breadcrumbs, nothing more. It seemed like stalling tactics to Kavanagh, but he would play this one out.

Valentine grunted as he struggled to manoeuvre himself. The back half of the van tilted slightly under his weight.

"Will you stop fumbling about." Kavanagh spat.

"Legs are numb," Valentine mumbled, defensively. The hulking brute made a face as he massaged his legs, kneading out stiff knots. Kavanagh turned his attention to the monitor screen. Divided into four segments, the cameras gave a wide scope of the building interior. It used to be an office building, with open plan spaces and large windows, but now just looked like any other derelict carcass found in London. In one screen, electrical cables were hanging from the ceiling like dead snakes. It showed a lift where they could identify who was coming and going with relative ease. The second screen fed them a long corridor leading into where they had placed the third small indistinguishable camera, a large area that may have once been filled with workbenches and ergonomic seats. This shot showed the entirety of the room, the drab carpeting, debris and graffiti on the peeling walls. The informant paced nervously around a broken vending machine that had been upturned and left on its side.

Another camera had been placed closer to where the kid was marching, so they'd be able to get a good look at his contact when the meeting went down.

Kavanagh probed the bridge of his nose with his thumb and forefinger. The swelling had eased over the last day, making it easier to breath without sounding like a broken whistle, but it still felt tender. His blackened eyes were already starting to saturate into a sickly yellow pallor, giving him a look of some jaundiced junkie.

Alice Paige was his drug. And he would find her. Oh yes, he had cast his net wide, and now he was reeling it in. He couldn't help but sneer at the thought of using members of The Movement to catch her. Two birds, one stone.

"What's that?" Valentine asked.

"Hmm?"

"You must submit to complete suffering to discover the completion of joy. That's what you said."

Kavanagh blinked. Had he said that out loud?

"It's nothing," he muttered, "just something drilled into my head when I was young."

Valentine nodded. "I used to think that I could move objects with my mind when I was a lad. I would focus all my energy into one spot...like the handle of a teapot, or the sharp end of a pencil. I'd spend hours locked into that spot, straining my mind to nudge it, just a little."

Kavanagh stared at the Agent.

"Never worked though."

Kavanagh arched an eyebrow. "Couldn't possibly imagine why."

Valentine shrugged.

The radio on the small table crackled to life.

"We've got movement on the east side," a tinny voice indicated. "Target has checked the perimeter and is now entering the building." Kavanagh picked up the radio and gave his instructions. "Wait for my signal. Absolute silence until the target has made contact."

He put the receiver down and looked at the upper left screen. The lift doors shortly slid open and a young girl filed down the corridor. Kavanagh's heart skipped a beat when he saw the leather jacket, the one Alice had been wearing since she went on the run, and unconsciously placed a hand over his chest to soothe the thrumming beat when he realised it wasn't Alice at all. He knew it wasn't going to be her – *but you could have ended it all here and now if it had been.* This girl was broader than Alice, different hair. He leaned into the screen and squinted his eyes.

She had a nose piercing.

The girl from the apartment block. The informant had been telling them the truth. Kavanagh steepled his fingers below his chin and smiled again.

Kaleb knew he was pacing up and down the empty office with manic energy, but he couldn't help it. He'd wanted to sit still, to exude power and authority. That had been an hour ago. Would she come? He'd text her the location on her burner this morning and had been glancing at his phone every couple of minutes since. If he messaged her again, that would look desperate. He didn't want to look desperate. She would come. The vids had splashed Parker's face...or what had been left of it, all over the news. She would come. Especially if he said he had information. Vital information for her cause.

He chewed his fingernail as he abruptly turned and strode down the same path he'd been walking up and down the last forty minutes.

He was surprised that he wasn't wearing the carpet down. His head was a mixture of emotions. He would tell her how he felt, that was the best thing to do. Get it out there in the open. That he had been in love with her the day he first laid eyes on her. He wouldn't have to mention anything about the deal he'd made. Not yet anyway. Once it was all done, once the dust had settled, then he would. First, he would tell her his feelings. He was sure she felt the same. And even if the worst-case scenario happened, he'd be okay with it. Because he knew what he was doing was the right thing.

But it wouldn't come to that. He had to think positively.

Not like on Monday. Monday had been a bad day.

The old guy at the pub, he was a mark. Nothing more. He was sure of it. Fairly certain. He didn't know why they needed him in the first place. Parker would never tell him the details. Never explained the full plan to any one member. That way, Parker said, if any of us get nabbed, they wouldn't be able to connect the dots. He'd always been like that. Shifty. But now Parker was dead. It wasn't his fault that had happened. Not really.

Parker brought it on himself.

Kaleb had been recently thinking a lot about what Parker said and what he did. There always seemed to be a different rule for him and others. Was that even his real name? Paranoid thoughts had made him jumpy. And what had Kaleb done, in the grand scheme of things? He wasn't a terrorist. He was just a guy in love, following the girl he loved into some political bullshit.

He'd despised the old guy the first moment he saw him in the pub. Looked too strait laced, too square for what they were doing. And he saw the way he looked at Carina, the way his gaze lingered on her for a fraction longer than necessary. That had got him mad.

Carina had a go at him in the pub too, and the old fucker had laughed. Not directly in his face, but in that 'trying not to laugh' way that seemed somehow worse. But Kaleb knew that she was just gaining the old guy's trust. Just taking a little jab at someone she could rely on to set the scene. Would've been nice if she would had let him in on it, though.

They'd gone to the party, and Kaleb was going to roofie the guy. That would show his true colours. He'd hoped the old fart would piss his pants and start convulsing on the floor. He hated the train journey getting there, listening to the guy prattle on about his job, like he was some big hotshot employee of The Network. Fucking creep. But Carina had been listening, laughing and nodding her head in all the right places. If it were up to him, Kaleb would have punched him square in the face and thrown him off at the next stop. But that wasn't the plan. The plan was to get him to the house party. He bit his tongue. He'd wanted to sit next to Carina on the train, but that dumb fuck had weaselled his way next to her. He saw the way his hand slid down to his leg, lightly touching her hand. He fucking saw.

Kaleb clenched his jaw at the memory. Remembered talking to him at the house party, said he would get him a refill. In the kitchen, he'd slipped the tablets into the plastic cup and returned to the living room, where the lights were strobing, and people were dancing.

But then he'd seen them go upstairs.

He imagined the things they had done up there.

He shut down the images in his head.

The idea had come so perfectly, so naturally. It was time to be done with these childish ideas, it was time for Kaleb to shine. He'd gone to The Network. Sat in Cassandra Rey's office, the vice president, no less. He'd taken something to mellow him out that morning, and he'd needed it. She was like a sphinx. He'd made a deal. A few names, a few people he knew from the parties, nothing in the grand scheme of things. Okay, sure - he'd made out he knew more than he did, but they'd never know. Did he feel bad that he'd given Parker's name? Well, only a little. Did it bother him that a day later Parker had mysteriously nosedived off a fiftieth story building...well, that had made him think twice. But he and Carina walked. That was the deal.

Then those two Agents. Man, those guys were a trip. The hulk smash motherfucker looked like he could snap a rebar in half with just a flick of his wrist, but the guy with the busted nose...there was something about him. There was malice in those shark eyes. More than just the thousand-yard stare. He was evil incarnate.

"What's the emergency, Kaleb?"

Kaleb looked over his shoulder. He'd been so engrossed in his thoughts he hadn't noticed Carina storm into the room.

"Hey Carina, how's it going?"

She seemed worn-out, as if her brain had been on a treadmill and was finding it difficult to find the stop button. Her fishnet tights had progressed from marginally ripped to full torn, revealing a pair of legs that Kaleb found trouble looking away from.

"Parker's dead. Communication's down. People are getting anxious. Soon it might be raining cats and dogs and I have a lot of stuff I need to be doing, so let's crack on with it, shall we?"

He didn't like the tone she was using. Like he was a nuisance, a box to be ticked off. He'd change that.

Kaleb stopped pacing and offered his hands forward, palms up. "I've got something you might like," he teased.

Carina sighed. "Kaleb, we've been through this. I don't know what kind of existential crisis you're going through at the minute, but I'm not going to fuck you. If you've brought me all the way out here –"

"No, no! Carina, you've got it all wrong! I've got the address for where they're keeping the *stuff*." He used air quotations for the last word.

This stopped Carina. She tilted her head, like a whistle had been blown that no other human could hear.

"What?"

"No jokes. Look, it's right here," he pulled out a small piece of paper and unfolded it. From where she was, Carina could make out an address. She stepped forward, narrowing her eyes.

Kaleb licked his lips. She was listening to him now. He was spinning his web and she was caught. Oh yes, for that moment he was the epicentre of her universe. And those Agent fools had given him the address like jackasses. He held out the note and she took it. Studied it.

"This is an industrial estate in Acton," she murmured. She bit her lip, as if trying to solve an impossible equation.

Kaleb grinned. It was toothy and wide.

She looked at him. Now he was no longer an irritation. Now he was the saviour. He was the master who had just delivered the skeleton key to open all her doors. He was the genie granting three wishes. He was God.

"Where did you get this?"

Kaleb shrugged. "Hey, you've got your sources and I've got mine, right?"

Carina paused for a moment and shook her head. "No, Kaleb. Someone doesn't give this intel to you on the street. You don't...you just don't come by this information. You're going to have to tell me *who* and *where* you got this."

Kaleb snorted. He couldn't believe it. Even in this moment, this paramount instant of importance, she had to act this way. It infuriated him. It rankled him to the bones. Just like the way she was in the pub. Making him feel inferior. Making him feel like nothing. But he could play the game. He did it with Cassandra Rey and she was the vice president of The Network. He gave her his wide-eyed innocent look.

"When I found out that Parker died...man, that just...it knocked me for six, y'know? Listen, I wasn't as close to the guy as you were and I know you think that I'm not serious about this stuff, but I am. I really am. Because I know how much it means to you. I did some digging. Went to a few bars, asked a few questions..."

"No."

Kaleb frowned. "No?"

Carina screwed up the parchment of paper and stepped forward, taking him by the lapels of his jacket. He staggered back, his heels knocking against the upturned vending machine, causing him to topple. Carina grappled him and leaned in, her face dark and full of malevolence.

"It took Parker years to set this up. Do you understand? *Years*. Do you know how hard it was to do that? How many documents had to be forged, palms greased, emails hacked in order for him to even get an application to be an employee? Do you have the *slightest* idea what sacrifices were made to get Freddy Henshaw's raw footage? And you're telling me you just walked into a few bars and got the address for where they're keeping the virus that will sterilise half the world?"

Kaleb laughed. He didn't mean to, it was nerves, but this incensed Carina further. Something struck Caleb's nose and he heard the delicate organ shatter. The attack had been so sudden and strong that pain didn't register straight away. Perplexed and startled, his head snapped back into position to see a fist retracting and *then* the pain came, followed by warm liquid gushing from his nostrils.

"You sud-of-a-bidtch!" he wailed.

"What did you do, Kaleb?" Carina shouted hoarsely. The blood streamed like a babbling brook from his broken nose onto his shirt. Kaleb blinked several times as if he didn't understand what had happened in the last few moments. She shook him to break his stupor, and he locked eyes with her.

"Ah dint thee you twing your fith," he rasped. "Badada."

"Yeah, and you won't see what's coming next if you don't start talking."

He put his hands up, the universal gesture of surrender.

"I'b bweedin,'" he croaked. "Badada!"

"Just tell me you didn't sell us out, Kaleb."

He clenched his jaw and stared at her. "I wub you."

Carina released him and let his body sag to the floor. Anger that fuelled her made way to a chilling realisation. Kaleb wouldn't be alone.

"Goodbye, Kaleb."

She turned on her heels and started running for the corridor.

Kaleb started sobbing. "Badada... Badada...." He closed his eyes and let out a strangled howl. How had it gone so, so wrong?

"Why does he keep saying that?" Valentine asked.

"It's the safe word you gave him, you moron."

Valentine's eyes enlarged in surprise. "Banana?" He made a move as if to leave the back of the van. Kavanagh stopped him.

"We were never going to jump in when he used that moronic word," Kavanagh said.

"But the boss lady -"

A flash of indignation rippled throughout Kavanagh's core. "I'm the boss here, Valentine. It would do you well to remember that."

The burly Agent hesitated for a moment, as if considering his options. He glanced at the monitor, where the girl had just entered the lifts. In a moment she would be outside the building.

"Do you know how you catch a tiger, Valentine?"

Department of Information public poll:

34% in favour of Agents retiring contestant Alice Paige before 5-day goal

61% in favour of Alice Paige surviving

5% Undecided

- From The Department of Information website

@minstry_info

26

THE OLD MAN

WEDNESDAY

49 HOURS REMAIN...

When you create the kind of legacy that makes the world better for all time, you start to think about what you're leaving behind for friends and family.

That's a nice thought, isn't it?

Second blog in a day. Feeling spritely. I've uploaded this past week's blogs to connect more with my family...the people of this country...

You.

Yes, that's right, I consider all of you a part of my family. The funny thing about family is that you don't have any control over them. However much you try to align things and make everyone happy, most of the time it'll never work. It's human nature, I suppose. The rebellious sister that stays out past curfew...the gameplaying brother that sits in front of his console all day and all night...the father who provides and the mother that cares for all of them. I would like to think that I'm the eccentric Grandfather who bestows gifts on all his family whenever he meets them, and I want to share with you one final gift before I finally take a bow and shuffle off the stage.

These past few months have been tough. I won't lie to you about that. It got me thinking: what would happen if things went back to the way they were? Before The Network? I realised then, that in my haste to try and plug the holes that were springing from the pipes, I never really took the time to look at the pipes themselves and think that we needed to install a completely new system.

That's a poor metaphor. Let me try something else.

Imagine there's a man. He owns a boat. He's the captain of the ship and he's sailing through the high seas. The waves are perilous and treacherous, and he comes across a small dinghy full of people. The captain knows that the people inside the dinghy won't survive for long, so he brings them on his ship. He continues his journey, and starts to find more dinghies in the ocean, with more people. Being the honourable Captain that he is, he brings them onto his boat, one after the other, but soon realises that there isn't enough space on his ship to hold them all. So, he starts building more decks on the ship to accommodate the people, and that's okay. Growth is good. The people are helping and extra hands make light work. They're also being trained in the ways of the sea and he finds that they're picking up more fish, exploring more islands, so he's becoming richer and that's also okay. The bounty is shared by all.

He comes across more people in the sea. He's bringing more people onto his vessel and he must build more decks to accommodate. He has a responsibility to the crew of his ship because they are his crew now. He builds another deck. And then another.

But the bigger the boat becomes, the more unstable at sea it is.

One of the crewmates comes down with a fever. It's nothing the doctor onboard has ever seen before. There's no medicine on the ship that he can use to prevent further contamination, so the fever quickly spreads and before long most of the boat has been infected.

It is during this time that the captain is caught in a terrible storm. The waves crash against the boat and because he has built too many decks, and too many crew members are incapacitated by the fever to help, the boat capsizes. Abandoned at sea, the people – his crew...all perish. The captain sinks to the bottom of the ocean, filled with regret and sadness that he was unable to protect his crew.

I think that's a better metaphor.

I referred to legacy before. The things we leave behind.

There's no real easy way of saying this, but I've never been the kind of person to shirk away from responsibilities or tiptoe around the matters at hand. I've always been the kind of person to rip a band aid off in one quick motion.

It's come to my attention that we could be facing down the barrel of another epidemic.

Now, firstly, don't panic!

Some of you may be too young to remember what it was like the first time round but suffice to say that wasn't a great couple of years. But we've learnt, we've adapted and there's hope for the future. This epidemic may not show its face in the next couple of weeks, the next couple of months or even the next couple of years, but it's coming. You can trust me on that.

My final gift to you, the great people of this country: my vaccination.

That's right, friends. Remember how I used to own a pharmaceutical company? Just because I sold the damned thing doesn't mean I didn't have shares. I had a voice still, and that voice shouted at the top of its lungs to invest in protecting our future. It keeps me warm at night thinking that we were looking forward this time. We're prepared for the next epidemic. There's already a facility with all the vaccinations required to combat this variation of the virus, and we'll be shipping them out to every house, every school, every community for immunisation relatively soon. Rest assured, your family will be safe.

We'll *all* be safe.

Cassandra Rey will be overseeing the whole process, and this is where I'm happy to announce my other legacy for The Network. Cassandra has been an absolute rock during all of this. From the moment I found out that I had a tumour, to co-ordinating all business affairs and roll out of the vaccine, Cassandra has been the lynchpin this company's direction need to take. She has never wanted for anything and knew that from day one no-one hands you anything. She's worked admirably for me for many years, and now it's time to hand over the baton, pass down the torch and fuckyfuckityfuckfuck- beebopshitty

Cassandra stopped for a moment, drumming her fingers on the table.

She wasn't pleased with the whole Captain/ship allegory. Sure, it was a nice lead up the main topic at hand, the vaccination – but it didn't sit well with her. That sip of coffee was too strong. It spoke the truth.

She stared at the words on her laptop for a moment longer, wondering if she should just scrap the entire document and start over. She hated writing these damned blogs, but it sent the right optics. The sheep had to know that things were changing, that the dynamic was being aligned for a new direction. It gnawed at her though, that the perception of The Old Man was some philanthropic sage, trying to save the people underneath him. He was just a charlatan. A crooked evangelist.

The truth of it was, he had been a cold, hard bastard.

He hadn't started The Network to communicate with the people. He was a ruthless businessman, willing to step on or over anyone who dared get in his way. He wanted what any other despot craved: control. Power. Cassandra had read somewhere that most CEO's of companies shared similar traits to sociopaths, and The Old Man hadn't been any different. She recalled her first memory of him, at a party following the premiere of some new show. She had recognised him from across the room. At that time, she had been a lesser-known PA for an executive producer, always a bit too grabby with her, with any photo opportunity resulting in a hand that trailed down an uncomfortable length to her backside.

The Old Man was greying then, his features gaunt. But his mind was still sharp. Like a serrated knife. Her natural reticence at the time was replaced by admiration and she had crossed the room to where The Old Man stood, surrounded by vultures and people that were too quick to laugh at his jokes. She introduced herself, expecting a quick handshake and a few perfunctory words at most.

She was surprised when he asked her opinion regarding a matter his group had been discussing.

"Thompson here thinks we should be aim for more light-hearted shows in the future. What do you think, my dear?"

Cassandra was acutely aware of The Old Man's steely eyes on her.

"The old ways are dead. People have been drip-fed formulaic content for decades. We need to shake things up. We need to be a sledgehammer."

Thompson guffawed at this and sipped champagne.

Unexpectedly, The Old Man's finger alighted on her exposed neck, cold as a cadaver. He ran it from behind her ear to the edge of her low-cut dress, and audibly sniffed like a wine connoisseur taking in a fine vintage. Then he withdrew and swung his arm low, his hand clamping and squeezing on Thompson's crotch.

Thompson juddered violently and dropped his flute of champagne. The other people in the group arched their eyebrows but said nothing. A pregnant beat ensued, and Cassandra could almost feel Thompson's heart pounding in his chest.

"*Jesus*," Thompson said, a hopelessly inadequate squeak.

"I just thought you might need a hand finding your balls, Thompson." The Old Man said. "Do you need me to find your balls for you, son?"

A glimpse at the man behind the mask let Thompson know that backing out wasn't an option. In this act, The Old Man had let the whole group know. Cassandra knew from that interaction that he never made a move on someone until he had some dirt on them, something they were ashamed of. The Old Man didn't need to be nice.

She learnt this.

That had been back then. She had worked diligently, she rose in ranks, and then The Old Man positioned her as his personal executive PA. Said he fondly remembered that evening and her conviction for the cause. And she worked. Hard. The Old Man held an air of indifference towards her, but she didn't mind. He was indifferent to everyone. Once a day he would make his way past her, a brief nod as he entered the gold-plated lifts to his penthouse suite, and once every night he would come back down and say something trivial as he left.

There were occasional parties and meetings that they both attended, but for the most part he remained cold and aloof. But in that time, she had become his eyes and ears. She had become his mouthpiece.

The Network's mouthpiece.

Cassandra sighed as she stared at the blinking line of her narrative cursor. She had been doing this for so long now, she wondered if she was just there to keep the wheels of their economy rolling. Every show, every Birthday Treat, every runner – all of it existed to facilitate the ratings and keep people under control. But there were more mouths to feed, always more. And new mouths demanded more bloodshed, more violence. It was a vicious circle she could ill-afford to end. She momentarily flirted with the notion of cancelling it all, to stop the juggernaut wheels from turning.

But that would be madness. All the jobs that would be lost, all the centres that would be closed, far more would die than The Network's regime could ever count.

No, The Old Man led the way. In that, he was right.

In the last year, he had been accustomed to spending more of his time in his penthouse suite, one evening bringing his wife Bea up with him.

The next morning, when Cassandra went upstairs to hand him

the daily news reports, she found them both slumped over each other's laps, dead. He hadn't left a note.

Cassandra registered this information and acted accordingly.

First, she disposed of the bodies in a quiet, methodical fashion. Afterwards, she went back to her office and carried on with business as usual. If she received any calls or messages, she would either deflect, divert or narrate a story as to why The Old Man couldn't respond. She started forging documents under his name and writing emails under his signature, as she was so accustomed to doing so for her usual role.

And in his name, she made herself Vice President.

It wasn't particularly hard to do. It wasn't like there was a board of directors that she needed permission from. The Old Man had been cunning and shrewd with all his business practices, and the last thing he needed was the red tape of a group of people dictating what he would do.

And then she had started the blog. Cassandra knew that she wouldn't be able to keep the pretence of his death at bay for longer than she already had – the lies and the deceit could only be spun so much. But in this way, she could make the public swoon towards her, as well as give them a martyr and cause they could fight for.

She'd seen the local polls. The people were starting to hope. The people were starting to cheer for Alice Paige.

And that was unacceptable.

Cassandra closed the laptop. She would continue with The Old Man's thoughts later. She had called Kavanagh and he hadn't responded. She didn't like that. The penultimate day of Alice's potential freedom, and she couldn't contact her main asset.

Things were unravelling. She couldn't abide that.

Brian watches the man and Roxanne leave the house. He followed them all the way to Chiswick when they left his flat in Hammersmith, staying as far away as possible without being seen. They went inside a house and have been in there most of the day. He feels cold and his legs are starting to feel numb, but he wants some answers – surely Roxanne…Alice, she'll be able to give them to her. After all he's done for her. Surely, she owes him that?

He takes out his phone and calls Charlie. He'll know what to do. Charlie always knows what to do. He's smart. When he spoke to Charlie earlier and told him that Alice Paige had been round his flat, his friend had laughed at him. A real throw your head back chuckle. Brian felt bad. His cheeks flushed the way they do when people asked him things and he couldn't understand them, but when he told Charlie to come round and saw all the Agents there…then he listened. He spoke to Charlie and told him they're on the move. Charlie ordered him to keep tabs and let him know exactly when they stopped. Brian said he would and hangs up the call. He felt like a spy, like in one of those old movies with the secret agent and gadgets.

Brian sings the theme tune of the movie as he follows his targets. That's what Charlie called them. The targets.

The man is older than Alice, and Brian wonders if they've had sex. He's heard that a lot of girls prefer older men, because they have more Social Credits and know their way around the cleet, or so he's been told. Brain's not sure what the cleet is, but he doesn't ask as people might laugh at him. Alice had been asleep on his sofa when he made her some beans, so maybe she liked sleeping on people's sofas. Maybe that was it.

The man keeps looking over his shoulder, as if he knows someone is following him. Brian can hear whoops and hollering from roving gangs nearby. There's an electric current in the air, he can feel that something bad is going to happen soon. Alice and the man turn a corner and walk down a street that opens out into a semi-circle of garages. The man pulls out a key and unlocks one of them, pulling up the shutter door. They slip in and close the door again.

Brian makes a note of the number. Writes it down so he won't forget it. He's always forgetting things, and this is an important case. A spy would never forget something as simple as a garage number. He makes another call to Charlie. It's dark now, and he knows The Ealing Slappers and Chiswick Choppers are out in full force tonight. They've had their fair share of tumbles in the past.

Charlie says that they'll be there soon.

Brian asks who is coming with him.

Charlie says: Everyone.

27

GEORGE

WEDNESDAY

47 HOURS REMAIN...

George had taken the duffel bag with the C4 and a few edible items, and they left the house. Alice wore a face mask and her wig again, and they moved quickly down the darkened streets. In the distance, he could hear hollering and cheering. They were searching for them. They were hunting them.

The garage wasn't far away, about a ten-minute walk. He'd purchased it years ago, his fortress of solitude, his escape from normal life. His inner sanctum. Over the years he'd started putting things in the garage, a couple of seats, his guitar, to make it look homely. Somewhere he could relax and read or just have some quiet time away from Elspeth, away from work, away from everything and everyone.

He constantly felt as if they were being watched from the

shadows. Dreadful thoughts of Agents adorned in black uniforms scuttling out of any nook surfaced, so he sped up his pace and Alice matched him.

Shortly, they arrived. The walls were concrete panels, machine vibrated and re-enforced with steel mats to give maximum strength. Nothing fancy, but it did its job. He unlocked and pulled the shutter doors up. He ushered Alice inside and secured it closed when he followed her.

He fumbled around in the darkness for the light switch and dumped the bag on the floor.

"You should be careful with that," Alice remarked.

"The detonators aren't attached."

"Still."

He shrugged. Alice surveyed the small garage. Coffee table with a laptop, a few cushions and seats. A mancave by any other name. Her eyes were drawn to the Les Paul upright on its stand.

"You play?" she said, incredulously.

"A long time ago, in a galaxy far, far away."

She nodded her head and went over to it. She looked at him to enquire whether it was okay to pick up and he nodded.

"Woah, dude. This is a gnarly model."

George went over to the corner, where he kept a mini fridge. "Played in a few bands when I was younger...but nothing spectacular. Just a few guys tearing it up, you know?"

Alice laughed. It was a sweet sound that cut the air. George smiled. He took out a couple of fizzy drinks and handed her one.

"I take it you know your way around one of those?"

"I play in a...well, I guess I used to play in a band. We did surprisingly good. There's nothing like it when you're on the stage. When you hear that roar from the crowd that blows you off your feet. When you're playing and everything comes together, synchronised. Symbols crashing...guitar shredding...everything up there feels epic. Magic. It's unlike anything else."

She strummed a few notes, plonking herself down on one of the chairs.

George plugged the guitar into the amp.

"Show me what you got then."

Alice's eyes widened.

"It's okay, the walls are virtually soundproof."

Alice grinned. Cracked her knuckles and began to play.

The next few hours continued with Alice playing the guitar. She would pause occasionally; they would talk and then she would play again. Sometimes she would play an upbeat song and George would watch her hands, moving so fast they were like liquid. Then she would play a guttural melody, all harsh angry rattles.

She sat up and winced.

"You okay?"

Alice carefully placed the guitar back in its stand and pulled up her shirt. A darkly red splotch had seeped through the gaze pad around her midriff.

"You're bleeding again," George said.

"Can you pass me the duffel bag? I put extra dressings in there before we left. Your bathroom is like a hospital. What's the deal with that?"

George collected the bag and rifled through it, bringing out additional gauze and wrapping.

"Let's just say that I like to be prepared."

"For the apocalypse?"

He sniggered. "More like I have...routines. Checks, to make sure I'm not dying."

Alice held out her hands. "Sounds like OCD to me."

George twirled his finger in the air. "Turn around, let me help you."

Alice stood still.

George started opening the packet. "What?"

"Newsflash, George: we're all dying. The day we're born the clock is ticking; you know what I'm saying?"

"Hey, did I say something wrong?"

"I can change the dressing myself."

"What are you talking about? It'll be easier if -"

"I said I can do it myself."

George handed her the pack. He stepped away as she awkwardly attempted to peel off the bandaging around her torso. An uncomfortable pause pervaded the small garage as she sucked in air through her teeth as skin came away with the pad. She dropped the fresh pack and let out a short cry as the bandage finally tore away from her flesh.

"This is ridiculous," George said, hurrying over to help. "Sit down. Slowly. Okay, looks like this needs to be cleaned up a little."

He squatted next to her on the chair, opening a bottle of water and splashing some on a fresh bandage.

"This may sting a little bit," he said as he carefully dabbed around her wound. She grimaced and let a *tsst!* of pain escape her mouth.

"What you said may be true," he said to break the silence. "But you seem in an awful rush to test that theory out. You said before that you chose not to take your Birthday Treat because you wanted to be different...but I don't think that's the case. I think you've been running for a lot longer than four days."

"We're all running from something, George."

He started carefully wrapping the new bandage around her. Paused.

"Maybe it's time for us to stop running."

Alice looked at him.

He gestured the duffel bag with a nod of his head. "Maybe that's what this is all about. I'm supposed to get my Birthday Treat on Friday. Maybe Carina wants me to blow something up."

"We take the fight to The Network." Alice said. "Freddy Henshaw made it. Years ago. People started to believe that they could make it on the show. More people stopped their Birthday Treats. It gave them..."

"Hope." George said. Alice turned and noticed he was looking at her neck. She stood up. Flexed her arm.

"That's a good field dressing, sarge."

George jerked his head up, as if snapping out of a dream.

"I...uh...once had to take first aid training. For my job. You should take some antibiotics."

Alice pulled down her shirt.

"But something Parker told me. The guy who...came off the balcony at the flats. Freddy Henshaw didn't make it. That was all a lie. They killed him, just like everyone else."

Alice's shoulders sagged. As if the wind had been taken out of her.

"How do you know this?"

"There's footage." He retrieved the USB from his pocket. He thought of Carina then.

This is where I give you absolute complete trust.

"Hang on," he said, flipping the case of his laptop open. He plugged in the USB and a video window popped up. He noticed Alice hovering over his shoulder.

"You want to see this?" He asked.

"Yes."

He pushed play.

The camera feed was a stationary. In a sewer.

"They have cameras down there?" Alice asked.

"They have cameras everywhere," George flatly responded. The footage timer in the top right of the screen elapsed a few minutes before a scared looking individual, gasping for breath ran into vision.

"Freddy Henshaw," Alice said, in a mild tone of wonderment.

Freddy Henshaw leaned against one of the walls of the sewer. He looked tired, his chest expanding and shrinking with each gulp of air. There was an ear-splitting *pang!* As a shot rang out. Freddy turned, ran down the narrow neck of the sewage system and another shot followed. George stared in disbelief at the screen as the bullet ricocheted off one of the venting pipes.

"We've got you, Henshaw! Dead to rights."

Freddy stopped. He put his hands in the air in surrender.

Three armed Agents entered the shot.

"Please man...just...let me go, aight?"

"Freddy, Freddy, Freddy. What do you think the last three days have been all about?" Said one of the uniformed Agents.

Freddy dropped to his knees. George knew what was about happen. But he couldn't tear his eyes away from the screen.

"Been down here, eating rats huh?" Said another Agent.

"Please, man. Please. I'm beggin' you. The only reason I'm doing this is my mum's sick. You know what I could do with all the-"

Another shot rang out.

Half of Freddy Henshaw's head exploded like a watermelon with too many elastic bands around it.

Alice turned away.

George closed the lid of the laptop.

"Real footage of what happened."

Alice closed her eyes. "Why would The Network send out a fake vid?"

"They knew that if the boot on our necks completely suffocated us, we would go back to square one. Riots...looting. It would be anarchy all over again. It would all unravel. They needed to give us just a glimmer of something else. So that we'd remain in this... subservient role."

Alice shook her head.

"I'm so close," she croaked.

He left the laptop on the coffee table and went over to her then. They hadn't known each other for long, but he felt an immediate parental need to protect her.

"No one knows where we are. I haven't told anyone about this place. Not even Elspeth. All you have to do is wait it out."

Alice laid down on the cushions scattered haphazardly on the floor.

"Can you play me something?" She asked.

George picked up his Les Paul. Started thrumming a soulful melody.

Alice closed her eyes. "I never said thank you. For all you're doing for me."

George continued playing as her breaths became shallow and she slipped into a deep slumber.

"And you'll never have to."

George didn't sleep well.

He was jolted awake by thoughts of the girl on the train platform being flung onto the track. Then he saw Parker's body slamming onto Samson's cab, pulverising him into a bloody, pulpy mess.

He checked his watch.

It was Thursday afternoon. Even though there were no windows in the garage, he could tell it was raining. There was a steady patter against the corrugated iron roof and the metallic panels of the shutter door. Alice stirred awake.

"I dreamt I was in a large castle," she said, "I was on trial. There was a queen judging me for all my sins. She sentenced me to death."

George took out the burner phone that Carina had given to him. There hadn't been any calls or messages.

"The last time I slept, I saw a white rabbit."

"You had a fever. How are you feeling now?"

"Better. Rejuvenated. If that's possible. What are we going to do?"

George rubbed his temples. "We wait. Carina will call with instructions. But for the moment we're in the safest place possible."

Alice sat up and stretched. "If you would have told me last week that I'd be camping out in a garage, one day away from finishing this fucking thing, I probably would have laughed. That Agent. Kavanagh. He'll find me. He's good at that."

George stood up. His stomach moaned and he went to the fridge to retrieve food.

"He'll have to get through me before he does." He wanted to sound strong for her, but the words felt hollow. She smiled thinly as she accepted a sandwich. He could tell that she didn't believe him, but that was alright.

"What do we do until then?"

"Tell me about yourself." George said.

She unwrapped the cellophane and took a bite.

"No mayonnaise. That's blasphemous."

"No deflecting. I can tell you've had years of experience."

Alice lowered the sandwich. She looked at George and opened her mouth. Before she knew it, all the years of hopping from foster home to foster home spilled out. The good families...the bad families. Mixing up with a bad crowd and jumping from boyfriend to boyfriend. Panic attacks. Playing onstage. All of it. George listened. When she finished, she let out a small shuddering sigh, as if expelling an anchored weight deep inside her.

"Feel better?"

"Actually," she said, "I do."

"That's good."

A silence descended over the small space, but it wasn't unpleasant. George listened to the rain pinging off the roof.

"Can I ask you a question, George?"

"Sure thing."

"Why are you doing this? You don't have anything to prove to the movement...or me. You could just walk away from all of it. Go back to your life."

George nodded, contemplating the question.

"My wife gave away our baby eighteen years ago." George said. His voice became strained. Slow. Thoughtful.

"This was during the transition period. I knew I should have gone to the police...but they weren't really the police anymore. We could have been locked up as we had broken the new rules. She just went out one night and...left her. She came home and was pretty much in a catatonic state. After trying to find out the location of where she went, I spent months looking for her. The first year was hard for both of us. Elspeth...put on this face. This façade. She came out of her paralysis and just started acting like nothing had happened. We went to therapy...counselling sessions. But we could never really *discuss* the root of the problem. Not without giving ourselves away. We stopped going. It was like this dark, dirty secret hanging over us. And then... we finally fell into a routine."

There was a pause, an awkward, lengthening pause, as George lowered his eyes to the ground.

"They told me...they told me you were my daughter."

Alice's face went white.

George raised his hands in a pacifying manner. "Don't worry, Alice. You're not." He let out a nervous laugh, a laugh of relief. "You see, Elspeth told me that she came in to check on you last night and looked at the back of your neck. Our...daughter had a small birthmark right about here."

George tapped the base of his neck. A single tear trickled down his cheek. "But when I was changing your bandage...I looked. Just wanted to make sure. She may be a lot of things, but Elspeth isn't a liar."

He cleared his throat, wiping away the tear with the back of his hand. "You ask me why I'm doing this...I guess it's because since that day it feels like my whole life stopped at that point. It's like...nothing good has happened since." He stopped and took a deep breath. "I owe it to her. I owe it Mary."

BRIAN WATCHES AGAIN

Brian is soaked and feels miserable. Charlie and the rest were meant to be here hours ago. Charlie told him to wait by the garages and report anything he saw, but that was last night. It's already dark, and he hasn't eaten anything all day. Nana would have made him some beans. Some lovely, hot beans. And toast. That was his favourite. Beans on toast.

The garage door has been closed all day. And it's been raining all day too. To avoid the downpour, he hid under a large Oak tree, somewhere where he could keep eyes on the garage court. But he'd gotten drowsy and think he may have nodded off for a few minutes. When he woke up, he was in panic mode, thinking that they may have left. He crept over to the garage door and put his ear to the panelling. He had let out a huge sigh of relief when he heard muffled sounds coming from inside. They were still there!

He took out his phone and called Charlie. His battery was nearly dead. Charlie says they're just around the corner. But Charlie always says that. He says he's just about to come round and then two hours later he'll finally arrive. Brain wondered if Charlie knew how to tell the time. He found it difficult, too – but you must practice, practice, practice. That's what his teachers always told him. Half an hour later Charlie and a few others of the Hammersmith Hardhats arrive. Brian doesn't know who came up with the name, but he likes it. He likes it because none of them wear hardhats. There's a name for something like that, but he can't remember what it is. Iron-something.

"What's occurring, Baldy Brian?"

"Told you not to call me that. I'm drenched, Charlie!"

"Stop yer whining, fuckface. Been any movement?"

"No, no not at all Charlie. They're still in there. Oh gosh, everyone's here. I've never seen so many of the gang in one place."

"Yeah, that's why I'm late. Got the whole charter together. No way those Ealing sapheads are going to get the drop on us when we stove in Alice Paige's head and broadcast it live for everyone to see."

"You didn't tell me we were going to hurt her, Charlie."

"Shuddup, Baldy. This is going to put us on the map, fella. We're gonna be numero uno around here. Ain't nobody gonna give us shit anymore, y'hear?"

"I'm not sure I like this…"

"Baldy…Brian – mate. You've done a good job. Stirling fucking effort, geezer. It's not going unnoticed. We had to make a detour and get a buzzsaw to open that tin can door, so why don't you help some of the other lads out getting it sorted and we'll –

"Gosh, the door's opening."

"Fuck. Boys…on me. Wait…it's just the old sod. What's his game? He's closing the door again. Now he's walking away…okay…okay…here's what we're going to do. Wait for the old fucker to leave and then we have her all to ourselves."

28

KAVANAGH

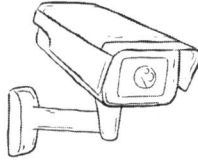

THURSDAY

11 HOURS REMAIN...

The bitch knew she was being followed.

She'd been trying to lose them for the whole day, but Kavanagh was a master of hiding in the shadows. First the emo girl with the nose piercing had gone to a public place. Kavanagh told Valentine to stay with the van as he followed her through the thronging crowds. He'd been growing increasingly agitated with Valentine's persistence to answer Rey's calls. Another bitch in a position of power that needed taking down a peg or two. He was glad of the short respite away from everyone.

It would also give him the opportunity to pick up some stimulants. He found his hand shaking uncontrollably in the van – an unfortunate but inevitable result from having been awake for more than ninety-six hours. He'd been having micro-sleeps in the van and felt haggard. He needed something, an edge to keep him focused.

The girl went into a coffee shop, glancing nervously over her shoulder. Kavanagh liked this. She should be afraid. She was going to meet another member of The Movement, or even Alice herself. And Kavanagh would be ready to pounce when she did.

The line for ordering was long, so Kavanagh risked slipping away for a moment. There was a Degenerate lurking at the mouth opening of an alley and he made a beeline for the punk.

"Two tickets," he snarled. The kid looked taken aback, almost jumped from where he was standing. He eyed Kavanagh suspiciously, taking in his harried demeanour and busted nose, but his expression soon changed when he saw the Social Credit reader.

"Forty creds," the snot nosed kid said. His voice was shrill and reedy. Kavanagh would like nothing more than to slam his face repeatedly into the brick wall. In other circumstances he would have just taken them from the kid, but he didn't dare risk causing a scene. Not when he was so close.

He scanned the reader on the kid's tablet and with a swift wave of the hand the exchange was done. The kid took off, likely to find another spot to sell.

Kavanagh opened the small baggy and did a couple of bumps. The effect was immediate: he felt energy surge into his brain and everything aligned into clarity. He knew it wouldn't last long, but he could keep taking bumps without Valentine noticing.

He went back and saw the girl ordering a coffee. After she left, she milled around, always looking around to make sure she wasn't about to be tackled to the ground. An hour later she felt confident to leave the crowds and several bumps later Kavanagh was feeling electric. He was chewing nothing in his mouth.

With self-discipline almost anything is possible.

He rubbed his chin and forced himself to stop chomping like a donkey. His eyes were dilated to pin needles.

The girl took him on a merry chase around the industrial sector and met up with more Degenerates. They were drinking and smoking, but they didn't look like they had any affiliation with her cause. Kavanagh noted it all down, nonetheless. Cassandra Rey would want evidence of his actions. And he wasn't going back to her empty handed.

It was evening when she made a phone call. This looked promising. Kavanagh dabbed more of the white stuff between his thumb and forefinger and snorted it. He would need all his attention.

She ended the call and started making her way out of the area. She was walking with purpose now; she had a plan in mind. Kavanagh called Valentine and told him to bring the van. The endgame was in sight.

A few hours later they were back in Chiswick. It had started to rain, the roads becoming a neon matt photograph, only to be washed as glossy as any magazine page.

Kavanagh's eye twitched as they passed a vid screen in a window shop – the ticker tape scrolling at the bottom exclaiming Alice Paige's journey so far. Gangs were roaming the streets, but he had noticed a shift in their jeers and chants. They were rooting for her.

Fools. All of them. All the stupid sheep.

This could make his job harder. He could feel the tension in the air, the trained foresight of a bouncer knowing that something was about to kick off. It was palpable.

The girl with the shredded tights was moving into the park.

"Okay, we'll walk from here. She's going to meet with a contact. Be prepared for anything."

Valentine sighed. "We should call this in. Rey's been trying to -"

Kavanagh turned on Valentine then, a look of pure hatred etched within the lines of his face.

"You answer to *me*! Do you understand that?"

Valentine's jaw clenched. It looked like he was about to say something, but simply nodded.

"Don't forget that it was me that got you reinstated. Now we track at a distance and wait for my signal. Do you understand, you bloody condom full of walnuts?"

Valentine nodded again.

"Good. Let's go."

They slipped out into the dark night. Kavanagh only realised the rain was cold because his skin carried the heat of his blood, otherwise he felt nothing. That would soon change. When he squeezed the life out of Alice, he would feel everything. He would be immortal.

Kavanagh slid to cover behind an oak tree. Watched for movement. The lamp posts were providing dull cones of light as the girl walked down the path. Kavanagh felt the comforting steel of his Glock tucked in his belt holster. He unclipped the safety clasp.

He moved forward, waving at Valentine to keep a safe distance. The big tree trunk of a man would give them away if she decided to turn and look in the direction he was facing. He wouldn't tolerate yet another failure.

Adrenaline was starting to coarse through Kavanagh. Or it could have been the cocaine. He was buzzed. Fresh as a daisy.

Fuck you dad, he thought. *I'm going to be somebody. You'll see. You'll see.*

She made her way to a small hexagonal bandstand in the middle of the park. He didn't have to wait long until someone appeared. A man. Looked in his mid-to-late thirties. He was unkempt, with a two-day stubble visible even in the darkness. They spoke for a while. Then they hugged.

Kavanagh rested his body against the bark of the tree. In this position, he could freely aim at the girl and the man. He took out his pistol. The rain was coming down heavy. He wiped his brows.

The girl gave the man something. Kavanagh couldn't tell from this distance. Something small. Something you could put in your pocket.

Then she came.

Alice Paige.

The man turned, looked surprised that she was there. She was carrying a guitar. Kavanagh took a moment to take it all in. There she was, no more than fifty feet away. The object of his mission. The pinnacle to which he aspired.

The man seemed upset. She was nodding at him, like she was being reprimanded, but she looked defiant. Kavanagh would soon see to that. He would see the fear in her eyes before the lights went out.

They were going to have a good chinwag. Oh yes, they were.

A snap of a twig broke him from his fantasy.

Kavanagh spun to his left. Valentine was looking down at his feet. The stupid imbecile. He snapped back to the bandstand.

They were all looking in his direction.

Even through the pouring rain, Kavanagh heard the girl scream for them to run.

He took aim and fired.

HAPPY HORGAN: Folks, we're back on the air. Action news reporter Patricia O'Neil was forcibly taken by Network Agents and we were removed from the studio. It's been absolute pandemonium here – but I was able to sneak back in before they could charter everyone off. Without my team I'm limited to what I can broadcast, but I'll keep the hits coming until they blow the door off the hinges and shoot me down. I've managed to barricade myself in but I'm not sure how long it'll hold. You guys have been incredible and I've been taking calls during all of this craziness – it appears that gangs are heading an masse to Chiswick, so it looks like something is definitely up. There's only a few hours remaining before Alice Paige wins her run and the switchboard is lighting up. Let's take a few calls. What's your name sweetie?

CALLER: Hi Happy! Sally here, so glad you're doing okay! OhmyGod it's crazy out there. I can literally see a tower of fire in Ealing. This is mental. You can hear them all chanting – my ex used to be part of the Ealing Slappers and I just want to tell him that if he's involved in any of the looting going on –

HAPPY HORGAN: Thanks Sally, next caller?

CALLER: I told ya bruv! You didn't listen to me, did ya? Thought you could call me names on air, well look who's sucking cock now you sonofa-

HAPPY HORGAN: Profanity is the lowest form of wit. Dickhead. Next?

CALLER: It's the end times, Happy! This is end of the world! Can you play something apocalyptic, mate?

HAPPY HORGAN: Run To The Hills by Iron Maiden coming up shortly, fella. Next?

CALLER: Alice Paige is in Chiswick Park, Happy! There's gonna be a fight to end all fights. Gangs descending upon the place right now!

HAPPY HORGAN: Well you've heard it here first, listeners. Under One hour to go…what will happen?

- From The Happy Horgan Live Show

@Happyhorgan

29

ALICE

THURSDAY

1 HOUR REMAINING...

George had left about three minutes ago and Alice didn't feel like sitting in the garage alone.

Not because she felt frightened or abandoned...quite the opposite. After playing the guitar again she felt that surge of energy, that 'something' she couldn't put her finger on, whenever she played. It was like she had chopped the last four days of Alice Paige and put them in the blender. The scared girl who ran away from Agents. The timid version of herself that ducked and weaved through dilapidated buildings and hung from balconies to avoid her troubles. The frightened shell who hid in cupboards in random people's houses.

They were all in a blender and when she played the guitar it was like turning the power button on. Those false replications of herself were sliced and cut into a million pieces. There wasn't much time left before she would have completed her running. She would be the first person in the history of Hunted TV to do it. All she would need to do is sit tight and count the hours away.

But something gnawed at her. George was risking his life for her. He had nothing to gain from that, not really. Maybe the last week had been a shock to his system, stirring something awake that had lain dormant for years...but that didn't mean he needed to throw his life away.

I signed up for this, she thought. *I consciously decided to forfeit my Birthday Treat. I knew the risks. George was forced into this. And now I'm letting him walk into...fuck knows.*

She'd thought Freddie Henshaw had been the gleaming spark of hope for her generation, someone she could look up to and admire for having survived. For having beaten the system. But he was just a smokescreen, something that The Network wheeled out whenever they felt they needed a boost to their ratings. Freddie Henshaw wasn't real. Freddie Henshaw was dead.

But she was alive.

Don't you even think it, Boss Bitch chided. *You go out there now and it's a death sentence. Gangs are out in force, Kavanagh's sniffing around... you know what that means. Just listen to George. Sit tight. Wait it out.*

Alice closed her eyes. Boss Bitch always had her best interests at heart. She'd been there from the start, all the way back in the fostering homes. Since Eugene. She'd been her voice of reason, assertive and dominant.

But Boss Bitch wasn't always right.

Alice stood. Opened her eyes. Grabbed the guitar and went to the shutters.

You're making a mistake. It was the last thing Boss Bitch said.

"I don't need you anymore." Alice replied.

She opened the shutters.

Charlie Ricoh stood outside the garage in the pelting rain, the buzzsaw heavy in his hands. His mob, the Hammersmith HardHats, were eagerly waiting behind him, armed with baseball bats, kitchen knives and other assortments of home-made weapons. He felt the anticipation of what was about to happen and he loved it – the thought of capturing Alice Paige and getting himself so many social credits. It was a game changer.

He'd be able to leave London, get himself a cushy little place in Hawaii or some other tropical island. Yeah, he could leave all this behind him, the dim-witted gang members, the incompetent friends that were too stupid to tie their own shoelaces, the constant nagging from his mum. All of it.

Baldy Brian was twitching next to him, his ERD pulsating several colours. He looked down at the chainsaw and realised that he didn't know how to work the thing.

He didn't want to look incapable in front of his mob. He hadn't stampeded through the ranks by asking for help. He took what he wanted and ordered others to follow lead. Because that was what it was like to be a leader. You had to take control.

"Baldy, this fucker's heavy. Start me up, will ya?"

Brian blinked as he looked at the contraption.

"Oh gosh, Charlie...I'm not sure what to do..."

Charlie grimaced in anger. This was exactly the thing he wanted to get away from. Weakness. Passivity. Loserville.

"Just come round here and push buttons until it starts," he said.

But in the end, he didn't need the buzzsaw.

The shutter doors started opening.

He felt the obvious energy from The HardHats behind him coil like a snake about to attack.

Alice Paige took a step out of the garage and looked at him directly. Her eyes scanned the crowd that had gathered around the garage, thirty-odd Degenerates all primed for a messy mosh.

Alice nodded, as if confirming something, then swung the guitar at Charlie's head.

The base hit him just above the ear, and he fell heavily, spreadeagled on the tarmac. The buzzsaw dropped to his feet with a loud metallic crunch. Alice paused a beat and looked at the rest of the crowd.

"What's your gang?" she asked. There was a cutting undertone to the question. She wasn't afraid.

"Hi Roxanne. It's me, Brian. We're the Hammersmith HardHats."

Alice gave Brian a quick smirk of acknowledgment. Charlie remained motionless on the floor. A few Degenerates started to come forward, raising their clubs in the air. Alice needed to act fast.

"HardHats...you've been lied to. We all have," she shouted. The crowd stopped undulating towards her. They were still moving, but slower. No-one wanted to be the second person to have the guitar smash against their skull. They were like hyenas, pacing the line waiting for an ample opportunity to attack. Their leader had fallen, so the initial spark of violence had been quelled, but it wouldn't be long until their courage returned, and she would be overrun.

"Freddie Henshaw never made his run. He was killed on the third day. There's proof."

The crowd stopped moving entirely. A few HardHats looked at one another with questioning expressions.

"Bullshit!" someone yelled from the back of the crowd. "Fucking get her!" another yelled.

But the first wave line remained still. Alice saw her chance.

"Listen to me!" She shouted. "The Network have lied about everything. That vid you saw earlier about vaccination. Lie! It's going to sterilise half the population of this country."

Alice could hear murmurs of dissent amongst the group. Their bats were no longer raised in a chilling war cry. The rain lashed down on them all now, and she looked out at the blank faces in front of her. If the first line rushed her, she'd be able to take out a few of them. But they had the numbers.

"The world is overpopulated. They did it twenty years ago with the first inoculation jabs. And look at us now. Most of us wear surgical discs on our heads to let others know what we're feeling! Don't you feel like you were cheated, HardHats?"

A few more grunts and quizzical glances to each other.

"Charlie said we'd get money by taking you in! Dead or alive!"

Alice felt the swarm growing restless.

"We want money!" came a voice.

"And social creds!" came another.

Alice could feel she was losing them. Soon their wails would crescendo to chanting and then they would come.

"Guys! Guys!"

The crowd's jeers dissipated. Brian stood next to Alice, his arms waving in the air.

"If we help her win, she'll give the Hardhats some money, won't you?"

Alice looked at Brian. Then looked back at the crowd.

"Uh. Sure. More money than Charlie promised you. If I win, I get five hundred thousand. You're more than welcome to two hundred thousand."

Incredulous noises were being made within the group. Alice arched her eyebrows. Obviously way more than what Charlie had promised them.

"If we help you?" said a voice.

"Help me get through to Friday, and I guarantee you when I have the money, I'll donate two hundred thousand to The Hammersmith HardHatters."

"It's HardHats!" someone yelled.

"Yep. Sure." Alice said.

Brian smiled.

30

GEORGE

THURSDAY

38 MINUTES REMAINING...

"I think I'm being followed. I know it's not safe, but you need this address. Do you still have the USB?"

George nodded at Carina. She looked exhausted. After spending the day in a garage, George thought that he probably didn't look so fresh either.

They were in the middle of the small bandstand, the one she had stood at a few days ago when he followed her to the antique shop. When he knew nothing about The Movement or Parker's involvement. Before everything.

Carina handed him a small slip of paper. He quickly looked at the address and stuffed it in his pocket. An estate in Acton. The industrial part. A warehouse, by the looks of it.

"Did you see the vid today?" Carina asked.

He shook his head.

"They're planning to roll out the inoculations soon. This is our only chance, George. We have to take out that shipment."

"That's what the explosives are for."

"You were never meant to be involved in that part. Parker wanted you to upload the USB of Freddie Henshaw's real footage. Using your credentials at The Network, you could access the AV section of the building and upload the data to be played as a live stream. That would be your Birthday Treat – corporate espionage. It was meant to be a three-pronged attack: one on the warehouse itself, destroying the virus, the second as the footage showing the people the truth and the third helping Alice Paige survive. Parker's intention was always to unveil the real face of The Network to everyone. He hoped Alice could be that catalyst."

The rain lashed down, machine gunning the roof of the bandstand. George turned, his eyes slowly sweeping past the amps and connection leads to Carina.

"You never knew where my daughter was, did you?"

Carina looked down at her feet.

"That was cruel. Just so you know, I didn't want to go with that approach. Parker needed something to galvanise you. To shake you from your apathy. When I argued, Parker asked me a simple question. 'What else can we use to open his eyes.' In a way, it was true. Harsh... but true."

George bit his bottom lip. In some way, he knew. He had always known. He would never see his daughter again.

"It's okay," he said. "The...thing that happened between us..."

"That was real." She looked up at him. They were silent for a moment. "After my brother died...all I've felt is hatred and anger. At The Network. At everyone around me. I've pushed more people away then I can count. I don't know...maybe knowing that all this...once this is all over, maybe I can move on. Or rot in a Network gulag somewhere. Maybe all I just needed was a hug."

George came forward and embraced her.

They stood there for a while, her head on his chest, his arms wrapped around her. It felt nice.

"Get a room guys," Alice said from behind.

George turned. "What are you doing here? You shouldn't be out in the open like this."

"George, trust me when I say this – I'm not safe anywhere. But it's okay, I've got a plan."

George frowned. "A plan? The plan is to survive, Alice. You've still got hours left. Anything could happen in that time. Anything at -"

A twig snapped.

Carina spun round, saw the hulking figure of an Agent trying desperately to hide behind a tree.

"Run!" she screamed.

A staccato shot reverberated throughout the park. George froze in a soundless thunderclap of shock. His breath sobbed out of his lungs in a pained whistle. His legs felt rubbery, as if someone had just taken all the energy from his body.

And in a way, they had.

Carina's hair jumped.

Gouts of blood burst from her nose and mouth and from the underside of her chin, where the bullet came out. She stared at George for a moment, their eyes locked in bewilderment and surprise.

Then she fell forward.

George felt himself move to catch her, but everything was slow. It was if he wasn't in control of his movements.

Her bewilderment shortly turned to a terrified shock, her eyes bugging out of her skull. Blood spurted from her neck and George clamped his hand over the wound. They both sagged onto the decking, now pooling with blood.

Carina said something but it came out as a choked gurgle. Her hands clawed at her neck, panic overtaking her.

"Try not to talk," George said. "Save your strength. Try not to talk."

He could hear more shots ring out in the darkened park. A chunk of wood exploded near his head. He didn't care about any of that.

She looked at him for a moment.

"Carina. Stay with me. Please."

Then she died.

He could feel the chill in his blood, coldness bringing the synapses of his brain to a standstill. Part of it was pain, but most of it was emptiness. A stark void left in his heart. He let out a guttural cry, something primordial and raw, a wailing that had been slowly building within him for years.

Carina stared vacantly at the bandstand roof. He gently laid her down and looked at his hands. They were shaking, slick with blood. He bunched them into fists. White knuckles from clenching too hard, his hunched form exuded an animosity that was like acid - burning, potent. His face was red with suppressed rage, and when George looked out to see Alice on the floor, wriggling in the grasp of the Agent, he swung around and mentally snapped.

"Get off her." He said. It was a calm tone, merely a whisper. He made his way down the bandstand steps, the rain stinging his face.

"I said get off her." His voice was rising now, like the fury blossoming in the pit of his stomach. He broke into a run, his focus laser sharp at the Agent straddling Alice, his hands wrapped around her throat, choking the life out of her. Ten feet away.

No. He couldn't lose another person.

"GET AWAY FROM HER!" He screamed, a banshee war cry thundering through the rain. Five feet away. His mind was detached.

George hit the cold, muddy grass before he felt the shockwave that had sent him sprawling. The other brute Agent had tackled him to the ground. Two feet away. He could hear Alice screaming, could see the manic look in the other Agent's face. It was the face of a man who had fantasised this scenario hundreds of times and was enjoying its actuality to the fullest.

The Agent with the bald head clamped his massive hands down on George's chest. The wind was knocked out of him instantly. Caked in blood and mud, he writhed under the colossal weight of the Agent.

He couldn't breathe. The burly man was smiling in child-like glee as he pushed down on George's crumpled body.

The Agent's hands crawled up his chest to his face. George felt his calloused thumbs dig into his eye sockets. The Agent was going to gouge out his eyes. He was going to pop them like grapes. He felt intense pressure and his vision went dark. George let out a garbled yell as he squirmed from the vice-like grip on his skull.

Searing white pain shot through his left eye socket. Did he just hear his eyeball pop? With all the might he could muster, George brought his knee up into the Agent's groin.

He heard the man grunt and a moment later the big man shifted off his body. George tried opening his eyes but all he could feel was the rain lashing down on him. He couldn't ease up, not now.

He heard the Agent let out a snort and he got to his knees, bunching his hands into fists. All the anger was back again, as he started reigning blow after blow onto the enormous man.

"YOU FUCKER!" He screamed. "YOU DIRTY CUNT FUCKER!"

He felt strength he never knew he had. His mind switched off. He didn't know how much time had passed, but he was vaguely aware of being dragged off the Agent. He tried opening his eyes again. The left one was destroyed. The pain would come later. He couldn't accept it yet.

Through blurred vision, he saw the scene in front of him.

It horrified him.

"Alice?"

31

KAVANAGH

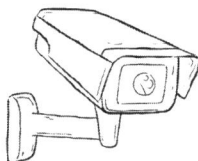

THURSDAY

10 MINUTES REMAINING...

Kavanagh saw the bitch in the bandstand go down.

He started sprinting after Alice. He fired another couple of shots, not really aiming, just suppressive fire. He motioned for Valentine to flank the bandstand.

He didn't want any distractions as he took Alice down.

She was running in the muddied park, and he took a pot shot at her. Saw the ground explode around her feet. The rain was in his eyes, the wet mud making him slip, but he persevered. She wouldn't get away this time. Not this time.

He was almost on top of her. He could shoot her there, but he wanted the full grace of watching the life ebb away from her in his hands. He raised the Glock again, maybe just to hobble her would be okay. A flesh wound would suffice.

But then she did something that surprised him.

She stopped and turned, swinging the guitar. Kavanagh's momentum couldn't stop in time. He crashed into Alice Paige and they were both sent sprawling. Kavanagh reared up off the floor and he pounced on her like an animal in the wild attacking its prey. Kavanagh's lungs were burning, and he could hear her shouting hysterically.

Such a lovely sound.

He straddled her; gloved hands clamped around her throat.

Her body was trying to jerk away from his grasp, but it was useless. He was in control now. He would squeeze and squeeze until he saw her life leave the body. He had waited patiently for this moment. Retiring old fuckers was nothing compared to this. They had accepted their fates. They never gave him the joy he so desperately required. But this...after a week of torment. A week of the chase and now the climax. It was exhilarating. It was nirvana.

He heard a sob coming from his throat, completely against his will.

Let's have a chat, son. The icy voice of his father. *Let's have a little chinwag, you and I.*

"Are you ready, Alice?" He said from some other universe. "I'm ready now. Yes, yes, yes." He squeezed his hands together, feeling the shuddering of her pulse quicken. "I've been waiting all my life. Yes. When father put matchsticks between my toes and lit them, I endured. Yes. When he made small cuts in those flexible parts of the hands. Yes. I waited. I grew stronger. We had some good 'ol chinwags, pops and I. But now. Yes. Now we have our little chinwag. Do you like it?"

Alice's face was crimson. Her eyes bulged from the sockets.

He needed to savour this.

"Fuck...you," she hissed through clenched teeth.

"The fire in you...it's bright. Shiny. Yes. I think I'll come when it goes out. But I'm being too hasty," he released one hand and ripped off the glove with his teeth. Alice tried to break free but his reactions were faster.

"Yes, Alice. Fight it. Fight for your life. Just like that. Daddy likes that."

"GET AWAY FROM HER!" Came a bellowing voice from behind him.

Kavanagh glanced round to see the man from the bandstand charging.

No! He couldn't have this moment ruined. He used his un-gloved hand to retrieve the Glock from his waistband but realised it wasn't there. It must have dropped to the ground when he collided with Alice.

Valentine tackled him to the ground.

He turned his attention back to Alice.

"No one can save you from me, Alice. This is what fate has dictated for us, can't you see that? You're not changing anything, you know. The clock stops for you here. Now. Yes." He pressed his thumbs down on her oesophagus. She made a choking, panicked noise, thrashing her arms to try and find purchase. She tore at his face, at his arms, but he was in a different realm now. Concentrating on her bulging eyes, looking through her.

"It's beautiful," he murmured. "It's so...beautiful."

He felt her life leaving her. He applied more pressure.

Kavanagh heard a whickering sound before something connected with his skull. There was a dull bonk, something that would normally be ludicrously comical in other circumstances. The sound of aluminium hitting a ball. Or in this case, a bat hitting his head.

Kavanagh half-turned, half sidled off Alice. His brain hadn't comprehended the force of the blow, but something had switched off up there. His body slumped to the muddy grass and he laid down. It felt good lying down.

A little smile played around the corners of Kavanagh's mouth. "Brian, my boy. Don't I have an appointment to see you soon?"

Alice gasped and choked for air. She sat upright, massaging her throat.

"You're not a nice man," Brian said.

Kavanagh's vision was out of focus, but he could see the

unmistakable glimmer of several ERD lights pulsating in the night. "Bring your friends, did you Brian?" He slurred. He tried to sit up but found he couldn't. "Helluva swing you have there."

Alice regained her senses and crawled on the muddy bank of grass. Kavanagh glanced over to Valentine. The man from the bandstand was battering him about the face with bloodied fists.

This wasn't how it was supposed to go.

He had been so near.

With self-discipline almost anything is possible.

The shock of the blow had subsided. Now came the pain. But he was no stranger to that. If anything, his father had taught him the real meaning of pain.

He grimaced and sat upright. Alice had found his Glock and pointed the barrel at his chest.

Force has no place where there is need of skill.

"You're not going to shoot me, Alice."

She tilted her head to the side.

"No?"

"No. You're not a killer."

"Tell that to the sleazy fuck who tried getting into my pants last week."

Kavanagh smiled. It was a smile of fervent malice.

"Strange. It must be the blow to the head, but I can't remember his name."

He felt strength returning to his body. He'd need to play this carefully. He still had his knife on him. He just needed an opening.

"Can't you see, Alice? We're alike, you and I. Outcasts. We've made something of ourselves out here. We're survivors."

His eyes flicked to Valentine. Some of the Degenerates were pulling the man off his partner. It didn't look like Valentine would be walking away from this. What used to be his head was caved in. A pulpy mess.

"You're right," Alice said. "I'm not a killer."

She handed the gun to Brian.

"But I can't say what I would do if I had a chance to avenge my gran's killer."

You must submit to complete suffering to discover the completion of joy.

Kavanagh's eyes went wide. They glittered with a mixture of fear and fury. I was supposed to kill you, those eyes said.

Kavanagh made his move.

Brian shot him twice in the chest.

He fell back onto the grass. Looked up at the starry night. Before everything went black, he thought to himself: *This isn't how I thought it would feel.*

32

ALICE

THURSDAY

5 MINUTES REMAINING...

Alice ran over to George.

"Fuck George, you look like shit."

George shrugged. He seemed detached from reality.

"Let's get you out of here."

George waved her away. "Think I'm going to sit here awhile." He looked at the group of teenagers that had crowded round them. "You should find somewhere safe."

Alice regarded Brian, who was looking intensely at the gun he had just fired. "It's okay, they're cool."

"I need to thank you Alice."

Alice frowned. "Thank me for what?"

George smiled. She thought he looked tired. So tired.

"For giving me something I haven't had for a while...purpose."

"Oh gosh," Brian said. "Looks like the Ealing Slappers and the Chiswick Choppers found us."

Alice looked where he was pointing. In the darkness, she could see silhouettes of figures moving out from the treelines towards them. A multitude of ERD's pulsating an ominous shade of vermillion. A low frequency of worry started to grow in volume.

Five minutes.

She had to survive another five minutes. Then this nightmare would be over.

She did quick arithmetic in her head. The HardHats constituted about thirty. From the west she could see at least double that number, and then from the east another forty or fifty people. There was no chance.

George tugged on her elbow and she bent down to him.

"There's something else you have to do," he said. Then he whispered an address in her ear.

"You've got to go. Now." Brian said nervously. The crowds were surging towards them.

"You've got a gun, Brian." She said after George had told her what she needed to do.

He looked at the weapon as if it were the first time seeing it.

"Yeah. I guess I have."

Alice looked at the guitar on the grass. She realised she had no choice. She grabbed it and ran to the bandstand. Grabbing the mic, she shouted:

My name is Alice Paige
If you wanna think of the future
Think of a boot stamping on your neck
Forever

Then she plugged in the Les Paul and started playing. The crackling speakers spat out VamPyrate's *Snot Grass City*, always a people pleaser. She just hoped that a butcher's knife wouldn't swish through the air and embed itself in her skull.

She looked out into the vast space of the park, saw the Hammersmith HardHats prepare themselves for a beat down.

Alice concentrated on her hands. Better to focus on playing rather than the crowd. All the old riffs, all the chord progressions and time changes came back to her like she'd played them yesterday. She found herself cranking up the set, her fingers sliding up and down the neck like they had some type of symbiotic mythical bond. Although the drums and bass were missing, Alice growled into the microphone like no-one was watching her.

She didn't even end *Snot Grass City* the way it was intended, she just melted into *Beat Me With Your Lovestick* as if the two songs were joined at the hip. She looked out of the bandstand and could see George bemused by something. She missed a chord and forced her head back into the song. She felt her body sway with the music, as if some ethereal power were driving her on. If she was going out, at least it would be on her terms. And with a guitar in her hands.

She could hear shouts now – as *Beat Me With Your Lovestick* ended she cranked it up even higher for *The White Dragon,* a favourite from their first album. The air seemed to vibrate as she played the fist pumping chorus, and she was deep into it now, like a spotlight was on her alone and she couldn't see anyone or anything out in the darkness.

Something swished past her head. A bottle. Then a shot rang out.

The mass undulating crowds were attacking each other. Sher tried to drown it all out. That's what she'd been doing her whole life. Just trying to drown out the static noise with her music.

Someone leapt on the stage and she swung the guitar with fury. The neck broke and the music abruptly stopped.

Now there was only shouting and screaming and gun shots.

More people swarmed the stage and Alice Paige felt hands and fingers grab at her. Soon, the bandstand was flooded with pulsating ERD lights.

33

GEORGE

FRIDAY

Even though he had lost the use of one eye, George couldn't believe what he was seeing.

Swathes of ERD's pulsed luminous colours as the gangs mobbed the bandstand stage. He coldly realised that it gone past midnight as the screams and shouting escalated to a primordial level.

The park was a mass of rippling bodies, writhing with pained demonic faces. The scene could have been a painting of hell.

He tried to limp towards the bandstand, but he was elbowed and jostled away. All his energy from battering the broad-shouldered Agent had left him. He let out another frantic call for Alice but realised there was no way he would get to where she was. Another shot rang out and people were running.

He had failed her. He had failed Carina and Alice.

He limped away from the bandstand, not even hearing the sirens and flashing lights of Network Agents as they came.

It was early morning by the time he reached home.
Two uniformed Agents stood at his door.
George Bryant fell to his knees and began sobbing.
Today was his birthday.

EPILOGUE

FRIDAY

The man adjusts the small camera on his boiler suit and looks at his reflection in the window. He took a handful of pills a few hours ago to stop the pain from his destroyed eye. He feels like he could float now.

The old version of himself would check for signs of scoliosis, or lumps where there shouldn't be lumps. This version of the man doesn't think that way anymore. He's lost so much in such a short space of time. The Free-Vee has been manic with activity. Reports coming in that Alice Paige was ripped to shreds and left in a pulpy mess at the park. Other reports that she escaped amongst the throng of crowds.

He picks up his duffel bag and leaves the house. He doesn't look back.

He walks to the train station, like he did every day for years. He notices people looking at him, in his luminous orange boiler suit. He doesn't care what they think.

He stands at the platform, with the duffel bag over his shoulder. Most people have left the platform after seeing him come up the stairs. The train arrives and the carriage is empty. It's been a long time since he's been in an empty carriage.

He sits and looks out of the window. He doesn't think of much.

Soon, he arrives at his destination.

He leaves the train and walks the same route to the Network building. He looks up and feels himself waver. Maybe he took too many pills.

No matter.

Upon entering the building, he hears a few shrieks from his colleagues. The security guard with the buzzcut hairstyle wants to do something but stands immobile. He goes for his walkie-talkie, but the man shakes his head. Buzzcut freezes. The man looks up at the railing and sees his old line-manager. He smirks as a stain blossoms from his line manager's crotch.

He takes the lift to the AV floor.

Walking through the corridors, he lets himself into a room.

"Holly Lucas," he says. His voice doesn't feel like his own.

The red headed girl turns and looks at him with wide eyes. Panic. Fear.

The man takes out a USB stick and hands it to her.

"You're going to play this on all streams in the next ten minutes," he says. Holly Lucas is breathing hard. With trembling hands, she takes the USB.

"Are y-you here to...k-kill me?" she stutters.

The man smiles.

Five minutes later he returns to the lift.

He punches in the button for the penthouse floor. He's never reached so high on the control panel before.

He reaches into his duffel bag and takes out a ceramic dog. It's one his wife found in a charity shop years ago. It's an ugly thing, chipped and hollow. The man knows how the dog feels.

When the lift opens, he wedges the dog by the opening, so that no one will be able to follow him. He assumes Buzzcut from the ground floor has called for reinforcements.

He doesn't knock at the door. He just enters.

The room is immaculate. Glass windows with a panoramic view of London. Cassandra Rey looks up from a file she's reading. She studies the man. Takes onboard the boiler suit.

*"You know it's an offence to use a Birthday Treat on a Network official,"
she says calmly. The man nods his head. He does.*

*"I would heavily suggest you turn around and walk out of here before
you do anything questionable."*

*The man closes the door. Takes out a short rod from his duffel bag and
slots it nicely through the handles. No one enters. No one leaves.*

*"I'd like to see the old man," he says. He's seen Cassandra Rey on the
Free-Vees many times before. She seemed to always exude a cold
demeanour. Today seems no different.*

Cassandra smiles thinly. "No-one sees him. Especially not you."

"I think you'll make an exception."

*The man walks over to one of the windows. Looks out and sees
billowing smoke way out to the west. Alice would have set fire to the
warehouse by now. He likes to think the fire is her doing. That she took the
address he gave her and blew up the estate in Acton where all the
inoculations have been kept. He has to think this is the truth.*

*He brings out the last item in the duffel bag. The C4. He put it all
together a few hours ago. Had to look up things on the internet. In the end,
it was relatively simple.*

*He looks at Cassandra. In one hand he has the explosives. In the other,
the detonator.*

"I think he'll see me now."

*Cassandra is silent. She watches him slowly move towards her desk.
He's impressed that she's still sitting there, as if she was dealing with a
bothersome colleague. She puts the folder down and leans back in her chair.*

"You don't think you'll actually change anything, do you?" she sneers.

The man indicates the Free-Vee on the wall behind her.

"You might want to watch that," he says.

*Cassandra narrows her eyes. She doesn't turn around right away, likely
thinking he might try something when her attention is diverted elsewhere.
But the man nods again, shrugging.*

With the remote, she turns up the volume.

*It's the raw footage of Freddie Henshaw, in his last moments before
Network Agents shoot him in the head, down in the sewer tunnels of East
London.*

"It's being broadcast on all channels," the man says. "Your factory has also been burnt down to the ground. No-one gets jabs this year."

Cassandra sighs. Turns the Free-Vee off.

"You can do that, huh?" The man says impassively.

"What's your name?"

"I have no name. Not anymore."

"Seems like quite the little operation. Must have taken quite a long time to set all that up?"

The man shrugs again. "Quit stalling. Get the old man down here. Now."

Cassandra steeples her fingers together. Negotiation time.

"What if I told you there was no CEO of this company. What if I told you that the old man died a few months ago? How would you feel about that?"

"If it was true, I'd say that you're probably running things around here."

She smiles.

"What if I told you that I was planning to change things?"

The man laughs. It was a howling fit that caused his head to rock back.

"That's a good one, lady. Planning to change things...oh man, that's good."

She looks at him levelly. "It's true. All I need is some time."

"Time? You've had your whole life."

"The people demand a certain-"

"The people? You know nothing about the people of this country. You sit in your ivory tower like some roman Caesar, looking down at the gladiatorial arena and you have your thumb turned down, all the time. Last week I saw a girl get thrown onto train tracks and watched her body explode and her bones get dragged for miles. This whole fucking planet is infected, and you are the carriers."

Cassandra grinds her teeth. The man can see the taut muscles in her scrawny jaw expand and shrink in rhythm.

"You know what the consequences are to what you're doing. Just think about that for a moment."

"I've got nothing left to lose. I can't be hurt anymore."

He sees her eyes scan the room. She's looking for an exit. A way out.

The door rocks as Agents try to get in. The pole holds.

"Miss. Rey! Miss. Rey! We'll be with you in one moment. Try to stay calm."

The man sighs.

"Looks like our time is up."

Cassandra stands. The once calm appearance has cracked.

"Think about your family," she says. "You must have someone out there, someone who loves you."

The man thinks about his daughter. He wonders where she is and what she's doing. Maybe she's in a band, playing music like he once did.

"You know what I've learnt, all these years down the line?"

Cassandra watches in horror as the man closes his eyes and squeezes the detonator.

"Love is sacrifice."

THE END

ACKNOWLEDGMENTS

This book wouldn't have been made possible without the support of two very dear friends – Tomek Dzido and Ross Jeffery. I also want to thank you, dear reader. Please do consider leaving a review on Amazon and GoodReads – every review helps!

ANTHONY SELF

Anthony Self is a London based writer. He Co-founded STORGY with Tomek Dzido in the hope of exploring the short story format and engaging with other artists and writers. He began writing theatre scripts and one of his short plays '*Maybe the moon didn't want Armstrong*' *was* performed at Hampstead Theatre. He has also directed several music videos and short films, one of which, *Anticipation* won an award judged by British film maker Shane Meadows. His first collection of short stories, *Catbox*, will be released in December 2021.

Twitter: @Mr_Selfy

Printed in Great Britain
by Amazon